W9-BUN-296

Compromised

KATE NOBLE

BERKLEY SENSATION, NEW YORK

THE BERKLEY PUBLISHING GROUP
Published by the Penguin Group
Penguin Group (USA) Inc.
375 Hudson Street, New York, New York 10014, USA

Penguin Group (Canada), 90 Eglinton Avenue East, Suite 700, Toronto, Ontario M4P 2Y3, Canada
(a division of Pearson Penguin Canada Inc.)
Penguin Books Ltd., 80 Strand, London WC2R 0RL, England
Penguin Group Ireland, 25 St. Stephen's Green, Dublin 2, Ireland (a division of Penguin Books Ltd.)
Penguin Group (Australia), 250 Camberwell Road, Camberwell, Victoria 3124, Australia
(a division of Pearson Australia Group Pty. Ltd.)
Penguin Books India Pvt. Ltd., 11 Community Centre, Panchsheel Park, New Delhi—110 017, India
Penguin Group (NZ), 67 Apollo Drive, Rosedale, North Shore 0632, New Zealand
(a division of Pearson New Zealand Ltd.)
Penguin Books (South Africa) (Pty.) Ltd., 24 Sturdee Avenue, Rosebank, Johannesburg 2196,
South Africa

Penguin Books Ltd., Registered Offices: 80 Strand, London WC2R 0RL, England

This is a work of fiction. Names, characters, places, and incidents either are the product of the author's imagination or are used fictitiously, and any resemblance to actual persons, living or dead, business establishments, events, or locales is entirely coincidental. The publisher does not have any control over and does not assume any responsibility for author or third-party websites or their content.

COMPROMISED

A Berkley Sensation Book / published by arrangement with the author

PRINTING HISTORY
Berkley Sensation trade paperback edition / March 2008
Berkley Sensation mass-market edition / February 2009

Copyright © 2008 by Kate Noble.
Excerpt from *Revealed* copyright © 2009 by Kate Noble.
Cover art by Alita Rafton.
Cover design by George Long.
Cover hand lettering by Ron Zinn.
Interior text design by Tiffany Estreicher.

ISBN: 978-0-425-22650-6

BERKLEY® SENSATION
Berkley Sensation Books are published by The Berkley Publishing Group,
a division of Penguin Group (USA) Inc.,
375 Hudson Street, New York, New York 10014.
BERKLEY® SENSATION and the "B" design are trademark of Penguin Group (USA) Inc.

PRINTED IN THE UNITED STATES OF AMERICA

10 9 8 7 6 5 4 3 2 1

To my mother and sister,
the two smartest, strongest women I know.

One

1829

THE grand townhouse on the corner had not been occupied in more than three years, its furniture covered in dust cloths, its servants a skeleton staff of retainers. But for the past two weeks, Number Seven Berkeley Square had been a beehive of activity. The head butler and housekeeper had been about hiring new parlor maids and footmen, scullery maids and porters. The Pickerings, who lived at Number Eight, learned from their valets and ladies' maids, who had heard from the cook, who had talked to the gardener, who had spoken to Number Seven's gardener, who had been informed by the head butler that Sir Geoffrey Alton and his family were to return from the Continent just in time for the Season. Naturally, the Pickerings spoke with the Garretts in Number Nine, who had heard the same information from their ladies' maids and valets, confirming this juicy tidbit.

Within the afternoon, all of Berkeley Square knew of Sir Geoffrey's impending arrival. Within three days, all of London Society knew. Almost everyone took the news with equanimity, and those that did not, did not know Sir Geoffrey and therefore could have no opinion. Those of the uninformed who inquired were quickly told the facts: Sir Geoffrey Alton was a very amiable man of middle age and held a moderate-sized estate in Surrey. He was well known to the king and had been sent on a number of diplomatic missions over the past several years. Through wit, talent, and determination, three colors that most London High Society eschewed, Sir Geoffrey had managed during the war with France to become an associate of the current prime minister the Duke of Wellington. Although his own background was somewhat lackluster (Sir Geoffrey was the third son of a country gentleman), his amiability and verve made him acceptable, his shrewd head for investments made him rich, and his marriage to a woman of a historical, if genteelly poor, family made him Ton. Nevermind that his wife's family never wholly approved of the match, for, even when he was knighted for services during the war, they considered Sir Geoffrey's money too new and his manners too modern for their traditional minds.

However, it was by all accounts a most happy marriage, as Sir Geoffrey had been devoted heart and soul to his wife, but was widowed a dozen years hence, left with two daughters. The eldest, my goodness she must be near twenty now, was reputed to be quite the beauty. Mothers with daughters bristled at this news, and mothers with sons perked up their ears. Beautiful daughters—however nouveau riche—had a pedigree all their own.

The occupants of Berkeley Square kept their eyes fixed on Number Seven from their front drawing rooms, and one morning—a Tuesday by most accounts, but some dissenting opinions swear it was a Thursday—their efforts were rewarded. A grand barouche pulled up to the front door of Number Seven, its lacquered finish and family crest shining in the sun. Several carriages followed, loaded down with luggage, all bearing the same signature crest. Only the Pickerings were able to make it out easily, reporting that the Alton family signature was very dignified, red lions crossed with blue banners. All watched as the coachman alighted, dusted himself off, and opened the carriage door. Sir Geoffrey emerged first, seemingly in good humor and none the worse for wear. Indeed, he looked in rather good form, a tall man with a straight back and a full head of dark hair verging on a distinguished gray. If his waist was thicker than when last seen, no one commented. Sir Geoffrey then turned and assisted, not two, but *three* females down from the barouche's height.

The residents of Berkeley Square strained their necks, trying to see if they counted correctly, and indeed they had, all excepting Miss Nesbitt, who later in the week purchased a new pair of spectacles. But try as they might, no one could make out the features of any of the ladies, for their traveling cloaks were heavy and they wore wide bonnets. All that could be said was two of the ladies were petite, and the third was nearly a whole head taller. In moments, the objects of so many eyes were inside Number Seven's white stone walls, and the carriages hurried round to the stable yard.

Speculation ran rife for two whole hours, until a scullery maid emerged from the side of Number Seven and was immediately pounced on by the servants of the other houses, sent out to await the news. When that news came back, the identity of the third woman was placed. She was not a cousin, a governess, or a spinster aunt as so many had guessed.

Sir Geoffrey, it seemed, had taken a wife.

* * *

"WELL! It's good to be back home, isn't it, girls?"

Sir Geoffrey faced the assembled staff, who stood rigidly at attention, as per the explicit orders of Morrison, the head butler. Sir Geoffrey, filled with ebullient joy from the moment he stepped onto English soil, was thrown into proper rapture at the sight of London, and his household staff were the first outside the carriage to be subjected to his delight.

"Morrison, old boy! How are you?" Sir Geoffrey exclaimed, pumping the old man's hand vigorously, much to Morrison's and the impressionable young staff's surprise.

"I . . . we . . . bid you welcome back, sir," Morrison said, trying to recover his dignity and straighten his coat at the same time.

"Thank you, thank you . . . Mrs. Bibb! How'd you do? How are your sisters?" Sir Geoffrey cried out, spotting the housekeeper's soft, wide form. Dissatisfied with her curtsy, he picked her up, hugged her close, and spun her in a circle, Mrs. Bibb shrieking like a little girl.

Truthfully, Sir Geoffrey was generally an amiable man, but never so much as on the day he arrived home from his diplomatic tours. He enjoyed travel and the connections and influence his work afforded him, but nothing was so good as the sight of his cozy, four-story London townhouse, its eight bedchambers, two drawing rooms, two breakfast suites, two-story library, three formal receiving rooms, dining room, ball-room, music room, conservatory, and one tree, in the rear. His servants were used to his peculiarities. His new wife, perhaps, was not.

The sound of a dainty throat clearing brought Sir Geoffrey's attention to the ladies behind him. Setting down his housekeeper, he hastened over to take the hand of the petite woman with thick auburn hair and gray eyes that matched her lush velvet cloak.

"My dear, I apologize. Everyone," Sir Geoffrey announced to the assembled staff, "I should like to introduce my wife, Romilla, Lady Alton."

Romilla nodded regally, a slight smile playing on her cool, otherwise expressionless face. All of the servants took turns being introduced by Sir Geoffrey, giving their most impressive bows and deepest curtsies for their new mistress. Romilla could not help but be impressed by her newest residence and was quite pleased with the dignity and deportment of the staff. The deportment of her incorrigible new husband, however, was something she was resigned to work on.

"I'm very pleased to meet you all," Romilla said, her voice bell toned and clear. "Mrs. Bibb"—at the sound of her name the housekeeper stood straighter—"I have heard so much good of you. I'm afraid I haven't been in London in a great many years, and I will rely on your knowledge of the house to help me find my feet in running it." Mrs. Bibb curtsied deeply, and Romilla smiled with gracious condescension. 'Twas always important to have the housekeeper on one's side, and a few compliments as to that person's ability went a long way toward greasing the wheels. "For now, would you please have someone unload the trunks and take them to our rooms?" A snap from Morrison had the footmen bustling the luggage up the stairs. Pleased with this efficiency, she turned to one of the maids.

"I am desperate for a cup of tea. Could you please bring it to the drawing room? Girls, come with me." Romilla looked behind her and addressed her two daughters of six months. A radiant beauty and a hopeless bookworm. The beauty seemed too tired from travel to do much beyond nod mutely, but the bookworm spoke up. "Ma'am, I'll lead you to the drawing room—you don't yet know where it is."

"Nonsense!" cried Romilla. "Abigail, must I remind you of your manners? The lady of the house always takes the lead. And I told you, please call me Mother."

Once Romilla was a few feet away, Gail allowed herself an eye-roll before following.

Romilla tried four doors before she finally gave up. "Abigail," she sighed, "which way is the drawing room?"

* * *

FINDING the drawing room in perfect order, bookish Gail, lovely Evangeline, and Romilla divested themselves of their cloaks and bonnets and sat down to tea. This was a habit of Romilla's that baffled both the girls: Every day, no matter what anyone was doing, tea was served at half past ten in the morning. Most of society was not yet awake at half past ten, but since the "Reign of Romilla," everyone named Alton most certainly was.

Once, Gail had summoned the wherewithal to ask Romilla about her odd habit. Romilla had replied curtly, "I am up before dawn every day and breakfast shortly thereafter. By half past ten I am *hungry*." A look of concern crossed her face, as she added, "Abigail, dear, it is most rude to inquire as to one's gastric tendencies—please don't make a habit of it."

This made Gail think better of asking why Romilla didn't simply sleep in later. She'd hate to be accused of questioning someone's somniferous tendencies.

Not that Romilla could, or would sleep in. She was a doer. A General, waging battle to shape the world to her liking. And the hours of the day were meant to be *used*. An oddity in any family of means, but, Gail thought, she rarely had a claim to normalcy herself.

That morning, as they settled on the sofas, the girls found

themselves reluctantly hungry, but Sir Geoffrey had to refuse. He had immediately met up with his steward and was locked in the library, discussing the Alton estate and interests. Without the buffer of their jovial father, both girls were left to the not so tender mercies of their stepmother.

"Well," Romilla said, looking about the room, "I see I shall have a great deal of work to do in here."

Evangeline and Gail looked around the front drawing room. They saw nothing at all unpleasant—comfortable walnut furniture and soft butter-colored fabrics. Evangeline, wearily silent since arriving home, finally found her voice. "Do you find something not to your taste in this room, ma . . . Mother?" she ventured, her color perking up under the influence of tea and Cook's best scones.

Romilla smiled indulgently. "No, my dearest, the room is quite lovely, if a few years out of date. It is simply that you will be receiving your callers in this room, and we want you to be in the most inspiring atmosphere imaginable. This yellow wallpaper, I'm afraid, is not enough for a flower such as you. A dusty pink I think, or a pattern of blue to match your eyes."

Gail regarded her sister. Evangeline was indeed a radiant creature. She was small and lithe, with a halo of blonde hair that, when unbound, streamed down her back in thick waves. Her face was a perfect oval, with a porcelain complexion that pinked in only the most becoming blushes. Big blue eyes framed in thick blonde lashes completed the tableau. All in all, Evangeline was the portrait of English gentility, a woman exuding spirit and a tremble-lipped vulnerability that evoked the desire to protect and cherish from any man within sight of her. Gail had to admit that yellow was not Evangeline's color, but she thought it more than a little silly to change a room's decor to match the eyes of one of its occupants.

Evangeline apparently agreed. "But Mother, I doubt anyone who calls will even notice if my eyes match the room. I find the butter yellow rather comforting, and besides, the color is nicely becoming on Gail."

Gail blushed awkwardly at the compliment. Evangeline smiled and winked at her sister, which only caused Gail's blush to deepen.

Shrinking back farther into the cushions, Gail thought how lovely it would be to not have to have a Season this year—to simply read at home or go to the museums or the park and be launched on society next year—when she wouldn't be in the shadow of her divine sister.

Yet, how she would hate to go through the thing alone!

And because she had reached the advanced age of eighteen, there was no putting off the inevitable. True, Evangeline had managed to turn twenty before attending a formal Season, but whenever Gail brought this point up, Romilla was adamant that Evangeline's advanced age was owing only to the fact that until this year, her options for marriage had been limited to foreign men, something society would surely understand. Gail's absence from the Season, however, they would not.

There was no getting out of it that way.

So she would have to flirt with gentlemen and make conversation with ladies. Gail honestly didn't know which would be more difficult. She had watched Evangeline blush and flutter with young men, and she knew she hadn't the ability. She was too direct to be coy with men, but also would have been hard-pressed to take part in speaking of current fashion and *on-dits* with ladies. It seemed the women of society in any country didn't realize there was an interesting world outside of their social circle. However, what truly baffled Gail, was that it seemed gentlemen of stature favored women with empty heads above those with useful ones. Surely she would never meet someone she liked enough, or who would like her enough, for marriage.

But that argument hadn't worked on Romilla, either.

Gail looked up and caught her stepmother regarding her intensely. Gail knew what Romilla thought of her less-impressive stepdaughter: pretty enough, with dark hair and the gold-flecked brown eyes of her father—her one good feature. But Gail was abominably tall, and she moved determinedly, as if always late for an appointment. She was often loaded down with books and could not be impressed upon to care about (or in fact, remember) the rules and dictates of society, much to her stepmother's constant exasperation. But it wasn't as if she meant to be rude or wry! Sometimes those things just popped out! And because Gail would not, or could not, mold herself into propriety, it was easiest to remain silent and let her sister shine. She knew Romilla was resolved that Evangeline should be the success of the Season. Meaning that no matter how well Gail looked in yellow, the decor of the drawing room had to go.

"No," Romilla replied, "the yellow simply must go. A robin's egg blue, I think. Now Evangeline, as early as possible tomorrow, we will go about outfitting you with a new wardrobe. The Season's about to begin, and you need to look your best."

"But, we just purchased new wardrobes in Lisbon."

Evangeline's protest, however, was smothered under the weight of her stepmother's insistence that foreign fashions would never do in London.

The girls resigned themselves to the conversation Romilla directed of how many flounces would be appropriate on a young lady of Evangeline's height, with whom Sir Geoffrey needed to renew his acquaintance, and what would spell the greatest success possible for Evangeline. Gail, knowing full well that this conversation would never miss her opinion, turned her gaze to the window, content to daydream.

Their home was in Mayfair, a pleasant, comfortable quarter of the city, with large houses on neatly kept squares. Sir Geoffrey had purchased Number Seven decades ago in something of a coup—a marquis had bankrupted his family coffers and had to sell off anything that wasn't entailed. Their father considered it an investment, but their mother, when they were in town, had considered it their home. Berkeley Square was a particularly fashionable address, although Gail had a suspicion that the astronomical prices of the homes drove the fashion more than the homes themselves did. Number Seven was situated on the southwest corner of the square, affording the front drawing room a panoramic view of their next-door neighbors and the park, defined by the cobblestone streets that lined it.

It was a bright, sunny spring day, with crocuses bursting forth from the well-manicured grounds—a day when people should be walking arm in arm and enjoying each other's company. But alas, it was not yet eleven in the morning, and most of the Ton were still consuming their breakfasts, if they were awake at all. And although the sunshine was calling to her, Gail only wanted to go back to her room and take a long nap. Sir Geoffrey had insisted on such an early start to the day that Gail felt like she had barely closed her eyes before she was roused again. She would enjoy the sunshine in the afternoon, she promised herself. If only Romilla would release her so she could get some rest!

Eyes turned to their neighbors to the north, Gail was happily composing a letter in her head, when she spied a twitching of the curtains from Number Eight's front windows. The curtains twitched again, and this time, Gail saw two sets of shining eyes peering in her direction. She leaned closer to the window trying to get a better view of who could be looking directly into their front drawing room, but could make out nothing more than two shadowy figures. She perched herself on the edge of the sofa, leaned closer and closer, and—

Whomp!

"Abigail, whatever are you doing? Get off the floor this instant!"

"Gail, are you all right?" Evangeline's sisterly hand helped her to her feet. Romilla looked disapprovingly at her clumsy stepdaughter, waiting for an explanation.

"I'm sorry, ma'am, er, Mother. It's the people next door in Number Eight . . ."

"The Pickerings?" Evangeline asked.

"Yes, the Pickerings, if they still live there."

"What about the Pickerings? And straighten your skirt. What if one of the servants should walk in? What would they think?" Romilla snapped.

"I imagine they would think I fell on the floor," Gail replied.

"Abigail," Romilla sighed, "*why* did you fall?"

"Well, it's just the people in Number Eight. I think they were spying on us from their front windows."

Romilla blinked once. Then twice. Then she burst out, exasperated, "Of course they were spying on us! This is London! It's what we do!"

FINALLY, finally, *finally*, Romilla noticed her stepdaughters were near to collapsing in their chairs and let the girls head upstairs to wash and rest. On the way to the large floating staircase in the middle of the front hall, Gail and Evangeline passed their father's library. Sir Geoffrey had dismissed his steward and was now speaking with his secretary (although who could tell, the two were practically interchangeable).

"No, no, no," the girls heard their father say. "I will be damned if I attend one of Mrs. Brenton's musicales. If they're the same as three years ago, they're a damned waste of time. I have no patience for such missish drivel, and neither do my daughters. I expect Romilla will want to choose from the other invitations on that day. Moving on to the twenty-sixth, I'll be in Parliament . . ."

As they passed the door, Gail caught a whiff of her father's cigar smoke, a scent that had seeped into everything that was Sir Geoffrey. Gail blinked back memories of being little and held by her father, inhaling deeply the sweet dark aroma that had settled into his shirts. Gail knew that long after her father was gone, the smell of cigars would stay in the leather of the library's books, the solid maple desk, the carpets, and the curtains. It was a thought that made her smile, albeit a bit sadly.

"Sounds as if Father will have no trouble falling back into London life," Evangeline remarked.

"He never has," Gail replied.

"Are you glad to be home?" Evangeline asked, taking her sister's arm affectionately.

"I'm glad that we are no longer on the road," Gail said, laughing. "But it is difficult to call London home. We've spent less time here than we have in other cities."

"Yes, but there we are the guests, the foreigners. There is something wholly relaxing about being a native."

"I suppose you are right on that score. No language barriers here," Gail mused.

"As if language was ever a barrier for you!" Evangeline laughed.

As the girls turned into the east wing, they were met by Mrs. Bibb, rushing down the hall with some mending in hand.

"Oh! Miss Evangeline, Miss Gail, you gave me such a start!" Mrs. Bibb proclaimed, hand to her breast. "But where are the two of you headin' now?"

"We are very tired, Mrs. Bibb. We are going to wash and rest for a few hours," Gail explained to the housekeeper.

"But, beggin' your pardons, dears, you're in the west wing, with the family rooms."

"Mrs. Bibb, are you certain? I'm quite sure our rooms were in the east wing, in the . . ." Gail's voice fell as she realized . . .

"The nursery, miss? La, you haven't been in this house since you were out of the schoolroom, have you? Your rooms used to be in the east wing, but now that you're not young girls anymore, you'll be in the west wing with your parents."

"Well." Evangeline cleared her throat. "Yes, I suppose that does make sense. Gail?"

Gail, a bit thrown by her own wrong presumption, recovered well enough to reply, "Yes, of course. How silly of me, Mrs. Bibb. Could you show us the way?"

More than happy to oblige the young ladies, Mrs. Bibb led

Evangeline and Gail to a pair of rooms in the west wing, across the hall from each other.

"They're not connected?" Evangeline inquired.

"Well, miss, Lady Alton thought you would be wantin' your privacy," Mrs. Bibb mumbled as she twisted the mending garment in her hands.

"But we always . . ." Gail's voice drifted off sadly. She couldn't remember a time she and Evie had not been together. If they weren't sharing a room, they at least had a connecting door so they could talk at all hours of the night.

But apparently, not anymore.

"Think of it this way, my dears," Mrs. Bibb said, as she opened the door to the room on the left, ushering Evangeline inside, "you'll be right across the hall from each other, not six feet away. Also, Lady Alton said you could each do up your rooms in any way you please. Seein' as the front drawing room and a few other rooms are going to be done over as well, it'll be no bother to have some new wallpaper or cushions in here."

Evangeline's room indeed wanted refurbishment. It must have been ten years at least since the walls had been covered in a pattern that alternated pink roses with pink stripes, and the color had faded in time to take on a hint of dingy gray. The linens were freshly cleaned, but dulled by time and disuse. Mrs. Bibb then crossed the hall and opened the door to Gail's room, a mint green, which was equally in need of touching up. Still, Gail was a little peeved to have been so maneuvered.

"Why does she want to change everything?" she blurted to the faded walls.

"Oh now, Miss Gail, when a lady enters a house she intends to make her home, she needs to put her own stamp on it. That's all her ladyship is trying to do."

"But this is my mother's house," Gail replied, her voice cracking under its own exhaustion and despair.

Mrs. Bibb looked Gail up and down. "Now, dearie, I know it's hard, but a house is a thing—a pile of bricks, nothing more. The only thing left in this world your mother can still lay claim to is the two of you. And she had right proper young ladies, ones who can weather any change that comes their way. Am I right?"

Gail nodded grudgingly and turned to her sister. Evangeline smiled bravely, determinedly putting a bright face on the situation.

"At least you got the view of the garden," she said. "I look out on the road."

Gail went to her sister's window. "No, you have a view of the park, I look out onto our one tree behind the house."

"We can switch if you like—" but Gail interrupted her.

"We wouldn't want to deprive all your suitors of the opportunity to serenade you in the moonlight, or break their necks scaling the sheer face of the front of the house," she grinned impishly.

Gail took a deep breath and pushed her shoulders back. Crossing back to her own room's doorway, and smiling just as bravely at Evangeline, she said, "You know, my room could use some new colors. What do you think of a butter yellow?"

Evangeline smirked. "I think the color is quite becoming on you."

Mrs. Bibb sagged in relief. Gail walked through her door and watched Evangeline enter hers across the way.

"We're going to lie down for a spell, Mrs. Bibb," Evangeline told the housekeeper.

"Yes, miss, never you worry. You two have yourselves a good rest."

"Thank you, Mrs. Bibb," the girls chorused, as they shut their doors.

"I'll have you up by half past two, because Lady Alton wants you both in the drawing room come three to discuss plans for your coming out ball," Mrs. Bibb said as she walked away.

As if on cue, two heads emerged from opposite sides of the hallway.

"What ball?"

* * *

"DO you have to snore through everything I say?"

The speaker kicked his subject a little less than gently with his heel, but all for naught. His faithful steed, Jupiter, who on any other day would have torn through Hyde Park like one of the mythical furies, simply would not move faster than a slug. Maximillian Augustus St. John, Viscount Fontaine, and future Earl of Longsbowe, let out a frustrated roar, which of course did nothing to speed Jupiter's step. Max dismounted and thought to pull the bloody horse along, but quickly discarded the idea. Knowing Jupiter's disposition, which today was one step above that of a stubborn mule, he would simply dig in his hooves and stop moving altogether. So Max, bereft of other options, decided that this indeed was a lovely spot to stop for a rest and tethered the black beast to a nearby tree, where he could mope to his heart's content.

A few minutes later, a tall, well-dressed gentleman riding atop a lively bay mare came galloping up to Max and Jupiter.

"Fontaine, what happened? The first time in my life I beat you in a race, I turn around to see you're not running it." Mr. William Holt dismounted as he addressed his friend.

"Sorry I couldn't oblige your desire for a little sport, Holt, but Jupiter here had other plans." Max looked daggers at Jupiter, who solemnly munched on a patch of clover.

"He didn't wish to race?"

"That's putting it mildly. He flatly refused."

"But Jupiter's a flier, if I've ever seen one! Is he injured? Or ill?" Will inquired, looking anxiously at his best friend's mount.

Max snorted. "Hardly. Jupiter is simply lovesick. He fell madly for a mare at the stables where I was boarding him. But she was sold, and so he mopes. Won't gallop, barely walks, and refuses cubes of sugar. It's the damnedest thing I ever saw. I told him there are other females out there and that we'd find him a sweet-faced chestnut to moon over, but he refuses to listen."

"But, Jupiter's a gelding," Will said questioningly. "He can't—"

"Yes, yes." Max frowned. "But I fear this has less to do with physical functions and more to do with—as disgusted as it makes me—affection."

Will looked thoughtful. "Why don't you buy the mare from its new owners?"

Max sighed, running his fingers through his midnight-black hair. "I don't have the blunt for a new horse, you know that. Besides, it's no use. The stable master's son was the one who handled the sale. He's barely fifteen and as green as they come. Doesn't remember a thing about the man who purchased her, just that he paid cash and was a gentleman."

"Well, that's something! How many gentlemen do you know who actually pay their debts?" Will smiled good-naturedly.

Max harrumphed. Trust Will to see the hope in every situation, no matter how desperate, or in this case, how silly. He was one of those sunny people that never failed to brighten a room, could contribute intelligently to a conversation, and always seemed to enjoy himself.

It was highly annoying.

"Fontaine," Will said, "you're scowling. Don't be so bloody dour! This is not something that requires the patented Longsbowe black humor. It's springtime. No wonder Jupiter is in love. We all should be! 'Tis the season to appreciate lovely females of all species."

Max's eyebrow arched cynically. He knew his friend too well. "And have you chosen which fair young miss you plan on falling madly in love with this year?"

"Not yet," Will grinned, "but there is no lack of choice."

"For you perhaps. Sometimes I believe you are the far luckier to be born without a title or a father who demands heirs in a timely fashion."

Will's smile faded. "You received another letter?"

Max nodded. "You're surprised? He's sent them once a week since I went to school. Now the old codger insists I be married this year and start producing offspring by Christmas."

Will sighed. "Do you know," he drawled, "I do not envy the nobility. Now, now—I realize that as I am in trade, I am naturally beneath your set and therefore should fawn at your feet." Max shot Will a sardonic look, who blithely continued on. "But I cannot. You have marriage forced upon you to continue your line—and therefore find it revolting, putting it off as long as possible. And forget love! That should only complicate matters. I, on the other hand, am free to fall in love as I please, whether she be pauper or princess. I look forward to falling in love every day."

"And you do. Every day, with a new girl," which was a statement to which Will could only agree.

Max raked his fingers through his hair, frustrated, letting Will's speech roll over him.

"So, I'm hopeless."

"Now, I didn't say—"

"So I suppose I should have it over and done with," Max determined. He untethered Jupiter from the tree, giving gentle tugs on the line to lead the recalcitrant horse back to its lonely public stables.

"Marriage? You're joking." Will laughed, meeting Max and Jupiter's pace.

"No no! First my father, now you—I'm convinced. I should choose a wife—any relatively well-bred young lady would do," Max said, shrugging off his friend's disbelief and smothering a smile. "You should look into settling down as well."

"Me?" Will squeaked, turning paler than marble, much to Max's amusement.

"We are getting on in years, you know," he intoned seriously.

"We are eight and twenty, if we're a day, not exactly diseased and decrepit," Will argued. "You're funning me, I know it."

Max's eyes were suspiciously wide and innocent. "Not a minute ago, you accused me of being dour. How could I not be serious?"

"I know you, Fontaine," Will said triumphantly. "As long as your father keeps haranguing you, you'll keep defying him in the only ways you can. No chance you will ever consider marriage." And with that, Will blithely nudged his bay mare into a canter, moving in front of his friend.

Although Max acknowledged Will's statement as true, Max's face still darkened, his thoughts focused on his father's most recent, and most pressuring, letter. It was amazing how easily a man whom he hadn't seen in years still managed to prick at his temper. Annoyed, Max pulled a little harder on Jupiter's reins than necessary, and suddenly the horse ground to a halt. He pulled all the more fervently and was soon tugging with all his strength. With Will chortling from ahead, Max let out a frustrated yell, capturing the attention of no small number of other riders.

"I don't know which of you is the more stubborn," Will said, chuckling.

"He is!" Max barked, still pulling at Jupiter's reins. "He refuses to believe there is nothing so foolhardy as love!"

* * *

GIVEN Mrs. Bibb's informative parting words, rest was difficult to achieve for both Gail and Evangeline, but for entirely different reasons. Eventually, Gail was able to close her eyes and relax into the faded green counterpane, and when she and Evangeline emerged from their rooms at three, they were greeted by an enthusiastic Romilla, ready to tackle London society in earnest. She, and a bevy of footmen, had spent the last few hours productively. Romilla had sent notes to make appointments with modistes, milliners, jewelers, and old acquaintances. She, with Mrs. Bibb's assistance, had begun interviewing the downstairs maids, to discern which would be most suitable to be trained as a ladies' maid for Evangeline and Gail. She had also sent inquiries through Morrison to hire painters and handymen, to redo no less than five rooms that were not to her taste. When Romilla did something, she jumped in with both feet and did not look back.

So it was with her desire to throw a ball for Evangeline and Gail's coming out. It would have to be a grand crush, surely, and with Sir Geoffrey's political contacts, it could be the smash of the Season. She had already begun making lists of prospective dates and whom to invite and sketching cunning little invitation designs. The idea of having a ball thrown in her honor, to have to be the center of attention (along with her sister), made Gail rather queasy. Her own anxieties about being looked at all the time and having to be interesting and polite at a moment's notice overtook any joy she would have in the project. But as nervous as the ball made Gail, it made Evangeline positively giddy. She had, of course, been reticent to begin with, but as Romilla spoke at length about the flowers and the courses, and oh, the gowns! Evangeline's interest could not help but grow, and soon she found herself swept up in the excitement of it all. When Gail excused herself from the conversation, Evangeline was debating the merits of decorating the ballroom with very fashionable orange trees, while Romilla was extolling the virtues of lemon.

Whenever Gail found herself in a confused state of mind, she went to seek out the one person who in the past had been a comfort. Her father. Quietly crossing the main foyer, Gail knocked on the library door, and was bidden a gruff "Enter."

She poked her head in, again hit with a wave of cigar-scented air, mixed with a springtime breeze, courtesy of an open window. The smell brought an easy smile to Gail's face.

Sir Geoffrey stood at the window, cigar stub between his teeth. He turned to see his youngest child, and smiled.

"Ah my Gaily girl! Glad it's you! Shut the door, shut the door. If Romilla caught me with this"—he wagged the cigar—"she'd string me up by my cravat."

Gail narrowed her gaze as she approached her father. "Is that woman trying to make you stop?"

"Now Gail, don't start. She's being a wife, worrying about her husband and the like."

Gail was immediately contrite. "I know Papa, it's just . . ."

"What is it, my little girl? Whatever's bothering you, you can tell your old father."

"Well . . . I mean, she keeps calling me Abigail. No one calls me Abigail, why should she?"

"Now, now, that's simply her way. But I think it would take a lot more than that to get you to this state, so you'd best tell me so I can go about making it right."

"It's just that . . ." Gail picked at the sleeves of her gown. "Romilla sees Evie as a perfect young lady, and Evie is so excited about being in town and throwing parties. And, well, look at me. Everything I am needs improvement."

Sir Geoffrey wore a look of shock. "No! Never say so!" he said, gathering his girl into a bear hug. "There's nothing the matter with you, dear, and well served will be those who realize it. Romilla just wants us to have the best of everything. And I will admit, I have some regret that I dragged you girls about the Continent. Our travels may not have been the best home I could have given you. If we'd stayed in one place, you could have made more friends, maybe had a beau or two. Evie might've been married off by now!"

"I loved our life!" Gail protested, pulling out of her father's embrace.

"As did I! A new place every year! What did the French call it?"

"Une annee de nouvelle vie," Gail spoke with easy fluency.

"A year of new life, exactly. But, my Gaily girl, what I would have given to have taught you how to swim in the lake at our house in Surrey. And what would you have given to have had a full stable of horses—ones you raised from colts? Eh?"

Gail had to smile at that thought. What joy a stable full of horses would have brought when she was a headstrong ten-year old intent on jumping every fence she could find!

Sir Geoffrey placed the stub of his cigar on the windowsill.

"Now buck up, my girl! London's ever so much fun! And this year, you get to enjoy it all."

At this, Gail went visibly green. "I'm not certain I'm as happy to attend the Season as Romilla and Evangeline are. I just wish to survive it."

But Sir Geoffrey simply waved this off. "Nonsense, just nerves, my dear. Now, I have a prospect to cheer you up."

Gail's face lit with curiosity. "What is it?"

Her father chuckled. "Patience, Gail, patience. You never could wait for your surprises. Be on the front steps tomorrow morning at seven o'clock."

"Seven o'clock? That's practically dawn! No one will be awake then." *Except Romilla*, Gail thought, but she fervently hoped her surprise would exclude her stepmother.

"Gaily girl, seven o'clock is the perfect time for some fun."

So, the next morning at exactly seven o'clock, Gail did exactly as she was told, and found herself on the front steps of Number Seven. She had been correct in her assessment that no other house would be awake at such an hour, as Berkeley Square was as quiet as a church on Saturday, and she did not notice any twitching of curtains from next door. Even her father did not await her on the steps. But Gail was most certainly not alone.

In front of the house was the most beautiful chestnut mare Gail had ever laid eyes on. She was roughly fifteen hands high, with white stockinged feet and a glossy brown coat that shone like sunbeams in the bright morning light.

A groom held her by the reins, and when Gail approached, he bowed and handed her a note in her father's familiar hand.

> *Gaily Girl,*
> *I knew you'd be itching for some exercise, so I wrote ahead to my steward last week and had him pick out the most beautiful and spirited mount for you this Season. I think he made a wise decision. Her name is QueenBee, and she is yours. I thought you'd like some time to become acquainted before the rest of the world rides out for fashion, hence the early hour. (I thankfully remain abed, for who in their right mind would be awake at this time?)*
>
> *So hurry up and get changed, my girl! I'll see you at tea—not before half past ten, please.*
> *Love, Papa*

* * *

"SHE'S really all mine?" Gail asked in a whisper, venturing a hand to stroke QueenBee's nose. She had never owned a horse before; their mounts were always let and sadly returned.

"Why, yes, miss," replied the befuddled groom. "Who else's could she be?" QueenBee nuzzled her hand, causing Gail to giggle through her awestruck adoration. So intent was she on QueenBee's shiny coat and steady gaze, she did not hear the groom's next question until he asked it a second time.

"Pardon me, miss, but will ye be wantin' to ride this mornin'?"

"What? Oh yes! I must change. Don't go anywhere, I'll be down in a trice!"

Gail ran up the steps into Number Seven, forgetting to even shut the door behind her. But it was of no consequence, as she was back down again faster than a jackrabbit, now wearing a deep green velvet riding habit and matching leather gloves. She carried an old, wide-brimmed leather hat in one hand, her riding crop in the other. Then, with childlike glee and perfect horsemanship, Gail was seated into QueenBee's ready saddle.

The groom could only gape. Gail grinned in delight, for never had a horse and rider taken so quickly to each other. They were five-minute friends, and already they moved and looked as one.

"Are you riding with me?" Gail asked the groom, who quickly shut his slackened jaw, and reached for his own mount nearby.

* * *

"ALL right, Jupiter, yesterday was unpleasant, but today we have the whole park to ourselves."

Max addressed his sulking horse as they entered the gates to the park, biting off a yawn. Here he was, up at an ungodly hour of the morning, after Holt dragged him to the Norrichs' card party last night, all because of his horse. His silly, love-sick horse.

Max had spoken to Mr. Wyatt, the stable master, and was told that, although Jupiter was in the best of health, he was uncommonly mournful. Wyatt thought Jupiter might pick up a bit if he were given free reign to run without large crowds about. Eager to get Jupiter out of his current disposition, Max found himself at the park hours before anyone else would think to be there.

It was a lovely morning—cool and crisp, the sharp sun melting the dew off the grass. It was a day to be outdoors, and Max almost felt sorry for those that weren't. Almost, for his head still ached a bit from partaking of the Norrichs' fine selection from their personal cellar.

Max shook the cobwebs from his brain, kicked his heels into Jupiter's flanks, and set forward at a brisk trot. Happily, Jupiter was improved this morning, and he took to the winding paths of Hyde Park with great aplomb.

"There. You see, Jupiter? Nothing in this world a good solitary ride can't make right."

Max was rather pleased with himself. Smiling, he and Jupiter reached an open field near a lake, and both horse and rider were more than ready for a full-out gallop. With another judicious kick, they set out across the expanse of green lawn, breathing in the beauty of the morning and the exhilaration of the ride. They were a magnificent pair, Max tall and strong, his body's rhythm flowing from horse to rider. Jupiter's midnight black hair matched that of his master, both shining in the sun from their exertions. After a good number of minutes, Max brought Jupiter to a trot again. Both horse and rider happier for their exercise, Max turned his mount to start across the lawn and toward the winding paths that led to the tall wrought iron gates of the park. He checked his pocket watch. It was a quarter to eight.

* * *

EVERYTHING was perfect. A beautiful morning, an empty park, and a wonderful horse that was all her own. As Gail wound through the wooded paths, QueenBee responded perfectly to her slightest touch. The groom was keeping a respectful distance, about twenty feet behind, giving Gail enough room to enjoy a sense of solitude. Jimmy's mount was older, slower, and so they walked at a meandering pace for several minutes before both Gail and QueenBee were itching for a good run.

"Jimmy, is there a field, or an open space nearby where we may gallop?"

"Well, er, yes, miss, right up here through these trees," the groom pointed. "But," he stuttered, "don't you want to wait a bit before gallopin'? Your horse being a new mount an' all?"

But Gail had already taken off in the direction Jimmy had indicated, leaving the befuddled groom and his lackadaisical mount in her dust.

She came up to the field, a great expanse of green about a mile square, sloping into a valley and edged by great maple trees on three sides, a lake on the other. Gail raised her hand to the brim of her weathered hat, shading her eyes. She beamed, taking in the view of the sun dappling on the water, and addressed her horse.

"Isn't it magnificent? Are you ready for a run?"

But QueenBee was not ready for a gallop. She had suddenly become very nervous, very skittish. For QueenBee had spotted something Gail had not. Across the field was a horse and rider, bearing down with all possible speed, and headed directly for them.

* * *

JUPITER whinnied, his upper lip curled back, and began to dance.

"What is it, now?" Max dropped his watch, trying to control his horse, but found himself barely able to keep his seat.

"Jupiter, calm down! Steady, boy! Steady . . . whoa!"

Jupiter took off at full gallop across the field. All Max could do was hold on for dear life. He tried to see what in God's name had spooked his horse, but the sun's reflection off the nearby lake blurred his vision. Suddenly, he saw her.

The young lady and her horse had just emerged from the clump of trees that shaded one of the park's many idyllic wooded paths. Her horse had seen Jupiter charging full speed ahead, but the lady had not. The lake to one side held her attention. Max pulled and pulled on Jupiter's reins, and Max thought he heard a snap. But Jupiter would not be deterred from his course, in fact, running all the faster. So Max did the only thing he could. He yelled.

"Move! Move out of the way!"

The girl started, and finally saw Max riding as if the devil was on his tail, not fifty feet away from her. A second passed, but then she flicked her reins and brought the mare around. She took off at a gallop, headed toward the water. Jupiter, the stubborn mule that he was, veered to follow the girl.

The white-footed mare was fast, but Jupiter was faster. He caught up with the girl too easily, and was soon keeping pace alongside them.

"Damn you, you stupid horse, stop!" Max yelled, but Jupiter had long since established that he wasn't listening.

"What's wrong with you, you idiot!" yelled the girl. "Pull up on the reins!"

Max, glowering, yelled back, "If you haven't noticed, I *am* pulling up on the reins!"

The girl looked over at Max with an expression of utter annoyance, as if he were a simpleton of the first order. Then she narrowed the space between them and reached out, grabbing the reins from Max's hands. Before he could protest, she followed the reins up to Jupiter's bridle, and pulled him toward her. Jupiter swung around to an abrupt halt, the girl's mare ground to a halt to avoid running into Jupiter, and both riders were thrown off their mounts.

Into each other.

And into the lake.

Three

"JUST what in the hell did you think you were doing?"

Well, apparently he wasn't dead. Neither was she for that matter, but Gail was definitely bruised. When she had taken the black beauty's bridle and swung him about, his rider had been thrown into her, and he took her down in his path. To be fair, he had done his best to soften the blow, embracing her in his arms and twisting about so he cushioned her fall. They had landed in a tangled mass of arms and legs about three feet out into the lake, shallow enough so they wouldn't drown, but enough water to soften the landing. Slightly. If she stood, the lake would be about as high as her mid-calf.

But they weren't standing.

After a few heart-stopping moments below the surface, the man pulled his head out of the water and propped himself up on one elbow. The other arm was wrapped firmly around Gail's waist, and she lying most unladylike across his lap.

Gail had never been this *close* to a man before, at least not one that wasn't her father. She could feel the hard muscles of his legs against her hip, feel the ripples of his solid chest and stomach through their wet, clinging clothes. Needless to say, she was speechless.

He must have (rightly) assumed he had startled her into shock, for his next words were far gentler in tone.

"Miss, er, are you all right? Is anything broken?"

She snapped herself back to her senses. Goodness, they were entwined! This would never do.

"Release me, if you please."

She wiggled a bit, trying to escape his grasp. Unfortunately, such movement only pressed her against him in new ways, and seemed to make him acutely uncomfortable. His scowl returned in full force, but his hands didn't move from her posterior.

"Remove your hand from my backside and release me now! Are you deaf?"

Promptly, he removed the offending hand.

"If I weren't before, I may well be so now." He shook his head, shedding rivulets of water before they ran into his eyes and ears. "Now remove *yourself* from my lap, you hellion, unless you want me to take what you are so carelessly offering."

"Oh!" was the angry reply, as she scrambled to get away from this loathsome person.

The gentleman gained his feet, the water pouring off his shoulders and down his back, forcing his clothes to cling all the tighter to his muscular frame. Oh my, he is tall, Gail thought, watching as he stripped off his soaked riding coat, wringing it out of excess water. She did her best not to notice, but her eyes kept returning to the nearly transparent white shirt plastered to the grooves and plains of an impressively male torso. Why, if she looked hard enough, she could see short dark hairs beneath the shirt . . .

"Are you going to get up, you daft girl?" he said, slinging the sodden coat over his shoulder. Gail shook her head clear and struggled to push herself up, but the green velvet habit had become so heavy, it was if it had absorbed the entire lake.

"The skirt. The habit, it's too heavy when it's wet."

The man (for she refused to think of those that had to be prodded into helping a lady as a gentleman) rolled his eyes and took her hand, ruthlessly hauling her to her feet. This had the unfortunate side effect of throwing Gail against the object of so much of her attention, namely, his chest.

Pressed against the hard, warm body, Gail felt him steady her with his strong embrace. She looked up and met his eyes—green, deep emerald green, and for a moment she was his willing captive. Then she saw those eyes go wide with . . . something, and he abruptly shoved her away, as if she were on fire.

Well, really! Like she could possibly be on fire with her clothes wet and clinging. Luckily she didn't fall again. Not waiting for the lady to precede him, not offering her any further assistance, the madman turned and stomped toward shore, grumbling something inaudible, and likely impolite.

That does it, Gail thought, affronted by his unaccountably abrupt behavior toward her.

"What in the bloody blue blazes did you think you were doing on that field?" she exclaimed, following him up to dry land.

He turned, aggravation shining in his fiery green eyes.

"What did I think *I* was doing? What in the 'bloody blue blazes,' as you so quaintly put it, were *you* doing on that field? What on earth possessed you to reach for my horse?"

Gail sputtered, fury steeling her body for the fight.

"What on earth possessed you to charge at me like that? Are you mad?!"

"I assure you, Miss, any madness that had taken hold of me occurred after you threw me from my horse and into that damn muddy lake!"

"I know what I saw, you were running straight for me."

"Good God, but your arrogance wears on my last hung-over nerve," he vented, rubbing his eyes. "It's my horse that's mad, not I." He pointed to the field, where his horse stood docilely under a tree, nickering softly to QueenBee. Gail watched his jaw drop as the black beast that had not a moment ago charged across the field, nip playfully at the mare's ear, who neighed coyly in return.

"Your horse seems quite gentle, which is more than I can say for his rider," she said, sardonically.

"Don't try me, missy, I'm not as nice as I look," he said,

his brows coming together in his most intimidating scowl. He loomed over her, something he did very well. She was a tall female, but he still had a good number of inches on her. *He's trying to intimidate me,* she thought snidely, demanding wordlessly that she apologize, submit, have sense enough to be a good, missish thing who cowed to his superiority.

But looking up into his face, that had rivulets of water dripping off of his nose and eyebrows two black wings of fury, Gail did the only thing she could. She laughed.

A peal of sparkling, beautiful laughter escaped her smile, taking all the wind out of his stance. For a moment, he could only blink.

"Listen, you . . . you . . ." he sputtered.

"You what? You've already used 'hellion,' 'daft girl,' and 'missy.' I can think of several, more interesting degradations, but then again, I'm not the one trying so hard to be intimidating."

"How about you maddening, foolish, moronic little chit?"

"Much better!" she applauded.

He took a deep breath. A very deep breath. "You grab the reins of an obviously frenzied horse and pull so violently that you throw both of us from our mounts. I could have been hurt or killed, my horse could have been hurt or killed."

"And what about poor little me?"

"You should be breathing a sigh of relief that I have not taken it upon myself to bring upon you what injuries you miraculously escaped in our flight into the freezing water! Now, what do you have to say for yourself?"

Gail took a moment just to stare at this man, righteous indignation radiating from his frame.

"Well? What do you have to say?"

"You're welcome," Gail replied pertly.

Really, she thought, *he should close his mouth when astonished. Else he looks like a fish.*

"You're welcome?" he repeated incredulously, once his jaw had regained function.

"Yes. You're welcome."

"Oh thank goodness, Miss! I was afraid you'd done yourself a harm. You are unhurt, aren't you, Miss?"

Amazing to fathom, but only a few minutes had passed since the madman and his horse had charged across the field. Jimmy had finally caught up to them, was just now dismounting and tying his mare to the tree by the other horses.

"Yes, Jimmy, I'm fine," she told the groom. "Just a bit damp is all."

Jimmy sighed in relief. "When I finally broke through the trees I couldn'a see you for a moment. Then I saw these two lovebirds by the lake and the two o' you in it. Thank goodness you're unharmed, Miss. Your father would have my head if you'd so much as sprained a finger."

"Her father should shackle her indoors until she learns some manners," the man said, but then something Jimmy said seemed to catch his attention. "Er, did you say lovebirds?" he inquired.

"Yes, sir. Your fella and her QueenBee. Anyone could see it from a mile away. They got an affection for each other."

He turned to Gail, a triumphant smirk on his face. "I told you my horse was a bit mad. Now, if Jupiter is in love with your QueenBee, is it?—it means she's the mare he mooned over at his stable yard. It also means that you purchased her quite recently. You've had that horse barely a week, am I right?"

"Actually, this was the first morning she had her, sir," Jimmy said, blithely unaware of his faux pas, giving his attention to QueenBee to make sure she had come out of the scuffle unharmed. Finding nary a hair out of place, the experienced groom moved on to the black beast next to her.

His green eyes glittered. "Your first day, eh? How bloody stupid do you have to be to try such a dangerous move as to grab my horse's bridle when your own mount is untried?" He ruthlessly advanced on his quarry, each step forcing her backward, into the water. "She could have thrown you without a care. Don't you know anything about horses?"

"Hang on a minute," said Jimmy, holding Jupiter's bridle, concern awash on his face. "This here bit is broken. Poor thing, musta hurt like hell."

Gail's own smile grew as the man's faltered. "You see, the bit of your horse's bridle broke in half. It probably hurt so severely, that every time you pulled up on the reins it only urged him into a deeper rage. I saw this and swung him around to a halt. Don't you know anything about horses?"

Gail was just shallow enough to take deep pleasure in seeing him and his argument deflate. His eyebrows came down into a scowl again. Obviously he was unable to even countenance that she could be in the right, and so he clung to his anger like, well, like his wet clothes were clinging to him.

"Wait a moment," he said, regarding her speculatively, "how can you see inside a horse's mouth?"

"I . . . uh . . ."

As Gail squeaked out vowel sounds, unable to come up with a reply, the man howled in triumph.

"You little liar! You had no idea what possessed my horse, did you? And yet you did something utterly foolish to stop him!"

"Well, I stopped him, didn't I? More than you managed to do." Indignant, Gail stood toe-to-toe with him.

His face softened as he reached out and tugged gently on a lock of her hair that had tumbled out of its coil. "You could have gotten us both killed."

Time stopped for a moment as she locked eyes with him. Then as his fingers wound around the errant lock of hair, Gail realized something was missing.

"Oh! My hat!" she exclaimed.

Gail turned back to the lake, scanning the shoreline for some glimpse of her brown leather hat. She finally found it settled amongst some reeds about ten feet away. Lifting up her weighted skirts, Gail marched over and picked it up. When she turned back, it was to find the madman regarding her peculiarly. His gaze raked up and down her body, and he looked to be enjoying the view. His regard rested the longest on her lower extremities, and Gail blushed furiously, realizing that when she picked up her skirts, her ankles had been exposed to his appreciative gaze.

Embarrassed beyond reckoning, she dropped her skirts and kept her eyes on the old, dearly loved hat in her hands, trying to poke it back into shape.

His attention followed hers.

"*That's* your hat?" he sputtered, incredulous.

Gail looked up. "Well, yes."

"Is it, er, ruined?" he ventured.

"No," Gail replied, "I think it will be fine."

Gail shook the hat up and down, ridding it of water and spraying everyone within a five-foot radius. Luckily, only the madman was within that radius. She then pushed her hair out of her eyes and placed the hat upon her head. She folded back the top brim, and raised her gaze to defiantly meet his.

He sniggered.

Soon that sniggering turned into a full-on attack of laughter.

Gail had the audacity to ask, "What's so funny?"

"You, miss," was the reply, "are utterly ridiculous."

Her cheeks flamed red, and she recoiled as if struck.

"Well, sir, at least I'm not the one walking my horse home!" she said, huffing. Straightening her back to the continual laughter, she marched to where Jimmy was holding Queen-Bee's reins. As gracefully as possible (a decided difficulty in a soaking wet habit), she mounted, turned, and said, "Good day, sir. I can't say it's been a pleasure."

And with that, she turned QueenBee about and nudged her into a gallop across the field, toward the path that led to the park's gates.

* * *

MAX was still laughing as he watched the retreating form of the impertinent girl, her back as straight as an arrow, her head never turning to look back. Jupiter, watched, too, but far more unhappily. Not wanting QueenBee to go, he tried to follow but he was tethered to a tree.

"So much for true love," Max remarked, between chuckles.

"I tied him up with a spare bit a' rope I had," Jimmy said, mounting his own horse. "You can use it to make a nice loose lead and walk the poor fella home. He'll probably need a few days mending time and a new bridle."

"Thank you, er . . ."

"Jimmy, sir."

"Thank you, Jimmy," Max said, and the groom tipped his hat to him, and sprinted off after his mistress.

It was only then that Max realized two things. First, that although he had had the manners to find out the groom's name, he and the girl had never exchanged theirs. More the better to never see each other again, he supposed. Still, she was an interesting creature—fire for eyes, and what a ridiculous hat! It was like something a farmer would wear, only worse.

No filter between her brain and her mouth, Max mused, rubbing the tension from the back of his neck. She was also either very brave, or very foolhardy, to pull that stunt on the horses. Likely both. And he certainly couldn't fault her ankles, or the way wet clothing stuck to her . . . A smile played around Max's mouth until he realized the second thing: The stable where he boarded Jupiter was nearly two miles away.

"Bloody hell," Max groaned. It was going to be a long, cold walk.

* * *

WHEN Gail traveled home that morning, she did not care one jot if any of their neighbors were awake and twitching back the curtains. The only thing she cared about was a good warm bath. That was, of course, until she heard the piece of news that greeted her the moment she opened the door.

Her debut ball was to be in three weeks. Invitations were already being printed.

Four

A week had passed since that infamous morning, and the occupants of Number Seven Berkeley Square were in a flurry of activity, what with calls to be paid and dresses to be ordered and fitted. Menus had to be arranged, flowers purchased, musical groups auditioned and chosen (Romilla liked the classic quartet and would not hear of Gail's impish desire for a grand trumpet processional), silver to be polished, and the refurbishing of now seven rooms. Of course during all this, Sir Geoffrey had to keep up his political acquaintance and pay calls on the Home Office. Therefore, Gail and Evangeline often found themselves left to the devices of Romilla, who did not deem it advisable for young ladies not yet presented to the Ton to go out to the British Museum, or to the opera, or Astley's Amphitheatre, or any other amusement that might keep their minds from dwelling too long on the approaching festivities. Evangeline bore it admirably, as she was in fact looking forward to the event and tried to throw herself as much into the process of giving a party as Romilla would hand over. Only occasionally did her fears of failure overcome her, but Gail was always there to talk her out of her low spirits.

As for Gail, she was not faring quite as well. Her nerves at the prospect of a ball were becoming increasingly worse, manifesting in a bout of awkwardness that had not been seen since the heyday of her adolescent growth spurts. Already, she had accidentally knocked over two very expensive vases and tripped on the corner of a rug, oversetting a tea tray. But whenever such mishaps brought forth scowls from Romilla and sighs from the servants, Evangeline was there to make Gail laugh at herself again.

One thing Gail did have to aid in escape was QueenBee. Romilla was staunchly against her riding during the Ton's most fashionable hours, but Sir Geoffrey had intervened for his daughter's sake, and struck a compromise. She was permitted to ride in the very early mornings, before the Ton was out strutting on horseback. Gail reveled in this solitary time, taking all of her frustration and channeling it into a glorious gallop across open fields. She came home refreshed, calmer, and more prepared to face whatever the day or Romilla thrust upon her. Of course now, while riding, she kept her eye out for tall, impossibly arrogant men riding mad horses as if the devil himself were on their tail. Not that she expected to see him. It was only that if she did see him, she would know to politely avoid the area he was in. She was very happy to not see him ever again. Not that she thought about him. Ever.

As for Maximillian Fontaine, he refused to think of that impossibly irritating girl who threw him into a lake. Unless of course, he happened by a lake. Or someone impossibly irritating. After recounting the tale of his watery misadventures to Will Holt, painting himself as the wronged party of course, Max was laughed at by his best friend and told most seriously to remove the rigid wooden object that occupied his posterior.

Max continued to ride as well, once Jupiter had recovered from the effects of his broken bridle. He thought it would be tempting fate to ride in the park in early morning, so he settled for the sunset hours. When most people were sitting down to dine, Max was taking Jupiter through his paces in some secluded corner. Happily, the solitary rides were beneficial to Jupiter's temper as well as his own. In fact, since having been in the presence of his beloved QueenBee, Jupiter's moods were much improved, maybe because he thought he might

happen upon her at any moment, even though Max was determined to avoid that at all costs. Even so, the horse and rider
would fly through the park's deserted paths and fields (avoiding the area of a particular lake) until they were both breathing heavily and happier for the exercise.

One evening, after a good bout of sprinting, Max and Jupiter wandered at their leisure and found themselves on a before
unknown bit of path. After twisting and turning through
wooded areas, they came upon a beautiful, shaded grotto,
with a newly installed gazebo in its center, in the popular ruined style. On that late spring day, the budding vines winding
up the gazebo's stone columns were a light green, but the
sunset made them glow as if on fire. Max found himself in
awe of the dazzling slices of red mixed with gold and hazels
cutting through the trees. The colors captivated him, the air
itself seemed to stop. He could only hear the sounds of birds
rustling and Jupiter shifting his weight, not the overbearing
noise of London's streets. In that moment, Max felt as if he
were the sole person on this earth.

All too soon, the light left the trees. He hated to leave the
peaceful grotto, but once the sun had dipped below the horizon, the park quickly became very dark, and very cold. Wishing he had some breadcrumbs to place so he could find his
way back to the serene spot, Max turned Jupiter about, and
headed for home.

Having deposited his horse back at the corner stables, Max
strolled the short distance back to his bachelor quarters. The
air of peace the grotto had given him still surrounding his
mind, Max hummed a bit of Beethoven as he walked up the
front steps.

His lodgings were located on Weymouth Street, near Re-
gent's Park and the grand winding avenue of the same name.
It was not the most fashionable part of town, but for Max it
was a haven for that very reason. His family connections and
title allowed him to mingle freely in society—although he
was never the star of any party, he was someone who could
fill an empty seat well enough, and therefore did not lack invitations. His club was most agreeable to his membership, as
long as his dues were paid. But when he came home at the end

of the day, Max's rooms were a sanctuary. There were no mews, but the rent was agreeable. His apartments occupied the ground floor of a thin, three-story house—the second and third floors were let to a young musician with a taste for the pianoforte and an old scholar working on his thousand-page treatise, respectively. He had a parlor with his bedroom beyond, and a small room for Harris, his valet. But what drew Max home night after night was the cozy study full of wonderfully musty books, and best of all—no stamp of his father's rigidity anywhere. It was all he required. It was all his own.

He strolled through the door.

"Good evening, Harris."

"Good evening, sir."

"I'm afraid I'm running late tonight," Max said as he handed his hat and gloves to his valet, "I'm dining with Mr. Holt at the club, so please send for a hack directly."

Harris cleared his throat and moved to intercept his employer. Harris had been with Max as long as Max had been in London, even through those years where pay was equivalent to that day's meals. He was getting older, but for a man of certain years, Harris moved uncommonly quickly when necessary. He cut a surprised Max off at the mouth of the drawing room.

"Sir," he said, "a guest arrived while you were riding. I installed him in the study."

Max finally noticed the gravity on Harris's face. The man was usually quite serious, bordering on dour, but today he looked downright bereaved.

A weight settled onto Max's shoulders, all the joy from his beautiful ride draining away. Only one person could unsettle Harris. He knew who was behind those doors across the narrow foyer, but not what kind of aggravations awaited him.

"Well then," he said, trying to sound jovial for his valet's benefit. "Best to get it over with, eh?"

Harris nodded, and Max managed a weak smile. Pushing open the study doors, Max encountered the one man he had long sought to avoid.

"Close the door, you dratted fool! A sick old man cannot be subject to a breeze."

His father.

Five

MAX closed the study doors behind him. His father was seated behind the large walnut table that served as a desk, which was normally covered six inches deep in various books, papers, and correspondence. Harris had obviously made quick work of cleaning it off before admitting the Earl, for it now shone with a polished brilliance. Max suddenly felt very much like a guest in his own home, and wondered where the study that he claimed as a refuge had gone.

"'Bout time you came back. I haven't the faintest idea what you think you're doing riding at such an hour. You haven't even changed your boots! Look at all the mud you are traipsing in, quite unseemly," said the Earl, not even bothering to rise.

Rising would have undone the image, thought Max, as he regarded his father. Oh yes, if he had risen to meet his son, it would have shown some consideration for Max as a beloved relative or at least as the master of this residence. Also, it would not do for a man who is supposed to be near his deathbed to stand upon someone's entry. That act of social nicety is reserved for the healthy.

Not that Max believed for a minute that his father was near

death's door—that ruse no longer worked on him. But now, seeing him for the first time in years, Max did have to admit that his father was looking older. The hair that was once a thick, distinguished gray was now limp, white, and thinning. His color was pale, and the normally strong frame seemed to hunch under its age. Max took note of a gold-headed cane in the corner, one he could tell was not purely ornamental.

But the eyes—the green eyes that mirrored his own, were as sharp and as cold as ever.

"Forgive me, Father," Max said stiffly. "I was surprised—I should not have wanted to keep you waiting."

"'Course you didn't," his father retorted. "I heard you through the door. You came in to 'get it over with' as quickly as possible."

Max's face reddened dully.

"I wouldn't have heard you if you were living somewhere with thicker walls," his father said.

"Somewhere like Longsbowe House, I suppose?" Sarcasm dripped from every word.

"Longsbowe House in London is there for the purpose of it being used. Why you insist on wasting your money on this unfamiliar place is beyond me!"

"It's my money, Father, I'll spend it as I choose. Tell me, what brings you to London when you have claimed to be too ill to remove yourself from Sussex? When you haven't been to town in over fifteen years?"

His father stared him down, placing his palms upon the desk. "Serious business brings me to this godforsaken town," the Earl said. "Since you don't respond to my letters, I felt it necessary to come and say what I have to in person."

Max suddenly felt very tired. "I'm no longer in short pants, Father. I have done nothing that requires a scolding."

The Earl brushed that aside. "It is precisely what you have not done that causes me to travel all over the country to speak with you."

The Earl lifted himself out of the chair, but leaned on the desk for support. He motioned to Max to have a seat. Max obediently took one of the chairs across from the desk, ready, if not precisely willing, to hear the Earl out.

But his father's first words surprised him.

"You don't like me. I know that. I confess I do not understand most of what you do either. You refuse to live as a Longsbowe, instead spending your time and life in this"—he waved his hand around—"place. You went to Oxford and the Continent, have been raised as a gentleman, and even though you insist on working for a wage, I daresay you enjoy your gentlemanly pursuits. But you have yet to take any responsibility for your station. You have not come back to Longsbowe Park and taken up the running of the estates. You have not pursued any woman of Quality who would make a suitable Countess for our distinguished name. Well, I have known for quite some time you were useless, but I refuse to have a wastrel for a son."

Max looked heavenward. "I'm well aware of your opinion of me, Father—this did not warrant a personal visit."

"I'm dying, boy," the Earl proclaimed irritably. "I am not long for this world. I know that, too. But before I go, you will step up and accept everything that comes with your title. You may not live off the money I allow you, but you live off the name I gave you. It is time you grew up and earned it. If you don't marry before three months are out, I will strip you of it."

For many moments, Max could not speak.

He was shocked at his father's pronouncement. He'd heard most of it before, being called a good-for-nothing and being railed at to get married and live at Longsbowe Park. But, dying? Max's father had said he'd been dying for the past decade. But as Max looked over the Earl's frail body, it was the first time he'd believed it. He pushed those thoughts out of his head. He had to.

Never had the Earl issued an ultimatum before—and what an ultimatum it was! Max finally exhaled when he realized his father wasn't capable of what he threatened.

"You can't strip me of the title, Father. Or the money that comes with it when you die."

"Oh no, that's where you're wrong!" chortled the Earl, creaking his body back into the chair. "If you had studied the legalities of Longsbowe you would have realized it. Nearly half of the estates and all of the money I have came from your mother when we married. That part is not entailed to you. I could very easily will the blunt away to your Uncle Alfred. What you would be left with is half a dozen estates, including Longsbowe Park and House, with absolutely no money to keep them running. You would go under within a month."

"So . . . so what?" Max bluffed. "I'll just sell off whatever isn't entailed."

"And then do what?" His father chortled evilly. "A desperate seller never gets the price he wants. You'd likely not earn enough capital to support Longsbowe Park—and that's one you can't sell. Besides"—his father's green eyes softened marginally—"you have always seen Longsbowe on your horizon. Admit it."

Max faltered. Then, "What about the title? You cannot take that from me."

"No, but I can seriously decrease its value. All it takes is one little whisper in the right ear, and suddenly everyone doubts your paternity. It would be quite a headache. Relatives you didn't even know you had would be clamoring to take your place. Try selling an estate when people doubt it's yours.

"Add that to your sudden lack of funds, and you would never be invited to another card party again. Do you think they'd even let you through the door of White's? You would be kicked out of all good society without your coat!"

Max stared at his father, whose grin had taken on a cold, Machiavellian feel.

"You would paint yourself a cuckold, besmirch my mother's name? You would destroy everything the Longsbowe name has meant for centuries?" Max said, disbelieving.

"I'll be dead. It won't matter to me any longer. And if the name means nothing to you as you claim, then what I threaten holds no weight. But if you do aspire to be Longsbowe . . ." The old man shrugged a withered shoulder.

It was a new low. It was a desperate manipulation.

It was classic Father.

"I knew you despised me seeking any small form of independence, but I didn't know you hated me this much."

"You sit around here, dawdling with your books, waiting for me to die. You will for once heed my wishes before I go."

A great sigh left the Earl. Now that he had said his piece, he suddenly looked much older, as if he had been saving his strength for this, and now that it was done he could rest.

Max let out a cry—half laugh, half disbelief, and placed his head in his hands.

"You will be married, within three months' time, else I will do as I said," the Earl stated.

Max knew the Earl was serious. That he had never doubted.

Six

ON the understanding that his future was decided and he had no choice but to comply with his father's wishes, Maximillian Augustus St. John, Viscount Fontaine, future Earl of Longsbowe, resigned himself to the inevitable and followed in the tradition of all distinguished gentlemen who found their hands tied.

He got very drunk.

After his father had hobbled his way to the door (he really was getting on in years, Max realized) and taken his crested carriage back to Grosvenor Square and the austere mansion of Longsbowe House, Max pounded his way back to his study, slamming the door. Harris visibly jolted at the sound, but gathered himself and went to fix a tray.

In the study, Max went furiously about righting his desk. He found the cabinet where Harris had stored his papers and books that had once littered the desktop, and ruthlessly put them back in their haphazard arrangement. When everything was in as close to order as he could recall, Max went to the sidebar and opened the heavy decanter of brandy.

Hours later, that was exactly where Will found Max, by the sidebar, with the decanter in hand. However, it was now nearly empty, and Max was no longer standing.

"Fontaine, where have you been? You never showed for supper at the club, never sent a note! I went ahead to the Reginalds' only to find you hadn't deigned to show there either. I had to leave Mathilda Cunningham, the most bewitching redhead to debut this year," Will said.

Max was seated on the floor, his coat and cravat undone, his muddy riding boots still on, utter misery awash on his face.

"I've seen you in your cups before, but something tells me this is different." Will squatted down next to his friend, who wobbled his head up to look through blurry eyes at the intruder.

"What gave it away?" he slurred.

A wry smile mixed with the concern on Will's face. The blue eyes crinkled. "No one drinks alone except for the miserable, Fontaine."

"That's not true," Max said, sloshing his brandy as he gestured. "Drunkards drink alone."

"I don't fancy too many of them are blissfully happy, do you?"

"Nope, don't suppose they are," Max sighed.

"Come on, stand up." Will placed his hands under Max's arms and lifted him to his feet. As Max outweighed Will by two stone of height and muscle, he nearly dropped him, but managed to hold on. Max, however, was unable to hold on to the brandy decanter, and its remaining contents splashed to the carpet below.

"Oh dear, my brandy. I should go back down and pick it up," Max said, weaving.

"No!" Will exclaimed, tightening his grip on his friend's shoulders. "Forget the brandy, I think Harris left you a tray by the door. You need something of more substance."

Will sat Max on the comfortably worn couch in the library and fetched the tray. "See, there? A nice tea. We'll have you fixed up in no time."

But Max was not paying attention. "I ruined the carpet. I ruin everything."

Will stirred four spoonfuls of sugar into the now quite chilled tea. "That's the talk of a man feeling sorry for himself. And utter rot, at that."

Max's blurred vision found his friend's face. "Am I a bad person?" he asked, sincerity and sorrow ringing from his voice.

"Now *that's* utter rot," said Will, as he handed the tea to his friend and uncovered a tray of cold cheese and ham.

"He's right, you know," Max replied mournfully. "I don't do anything. I ride my horse, I go to parties, and I play cards. But what good is that? I don't run the estates, I don't care to. I am worthless."

"You are not worthless. So you attend parties and live in society. Surprisingly, most of our acquaintances do as well."

"That's not the whole of their lives. They do other things. You do."

"Yes, but not everyone is like me. I have to be in trade. It's just happy luck that I have a taste for it. Besides, you have your translation work."

"Not enough money in it. And he knows it."

"Now I understand what has gotten you into this state. Your father send you another letter, did he?" Will said, setting the tray of food in front of Max.

Max shook his head. "He came."

The knife Will was holding clattered to the plate, but his face remained impassive, his jaw set. "He came? Here? Your father?"

"Yes, yes, and yes, my good man." Max absently picked up a piece of meat and placed it down again. He was in no mood for food. All he desired was another drink.

"What the devil did he say to you?"

Max took a deep breath. "Among other things, that I must reform my way of life."

"There is nothing wrong with your life." Will sighed. "For some reason your father thinks you are a wastrel of the worst reputation, who gambles and drinks himself into oblivion. I happen to know you enjoy a very average reputation, don't gamble more than a penny a point, and as for the drinking, well, not including tonight . . . In truth, I don't really know why he's always been so angry with you, and vice versa."

"We . . . just never got on," Max muttered, staring coldly into his teacup. And indeed, after Max had turned ten years

old, this had been true. They had always argued. At Longsbowe Park, the Earl always tried to bind Max too tight. And
as Max got older, the arguments broadened in topic and purpose.

The Earl never consented to see the future as any more
than the next day. Whereas Max, stuck in a relic surrounded
by relics and drilled in the ways of the past, craved his own
life. So they'd fought. Sometimes it's the littlest thing that can
fracture a bond. The weight of one grievance piled on top of
the last.

The fact was, the world moved forward, and Max's father
could never forgive his son for moving with it. And Max could
never forgive the old man for so resolutely standing still.

"Am I . . ." Max coughed, nervously started again. "Am I
simply waiting for him to die?"

Will sucked in his breath. "No," he finally replied. "Don't
even think it."

"He says I must get married in three months' time, else I
will be cut out of my inheritance and he'll declare to the
world I'm a bastard," Max stated.

Will just stared at Max, unable to comprehend.

"Bloody hell," Will managed to breathe out. "Where did
you put that brandy?"

Some time later, after a great many half-started but never
finished questions, Will finally put together a coherent sentence, and posed it to Max.

"It seems rather prophetic. We were just joking about this
the other day."

"I know. Fate has annoying timing," Max answered, so-
bering up a bit. "It's easy to joke about taking a wife. To actually have to do it is an entirely different thing altogether."

"And not on your own terms," Will finished for him.

"Yes, quite," Max reasoned.

"You could always say that you don't care about the stupid
inheritance," Will mused. "He'll never do it. He can see
you've lived without the money and don't need it."

Max looked at Will with a certain degree of cynicism.

"Yes, he will. I know my father. His skills at manipulation
are ruthless and unsurpassed." Then Max's face softened,

sarcasm giving way to worry. A brief thought flitted across his mind. *What is the old man afraid of? That I'll disappoint him in this, too?*

He let that question go with a shake of his head, saying to his friend, "There's a decided difference between being cut off and being disinherited. I may not use his money, Holt, but the old man is right. I enjoy the life I lead partially because of the prospect of it. He takes that away, and he takes away my good name . . ." Max leaned his head against the paneling of his study wall. "I am no good at being anything but a gentleman. The truth of the matter is, I like it. I think about all the things I could do with the title—modernize Longsbowe Park, for once make a decent turn over on the crops, I could still dally with my work even . . ." Max looked thoughtful for a moment, and then, "He's probably right, you know."

Will glanced at Max. "Your father? How?"

"Maybe it is time to grow up. I've been avoiding stepping into his shoes for so long, I—"

"Never really found your own place?"

Max nodded silently. "Now I have to find a wife."

"Well then," Will replied, lifting his own cup of chilled tea. "A toast. To your future wife. Whoever she may be."

"To my bride." Max drained the remains of the too-sweet, too-cold tea. The taste had him grimacing.

To his bride. The search would begin in the morning.

Seven

THE ball was a smashing success. Romilla could not be happier. Well, she could be, she supposed, if she had been able to secure a royal or two as guests, but her husband assured her that the court was far too busy while removed in Brighton to attend. They would have to content themselves with ordinary aristocrats. But other than that, Romilla was a very pleased hostess.

As she looked out across the ballroom, which was teeming with colored silks and black evening coats lit by a thousand crystalline candles, Romilla took a great sigh of relief. All of her guests were enthusiastic and happy, all of the best character. The musicians kept the dancing going, and she was certain no other hostess this Season would be able to boast of such a fine punch—from her mother's own recipe. And if a whisper of the words *nouveau riche* floated through the air, Romilla was content to ignore those snobbish remarks in favor of seeing the better side of the snobbish guests who said them. After all, a person is only looked down upon until they are looked up to. And everyone had to admire the Alton ball—whether they wanted to or not.

All might not have turned out so well, Romilla thought. There had been a potential disaster just that morning while calling on Lady Charlbury, when Gail accidentally spilled tea on that lady's favorite cat. Gail had apologized quite sincerely, but Lady Charlbury almost refused to attend the ball, and without her attendance, half of London would have considered the event not worth the effort. Lady Charlbury managed to be reclusive and yet quite ruled society in a way Romilla aspired to.

Luckily, Lady Charlbury accepted Gail's apology. Romilla grudgingly gave the girl some respect for the way she handled the old woman. Gail had simply picked up the teapot while the cat and its owner were making a mewling fuss, and said, "I'm so sorry, ma'am. At least now your cat won't try to take tea with you again. Perhaps he'll just settle for the cream."

Lady Charlbury had blinked at the audacious girl. Romilla was afraid she had made the situation all the worse, but suddenly Lady Charlbury started to chuckle.

"Why, young lady, I never looked at it that way! I've been trying to break him of the habit for years!"

"Did you know," said Gail, sitting beside Lady Charlbury, "that some ancient cultures revered cats as equal to humans? Sometimes gods? I daresay they would have been honored to have had wise old Tom for tea."

And from that point on, Lady Charlbury and Gail spent the morning thick as thieves, discussing cats throughout history. When Romilla and Gail were taking their leave, Lady Charlbury made a point of saying she was eagerly anticipating that evening's ball. Once the door to the carriage had closed, Romilla made certain she paid the child a compliment.

"My dear, that was a very successful morning. I was impressed with your poise. I do hope it won't escape you by nightfall. And for once your penchant for useless knowledge has come in handy!"

Gail and Evangeline shared a glance.

"Father always told us that everyone has their own special interests. To carry on a conversation all one needs to do is to find it," Evangeline replied, smiling at her sister.

"How did you know her interest was her cats?" Romilla inquired.

"Well," Gail drawled, "she does have six of them."

"Ah. Now, Gail," Romilla said, as she settled herself against the cushions of the carriage seat, closing her eyes, "if only you could speak as well to men or people your own age. And mind you, most of them don't care at all for young ladies who read overmuch. Lady Charlbury is an oddity, and charming old ladies are not what will get you married."

Gail looked down at her lap and twisted her fingers about nervously. "I know," she whispered.

Evangeline took hold of her sister's hand. "Gail, I didn't know that cats were sometimes considered gods. Was that in India?"

"Egypt. The Hindu in India revere cows," Gail answered.

"Cows?" Romilla opened an eye. "I wonder if they eat a great deal of beef?"

* * *

NOW that she had a moment to reflect, Romilla thought Gail was doing remarkably well at the ball that evening. Although she was not continually dancing, she had not tripped on or spilled anything; and she had not once said some wholly inappropriate remark that revealed her unusual upbringing. She even looked remarkably well in a gown of pale yellow silk. Romilla had even seen one gangly young gentleman eagerly fetch Gail a glass of punch. But nothing could compare to Evangeline's success.

Radiant in a deceptively simple ivory silk and lace gown, Evangeline was completely surrounded by every eligible bachelor in attendance. From her position at the front of the ballroom, Romilla could see her beautiful stepdaughter quite clearly, and was immensely pleased.

Evangeline's incomparable beauty, matched with her genuinely sweet and open personality, was a heady combination. Romilla had made certain that she was taken around to every society matron and made proper introductions. Aside from Lady Charlbury, who had already been introduced and so took the time to ask pointedly after Gail, every single one of the old biddies was absolutely charmed by Evangeline. After that, she was given carte blanche to be introduced to and dance with any man in attendance.

Needless to say, all of the gentlemen present were quite eager to make her acquaintance.

Romilla took her feathered fan and lightly tapped her husband on the arm.

"Well, my dear," he said, offering his arm, "you seem to have pulled off the coup of the Season. I congratulate you."

Romilla gave him a pretty smile. "Thank you, my husband. But I will give credit where it's due. A great many of your political acquaintances are here tonight, and they lend a certain sparkle to the event."

Sir Geoffrey grinned. "You and my daughters are all the sparkle I'll ever need," he said in hushed tones, causing a warm blush to flow over Romilla's cheeks.

"I see Evangeline is making quite a few friends," Sir Geoffrey remarked, turning his eyes back to the ballroom floor, nodding to a few parliamentary types as he did.

"She will make a great match," Romilla whispered fervently, as if saying it enough would make it true.

"But where has Gail gotten off to?" Sir Geoffrey scanned the crowd. "Oh there she is, I see her. She is talking to young Ommersley."

A sense of dread overcame Romilla. She turned and saw Gail on the far side of the ballroom, lecturing to the painfully thin young man with more Adam's apple than head. "Ommersley? Who lives at Number Twenty? His family's name is older than Moses! God spare us if she is speaking nonsense about ancient cultures or industrial technology or Wollstonecraft. His mother will make certain we're never received in any house on the Square."

Sir Geoffrey looked at his youngest daughter, took in her rapid speech, her companion's rapt expression, and chuckled. "I doubt he's even listening, my dear. Now come. We have greeted all our guests, the punch is absolutely delicious, and the musicians are playing a waltz. I request a dance with the best hostess in London."

Romilla gave one last worried glance toward Gail and relaxed against her husband's arm as he led her to the floor. Sometimes, she thought, as he spun her out with the other couples, she was so very happy to have married him.

* * *

SIR Geoffrey was mistaken in one of his declarations. The host and hostess had not yet greeted all their guests, because a few were very late to arrive. Two, in fact.

Wearing his finest black evening dress, his dark hair ruthlessly pushed back from his face, Max's hawk-like gaze scanned the throng that crowded the ballroom floor of Number Seven Berkeley Square.

"How are we acquainted with the host this time?" Max said, his green eyes continuing to scan the crowd.

"We met Sir Geoffrey in Vienna on our tour of the Continent, remember? He was attached to the British Consul's office," Will answered from beside Max, quite dashing in his own evening kit. "I received the invitation a few weeks ago, but not until your bride hunt began did I decide to attend."

Max's gaze narrowed. The "bride hunt," as Will so aptly called it, had consumed the majority of Max's time since it began in earnest more than two weeks ago. He had always been a mildly social creature, but since his father had issued the ultimatum, Max had been to more balls, musicales, afternoon teas, public assemblies at Almack's, and theater performances than he cared to count. He had met numerous young ladies, some fresh out of the schoolroom, some in their second or third Seasons, some decidedly upon the shelf. They were variously short, tall, plump, thin, dark, fair, pleasant, pretty, plain, intelligent, and insipid. Max had been courteous to all of the above, happily flirting with the mamas as much as the daughters, working his way into the good graces of every eligible female in London. Suffice it to say, Max had found every single one of the girls he met lacking. He was fast growing weary of the hunt.

"I am fast growing weary of this hunt," he remarked.

Will rolled his eyes. "You are the one who has rejected every eligible young lady out of hand! What was wrong with Miss Plimpton, dare I ask? I thought her remarkably good natured."

Max shot his friend a hard look. "She had a gap between her two front teeth, and when she spoke there was whistling."

"Well, then of course she is beneath your notice," Will replied sarcastically. "Sir Geoffrey has two daughters, if I recall. Do let me know if either of them has a nose that doesn't meet with your approval? Or chews her food too many times before swallowing?"

Max smirked. "Have you made the acquaintance of Sir Geoffrey's daughters?"

Will shook his head. "When we were in Vienna, they were still in the schoolroom. And, uh, I was otherwise occupied in Vienna, if you recall."

"Oh, yes. *Otherwise occupied*. That's a new term for it."

Will shot him a look, but Max just squared his shoulders and took a deep breath. "The misses Alton must be the only two young ladies in London we haven't met."

"Shall we seek them out, then? Who knows, you could fall madly in love with one."

Max gave his friend a very cynical glare. "God help me if I do. Love doesn't come into this bride hunt, Will. Come on, let's find our hosts and get this over with."

Max headed into the maddening crowd of Society's beautiful people, with a smirking Will close at his heels.

* * *

GAIL stood on the far side of the ballroom, close to the balcony doors, quite happily unaware of the latest arrivals to her and Evangeline's debut ball. She had been so nervous before, but now Gail was quite certain she'd never been in such a good mood in her life.

It was working! Evangeline had given her explicit instructions before the ball began.

"Gail, darling," she had said as Polly, the newly promoted ladies' maid, worked a seed pearl into her elegant coiffure, "I want you to try an experiment tonight. I want you to try conversing with a gentleman for more than two minutes."

"But—" Gail had started to say, but Evangeline cut her off with a wave of her hand.

"Give him your full attention for more than two minutes, and any gentleman will become taken with you, I promise."

And now, Gail stood with young Lord Ommersley, cheerfully lecturing him on the presumptiveness of Lord Elgin, who had retrieved the friezes from right off the side of Greece's Parthenon.

"And did he not realize that he is contributing to the global impression that England is nothing more than a conquering giant, pillaging every country we choose? Those marble friezes belong in Athens, they are part of their history! And if—"

"Miss Alton!" Lord Ommersley interrupted, his Adam's apple bobbing on every cracking syllable. "I wonder, would you care to step out onto the balcony?"

Gail furrowed her brow. "The balcony? Why?"

Ommersley immediately backtracked. "Or, perhaps, a, er, a dance?"

"Dance? Oh, well, thank you, Lord Ommersley, but I'm afraid I don't dance well. I mean, I danced the first few because it would be unseemly of me not to, this being a ball for Evie and me, but I am not very—"

"Well," he interrupted, completely unfazed, "perhaps I can fetch you another glass of punch. After, maybe I can convince you otherwise."

Gail glanced down at her cut glass cup and saw that it was drained to the very bottom. *How on earth had that happened?* she thought with a small frown. The punch was especially delicious tonight, but this was the third glass Ommersely had brought for her. Or was it the fourth? She shrugged.

Gail gave Ommersley a brilliant smile and handed him her cup. "Thank you ever so much. Another glass would be delightful."

* * *

MAX and Will located their hosts, quickly introducing themselves. Lady Alton was most pleased to have a guest with a name as old as Longsbowe. Sir Geoffrey was quite jovial in his greeting, shaking hands with both and, with a politician's knack for names and faces, took care to remember Will and Max from their travels.

"Vienna, wasn't it?" Sir Geoffrey voiced, smiling good-naturedly. "As I recall, Mr. Holt was particularly enamored of their opera house."

"I doubt it was the opera house, per se," Max drawled. "More likely a certain dan—"

Will interrupted his smirking friend quickly. "Sir Geoffrey, how are your lovely daughters? We must beg an introduction, the ball being in their honor, after all."

"I believe they are on the ballroom floor at the moment. At least, Evangeline is," Romilla answered, her discerning gaze entirely focused on Viscount Fontaine. "If you like, have a glass of punch, it is particularly excellent. This set will conclude shortly, I will be happy to introduce you after. And you as well, Mr. Holt."

Both gentlemen bowed in acquiescence.

"Well," remarked Will, as they found their way to the refreshments table. "We have no doubt that you have the mother's blessing."

"Stepmother," Max grumbled. He reached for the ladle from the punch bowl, but a long narrow hand had reached it first. Max watched as the tall, painfully thin young gentleman filled a glass halfway with the red punch. Replacing the ladle, the young man placed the cup on the table, and then, by means of some container concealed up his sleeve, poured a clear liquid into the cup, diluting the punch until it was a light pink. He looked around nonchalantly as he did so, only blushing when he saw Max watching him openly. As no one else seemed to have noted the oddity of his behavior (or the oddity of what was hiding in his sleeve), the tall young gentleman gave a wry smirk.

"Some girls need a little encouragement to, ah, enjoy the festivities," he said, placing his hand in his breast pocket, and transferring his sleeve's occupant there, while giving Max an easy wink, his sandy hair falling limply over his brow.

Watching the prankster make his way through the crowd, Will inquired, "What was that about?"

"I believe he's trying to improve his odds with a particular young lady."

"He spiked the punch?" Will asked.

"Quite." Max took a sip from his own glass. Lady Alton had been correct; it was very good—in its undiluted state.

"Fontaine," Will said, eyeing his friend.

"Holt," Max replied, taking the same innocent tone.

"You're not going to let him take advantage of some unfortunate girl who has had her wits tampered with?"

"What would you have me do, William? Charge in with my sword drawn and save the day?" Max quipped, quirking an eyebrow.

"Precisely."

"Did I hit you too hard round the head at Gentleman Jackson's today? I am going to wait right here, be introduced to our newest debutantes, dance one dance, and leave. You go save the unknown young lady from the perils of drink, if you feel it necessary."

"Well, I could do that," Will reasoned, his gaze leveled over Max's right shoulder. "But, I am going to do you a fantastic favor and head off Mrs. Plimpton and her whistle-toothed daughter."

Max turned and glanced behind him. Mrs. Plimpton had her daughter by the hand and was quite literally cutting her way through the crowd. Her intended target was obvious.

Max shuddered and turned back abruptly, hoping to God that the old bat hadn't noticed he'd spotted her. He ducked underneath Will's arm and walked away as quickly as he could without drawing attention to himself. Max heard Will call after him.

"Rescue the girl and save the day, my good man! Ah, Mrs. Plimpton, how pleasant to see you again. And your lovely daughter as well."

* * *

GAIL stood alone by the balcony doors, listening to the orchestra play an absolutely beautiful waltz. Not a confident dancer, she was somewhat surprised to find herself swaying to the music. She felt loose, bemused, studying the colors on the dance floor swirling in rhythm to the waltz. As she watched under heavy lids, entranced, Gail picked at the sleeve of her gown. She never realized just how interesting the feel of silk was. The feel of anything, for that matter. She ran her hand over a fluted column relief in the wall, reveling in the cold touch of marble.

This warm, amused feeling was quite foreign to Gail, but instead of being suspicious, she decided to enjoy it. The occasional giggle escaped her lips, which amused her even more. She went on swaying to the sounds of violins and French horns, until her yellow slipper caught the edge of her hem, and she stumbled face forward . . .

Into the arms of Lord Ommersley.

"Lord Ommersley! Thank you." Gail spoke in between heavy breaths. "You are apparently agile enough to catch a stumblik . . . stumbling yellow debutante and not spill the drink you had taken the trouble to fetch for her."

He had manners enough to seem taken aback, but Gail was too intent on righting herself to catch the mischievous glint that passed through his eyes as he studied the entrancing rise and fall of her breast. She pushed herself away from the young man's embrace. He, however, was a bit more reluctant to let go.

"I had thought to bring you another drink," Lord Ommersley drawled, "but now I think you may not need it." His free hand closed over Gail's wrist in a gentle but firm grasp.

"Oh, but I am thirsty," Gail protested, trying to ease her wrist away from its captor, but finding herself caught.

"Well then," Ommersley said, "come out onto the balcony, and I shall let you have your drink."

Gail narrowed her eyes, but could not hone in on what was raising her suspicions. Before she had been enjoying her fuzzy mind—now it was becoming somewhat of a hindrance.

"The balcony?" Gail questioned. "But t'would be improper."

"Come now," Ommersley cajoled, tugging Gail along to the terrace doors. "We are going to be great friends, you and I. After all, I live right across the Square. I promise, a bit of air will be refreshing."

Gail's brow remained set in a furrowed frown. Something wasn't right here. Before, Ommersley seemed to be very attentive, in a harmless sort of way. But now Gail could see the wicked intentions in his face, hear the fevered determination in his voice. A heavy velvet curtain separated them from most of the party, and suddenly her mind latched onto the fact that she was very alone with this man. And Gail had had enough.

With all the force she could muster, she wrenched her arm free of Ommersley's grasp, pulling at him with such force that he spilled the drink he carried—all down the front of Gail's dress.

"Oh!" Gail cried, as the cool liquid drenched through the cloth and hit her skin. "My dress! How awful!"

Ommersley, however, seemed to be more enraged at the thought of her breaking his grip than the ruined state of her gown. Quickly, with a snarling ferocity his hollow frame disguised, he grabbed Gail by the forearms with bruising force and attempted to shake her into submission.

Through the pounding in her ears from being so shockingly handled, Gail heard a growling whisper.

"Enough!"

As suddenly as the shaking started, it stopped. Gail was given to the wall to lean against, whilst a dark, and somehow familiar form dragged a whimpering Ommersley off by the scruff of his neck, opened the French doors to the balcony and disappeared for no more than twenty seconds. Gail could hear nothing but a few grunts through the doors, but when they reopened, only the form of her savior reemerged, wiping his hands with a handkerchief. The long figure walked toward Gail, his strides quiet but strong. As he passed a lit wall sconce, she could discern his features, and her eyes widened in shock.

Bloody Hell.

"I honestly thought you had him when you broke his grasp but he was a bit too fervent for his own good." The man spoke as he approached, his eyes still on the balcony doors. When he turned his head, his concerned, good-natured smile quickly faded.

"Bloody Hell," he breathed.

* * *

"WHAT the devil are you doing here?" Max, after a moment of shock, finally spat out.

"Me?" she expostulated. "What the devil are you doing here?"

"I was invited to this party!" Max replied, which was (marginally) true. "Although I would have thought twice about attending had I known they let in bumbling headstrong nitwits who get themselves attacked."

"Hah! I can only question how such a conceited, overbearing ass received an invitation!" she shot back.

"Look around." Max waved his hand to the assembled crowd, who happily went on dancing without any thought or care as to the spitting match that was going on by the balcony doors. "Everyone here is a conceited, overbearing ass!"

A snort of laughter escaped her lips. Max's eyes narrowed as he leaned over her, placing his hand on the wall beside her head. He knew his frame to be quite imposing and, this time, as he judged by her widening eyes, she might actually take him seriously.

"The man who is currently bleeding on the balcony is a conceited, overbearing ass," he growled, forcing her golden eyes to hold his gaze. "He could have hurt you, and would have, had I not been here."

The girl steeled her spine. "I was doing just fine before you came."

Max snorted. "Oh yes, you had him in your clutches. He was deeply fooled by your impression of a rag doll, unaware that at any moment you would strike."

Aggravated, she looked up into his face—but for some reason her eyes couldn't focus on his properly. Her hand went to her head, as her knees bent involuntarily.

"Careful there. I've got you." Quickly, his arms went around her, catching her before she could fall. Max could not help but be reminded of the last time he had this woman in his embrace; she was as soft then as she was now. And as wet—he could feel her form pressing through the damp, sticky barrier of her dress. She was almost pretty, almost likeable . . . if only she didn't feel the need to set his back up with every sentence.

"What's your name?" he wondered, looking down into the hooded golden brown eyes.

She refocused and determinedly met his eyes, steadying herself there. "Propriety dictates the gentleman offer his name first."

"You wouldn't know propriety if it came up and shook your hand," Max countered, but conceded to her unwavering stare. Making certain the girl could stand on her own two feet, Max stepped back and gave a very smart bow. "Maximillian Augustus St. John, Viscount Fontaine, future Earl of Longsbowe, of Longsbowe Park, manor, and estates, at your reluctant service."

"It makes sense for you to have a name as pompous as you are, Max." Her smirk was drunkenly lopsided. "I am going to call you Max from now on—I doubt I care to remember all the St. John Augustine nonsense."

There it is, Max thought, *there is the reason I find you so terribly provoking.* That thought, however, he managed to keep to himself.

"And what, pray tell, is your name, brat?" Max gritted out. "Hester? Prudence? Mabel? Something as irritating and headstrong as you, perhaps?"

Her eyes lowered. "Gail," she mumbled, worrying the lace netting of her dress.

"Just Gail?"

"Just Gail," she countered, lifting her head again, with renewed fire.

"I think I like Brat better. More fitting. Haven't you a surname? Some poor family must be forced to survive you."

Gail visibly bristled at this jab and opened her mouth to answer, but was quickly interrupted by a muffled giggle. The giggle was soon joined by a masculine voice, whispering inaudible but heated phrases, eliciting more giggles. Both the giggle and the heated masculine voice were headed toward the balcony doors.

Max put his hand over Gail's mouth and quickly dragged her into the shadows, behind the curtain.

His mouth at her ear, he whispered, "Believe me, Brat, neither of us wants to be found having private words with the other. It would cause only embarrassment . . . and possibly marriage."

Wisely, Gail kept silent.

They watched as a voluptuous Titian-haired woman in an extremely well-formed dress tiptoed past on the arm of a gentleman, who seemed to delight in putting his hand in the most inappropriate place on her posterior. The lady, however, didn't seem to mind.

Once the frisky couple had closed the doors behind them, Max released his hand from Gail's mouth, set his head back against the cool stone, and breathed a sigh of relief.

"Well," he said, "since there were no screams issuing back at us, I gather they didn't see that conceited, overbearing ass I left behind the potted lemon tree. Although why the Altons have lemon trees outside in this climate is beyond me." He returned his gaze to the girl. "What, nothing to add? No witty rejoinder?"

Max took Gail by the shoulders and turned her about to face him, which turned out to be the wrong idea. The sudden movement combined with the recent lack of air behind the stuffy curtain and Max's hand, and none too few glasses of punch, had brought forth a wave of nausea that could not be denied.

There, behind the curtain, near the terrace doors, Gail lost control of her stomach.

All over Max's only pair of dancing shoes.

"Oh for the love of . . . !"

Max swore with a fluency Gail likely would have admired if she hadn't been in such a state. His face flushed to a bright, mottled red, he strained to keep his voice to a fervent whisper.

"Brat! Er, Gail! Are you all right? Can you take some deep breaths for me? Good. Now what's your family name? Where are your parents?"

She didn't answer him, instead her face turned pale and waxen as she leaned back against the cool wall behind her. He gently took her chin in his hand, but she pushed it aside and let her head fall to her chest. She was not handling her liquor well at all. Covering his face in his hands, Max took a deep breath (through his mouth, of course), turned on his now slippery heel and walked out from behind the curtain and into the throng of partygoers.

Luck was on his side, for he avoided having anyone notice his shoes, by grabbing the first passing servant he could find. Pulling the poor man toward their hidden spot, he ushered him behind the curtain and spoke in low tones.

"What is your name?"

"Grisby, sir."

"Grisby, do you know who this young lady is?"

"Why, yes, sir, she's . . . blimey, she's—"

"Can you escort her to her family?" Max interrupted. "Someone to take care of her?"

"Why, yes sir, of course."

Max discreetly slipped a coin into the astonished Grisby's hand. "That is for your discretion."

Grisby blinked several times. "Sir, as a member of Sir Geoffrey's household, I never—"

"For your services, then. Please take care of her before anyone sees. She'll need a good deal of water and air."

"Yes, sir, I'll take her directly. Come on, now, miss, we'll fix you right up," Grisby said, as he gently took hold of Gail's arm, steadying her against the side of his body. For a man with graying hair and a lean frame he took hold of her inert weight remarkably well. Max watched with concern as Grisby led Gail through a door paneled into the interior wall just to their right, hidden behind the curtain. It blended perfectly, indiscernible, if one hadn't known to look for it.

Trying not to breathe too deeply (the smell of his shoes being pervasive), Max took a moment to gather himself. It had only been minutes since he had had the misfortune to again be thrown into the presence of Miss Gail . . . er, something or other, but it felt like hours. She had never failed to aggravate him to his breaking point. This ball was a complete waste of time, Max thought, and suddenly, he was very tired. As much as he did not wish to offend his hosts, Max could not bring himself to face another set of debutantes. There was no bride hunting to be done tonight, it seemed, and Max decided the time had come to head home.

However, he hadn't taken two steps toward the party before he realized he could not easily cross the ballroom floor without causing a complete scandal. That is to say, without the state of his shoes causing some crinkled noses.

Max cursed himself for not asking Grisby if he could get his shoes washed or at least asked him the direction of the nearest water closet. His eyes flicked to the hidden, paneled door. Where did it lead? Suddenly, a niggling worry entered his brain. *Damn*, Max thought, *I hope I didn't dump the poor girl on someone who is just going to dump her behind some potted tree.* His conscience getting the better of him, Max made certain no one was coming toward the balcony, then quickly stepped behind the curtain again, found the door's latch and slipped through.

He stepped into another world. Was it a conservatory? A hothouse? The room was twenty feet high, cased by glass and filled with the most beautiful flowering trees and plants Max had ever seen. It was warm, humid, exotic. Down a wrought iron spiral staircase was a small stone path that wove its way through this enclosed forest, hiding its curves in the shade of wide-leafed palms. Moonlight filtered through the glass walls and played across the branches of the tallest trees, hung with leafy vines that flowered white bells. The tinkling of water mixed with the faded strains of the music, and Max breathed in the heavy perfume of the bright orange lilies that peppered the edge of the path.

Obviously, the hidden door did not lead to the kitchens. Not directly in any case. But as there was no sign of Grisby or Gail, Max had to assume there was another way through, and the old man had used this merely as a hallway, likely to the servant's quarters. Max wound his way down the stone path, forgetting about the awful state of his shoes for a moment, while he took in the beauty of this isolated spot in the middle of the teeming city. At the far end of the path, closest to the rounded end of the glass enclosure, was a stone fountain peppered with naughty little wood sprites pouring pails of water over unhappy looking stone frogs. Each sprite had a roguish wink in its eye and a pair of wings too small for its rounded cherubic body. But in the moonlight, they seemed to take flight. The fountain flowed down from higher tiers but ended in a wide, low pool. A pool he could easily step into.

Max looked around to make certain he was alone and sent silent thanks for an easy way to clean his shoes. Throwing any lingering caution to the wind, he stepped into the fountain, splashing about happily. He let the wood sprites pour water over the filth on the once-soft leather. They were clean in no time, and Max was about to remove himself from the pool and the party, when a shadowed figured walked through the trees, and jumped back, startled at his presence.

"Oh!" a female voice exclaimed, lifting her head from her own private reverie.

Max was dumbstruck. She was the most glorious creature he had ever laid eyes on. A small, delicate-looking female, swathed in a delicious confection of silk and lace that shimmered in the moonlight. Her hair was a sweet honeyed blonde, piled artfully upon her head, a long curl escaping over her shoulder. She had a blue-eyed gaze that speared him, a slightly sloping nose that curved up in a fetching manner at the end and a pert rosebud mouth that Max ached to taste. He couldn't help but notice the sleeve of her gown was torn and trailing off her shoulder.

"Excuse me," she said, casting her gaze again to the floor and turning away.

"No! Wait!" Max exclaimed, rushing out of the fountain's pool with a resounding splash. He caught up to her as she turned to face him. He dared not touch her, for fear she might disappear, but gathered himself enough to bow.

"I'm sorry if I disturbed you, miss, you should not have to leave such a lovely garden just because I am here." Given his unexpected jumble of nerves, Max was surprised at his own eloquence. "Er—are you quite well?" He indicated her shoulder, ready to do battle with anyone who had caused such a glowing beauty harm.

"Oh! Yes, I'm perfectly fine," she blushed, her mouth forming an *O* of surprise as she held the shoulder of her gown together with her hand. "This—I'm afraid the stitching on this gown is not very strong. I was dancing, and . . . well . . ." The young lady ventured a sweet smile to Max, the warmth of her expression flooring him.

How was this possible? Max hadn't felt so undone since he was a green lad, girding himself up to talk to a girl for the first time. Propriety dictated he leave the lady to her garden, but somehow, he couldn't. Max was caught up in her dazzling gaze, and she had forgotten her feminine blushes and found herself staring, entranced, in return.

A comfortable silence descended, and a sudden need to fill it. She spoke first.

"Um . . . what were you doing in the fountain?" she asked, awkwardly folding one hand to her waist, while the other was occupied holding up her sleeve.

Max looked down at his shoes, clean now, and the footprint puddles that tracked back to the fountain. He had been in quite the hurry to stop her from going, hadn't he? "Some, er, food was spilled on my shoes. I came through the door looking for a servant and found this marvelous place, and uh, washed off my shoes." Max grinned ruefully at his own story. It sounded so silly now, his anger at his ruined shoes and that damned girl.

Oh, no, Miss Brat Whomever, Max thought, *I shan't think about you. You and your irritating mouth and golden eyes won't intrude on my time with this captivating beauty.*

"Was it pudding?" asked the captivating beauty.

"Pardon?" Max said, startled out of his reverie.

"On your shoes, did someone spill a pudding?"

"Probably."

Again, they found themselves lapsing into that comfortable silence. He was so enchanted with this vision before him, the magic of the glass garden, that he couldn't help but devour her with his eyes. She met his gaze with one of equally fascinated interest.

"What's your name?" Max murmured, not realizing he'd said it aloud.

Suddenly she smiled, giving a surprisingly low, husky laugh, exuding a sensuality that had Max's full attention.

"My stepmother would tell you that propriety dictates the gentleman introduce himself first," she said coyly, looking out from underneath her lashes.

Where had he heard that before? It didn't matter.

Max bowed, not extravagantly, but warmly, bending at the waist, but always keeping his eyes locked with hers. "Maximillian, Lord Fontaine, at your service, ma'am."

"I think I saw you enter the party tonight, Lord Fontaine. You and a blond gentleman, who looks to be perpetually happy."

"Oh, you're mistaken. My friend is really quite dour." Max

smiled. When she looked at him quizzically, he continued. "Sometimes, there are whole minutes when he's not smiling."

That elicited a giggle from his companion, entrancing Max even further.

"I am Miss Evangeline Alton." She dipped into a curtsy. "A pleasure."

"So you're the daughter of the house!"

"One of them," Evangeline replied, nodding sweetly.

"Elder or younger?" Max inquired.

When she replied elder, Max asked if this was her first outing in society, for he did not recall having seen her before.

"In London, yes," she replied. "But I have been in Portugal for the past year, and Paris and Madrid before that, so . . ."

"Yes, I doubt you are unfamiliar with the ways of society," he chuckled. "But you should be out enjoying the party."

"I was. I mean, I am. Romilla—my stepmother—was dancing so merrily, I didn't wish to bother her. So I thought to simply cut through to the kitchens, to see if I could get my dress stitched. I didn't think anyone would be in here. How do you know my family?"

He told her of meeting her father in Vienna. "You were still in the schoolroom at the time, else I certainly would have remembered you." Yes, he would have remembered her, very well indeed. What if, what if he was so bold as to touch her? Would she disappear like smoke?

Overcome by the idea, Max held out his arm in a courtly gesture, inviting her to take it. "Miss Alton, you must know all about this lovely conservatory. Would you be so good as to show me some of its secrets?"

She hesitated at first, likely not used to being left alone with a man. But, he wanted no more than he asked, and smiled to urge her on—and saw in her answering smile the moment she lost all hesitation and decided in his favor.

Her free arm slid through his, and warmth flooded Max's body. She started speaking, idling through the path and under tree branches, and Max was determined to remember every word.

"This was my mother's garden. She loved to sit in here. She loved different kinds of plants, so every time my father came home from his travels, he brought her something new and exotic. These vines, with the white flowers? They're from Greece. The olive growers plant these vines beside the olive trees, because they make the fruit sweeter."

Max reached up to one of the white-belled flowers and, with a firm hand, plucked it and presented it to Evangeline. Although she had no free hand with which to take it.

"Allow me," Max said softly, and at her acquiescing nod, tucked the flower behind her ear, tracing her jaw as he withdrew his hand.

She smiled at him, his eyes never leaving her face. He could get lost in that face.

"My mother died when I was young," she continued, "but my father dictated that the garden should always grow, even when we weren't here. I'm impressed you managed to find it—the doors are well hidden."

"I consider it fortunate I did so."

They had stopped walking, although Max hadn't noticed. His feet had stopped touching the ground long ago. They stood in that garden, with the muted strains of music lilting through from the ballroom, moonlight drifting through the trees, and his mind filled with her.

He didn't plan it. But as easily as Evangeline had taken Max's arm, as hopefully as he'd offered it, Max and Evangeline found themselves leaning into each other. Her hand abandoned her own torn sleeve, transferred to his. His face was a hair's breadth from hers, her mouth tilted up. He could feel the warmth of her breath on his skin, and when their lips met, it was simple.

It was sweet.

"Oh, Miss Evangeline! Thank goodness!"

Evangeline pulled away from him quickly, her jerky movement breaking the spell that held them both. The darkness hid most of them, but Evangeline's pale hair and dress had caught the moonlight, making her glow like a beacon, which attracted the very person searching frantically for her. Evangeline quickly tried to rearranged her torn shoulder, but to no avail.

A servant, the housekeeper by her dress, stood in a second doorway, one that led down to the kitchens. She rushed forward, the jangling of her pockets announcing her arrival to everyone near and far. She approached her quarry nervously, her eyes flitting from Evangeline to Evangeline's sleeve to Max in quick succession.

"I, uh, I beg your pardon, sir," the housekeeper said, stooping into a curtsy, "but might I have a word with Miss Alton?"

Evangeline nodded, and Max, receiving his signal, bowed to her and walked back along the narrow path toward the fountain.

"Mrs. Bibb, I know it seems strange, my being here alone with . . ."

That was all Max could hear. The housekeeper took over the conversation in a series of furtive whispers. Max tried not to eavesdrop, but he didn't want Evangeline to be scolded or belittled in any way for her actions this evening, and so found himself straining to hear what was being said.

A few moments later, Evangeline burst through the thicket of branches that hid the path from the fountain.

"I have to go," she stated, her manner completely changed. She was brisk, worried. "I'm very sorry, but there is a pressing matter I must see to."

"Please tell me you're not in trouble. I didn't intend to cause you any difficulty," Max whispered, his concern genuine.

Her expression softened. "Oh no, nothing of the sort. But I have to attend to something."

He closed the gap between them and ventured so far as to take her free hand.

"May I claim a dance with you later?"

"I'm sorry, but I doubt I'll be dancing anymore this evening."

Max would have taken that as a setback, except that she squeezed his hand as she said it. She was truly worried about something, and just as truly sorry to have missed the chance to dance with him.

"Then may I call upon you and your father tomorrow?" Max asked, holding her hand firmly, afraid that if he lost the connection, it would be he himself who was lost.

"Yes," she breathed. "Please do."

Max took the delicate gloved hand to his mouth, kissed it with a reverence reserved for cherished objects. His sharp gaze never left her as she disappeared through the thicket of the path, like mist in the air.

Max didn't remember leaving the conservatory. He didn't remember strolling through the ballroom, thick with dancers and the merry spirit of wine and song. Didn't remember retrieving Will, who was backed up against a wall like a startled fawn, forced to listen to the never tiring font of ignorance that was Mrs. Plimpton, while her daughter did a respectable imitation of a statue. What he did remember was a lovely mouth, a sweet smile, and a pair of brilliant golden . . . no, blue eyes.

"This is it, Holt!" Max said, slapping his friend on the shoulder once he had quickly and safely ushered them into his friend's carriage.

"What is it? And where did you disappear to for a half hour?" Will said, crossing his arms, petulantly. "I had to listen to every word that old biddy had to say about how this Season's neckline was indecent, especially for her 'pure, virtuous daughter.' It doesn't take that long to save one girl from a young cad's intentions."

"Beg pardon?" Max said, not knowing for a moment of whom Will spoke, his mind was much otherwise engaged. "Oh, that. Yes, that took hardly any time at all—and it doesn't matter now anyway. I've done it! I've found her! The hunt is over, I found one female in this town worth pursuing!"

Will looked at his friend, utter disbelief on his face. "Who?"

* * *

ROMILLA burst through the doors of the newly butter-yellow bedroom Gail claimed as her own. There she saw quite the tableau. Sitting on the bed was a very green-faced Gail, holding a porcelain bowl in her arms, while Evangeline, still startling in her ivory dress, her sleeve torn, busied herself by smoothing back Gail's fallen locks of hair and keeping a wet cloth to her sister's forehead.

"What on earth is going on here? Girls, why aren't you

downstairs? The house full of guests—Evangeline, what happened to your dress? Your dance partners are asking after you."

"I'm sorry, ma'am, er, Mother," Evangeline said, "but you see Gail has fallen quite ill."

A wave of genuine motherly concern came over Romilla as she rushed to the bedside.

"Ill? My dear girl, what's wrong? What has made you feel so poorly?"

"I don't know," Gail answered weakly. Romilla worried her lower lip, leaned in to feel Gail's forehead, and caught a whiff of a suspicious aroma on Gail's breath and dress. Romilla drew back quickly, frustration and annoyance replacing any concern in her voice.

"Ill," she stated flatly. "Well of course you're ill—you smell like the inside of a whiskey barrel."

"Ma'am?" Evangeline questioned. "Whatever do you mean?"

"Never fear, Evangeline. Abigail will survive. It's a sickness she'll soon get over. Your sister has gotten herself drunk. Quite in her cups. Oh, how could she? God forbid anyone hear about this—we'll be the laughingstock of Society before you can say *scotch*."

"Drunk?!" Evangeline exclaimed. "No! Gail has never had a drink of liquor in her life!"

"I sincerely doubt that," Romilla replied. She went to the pale, hunched form of her incorrigible stepchild. "Abigail! What did you have to drink? And how much?"

She was answered by a horrible retching, followed by a splash in the porcelain bowl.

Gail lifted her head.

"I swear," she said, her voice breaking miserably on each word, "I only had punch."

Eight

"THAT girl is lying. There was absolutely nothing intoxicating in that punch. It's from my own recipe!" Romilla exclaimed to her husband, indignant at the very thought of her punch being the cause of all the trouble. She was still seething the morning after the ball.

Following Romilla's diagnosis of inebriation, Evangeline had staunchly refused her stepmother's firm request that she go back down and join the merrymaking. She said she was quite sure there was no one left she cared to dance with in any case. Romilla had wheedled, cajoled, and outright demanded that Evangeline release Gail to the tender care of Mrs. Bibb, but Evangeline would not be persuaded to leave her sister's side. Romilla had eventually thrown up her hands at this display of sisterly devotion, convinced in her own rightness that Evangeline should be as outraged as she, and Gail was to blame for every wrong thing in this world, from influenza to the French.

Of course, Romilla calmed herself quickly. It was extremely judgmental to blame the girl for all of society's ills—besides, the French were their own problem. Taking herself back downstairs, Romilla rationalized her thoughts. Gail had been extremely nervous before the ball, this being her first outing in London Society; the parties in Portugal and Paris had been quite small and intimate compared to this grandest of events. Romilla could understand if she had had a nip or two of something to calm her nerves. But to claim she had only had punch! Romilla felt her ire work itself back up again. The least the child could do was be honest!

Which was exactly what she was saying to her husband in the library the following morning. She was supposed to be guiding the girls through their first morning of callers, but Gail was still abed, and Romilla was so upset she had abandoned Evangeline to Miss Nesbitt's spinsterly chaperonage in the drawing room while taking calls from eager young gentlemen.

"Drunkenness is unpardonable! Abigail is unpardonable!" Romilla said in a huff. "It's as if . . . are you even listening to me?"

Sir Geoffrey sat behind his desk, his thumb idly tapping the arm of his chair, his eyes straying to the paper in front of him. Romilla stopped mid-sentence, jostling her husband into looking at her. What he saw was a woman who could not be placated. Romilla was spitting mad, and she would be hanged if he thought he was going to read the paper today.

"Yes, dear," he sighed. "I'm paying attention."

* * *

MAX was admitted to the foyer of the Alton household in high hopes. In his hand, he carried a bunch of white-belled flowers, as close to the trailing vines Miss Alton had shown him in the conservatory as he could find in London's hothouses. He had barely slept a wink the night before in anticipation of meeting Evangeline again and presenting his rather hasty request to her father. He was about to do something he could hardly believe—asking a man permission to court his daughter. It was a day that had to arrive in any gentleman's life. And Max liked Evangeline, he truly did. She was perfection incarnate. Surely this feeling he was stepping off a cliff would pass.

Max handed his overcoat to the butler, a very formal and disapproving-looking fellow, who placed it in a cupboard with several other gentlemen's coats and hats. It suddenly struck Max that he must not be the only caller this morning. All the young gentlemen who'd had chance to dance with the Alton daughters were sure to be vying for their attention, and the rest of the day would be filled with visits to and from other ladies. Such was life in the world of the Ton. Absolutely no time to yourself to sneak out to the conservatory.

The butler turned imperiously and started toward the drawing room. Max followed, but was brought to a jolting stop by the sounds coming from behind a set of wide-paneled doors across the hall.

"Her behavior last night was absolutely scandalous!"

The heated female voice made Max wince. Obviously, the new Lady Alton was in a great temper about something.

"I'm not disagreeing with you, dear," came Sir Geoffrey's deep rumble, "but . . ."

"Could you believe a young lady could act so outrageously, *at her debut ball no less*?"

Max froze in his tracks. Evangeline had assured him that she would be perfectly all right, that she wouldn't be in trouble for being alone with him in the garden. But now, having heard those snippets of conversation, Max knew she had been wrong. Her parents, her stepmother in particular, were in a froth over it.

Max looked from the drawing room door, where the butler stood waiting to show him in, to the other door across the hall where the emanating sounds had been quelled to murmurs. He made his decision.

"Do you have a pencil?"

The butler looked at him curiously before reaching into his pocket and producing a short, nubbed pencil. Max took a calling card out of his own pocket and scribbled a quick note on the back. He handed the trailing white flowers and the card to the butler.

"Please see that Miss Alton receives these immediately. I'll wait right here for a reply."

The butler took the bundle, barely sniffing at his peculiar behavior.

"Yes, sir."

And with one quick glance over his shoulder the butler disappeared into the drawing room. Max caught a glimpse of a light blue room filled with flowers, morning sunlight, and too many gentlemen for his peace of mind. But he couldn't worry about that right now. It would only be a few moments before the butler returned, and he would rather not have to explain himself to the formidable family retainer.

Max quickly crossed the hall, and knocked on the wide paneled doors.

* * *

GAIL lay very, very still. The bed curtains were drawn. The window curtains were drawn. The covers were drawn up over her head. Sunlight was the enemy. As was noise, food, and any movement whatsoever. But she was awake. She had woken up just after dawn and tried to fall back asleep, but it was no use. Her body wouldn't allow herself the luxury. But she couldn't get out of bed—not now, not ever. Her head was pounding with such force that she was certain any sudden movement would dislodge her brain. She wasn't going to be riding QueenBee today, that was certain.

At the thought of QueenBee, her mind automatically followed a course from her horse, to the black horse that had nearly run her over, to its rider. Gail cringed—which hurt.

At least she knew his name now: Maximillian Something Something Fontaine, future Earl of Longsbowe. Oh, how could she have acted so damned stupidly? She had been doing so well, she had dressed appropriately, and she had spoken and danced with at least three gentlemen. But then her natural tendency for disaster had to strike. Getting drunk was bad enough, but to be rescued by *him*?

And he's a peer of the realm, a Viscount, an Earl-to-be! Doubtless Max took no small pleasure in telling any and all of the guests last night that the young lady who was so abominably rude to him a few weeks earlier had gotten completely in her cups, nearly assaulted, and then cast up accounts all over his shoes.

A tear leaked out of the corner of her eye. One day, *one day* out in London society, and she ruined it all.

She lay like that for hours, unable to think beyond her own misery. And rightly so, too! How much damage had she done to her own reputation? How much had she embarrassed her father, Evangeline, even Romilla . . .

Gail cringed, and then cringed again at the pain the first cringe caused in her forehead. Movement was tricky.

Romilla. Gail certainly remembered that her stepmother had been on an awful tear the night before about the punch. Hindsight was always annoyingly clear, and Gail could now see that young Ommersley was certainly no gentleman, and had likely tampered with the refreshments he was so diligent in procuring for her. Gail fumed. She dearly wanted to give that overentitled, unscrupulous little twit his comeuppance, but would have to think of exactly how later. The bloody nose Lord Fontaine had delivered would certainly not suffice.

As Gail's brain threatened to loop back onto Max again, suddenly, the deafening squeak of door hinges exploded in her brain, followed by the positively earsplitting noise of someone bustling about the hearth.

"Please . . . not so loud," she croaked out, her voice muffled to a whisper by all the cotton taking up residence in her mouth.

Sunlight burned a path into Gail's tortured eyes when Mrs. Bibb unceremoniously pulled the bed curtains back.

"Ah! Good mornin', Miss Gail!" Mrs. Bibb proclaimed cheerily, as Gail turned her frail head away from the light. "Glad to see yer awake. Quite a night you had, I'm surprised you dinna sleep till nightfall."

"Please . . ." Gail whispered, "just let me die."

Mrs. Bibb clucked her tongue. "Miss Gail, you always did have a knack for dramatics."

Then, the loving housekeeper flung back the feathered quilts on the bed, forcing Gail to curl into a ball to keep warm.

"Now," she began blithely while opening the windows, letting in a mild spring breeze. "All you need is some fresh air. Lord, you think yer the first person to feel their head after a night of too many? Stuff and nonsense, missy. Now, as I was sayin', you just need some fresh air, a hot bath"—Gail looked bleary-eyed to the hearth where two maids were filling a copper tub with steaming water—"and, of course, *this*."

Mrs. Bibb brought forth a tray, upon which sat a glass full of the vilest looking liquid Gail had ever had the misfortune to lay eyes on.

"What on earth is that?" Gail blurted out, eyeing the glass with clear distain and rising nausea. "Blood?" she ventured cautiously.

"Lord, you are a silly girl some days!" Mrs. Bibb proclaimed. "It's none but tomatoes, an egg, some other kitchen things, and a bit o' hair of the dog."

"There's dog hair in it?!" Gail looked aghast.

"Miss Gail, no!" Mrs. Bibb sighed, exasperated. "By that I mean a bit of the liquor you took upon yourself to guzzle last evenin'! It's a time-tested true cure for your complaints this morning. No dog hair, no blood. I swear on the grave of my dear Mr. Bibb."

Whenever Mrs. Bibb's late husband's grave was brought into the picture, her word was solid as scripture. But still, the drink looked absolutely evil.

"Now," Mrs. Bibb was saying, "drink up, hop into that tub, and you'll feel right as rain in no time."

Oh, she couldn't. She nearly lost her stomach just looking at it.

"Please," Gail begged, "may I just stay in bed today? Papa will understand."

Mrs. Bibb's eyes narrowed. "Your papa might let you lay about"—her voice had the steeled edge that Gail knew not to ignore—"but I guarantee her ladyship would'na stand for it. She told me if yer not downstairs in a half hour's time, she's comin' to get you herself. And she won't be as nice as me, miss. If you think she was displeased last night, you donna want to see her this mornin'."

Gail didn't have to be told twice.

Nothing could have induced her to move faster than avoidance of the scolding she was bound to receive from her stepmother. Gail would do anything if it meant she could feel well and presentable enough to leave this room before Romilla entered it.

She took the glass, and with a murmured toast of "cheers" to Mrs. Bibb, Gail mustered her courage, and swallowed the contents in one long gulp.

* * *

"IT will be impossible to get the girls vouchers for Almack's now—"

Romilla's fevered rant was interrupted by a knock on the library doors.

"Oh, what now?" she cried. "I told Morrison not to disturb us unless it was particularly important!"

"Well, if I knew there was a 'do not disturb' order in place, I would have found a way to use our time to better advantage," Sir Geoffrey replied, giving his wife a distinctly lusty look as he crossed to the door. As peeved as she was by her husband's flippancy while she was trying to discuss something of great import, Romilla could not help but flush.

"Morrison, I hope this is urg . . ." Sir Geoffrey's voice died as he opened the door. Lord Fontaine stood, his back straight, hands at his sides, his face a picture of noble surrender.

"Uh, Lord Fontaine, isn't it? Lost your way to the drawing room, have you?" Sir Geoffrey inquired.

"No, Sir Geoffrey. I do apologize for interrupting your private conversation," he said as he made a sharp bow to Sir Geoffrey and then Romilla, as she joined her husband at the door. "But I'm afraid what I have to say will bear weight on your discourse."

Lord Fontaine paused, but since neither of his audience made a sound (beyond some raised eyebrows—which don't make much noise in the first place) he took a breath and said, "I am the man who compromised your daughter last evening."

* * *

THERE were so many flowers, the maids were having trouble finding enough vases to hold them. Evangeline had never seen such a quantity in her life—it was like a sea of color. She sat on a marvelously sculpted sofa in the blue drawing room, papered and furnished to match her eyes and complement her complexion. Surrounding her were fields of peonies, daisies, daffodils, tulips, day lilies, but most of all roses and roses and roses. All in complex arrangements, all from the best hothouses. The blooms were as showy as the gentlemen that surrounded them tried to be.

There was Mr. Fitzwilliam, squeezed in a blue coat and buff trousers. She had danced the quadrille with him, Evangeline remembered, and he had flushed so dreadfully she thought he would expire from the exertion. His face was just as red now, as he attempted to tell a story that cast himself as the rescuer of a child in the street. Mr. Thornley, Captain Sterling, and Sir Quayle all wore sedate coats of deep mauve. They did their best to avoid standing too close to one another, although they rolled their eyes in time with each other to Fitzwilliam's story. Then they proceeded to try and best him with tales of their own exploits, interrupting each other as they did so. A good half dozen other gentlemen tried to stand out in the throng by offering to fetch a pillow, or detailing their exploits at St. James's Court, every last one a peacock strutting for the female's attention.

Evangeline smiled, laughed, and played the gracious and demure young lady to perfection. But on the inside, she was a bundle of nerves. She desperately wished Gail would come downstairs and act as a relief from all of these young men trying to catch her eye. If only Romilla wasn't shut up in the study with father, she could come and deflect some of the more over-eager lads that crowded Evangeline's shoulders. Romilla had the good sense to invite Miss Nesbitt to sit with them today, so at least there were some chaperonage in the room, and thus the semblance of propriety. But Evangeline could hardly claim to know Miss Nesbitt well, and she desperately wanted the support of a familiar face.

One particular face floated across her mind. Dark hair and green eyes that shone in the moonlight, a strong countenance that made her stomach flutter with anxiety. Would he call today? Lord Fontaine had asked permission to call upon her and her father, but would he? If he did, moreover, would she be happy to see him? Evangeline's mind was unsettled on the matter. After all, she knew him less than she knew Miss Nesbitt.

At that moment, the familiar stutter of a throat clearing interrupted Evangeline's reverie. Her mind snapped back to the present, and she realized that several pairs of eyes had come to rest quizzically upon her in the intervening moments. One of which was the butler, Morrison.

Giving the room her brightest smile, she excused herself from the crowd. They continued chatting along without her, but Evangeline knew full well that she was still the object of much attention.

"Another bouquet for you, miss," Morrison said in his most imperious tones, handing her the flowers. Then, lower, "And a note."

She smelled the blooms—quite the least traditional flowers she had yet received, so very exotic! They looked just like the vines she showed . . .

It took all Evangeline had to appear outwardly cool as she took the plain card. On it was printed only a name: *Viscount Fontaine.* But underneath in a scrawl of pencil, was written: *Meet me in thirty minutes. You know where.*

She did know where. Oh, so very reckless to be meeting the man again without any chaperone! The war of Evangeline's propriety and her curiosity was hard fought, but quickly resolved. Where was the harm in a brief meeting, wherein Evangeline would be sure to scold him lightly for his forward manner, followed by an invitation to stay and chat—chaperoned, in the drawing room, of course.

She looked up. Morrison stood straight as an arrow, expecting her reply.

"Tell him I shall be delighted."

* * *

"WHAT do you mean, you are the man who compromised my daughter last night?" Sir Geoffrey said, his face impassive, his arms relaxed on the desk. Max could see how this man was able to move up through the spider web of politics. He could freeze you in your tracks with a look and conduct an interrogation without emotion, even when it was his own daughter in question. This was a man he wanted on his side, for he would be a very sharp adversary.

Unfortunately, Max's doorside proclamation had declared him the enemy. He had been ushered into the room in all politeness and asked very genteelly if he should care to take a seat. Sir Geoffrey had ordered a low, uncomfortable wooden chair brought forth and placed in the center of the room. Max had little choice but to accept it. Romilla had positioned herself on a sofa, not saying a word, just watching with piercing eyes and a rigid posture of which few headmistresses could boast. The hands in her lap were gripped so tightly the knuckles turned white. Max had a feeling she was forcing herself to not jump up and hit him over the head with a handy piece of statuary.

"I mean to say, sir, that I am the reason you are up in arms. I am the man your daughter was found with in the conservatory." Max confessed in measured words, looking Sir Geoffrey straight in the eye. Well, as straight as he could, from such an awkwardly low chair.

This was met with astounded silence. Then—

"What on earth . . ." was all that could break free from Lady Alton's mouth before her husband held up one hand to silence her. He kept his eyes focused on Max.

"Would you care to, uh, explain the circumstances of how you came to be in the conservatory with my daughter?" Sir Geoffrey said, as he took a seat behind his desk in the large leather chair and steepled his fingers. It was probably a very comfortable chair, Max thought briefly.

"Well, sir, I was in attendance at your absolutely delightful ball"—Max made a point of looking to Romilla with this compliment; her eyes simply narrowed—"and I was following a servant through a door that I thought led to the kitchens, never mind why, and I found myself in your indoor garden. A very beautiful place, sir, I congratulate you on it. I wandered around for a bit, and was about to leave when your daughter entered—"

"And then you gave her the punch?" Sir Geoffrey interrupted.

"Punch? No sir, I certainly didn't punch her!"

"Then when . . ." Sir Geoffrey let the question die. "Please," he said, waving his hand, "continue."

Max took a deep breath.

"Your daughter and I chatted for some time and then we were interrupted by, I believe, your housekeeper. I must say she is a most amiable female."

"My housekeeper?"

"No, your daughter. Although I'm sure your housekeeper is very pleasant."

"Ah. So, let me understand this. You were 'chatting' in the conservatory with my youngest girl . . ." Sir Geoffrey summarized.

"No, sir."

"But you just said you were," Romilla said, her brow furrowed.

"It wasn't your youngest daughter," Max stated firmly, " 'twas your eldest, Evangeline."

A muffled shriek escaped Romilla's lips, caught by a covered hand. Sir Geoffrey was no less surprised, but hid it better.

"Evangeline? You were alone in the conservatory with *Evangeline*?"

"Well, yes, of course, Evangeline. Who did you think I was speaking about?" Max declared, rising out of his seat. He simply could not take sitting any longer.

"Lord Fontaine, I have recently come to the conclusion that I haven't the faintest idea what you're talking about and why you're confessing to it, but I will have the whole of the story *now*. You say you went to the conservatory alone. You met my daughter, my eldest daughter Evangeline, there. You talked. What else?"

"And we were interrupted, discovered, by your housekeeper," Max said.

Sir Geoffrey looked closely at him. Max felt as if his skin was being peeled away and the man could see right through him.

He stood stiffly, watching as Sir Geoffrey crossed the room to his wife, and they spoke in low voices. Romilla nodded, and then excused herself from the room, keeping her eyes forward and her chin up as she passed Max. When the doors shut with a firm click, Sir Geoffrey turned back to his quarry.

"What else?" Sir Geoffrey asked, his voice deceptively calm.

"What . . . else, sir?" Max replied, keeping his voice as cool as he could manage.

"Yes, what else happened between you and my Evangeline? You came here to confess to something, I know not what, but I can tell you that if nothing damaging had transpired between you and my daughter, you wouldn't feel so burdened to speak."

"I feel burdened to speak, sir, because being found alone with a man is damaging to any young lady's reputation, no matter the behavior of the gentleman. When I walked into the house today, hoping to call upon you and your daughter, I could not help but overhear your conversation with your wife. I did not want Miss Alton to be in disgrace for something that was in no way her fault," Max declared vehemently.

"An excellent argument," Sir Geoffrey conceded, "but I know as well as you that something else happened."

"Sir, whatever occurred between your daughter and I was innocent, and therefore, does not bear on this conversation." It was only a kiss after all. One little kiss, it was nothing.

Sir Geoffrey paused and gave Max such a look—a cold, intense stare, unblinking, unwavering, attempting to break Max down into a pile of dust. Max simply met the gaze. Sir Geoffrey's eyebrow twitched up, in . . . could it be a twinge of respect?

"We shall see." The older gentleman spoke in clipped tones.

Both men took a moment to breathe. Max watched as Sir Geoffrey checked his pockets, patted them down, and pulled out a cigar. He held it to his nose and took a deep breath.

Sir Geoffrey noticed Max's attention. "I would ask if you would care if I lit a cigar, but my wife will be back any moment, and I know her answer to that question."

Max's mouth quirked of its own accord, and the two gentlemen shared understanding looks, forgetting for a moment the reason they were in this room together.

Max had to break the silence.

"Sir, before your wife returns, I should like to discuss a certain matter with you."

"And what matter would this be?"

"Marriage."

If Sir Geoffrey had been permitted to light a cigar, he would have surely choked on it. As it was, his face turned an impressively mottled purple.

"Does marriage *need* to be discussed?" he asked angrily.

"No! No, sir! But I should like to discuss it all the same."

"Why?"

"Because I should like to marry your daughter."

Sir Geoffrey lifted a hand to his head, as if it had suddenly begun to pound.

"Quickly, if you don't mind," Max added.

"Honestly," Sir Geoffrey growled, "right now I'm not inclined to let either of my daughters out of their rooms until Kingdom Come!"

A terse knock cut off any rant Sir Geoffrey may have been persuing, and Romilla entered, followed closely by Mrs. Bibb. The good-natured and efficient housekeeper was worrying the edge of her apron, the only outward sign of her nervousness at being summoned abruptly to the master's library.

"Mrs. Bibb," Sir Geoffrey said calmly, his voice pitched to soothe frayed nerves, as he sat on the edge of his large mahogany desk. "Do you recognize this man?"

Mrs. Bibb turned to look at Max, who had positioned himself against the far wall. Max knew the instant recognition hit.

"Ah. I'm afraid I do, sir," she said, turning her eyes to Sir Geoffrey, her hand never leaving her apron. A nod from Sir Geoffrey told her to continue.

"He, ah, he was with Miss Evangeline in the conservatory, when I, ah, had to fetch her last evening," she stated.

Sir Geoffrey's jaw hardened—this was the question he had been dreading.

"And what were they doing in the conservatory?"

"Doing, sir?"

"Were they talking, or perhaps walking about?"

"No, sir," she replied.

"Then what were they doing there together?"

For the first time Mrs. Bibb broke eye contact with Sir Geoffrey and looked at her hands.

"They were kissing, sir."

A small sound came from Romilla as she put her hand over her mouth, her eyes burning fire. Max's jaw worked something fierce. Sir Geoffrey's countenance, however, remained impassive.

"Why didn't you tell us before, Mrs. Bibb?" Romilla asked from her position on the couch.

"I'm sorry, ma'am, I truly am," Mrs. Bibb replied, misery in her voice, "but I'm afraid I forgot, with, er, with other things goin' on last night."

Sir Geoffrey nodded. Romilla simply looked hard at Max, as if she were calculating a long sum of numbers.

"Mrs. Bibb, one more question before you go, I know you must be busy," Sir Geoffrey said, bringing her attention back to him. She nodded slowly.

"Did you mention to anyone how you found Miss Evangeline and this, er, gentleman?"

"No, sir!" Mrs. Bibb replied indignantly. "I'd never spread tales about Miss Evangeline, yer Lordship!"

Sir Geoffrey gave a great sigh of relief. He was about to dismiss Mrs. Bibb and this whole awful affair, when . . .

"Except that . . ." Mrs. Bibb said softly.

Sir Geoffrey, Romilla, and Max all stiffened.

"It's just that, I might have been scoldin' Miss Evie a bit as we're walkin'. And we did pass one of the newer maids in the hallway. And, er, there was the issue with the dress."

Romilla's head snapped up. "Her sleeve! I saw it—it was torn and hanging past her shoulder." She turned accusatory eyes on Max.

Sir Geoffrey turned white.

"Her sleeve, madam, was torn dancing, or so she told me," Max replied evenly.

"We did have such trouble gettin' it to fit right earlier, if you recall, my Lady," Mrs. Bibb piped up, but Sir Geoffrey held up his hand.

"Thank you, Mrs. Bibb—you may go," he said wearily.

"Well, Lord Fontaine," Sir Geoffrey said, after Mrs. Bibb left the room, "it looks like you may get your wish after all."

"What wish?" Romilla inquired.

"To marry Evangeline, my dear. And quickly."

Nine

"I don't like this, not one bit."

"I know dearest, but what are we to do?"

It had been such a nice party last night. He didn't need this, Sir Geoffrey thought, he really didn't. He had issues to discuss with his estate manager and reports to give on Portuguese cooperation to Parliament, and he desperately wanted the comfort of a cigar. But suddenly he was mired waist deep in domestic mess. First Gail, now Evangeline, and this man asking to marry her—quickly!

"We? You were supposed to ensure their debut!" Sir Geoffrey thundered. "You were supposed to make certain everything my daughters did reflected well upon themselves and on me!"

He had dismissed Lord Fontaine from the library, but instructed him not to leave the house. Sir Geoffrey also warned Morrison that Lord Fontaine was not to go anywhere near Evangeline or the drawing room. When Morrison knocked on the door and assured them that the young gentleman had wisely decided to take a tour of the music room, Sir Geoffrey and Romilla began their discussion in earnest.

Sir Geoffrey talked. And paced. And yelled. And desperately wanted a cigar. Romilla sat on the couch and watched.

"And not only Gail—whose injuries to herself are comparatively minor—but Evangeline!" Sir Geoffrey raged after a great long while. "I know it was 'circumstance,' but she should have known better! She always knows better!"

Romilla sighed. "I almost wish it was Abigail who was in the conservatory with him. Evangeline has so much promise . . ."

Sir Geoffrey crossed his arms over his chest. "Not everyone dismisses Gail as easily as you do, my dear."

Romilla blanched, then stuttered. "I . . . I don't dismiss her. I just meant—" But Sir Geoffrey had already moved on.

"The pertinent question now is what are we going to do?" He smacked his fist against the desk, causing all manner of quills, jars, and papers to jump. Romilla watched as Sir Geoffrey's hand found its way into his breast pocket and pulled out a cigar. She frowned as he cut and lit it.

"I do wish you wouldn't smoke, dearest."

"Right now, darling"—Sir Geoffrey exhaled a long tendril of blue smoke—"I really don't give a bloody damn."

A long silence ensued. The clock ticked on the mantel. Romilla concentrated on smoothing an indiscernible fold in her skirt, while her husband rolled the cigar between his fingers, creating patterns in the escaping smoke.

"I'm sorry," he said after a while, "for yelling just now."

Romilla smiled at him, her eyes softening with forgiveness.

"Do you believe anything actually happened between them?" she asked.

"Do I think my daughter's person has been compromised beyond all redemption? No. Any cad who would do such a thing would never come and confess to her parents the next morning."

"What about the sleeve?" Romilla asked.

Sir Geoffrey let his breath go in a long sigh. "That's a problem. Gossip is ever so much more interesting with visual details."

"It is possible it ripped on the dance floor," Romilla added hopefully. "It came back from the dressmaker's tight across the shoulders, Mrs. Bibb was correct there."

"If so, why weren't you informed? Why didn't a lady's maid attend to Evangeline in the powder room?"

"Dearest"—Romilla held up her hands—"I simply don't know."

Sir Geoffrey, all out of sighs and blusters, resigned himself to slumping in his chair. "She may not have been compromised physically, but her reputation is a different story. If this gets out . . ."

Romilla gave a ladylike snort. "Darling, we've been here three weeks, and I can already tell you the latest gossip about everyone on this square, from the name of Mr. Watling's latest opera dancer, to how many kittens the Pickerings' tomcat sired. Believe me, rumors will get around. And by the time they get back to us, it won't be kissing in the conservatory with a torn sleeve, it will be ravaging in the bedroom naked to the waist. An allusion's all that's needed to seem real."

Sir Geoffrey went white at the imagery—then red. "Her sleeve, what if he did . . . by god, she's just a child!"

"She's twenty, not a child," Romilla replied quietly.

"She's my child."

Romilla was silent for a moment, lost in thought. Then—

"It could be worse, you realize. No dearest, listen to me for a moment." Sir Geoffrey had begun a scoff of disbelief. "While Lord Fontaine would not be my first choice, consider, he has funds—or will once he inherits. True, he is not the toast of society, but I know of no unappealing rumors attached to him. His birth and breeding are impeccable, and although his father hasn't deigned to sit in the House of Lords for years, maybe Lord Fontaine is not wholly without merit. With the exception of his behavior last night, he seems intelligent. And Evangeline would be a countess. A peer no one could disparage."

A look of consideration played over Sir Geoffrey's face. "What-ifs" drifted in front of his eyes. But . . .

"A hasty marriage would do terrible damage to my prospects—Countess or no."

"Then maybe we can buy some time." Romilla rose and

began to pace in the same circle Sir Geoffrey had before. "You're right, if a wedding were to take place tomorrow, it would only serve as proof of some indiscretion. And that would reflect badly on us all. But, if we ignore the rumors and refuse to allow Lord Fontaine anywhere near us, the rumors would be fueled and still blacken our name. We are lucky in one regard—that any gossip would have originated with the servants. If one of the guests had discovered them, we would be done for."

"Why is that lucky?" Sir Geoffrey groused. "You've told me a dozen times that the best and most useful information originates downstairs, not up."

Romilla dismissed this with a shrug. "It's one of the great ironies of Society."

She stopped pacing and came to stand before her husband. He reached for her hand.

"What we'll do," she said softly, "is allow Lord Fontaine to outwardly court Evangeline, while they are secretly engaged. Only the family will know, not even the servants. The fact that he is so attentive to Evangeline in a gentlemanly fashion will stem off some of the meaner gossip. When we announce the betrothal in, oh, a month's time, and when the wedding occurs, it will seem to have happened naturally."

Sir Geoffrey looked at his wife, impressed. "You put the schemings of Parliament to shame, darling," he said with appreciation.

"I'll take that as a compliment, dearest." She hesitated a moment. "My only fear is if he doesn't take to her. What if they don't get on well?"

"He's the one who wants to marry her. Besides, from what was reported last night, they get on very well indeed," Sir Geoffrey replied. And his wife was forced to agree. He looked at the smoke escaping from his cigar, considered the options for a moment—and saw very few.

"I will allow this," Sir Geoffrey said, rising from the side of the desk, "on one condition. That Evangeline agrees, of her own free will. After all, no one has asked her if she *wants* to marry him. But I warn you, my dear, if she says no now, we will support her, and we will weather the scandal as a family." Sir Geoffrey stubbed out the cigar, muttering, "Although she had better say yes." He stood and crossed to his wife. Placing his hands on her shoulders, he looked her dead in the eye.

"So my dear, what do you say?"

Romilla rubbed her chin, thoughtful. "Send for Evangeline."

* * *

JUST outside of the library, Gail tiptoed downstairs. She was clean, dressed, and surprisingly bright eyed, given her physical state not half an hour ago. Mrs. Bibb's cure-all really did have restorative powers. Perhaps she could bottle and sell it, like so many medicines Gail saw advertised in the *Times*— all promising freedom from such ailments as gout, pneumonia, and women's complaints. Making certain to step over the third stair from the bottom (for it squeaked abominably), Gail walked quickly down the hall, careful to avoid the library doors, where she could hear the rumblings of her father's voice. She thought briefly about going into the drawing room, knowing Evangeline was there—and Gail wouldn't mind a friendly face. But the fear of meeting Romilla, who was surely sitting next to her protégée, outweighed any reassurance she could receive from her sister. Gail knew that she would eventually have to meet with her stepmother, but she would prefer to avoid it as long as possible.

Deftly stepping into a cupboard to avoid being seen by a pair of maids making their way to the stairs with fresh linens, Gail poked her head out only after she heard their footsteps retreating. She wasn't going to chance running into anyone. Unfortunately, there were very few places for privacy in Number Seven. Servants were everywhere, righting the house from last night's festivities, as were morning callers spilling out from the drawing room into the hall. She could go to the music room, but if she were to play one note, Romilla would come charging up the stairs. There was only one place that Gail thought might be unoccupied.

Seeing the coast was clear, Gail slipped down the hall into the ballroom and across the floor to a hidden door by the balcony.

* * *

MAX did as he had said he would, retreating to the music room, which overlooked the rear gardens—more accurately, overlooked the one tree Number Seven had claim to. The window was open, but Max barely registered the sweet spring breeze in the air, as he kept checking his pocket watch at obscenely close intervals.

Ten more minutes. Nine and three-quarters. Nine and a half . . . He couldn't even properly enjoy the brilliant beauty of the music room—its pianoforte gleamingly grand in the room's center. Nor could he see the loveliness of the new buds on the lonely tree, the small, light green leaves that hinted at something richer. Nay, his mind was far too preoccupied.

Max guessed Sir Geoffrey and Lady Alton's discussion could go on some time. They would either have decided immediately (and if so, he wouldn't be standing in the music room right now, or standing period, most likely), or they would be debating his future for hours. Actually, Max wasn't as worried on that score as he probably should be—in fact the accidental revelation of last night's indiscretion might have furthered his actual purpose to marry Evangeline—albeit not the way he had hoped. Parents were never inclined to think well of men who compromised their daughters, even if they did get married.

Nay, Max wasn't concerned about his future in-laws. In truth, he was counting the minutes till he met with his future wife.

Eight and a half minutes. Eight and a quarter . . . Max plunked himself on the pianoforte's bench, accidentally resting his elbow on the keys, producing a horrid chord. He promptly stood up again. His body was a bundle of nerves, and he had twice his normal energy. He didn't know what to do with himself when time refused to move at its proper pace.

He was banned from the drawing room, but that did not prevent Evangeline from leaving it, if she was so inclined. Max desperately wanted to see Evangeline again—not only to ascertain that she was well after leaving so abruptly the previous evening. He needed to look into her eyes, to make certain that what he saw there before wasn't just a trick of moonlight. He paced his way back to the window. Next to the one tree was the glass conservatory's outer wall, which took up most of the rear of the house. Was it possible he spied movement within its translucent shell? He checked his watch one last time before dropping it into his pocket.

Seven minutes, fifty seconds.

Close enough, he thought, as he headed toward the door, barely restraining himself from breaking into a run.

Across the hall, tiptoeing through the already immaculate ballroom, Max found the hidden door rather neatly in the sunlight, as opposed to the warm glow of a candlelit ballroom. He found the latch and turned it with an easily recalled flick of the wrist, stepping into his remembered heaven.

The garden looked different in the daylight. The tall trees that had loomed like shadowed gatekeepers now stood proud and thick with leaves, reaching for the sun coming through the glass ceiling above. The moonlight that had cut through the mist of the heated atmosphere was now gone. He could see the dirt surrounding the plants, the seams of the cobblestones in the winding path. His footsteps clipped against the stone, through the trees, under the bower of white-belled flowers, that were tinted pink by day, and he could see the green painted trellis that supported them beneath the vines. It was still a beautiful garden, a remarkable conservatory in an English climate. But it lost some of its magic when one could see the puppeteer's strings.

Max tossed these thoughts aside. What did it matter that the garden looked different in the harsh brightness of day? It was still the conservatory where he had met with his future (and desired, he told himself) bride, Evangeline. He could still hear the trickle of water from the fountain he had been standing in when he first laid eyes upon her. Max turned sharply on the path and let his feet go where his thoughts were taking them. As he approached the fountain, he heard a rustling ahead.

Could it be?

Was she here?

He moved faster, rounded the corner of the path and emerged from its shadows.

She sat in a high-backed stone bench, the wings of its sides obscuring her face from view. But he could see the length of her yellow skirts swirling about the flagstones, a toe of her leather shoe sitting against one of the surlier stone frogs edging the fountain.

Max smiled in relief, in hope, in anticipation. She came. Obviously she was as eager to meet as he, for she was there a full (he checked his pocket watch) four minutes early. Max took a deep breath and ran his fingers through his hair to make sure it was presentable before he ventured to speak.

"You came." His voice was filled with warmth. "I was so afraid you wouldn't be able to slip away." Max took three steps toward the bench.

And stopped dead.

"What are you doing here?" two very surprised people asked each other.

He stood stock still, while his eyes, which had been filled with such hope as he walked out from the shade of the trees, now narrowed in suspicion.

Gail—Just Gail, Brat, whomever she was—sat frozen, staring like a fox caught in his sight, and ready to bolt at any moment. Golden eyes were wide with shock, and her color pale. Although, he could attribute her pallor to her previous evening's imbibing . . . But this was madness! What was she doing here?

Maybe she was an apparition. The firebrand that had thrown him into a lake and thrown up on his shoes had somehow violated his thoughts and made herself formed flesh when he expected to find his darling future bride.

Obviously he was hallucinating because of lack of sleep (although he had slept quite well) or something he ate (although he only had coffee for breakfast, such was his hurry to get Evangeline's flowers). Yes, he rationalized desperately, that was it! It was the lack of food; he really should have heeded Harris's advice and eaten heartily before he left this morning . . .

"Uh . . ." came her voice. It was surprisingly rough, and shy. As if the firebrand who had scorched his ears twice before didn't know how to start a sentence. Max felt his hallucination theory deflate, as something cold ran down his spine. She was real. If she were a product of his imagination, she would have shrewishly torn him down by now.

"I live here," Gail answered his question. Her voice was stronger now, but still small.

That cold line running down his spine? He knew what it was now. Dread.

Realization dawned, a crashing spiral in the pit of his stomach.

There were two Alton daughters.

Evangeline had a sister.

"There are two of you . . ." he moaned, his own stupidity crashing about his ears.

"No," she said softly, a slight smile painting her full mouth, "I assure you, there's only one of me.

"But what are you doing here?" Gail, Evangeline's sister, asked. Her timid voice was fast gaining its normal strength, but without the defensive tone he was accustomed to.

"I . . . I, uh . . ." It was Max's turn to stutter. He looked everywhere about him. At the dirt around the base of the trees, at the vines overhead—anywhere but at her.

A rustling down the path saved him from answering, or looking any more the fool for stalling. Two sets of footsteps, one moving quickly, one trying to keep up, echoed through the trees. Seconds later, Romilla emerged from the shadows, followed closely by a subdued Evangeline.

She was paler than last night, but Max could guess the reasons for that—no doubt she had just come from a rather paling interview. Other than that, however, Evangeline looked exactly as she had: beautiful, demure, ethereal. The perfect Countess of Longsbowe.

Evangeline's attention did not stray to Max but was fixed

on Romilla, whose normally pleasant manner was marked by a brittleness she didn't bother to hide.

"Lord Fontaine," she said immediately upon seeing the unexpected tableau before her, "I would ask that you stop meeting my daughters alone in this conservatory. Once is accidental, twice is stupidity."

Max wisely said nothing, just bowed his head.

"Gail, I'm surprised to see you out and about this morning, but I'm glad you're here."

No one moved as Romilla took a breath.

"I should like to introduce you to your future brother-in-law, Viscount Fontaine."

Ten

"YOU were compromised? How the bloody hell did you get compromised?"

"Gail, don't swear. She'll hear you." Evangeline shushed her sister.

But Gail paid her no heed. "You didn't have time to get compromised, you were with me all night!"

Max entering her sanctuary that morning had been the embodiment of her nightmare. She had feared she would cast up accounts again, such was her shock. And he . . . he had looked so boyish, so hopeful. Of course, she thought grimly, all that had changed the moment he saw her.

When Romilla had arrived and, instead of berating her for drunkenness as Gail had feared, declared Max was to marry Evangeline—well, suffice to say, if Gail hadn't been sitting, she most certainly would have landed on the floor.

After the surprising announcement, Max was summoned back to the library and shut in with Sir Geoffrey. That had been this morning. It was now sunset, and Evangeline and Gail peered out the window of Evangeline's bedroom, watching the rear of Max's hack roll away down Berkeley Square.

Gail and Evangeline, on the other hand, had spent the day

with Romilla, who had in turn surprised them both. There were no vehement lectures about their behavior at the ball, no vases thrown at their heads, literally or metaphorically. Gail expected to be shut in her room for at least the rest of the Season, but was bewildered when, immediately, the opposite occurred.

Once the Viscount had been ushered out of the conservatory, Romilla had turned to the girls and ordered, "You have five minutes to go upstairs, arrange yourselves, and report back to the drawing room," and swept out of the room.

The girls didn't need to be told twice. They ran up the stairs, splashed water on their faces and pinched their cheeks, checked their hair in the looking glass, and presented themselves in the drawing room exactly five minutes later, looking the bloom of health and vitality. Indeed, it was crucial that they do so, because Romilla was insistent upon taking them through the day as if nothing odd had occurred.

They visited with the callers in the drawing room, about whom they had nearly forgotten, although in truth only a quarter hour had passed since Evangeline had left.

Romilla made a great show of presenting Gail to the party, whom she claimed Evangeline had excused herself to fetch. Such a reasonable excuse was taken to heart by all present, and the party continued chatting amiably, including Gail in their circle, though she was characteristically silent.

The morning was unending. Gail glanced at the mantel clock every five seconds, and while Evangeline was a bit more subtle, she was no less aware of the time. Fortunately, the assembled party did not take notice of either girl's distraction, and soon enough Romilla skillfully ushered the guests out the front door, with promises of return visits and meeting at balls and musicales later in the week.

However, just when Gail thought she would finally have an opportunity to question, throttle, and consolingly hug her sister in turns, Romilla swept them out of the drawing room (Gail was quick to note the library doors were still shut tight), and after a change of dress, out the door.

The afternoon was spent visiting such a collection of Society ladies, their giggling daughters, and eligible sons that

Gail and Evangeline barely had an opportunity to say more than three words to each other.

Only after all the calls had been paid and they returned to their house and rooms (on pretense of changing for dinner—oh, how many clothes were required to be out in London!) were Gail and Evangeline finally able to speak.

Gail spoke first and loudest.

"How on earth did *you* come to be compromised by *him*?"

Evangeline gave a deep sigh. "Well, you see . . . I'm afraid I gave in to a moment of, romantic . . . curiosity."

As Evangeline explained, Gail felt her stomach sink and her blood rise. It was her fault. If she hadn't been intoxicated, Max would never have wandered into the conservatory, never seen Evangeline . . .

But oh, how hypocritical was a world that thrived on gossip and then condemned its subject? That forced a girl into marriage to head off a rumor?

For a rumor had indeed gotten out. It seemed the new maid had mentioned it in passing to her friend in the laundry, who told it to the young footman she was keen on, who laughed about it with other blokes while they waited for their employers to emerge from the Alton's ball. From there it became fodder that was passed to various valets and ladies' maids to their employers, who spread it like jam on their morning toast.

By the time the Alton party had reached the residence of Lady Hurstwood at two in the afternoon, no less than three people had hinted at distorted versions of an indiscretion to Gail. Always protective and understandably confused, Gail had nearly unleashed a hot scolding on Mrs. Plimpton before Romilla's pointy shoe connected with her ankle. Then Romilla had magnificently fended off untoward questions with feigned ignorance and a smooth change of subject. Gail was not required to feign ignorance, and not one word was said to Evangeline. No, the vultures let the rumor swirl around like mist, without actually approaching its subject. And all because that loathsome Max Fontaine had forced himself on her sister!

"Gail, he didn't force himself upon me. But we were alone,

and when Mrs. Bibb caught us"—Evangeline sighed and pressed a hand to her temple—"I doubt it looked good. It stands to reason that people would find out somehow. It doesn't matter what did or didn't happen because the taint will exist regardless. It was actually very . . . very generous of Lord Fontaine to offer marriage."

"Who told you such antiquated nonsense?" Gail wanted to throttle her sister, to cry, to reverse time. Alas, there was nowhere to move but forward. "You hardly know him!"

"I agreed!" Evangeline cried. "Father called me to the library, told me the predicament, and I agreed to marry."

"You . . . agreed?"

"Papa offered me a choice."

"And marriage to a stranger was what you chose?" Gail nearly screeched, such was her disbelief.

"Better marriage than rejection from all society and ruining Father's career with it!" Evangeline had maintained serenity throughout the whole day, but here, alone with Gail, her calm facade cracked and fell.

"I'm sorry!" she gulped, "you're the only person who I can talk to . . ." As Evangeline broke down in sobs, Gail rushed to put her arms around her. Understanding dawned as tears soaked the front of her gown. Evangeline, serene, lovely Evangeline, was scared beyond measure.

"Hush now," Gail rocked her sister back and forth. "I'm sorry—I shouldn't have yelled."

"Gail, it's just . . ." Evangeline said between sobs, "there was moonlight last night. What if I spend the rest of my life regretting that moonlight?"

Gail smoothed her sister's hair and murmured comforting sounds, while Evangeline cried on her shoulder. When most of the sobs had subsided, Gail asked, "What do you mean? About the moonlight?"

"What if Lord Fontaine and I don't suit? You're right, I hardly know him. What if everything I was feeling was due to the moonlight and not to him? I want to love my husband, and I'm so afraid that I won't . . ."

Torn between a chance to belittle Max and assuage her sister's fears, Gail reluctantly but swiftly chose the latter.

Bracing her sister by the arms, she said, "Evie, listen to me. Dry your eyes. I'm sure that everything will be just fine. So you don't know him very well now. You will come to know him! You have, what did Romilla say, a month? A month before the announcement. That's plenty of time. You and Max, er, Lord Fontaine, will spend a good amount of time alone together, and . . ."

"No! No, Gail, I can't be alone with him!"

Gail simply stared.

"What do you mean you can't be alone with him? You're going to marry him *because* you were alone with him!"

"I need your help. I respect your sense and judgment above all others. I need you there so you can tell me what you think of him."

Thinking she could very well tell Evangeline what she thought of Max right now, Gail wisely held her tongue.

"Gail, just promise you'll stay with me. Please."

The imploring shine from those still wet eyes, combined with the death grip Evangeline had on her hand, told Gail that she wasn't going to be able to respectfully decline.

"For as long as you need me, I'll be there. I promise."

* * *

A promise is a promise. A gentleman is only as good as his word. These were the phrases that ran through Max's head after a day such as the victims of the Spanish Inquisition never had. Though his morning had started out full of hope, anticipation, and trailing white flowers, Max felt like a crumpled weed pulled ruthlessly out of the ground. He closed his eyes and let the carriage sway his fatigue away. That morning, when he had been escorted so adamantly out of the conservatory and into the library, he had been reeling. The only woman in the world who annoyed him beyond reason was going to be related to him through marriage. How could he have been so blind, so stupid as to not guess that Gail was Evangeline's sister? In hindsight, they did have some remarkably similar features. The shape of their eyes (although not the color) and their noses were very close. Max supposed he had been thrown off by the difference in their heights. Where Evangeline came to below his shoulder, Gail was a head taller. An easier distance from which to spit in his eye, he thought spitefully.

Max had been ushered into the library again, this time by a small, efficient-looking secretary in spectacles. Sir Geoffrey gave that man instructions to clear his schedule for the day and shut the door on the way out. Max was then left to face Sir Geoffrey, his future father-in-law, alone.

A daunting prospect, to say the least.

Sir Geoffrey was not an imposing figure in political circles for nothing. His reputation as a man of rising influence was only exceeded by his reputation for extracting information. It was whispered that he had had a surprisingly large role in Napoleon's exile to Elba, although no details could be ascertained. But it was a fact that he had been knighted shortly thereafter. No, Sir Geoffrey was known as an amiable man, but his business was his reputation. And business was good, due partly to his family's name. They might be new to the higher circles of society, but they had never been attached to any form of scandal. And now, because of Max, all that could change.

Sir Geoffrey's gaze was direct over the top of his steepled fingers. He sat at his vast mahogany desk, whose gleaming surface was free of any clutter; no obstacles sat between the hunter and his cornered prey.

The interview started off innocently enough. Sir Geoffrey asked about Max's family, his connections, and the prospects of his fortune. Max answered in polite, standard form. His mother passed on some years ago, his father is currently in London, although he spends most of his time at Longsbowe Park on the cliffs in southeast England. His family owns a half dozen estates, mostly farming properties, but yes, Longsbowe Park is the ancestral home. Yes, he attended Eton. Yes, he attended Oxford. Yes, he was fond of dogs, but not cats.

After a few hours of this, Sir Geoffrey thought enough of his guest to ask if he should like a chair.

The interview then turned far more personal, and far more uncomfortable for Max. Who are his chums? What clubs did he belong to? Are there any young ladies in his past who he's compromised as well? Did he keep a mistress, and did he intend to after the wedding? Is he certain he hadn't contracted any disease from an opera dancer or lightskirt that could come to prey on his daughter?

After a few hours of this line of questioning, Sir Geoffrey called for luncheon. His luncheon.

Max did his best to keep his composure answering these questions, and eventually, he almost found it amusing. He answered Sir Geoffrey with blunt honesty, a tack that man seemed to appreciate. Only once did Max's annoyance show—after Max had answered negative to all the lightskirt and opera dancer questions, Sir Geoffrey leaned back in his chair and asked in an astonished voice, "Well, then what on earth do you do for amusement?"

"I attack girls in conservatories," was Max's curt and unrestrained reply.

Sir Geoffrey's gaze remained steady, but narrowed over the top of his hands. For once, Max was not able to hold his eyes. Mumbling apologies, he looked away.

"Humor has its time and place. I doubt this is it," Sir Geoffrey said gruffly, leaning back into his chair. "Now, tell me about your ambitions in life."

Max looked up. "My ambitions?"

"Yes, what you wish to do, to be."

"I . . . I am to be an earl . . . I will inherit a great estate . . ." Max stuttered out. What did he want to be? It was a question no one had asked him before. As Max stumbled over the speech he had been programmed his entire life to say, about family duty, responsibility, and the continuation thereof, he watched a cloud descend over his future father-in-law's face.

"Young man," Sir Geoffrey interrupted him, "I asked you what you might contribute to the world—not how much of it you will own. I am a great believer that every man should be of some use. And I can't put much faith in anyone that bases their worth on that of their forebearers."

* * *

AS the hack rumbled to a stop in front of Max's nondescript lodgings, his mind was too tired to review his answers any longer. His one solace was the fact that, yes, it seemed as if

Evangeline would be his bride. After the lengthy debriefing, Sir Geoffrey had outlined the whole plan for him—a social strategy devised to keep the truth hazy and the gossips at bay. To openly and honestly court his bride-to-be for a month would leave the Ton with the impression that the gossip was false, and there was nothing untoward about their relationship, and the marriage would invalidate any leftover critics. Romilla was to be complimented.

But still, a month seemed an awfully long time to wait, especially when he had his father breathing down his neck.

Max alighted from the carriage, and as if fate had read his thoughts, he saw another carriage parked in front of his red-brick building. Even in the low light, the crest of Longsbowe was unmistakable on the side of the lacquered black carriage.

"From one fatherly interrogation to another," Max stated to no one in particular as he headed to the house. Harris greeted him at the door, a rushed formality about him.

"Sir! You have returned. I sent word to your club and the museum, but they came back saying you were not in attendance. May I ask where—?"

"Don't worry, Harris, I wasn't kidnapped," Max said, trying for a bit of levity, but his weariness showed through. "Actually, I was kidnapped, but never fear, I survived. Where is he?"

Harris closed the door and took his master's coat. "I was able to avoid putting him in the study this time, sir. He's in the drawing room."

Max nodded, sighed heavily, and went to face his father.

"Good gravy, young fool, what tangle have you gotten yourself into now?"

The Earl sat in Max's favorite large, deep green winged armchair closest to the fire. His walking cane leaned against the mantel, its golden handle gleaming in the firelight. The Earl was painfully hunched, but his eyes held the sparkle of the engaged mind. And the Earl's gaze was glued to his son.

"I take it you've heard," Max drawled.

"Heard? I haven't stopped hearing! There was no other topic of conversation at the club!" The Earl banged his arm on the chair.

"You went to your club?" Max asked, incredulous. "You went out of the house?"

"Well, no," the Earl admitted. "I sent Rentworth, and he reported back to me."

Max nodded. Rentworth, his father's longtime glorified servant, was actually a minor baron, and wholly loyal to the Earl. Rentworth's baronetcy allowed him into the clubs, into the music halls, and even into Almack's, from which he reported the most powerful information in London: gossip. The Earl never left his home if it could be avoided. Obviously, tonight that was not possible.

"Maximillian, this is solvable. Listen to me, sit down." The softened tone of the Earl's voice caught Max off guard, and he reflexively moved to the chair across from his father. He hesitated halfway there, but his father's imploring look had him sitting in a trice.

"No one knows it was you. The report is a tall gentleman with dark hair and green eyes was caught ravishing Sir Geoffrey's daughter."

Max was taken aback. "How, then, did you know it was me?" he asked slowly.

"Dark hair, green eyes, and the stupidity to be caught. Call it parental intuition."

Ignoring the jibe, Max was a little surprised the Earl knew the color of his eyes—but then recalled they were the same as his father's.

"Then I am shocked, Father," Max said as he leaned back in his chair, "that you think no one else will figure it out either."

The Earl waved a gnarled hand in front of him. "Bah! Londoners are remarkably dull-witted en masse. You will simply go about your regular routine, as if nothing occurred. Do not visit the Altons again, and if you run into them in society, be polite, but unfamiliar—people will never suspect you."

"It occurs to me," Max started slowly, "that if I deny my involvement, it would be exceedingly rare for me to run into the Altons out in society. They would never be allowed to associate in it."

"That, while unfortunate, is their problem."

"*Their* problem?" Max repeated, incredulous.

"The point is, you shouldn't be forced to marry her because of one stupid incident!" the Earl roared.

"You *want* me to marry!" Max exploded, nearly oversetting his chair as he stood. He descended on his father, leaning over him with shaking frustration. "*You* have employed blackmail to get me to marry! You were here for that conversation, weren't you? It took place right across the hall, in the study. You said, 'Get married, Max, or I'll ruin your life from beyond the grave!' And now that there is a bride on the horizon, you tell me to make a fool out of her? To refuse to marry her, to even be seen in public with her after egregiously harming her reputation? How dare you? How bloody dare you?"

"I do it because, believe it or not, I care about your future," the Earl shot back with stuttered breath. "If you require more time to search your marriage options . . . I'll give you another month. But this Miss Alton is obviously a harlot! A girl who gave herself up at her first ball in society? She's probably a fortune hunter! Her father's a grasping opportunist . . . She is obviously unworthy of the name Longsbowe!"

Max was seething. He paced, prowled the room. "She didn't 'give herself up,' damn it all—it was just one harmless kiss!"

The Earl raised an eyebrow, but said nothing.

"She is not a harlot. The incident was innocent and entirely my fault. Get that through your head, Father, right now. I am a gentleman, and it was entirely my fault."

"Then the girl is exceedingly stupid to have allowed it to happen," the Earl argued. For a weak old man, he could put up a fight when necessary. "Besides, a woman raised on the road? She's practically a gypsy. That's no life for you."

"Father, only the impracticality of disposing of your body is keeping me from patricide at the moment," Max said with a dark gleam in his eyes.

"She is not good enough for you, for Longsbowe. I have had Rentworth draw up a list of suitable ladies—Evangeline Alton is nowhere on it," the Earl said with finality.

"That's what this is about," Max said, with dawning realization. "You do not approve of Miss Alton, because you didn't choose her yourself! Well, not to worry, you have nothing to complain against. Evangeline Alton is beautiful and kind, and I happen to like her very much. Her family is wealthy—"

"Grasping nobodies—bah! Vagabonds, the lot of them, traipsing around the world!" the Earl snorted.

"Vagabonds don't tend to have an estate in Surrey and a house on Berkeley Square."

Silence reigned as the Earl's eyes searched the room, looking desperately for his next argument.

"I don't like it," he finally grumbled.

"You don't have to like it," Max stated. "I'm the one marrying her. And I will, Father. That was one of the terms of your blackmail."

"But, son, I—"

"Don't call me that," Max spat out, his hurt showing. "We haven't anything in common any longer, except blood."

And with that, Max silently left the room.

* * *

THE Earl sat awhile, watching the fire embers crackle in the hearth. He was too hard a man to weep, but too cut by his son's last words not to feel the cold. So, he watched the fire until it died, rose on gnarled and shaky legs, and left the house.

Eleven

THE next morning, Max woke surprisingly sated. He had slept deeply as always, but more so because for the first time since he left Longsbowe Park, he had stood up to his father. Any wince of regret he felt at that last parting comment was quickly swallowed by the thought of his upcoming day.

Max was going to the Altons' to pay court to Evangeline. Somewhere in the mass of confusion that was yesterday, he remembered something about agreeing to a carriage ride in the park at high riding hours. This presented a problem, as he had a feeling he was expected to provide a carriage. Having his horse boarded and occasionally hiring hacks had its advantages, but impressing young ladies with his frugality was not generally among them. He would be damned, Max thought, if he would call round to Longsbowe House and take one of their carriages, especially after last night—so he turned to the next viable option. He sent a quick note off to Will, begging for the favor of his smartest conveyance, and salvation was delivered to Max's doorstep at precisely one o'clock: a shining gray open barouche, Will's best whip neatly in control of a lovely pair of matched bays. Max took a moment to question whether or not a barouche of this size was too much, but ultimately decided that as his note was nonspecific in the type of carriage, Will assumed best meant best. Besides, they could stretch out their legs.

So it was that at precisely two thirty, Max pulled up in front of Number Seven Berkeley Square in his best afternoon coat and hat, a basket of nibbles Harris had packed personally sitting on the seat beside him.

Max alighted and was promptly admitted. He waited in the drawing room the proper number of minutes, and then ten more, before anyone came to greet him. And even then, it was not the lady he had come to see.

It was Lady Alton.

"Lord Fontaine," Romilla said, giving a cool nod as a greeting.

Max gave a deep bow and replied in kind.

"I should like to lay some ground rules before my daughters come downstairs."

The plural of "daughters" caught Max's interest, but he ignored it, wisely remaining silent.

"When you are in public with Evangeline, you are to be polite and attentive, but never overbearing. Never are you to attempt to even grasp her hand, beyond assisting her into and alighting from the carriage. Luckily, I will be on hand to keep things proper, and—"

"Excuse me, madam?" Max couldn't help but interrupt. "You are attending the carriage ride today?"

"Yes, of course. Abigail will be riding with us as well. Not just today, either. A family member will be present at all times you and Evangeline are in public together—a maid will not suffice. What good is your appearing in each other's company if it is not known to be sanctified by her family?" Romilla said, waving her hands about as she spoke, as if dismissing bothersome insects. Max's teeth started to grind. Not for the first time, the niggling question echoed in his head: What had he gotten himself into?

"I thought, madam, that the purpose might have been the

opportunity for Evangeline and I to get to know one another more intimately."

Romilla's face hardened. "Yes, well, I'd say you already know her intimately enough."

Max had to admit, he had walked right into that one.

"And another thing, my Lord—I noticed your carriage in the drive. A lovely vehicle to be sure, and I'm very pleased it will seat us all—so Abigail and I will not have to follow in our carriage—but not your own, am I correct? Please from now on, would you be so kind as to bring your own carriage? To be seen under the crest of Longsbowe would go a good distance in solidifying to the public eye the respectability of your intent."

"Madam, I do not have a carriage," Max said with deceptive calm.

Romilla blinked. "Of course you do. Longsbowe House has quite the stableyard."

"Lady Alton," Max answered, "the Longsbowe stables belong to my father. I personally own one horse, and he is boarded near my lodgings, which I rent."

Romilla placed her hands on her hips, frustrated. "Would your father begrudge you the use of his stables?"

"No, but—"

"Then next time you take us for a ride in the park, borrow a carriage from your father."

"Respectfully, madam, I will not. My father and I—"

"Lord Fontaine!" Romilla interrupted. The frustration purpled her face, but she took a deep breath, calming herself before she spoke again.

"This is an unusual situation for us all." She sighed, tired already. "I apologize if my instructions seem rude, but truth be told, we don't know you, and what we know of you so far doesn't necessarily make us inclined to trust you. Understand that everything, *everything*, that I am attempting to do today and in the future is to protect my daughter and family. Someday soon, I hope to be able to chat amiably with you, to respect you, even to like you. But for now, I have to ask you to bend a little and go along with what I ask."

It was an honest appeal—something Max encountered all

too rarely. He could appreciate that, he thought, even if he didn't like what it asked him to do.

"I'm sure I'll find a way to accommodate us both, ma'am," Max said, meaning it, and bowing.

The hard lines of Romilla's face broke into a smile for the first time that afternoon, just as the drawing room doors opened again, admitting the Alton sisters. Evangeline was in the lead, breathtakingly beautiful in a pink day dress and carriage coat of deeper rose, but her cheeks did not pick up the color. She was pale and kept her sparkling blue eyes downcast. If one didn't know better, it seemed as if she were nervous, even scared.

Gail Alton stood behind her, closest to the door, her golden gaze direct, if expressionless. She was studying him, he realized. And Evangeline was avoiding him. Somehow, Max thought, those roles should be reversed.

Realizing perhaps he shouldn't be staring, or if he did, he should limit his sightline to his intended, Max bowed, murmuring his greetings. Evangeline and Gail both curtsied, replying in kind. They rose.

And . . . no one said a word.

"Well," Romilla broke the silence, perhaps a bit too brightly, "we should be off then. Evangeline, Lord Fontaine has the loveliest barouche awaiting us, and I cannot wait to be out in the fresh air today."

Max glanced out the window. The sky was slate gray, and London air was rarely described as "fresh"—too much coal dust floated over the city. As he turned back, he caught a glimpse of Gail turning her eyes back from the window, too. He could guess that her thoughts were similar to his own, and a small wry smile escaped his lips.

They went into the foyer, and Max retrieved his articles from the butler, while the ladies pulled on their bonnets and gloves.

Suddenly, a small ripping noise broke the silence as they just stepped outside the door.

"Oh drat," Evangeline's sweet breathless voice filled the air. "It seems I rent my glove," she said, a slight frown lining her brow.

"Oh dear." Romilla sighed and went to examine the damaged garment. The seam connecting the thumb to the palm of the glove had split.

"At least it's repairable. Run upstairs and put on another pair, quickly dear."

"I'm afraid this is my last pair of white gloves"—Evangeline lowered her voice discreetly—"today is laundry day. The rest are in the wash."

"Borrow some of Gail's, then," Romilla quickly suggested.

"I apologize, ma'am," Gail interjected, "but I'm fresh out, too. Indeed, Mrs. Bibb made certain we had these for our outing today—but all our other things are being cleaned."

"Besides," Evangeline added, "Gail's gloves are too large for me."

Romilla sighed, and rolled her eyes to the heavens, as if bargaining with God to get her through the afternoon. "All right. Evangeline, come with me, I'll find you something from my wardrobe. Lord Fontaine, Gail—we'll be back shortly." And they went back into the house, leaving Gail and Max alone on the steps.

Shocked by the sudden advent of Gail's sole company, Max slid his eyes to his companion, to gauge if her reaction was similar.

Gail, in turn, slid her eyes to Max.

Quickly, they both looked away.

It was acutely uncomfortable.

Max crossed his arms over his chest, looking around at the stone steps, the potted urns of early spring flowers that flanked the door, his shoes, anything was safer than Gail. Likewise, Gail kept her gaze straight ahead into the park square.

Well, someone would have to venture some sort of conversation, Max decided, and it might as well be him.

"What I don't understand is why your stepmother is so adamant that I not be alone with your sister, and yet, here I stand, alone with you."

"But we're not alone," she answered without any inflection.

"We're not? I could have sworn only you and I stood here. Did you bring along an imaginary friend?" he said mockingly.

Gail slid him a wry glance, but kept her head straight. "Right now, there are a dozen eyes on us. The Pickerings in Number Eight are twitching back the curtains. Indeed, there are more people watching us now than were watching us at the ball."

Max's head came up involuntarily, immediately looking toward Number Eight, and saw the curtains mysteriously swing back into place as he turned his head.

"We're being spied on?"

"I have it on good authority that in London spying is what people do," Gail said, finally turning her head to look at him. A slight smile played at the corners of her mouth, as if she were mocking him—but for once, he didn't mind. She seemed less frightening, less confrontational. She was just as tall, her back ramrod straight, and yet she was smaller somehow. Maybe because she wasn't drunk or as mad as a soaking wet hen.

"Speaking of that night at the ball . . ." Max started. He looked to Gail who kept her face schooled in impassivity. He coughed and sputtered a little and started again. "Yes— ahem—while we're on the subject . . . the ball."

Gail froze—but as she really wasn't moving to begin with, it was quite imperceptible.

"The ball," she repeated.

"Far be it from me to instruct you on the ways of proper conduct . . ." Max said, in his most imperious tone—the one that always worked for his father.

"Yes, it would be very far from *you* to instruct *me* on proper conduct," Gail noted dryly.

Max felt the heat rise to his cheeks and glowered to hide his blush.

"Perhaps you should take more care of who you have fetch your drinks—and being lured into dark corners and . . . and lecherous men with only one thing on their minds."

Now was Gail's turn to blush and glower.

He saw her eyes narrow, her shoulders hunch as if ready to pounce. He could see the scathing she would give him, held just behind her voice. But she held her tongue.

Max smirked. She was trying so hard to hold back, he realized, for the sake of propriety. And yet all she wanted to do was brain him with her reticule—her fingers twitched on the strings.

A little demon on his shoulder told him to prod her further.

"Well, what do you have to say for yourself?"

As if those were the magic words that opened the gates to her opinion, Gail turned to him, eyes flashing, mouth quirked in a predatory twist. He was all too aware of the intensity of her golden gaze (and the little lurch of anticipation his stomach gave at encountering it) when he saw her pull back. Rein in.

Taking a deep breath, she spoke.

"Thank you."

He blinked.

"I beg your pardon?"

"I said, 'Thank you.' I was veering toward disaster that night, and you came to my rescue. You also held your tongue, when you could have told my parents or any number of your acquaintances, who would have no doubt delighted in a morsel of gossip. I appreciate your reticence. Given our previous encounter, I would have preferred anyone else in the world to witness my, er, state. However, it was you, Max. So I say thank you."

Max leaned back against the door, all of the ready engagement he had brewing diffused. Disarmed.

Well, that was no fun.

"Oh," he mumbled. "Don't mention it."

Silence took over for a moment as Max went back to crossing and uncrossing his arms and looking at his toes. He was just beginning to bear the quiet, leaning back against the door, wondering just how long it took to fetch a silly glove, when Gail opened her mouth.

"It does beg the question, however," she said.

"What question?"

"What do *you* have to say for yourself?"

Max's eyebrow went up. "I beg your pardon?"

"You keep begging my pardon, and really, I'm not inclined to give it. What do you have to say for yourself?"

"For what?"

"For being caught kissing *my* sister in *my* conservatory!"

Gail hissed, trying not to be overheard. Max couldn't see any potential eavesdroppers, but sound had the annoying habit of carrying to all too-interested ears.

"You are the most hypocritical man I ever met," she continued. "You take me to task for being preyed upon and then go and prey upon my sister! You went from being the rescuer of one to the seducer of the other, in the span of a quarter hour!"

"My actions, regarding your sister," Max said slowly, his voice cold as steel, "are none of your business, Brat."

"My sister, my conservatory," Gail countered. "My family. I'd count myself as an interested party."

"Miss Alton," Max said, turning to her, his shoulder leaning against the door in a relaxed pose of false calm, "I'm not answerable to you."

"No, Max, you're not, sadly. Are you answerable to anyone? Is there anyone in this world who keeps you and your tremendous ego in check?" Gail looked into his face, and he was surprised to see the beginnings of real tears. "How could you? How *could* you? You are no better than Ommersley, getting a girl alone and then forcing your intentions on her! And you can't deny it."

"Of course I can deny it! I didn't prey on you, did I?" Max said, perhaps more loudly than was proper, causing Gail to stare him into silence.

"But you don't like me, Max. I cast up the contents of my stomach on your shoes. Preying on me was probably repulsive, even to an unethical blackguard like you."

An image of the way Gail had looked that night drifted across Max's mind. Bleary eyed, tipsy, and eventually covered in vomit. Not at all appealing.

And yet, that had been an awfully fetching yellow dress.

"Why did you have to prey on my family?" Gail asked in a furious whisper, eyes gleaming. "Why couldn't you leave us alone? Sometimes you really are a . . ."

She managed to stop herself, but not the tears. Max was caught by those watery golden brown eyes, stoically fighting as one glistening tear lazily rolled its way down her flushed cheek.

He felt all the air leave his body. She was right—somewhat. He *had* blithely tripped into her family for his own reasons. He had sat through an uncomfortable interview with the father, and the stepmother, but until he encountered Gail's frustration and anger, Max hadn't really considered how his actions had affected this family. And here he'd stood on the steps, playfully snide and superior, prodding Gail into tears.

Sometimes, he really was a—

Suddenly, the door that supported most of his weight opened.

Luckily, he managed to catch himself on a nearby urn before falling completely, but he did make a few stumbling steps that Romilla looked upon most disapprovingly.

As both ladies emerged into the bleak afternoon daylight, gloves on and intact, Romilla gave a great smile. "Well," she said, false cheer in place, "shall we be off, then?"

* * *

IF it was thought the excursion had started off badly, the carriage ride itself could only be classified as a complete disaster.

Not outwardly of course—Romilla, a master at keeping up appearances, had made certain that they looked happy and jovial to anyone spying from afar. But if anyone had gotten close enough to read the subtleties, they would have come to realize one truth: No one here was having any fun.

Part of the reason, nay, the whole of the reason people rode in the park in the afternoons was that it was terribly fashionable. Gentlemen were there to look at the Young Ladies. Young Ladies were there to catch the eye of the Gentlemen and make themselves known to the many Matrons that ruled the Ton. The Matrons were there to ensure that no one faltered on the steps of the social ladder, and if they did, to be able to claim themselves an eyewitness to the occasion. Exercise was secondary.

The Alton/Fontaine party was no different, however much one or another of its occupants wished to be riding freely at a gallop on their own horse. Even in this unremarkable and somewhat chilly weather, the mass of fashionability turned out in fine style, crowding the neatly graveled paths and rolling lawns of Hyde Park. Gentlemen on fine horses, many of whom had more prestigious breeding than their owners, flanked carriages with ladies lounging in the seats. Lord Fontaine's carriage joined the unofficial queue of people dancing attendance on each other.

They smiled and nodded to Lord and Lady Garrett and the Pickerings, who giggled as they passed by. Mr. and Mrs. Fortings waved coolly as they went along, and several gentlemen greeted them genially. Indeed, from afar, it all looked so very amiable.

However, the insidious rumors had reached more and more ears in the past day, and the Ton was getting more and more curious.

Some of the gentlemen who stopped at the barouche's side were either complete rakes sensing easy prey or young bucks trying to earn dissolute reputations. Some people simply passed by with their noses in the air. Lady Hurstwood gave Lord Fontaine the most suspicious glance as she chatted with Evangeline. She had gone so far as to hint at the notion of a wedding, but out of necessity, not romance. Romilla had, of course, handled such inquisitions smoothly, until she had the opportunity to chat with Lady Jersey.

Lady Jersey was one of the leading matrons of the Ton. She and a handful of other ladies held supreme social power because they held all the vouchers for Almack's. Without a voucher, a young lady might just as well go home for the Season and quietly cry in the corner, such were her chances for social success. Most of these matrons were narrow-mindedly pompous, prudishly strict individuals who believed unequivocally in their own rightness. Lady Jersey was no different—but, perhaps, the nicest of the lot.

"Lady Alton. I must congratulate you on your ball the other evening," Lady Jersey began after being hailed by Romilla, her pair of horses coming to a smart halt at the lightest flick of her wrist. "It was not lacking in interesting events, I understand."

Romilla wisely ignored the bait. "Thank you, Lady Jersey, I'm so glad you enjoyed it."

"I daresay I wasn't the only one," Lady Jersey continued,

her eyes flitting to Lord Fontaine, as Gail and Evangeline exchanged quick looks.

Romilla cleared her throat and dared the next sentence. "Lady Jersey, are you acquainted with Lord Fontaine?"

Lady Jersey looked at Max, quirked her eyebrow, and extended her hand. "Lord Fontaine and I have never met, although I have seen you at several functions around town."

"Of course," Max answered smoothly. "Your servant, ma'am."

She nodded, regarded him a moment, and then asked, "Do you attend Almack's, my Lord?"

"But rarely, ma'am. I haven't had much cause to go until recently."

"Yes, of course. Few young gentlemen attend until they meet a lady worth pursuing there," Lady Jersey said coolly, but politely.

"Perhaps you'll see more of me then." Max smiled charmingly, and Lady Jersey responded in kind.

Romilla took advantage of the easier interaction Max had provided and took the next step. "Lady Jersey, I do hope that we may call upon you later in the week, I so admired the facade of your home."

Max knew Lady Jersey lived just across Berkeley Square, and therefore was required to maintain a neighborly connection with the Altons. But she could so easily say no. No one could be blind to Romilla's motivation, least of all Lady Jersey: vouchers for Almack's. Max saw Romilla catch her breath, Evangeline go white under her placid smile, and Gail raise a curious eyebrow, as Lady Jersey took a long probing look at their party. Finally, she smiled again, albeit thinly.

"We'll see," was all she said, before conveniently seeing that she was being hailed by another carriage and took her leave.

Romilla's face was impassive as stone, but her eyes flashed with intensity and anticipation. This was war, socially speaking, and she was ready to face down all the challenges. But she smothered the look so quickly, if Max had blinked he would have missed it.

And so it went on. Everyone that stopped by the carriage

gave cordial greetings to Romilla, smiling warmly at Evangeline and acknowledging she looked particularly well, with sly looks toward Max. Everyone got a good look at Max riding with the Alton girls and under the supervision and approval of the stepmother. However, Max noted no one said much to Gail. Odd, that. She was irritating for certain, but she also had obvious intelligence, a keen and ripe sense of humor, and was pretty, in a manner. But no one looked her way.

The Fontaine/Alton party soon left Rotten Row, and made their way at a brisk pace around the park, far enough from the main roads, but still in sighting distance of those who made it their business to watch. They were now free to converse openly, although Romilla instructed everyone to keep a congenial look or smile on his or her face the whole ride.

Once they were able to speak freely, however, a problem arose. No one had anything to say.

Oh, Romilla tried to engage in conversation. She started by noting, however sarcastically, how polite Lady Jersey had been and how nice the Pickering girls looked in their matching habits, adding that no one will ever be able to tell them apart until they start making use of their differences. She even tried to draw Max and Evangeline into a dialogue by discussing plans for the next few days and evenings, but to no avail.

Max's mind was curiously drawn to his earlier behavior toward Gail and gave short answers. Evangeline's answers were even shorter. She kept her eyes down and over, anywhere but on the three other people in the carriage.

Romilla finally gave up on her social graces and gave Max a solid kick on the toe to get him to talk.

And he did, once he realized through Romilla's remarkably pointy shoe that, as their de facto host, the burden of conversation was rightly on his shoulders. He tried to think of anything to say to Evangeline—but found his mouth dry and his mind blank. What to say? What were her interests? He couldn't even move to touch her hand under Romilla's watchful eye, and he certainly couldn't mention their previous meeting in range of her attentive ear.

And of course, there was the added presence of Gail.

How did he court Evangeline with the irksome sister always

watching, her sharp eyes and wit on hand and ready to slay him down to size? She would smirk and say something smart, and it would hit him dead in the chest.

Then again, Gail had barely said a word since her nearly tearful speech on the doorstep. She had observed his and Romilla's attempts at conversation, but never entered it, nor, he noted, had she been invited.

Hard to think this hellcat would wait for an invitation. But if he didn't know better, he'd think Gail was rather . . . subdued.

Her sister wasn't fairing much better. Max had tried subjects he thought might pique her interest. Fashion, the countryside, music.

"What did you think of Mrs. Reed's latest Gothic novel?"

"I'm sorry, I haven't read it."

"What's your opinion of the tragedy in Norfolk?"

"It's, ah, terribly tragic, indeed."

"Do you enjoy being back in England?"

"Very much, my Lord."

None of her answers were snappish; they were simply short—as if she couldn't think of a thing to say, either.

Nerves, it seemed, had overtaken the whole carriage.

Victuals that had been packed in a basket were opened in the hopes everyone would comment on the food, but no one was hungry.

After a turn and a half round the park, they admitted defeat. They waved good-bye to the afternoon riders they passed and returned to Number Seven Berkeley Square in silence.

* * *

AS Max escorted the ladies to the door, Romilla turned and asked him to stay for dinner.

It was an order, not a request, but Max couldn't think of anything he cared to avoid more. Claiming a previous engagement, Max made his regrets and promised to call in the morning. He bowed to Romilla and then turned to his intended. Evangeline looked fraily beautiful, but was still appallingly silent. She seemed outwardly serene, but had a death grip on her sister's hand.

He looked at that hand, holding on to Gail's as if she derived all her strength from that connection. Evangeline was acutely uncomfortable, and Gail was the only thing holding her together. Funny, Max mused. Given that on his previous meetings with Gail she had been a complete mess, he would have thought Evangeline the stronger of the two.

Max bowed to her, but dared not try to kiss her hand. As he took his leave of the Alton ladies and rode down the street, he reviewed the atrocious afternoon in his head.

Although Romilla's presence had done a great deal to stable their connection socially, it did nothing to help it grow. Indeed, a parent's presence could cause any growing tendresse to falter.

Gail's presence didn't help either.

What he needed was a way to rid himself of Romilla and Gail for the duration of the courtship. Then, the image of Evangeline's hand securely in Gail's flashed into Max's mind. Evangeline would probably want her sister there, at least for a bit, for her own peace of mind, even if it meant he would have to face her. Romilla's earlier dictate was that there always be at least one family member present. Gail was marginally the lesser of two evils, but he would at least need a way to distract her—and maybe keep her obnoxious comments away from him.

Max made a decision, and a sharp turn off his intended path.

He needed help.

He needed a friend.

Twelve

"GOOD God, Fontaine, can't you even court a girl on your own anymore?" Will rolled his eyes as he and Max walked up the steps to Number Seven. It was the next morning, and they were late for tea. Romilla would surely have his head.

"I just need the opportunity to talk with Miss Alton on my own," Max pleaded as he knocked on the door. "With you there, the stepmother won't need to be present all the time, and the sister—well, maybe she'll be less bothersome."

Will guffawed as he straightened his cravat. "Let me get this straight," he said, "you want me to give up any personal pursuits I may have for the next month, which will severely ruin my chances with any lady for the rest of the Season, and follow you and your intended around, just so you can avoid the stepmother. And on top of that, you want me to be saddled with the task of entertaining the *bothersome* sister? Goodness, Fontaine, this just sounds more and more appealing."

Max rubbed his temples. It was far too early in the morning. "Are you trying to make my life harder?"

"Every chance I get." Will smiled. "But not to worry. I'll do my best to keep the toothless, haggard, bothersome bluestocking sister away from you and your lovely intended. But you'll owe me."

"She's not haggard, or toothless," Max protested. "Actually, she's . . ." but before he could argue any further, the door opened, and they were admitted to Number Seven.

* * *

NOT an hour before Max raised his fist to knock on the door, two very tired girls had descended the staircase in Number Seven. After they were deposited back from their carriage ride the previous afternoon, they had once again been swept about London on the orders of their stepmother. While Max had scurried out the door as quickly as his legs would carry him, the Altons had quite the evening in front of them. It took an hour at least for each girl to dress, while Polly ran frantically between the two rooms as she assisted the young ladies. And, of course, it was impossible to get a word in edgewise with Romilla lecturing on the need to be happy and cheerful that evening. She went through, once again, the Dos and Don'ts of public behavior (Do stay in the ballroom, Don't be caught kissing a man in the conservatory) then gathered up her husband, and the whole party headed out.

After Lady Carmichael's rout, they went to the Quayles', and then on to another at the Rutherfords', who were very old friends of Sir Geoffrey's. The family did not return to Number Seven until three in the morning, and finally, the girls were able to speak on their own.

In her dressing gown, Evangeline snuck into Gail's room after their parents had said their goodnights. This was the first chance they had to chat privately, and Gail was not one to misuse it. She plunged right in.

"Evie, what was that?" Gail asked immediately.

"What was what?" Evangeline evaded.

"This afternoon! You were hoping I wouldn't remember back that far, weren't you? Well, I remember the grip you had on my hand—I nearly bruised from it."

Gail made room on the bed for Evangeline, who curled up in a ball, knees to her chest.

"I was just so nervous! I couldn't think of a thing to say

that wouldn't make me sound like a complete twit, so I ended up saying nothing—"

"And not surprisingly, sounded like a complete twit," Gail finished for her. Evangeline held her head in her hands.

"You get away with saying nothing all the time!" Evangeline sighed. "It *was* awful, wasn't it? Romilla was staring at me the whole time, making small talk, trying to get Lord Fontaine and me to speak. She even kicked me on the toe once. Honestly, Gail, I don't think I can ever face him again."

"Really?" Gail said, her hope too abundant to be disguised.

"Gail! Could you try to be nice? You shot Lord Fontaine daggers all afternoon, when you bothered to look at him. He's a very amiable gentleman. I think." Worry creased Evangeline's brow. Gail could read her thoughts—if her sister and her intended were always at odds, it would tear her apart inside.

"I'm sorry. This is difficult for us all," Gail spoke carefully. "I don't like this situation, and he is very much responsible for it."

"Only in part. I was there, too," Evangeline intoned seriously.

"I just think it's all wrong. And he's wrong for you," Gail said, in nearly a whisper.

Evangeline rose from the bed and stood by the window. The full force of Evangeline's beauty hit Gail, as it did from time to time. She loved her sister with the whole of her heart, and would never begrudge her a thing—after all, it's not as if Evie *asked* to be made beautiful—but there were times that Gail couldn't help but feel a twinge of envy. Why couldn't her mouth tilt in just that way, or the line of her shoulder be that graceful? Oh, to be so lovely, so admired!

But tonight, that beautiful face wore an expression of seriousness, determination, and a hint of sadness. Before Gail could ask what was wrong, Evangeline turned from the window, framed in the silver glow of the waning moon.

"I agreed to it. I'm going to marry him," she said quietly.

That sentence settled in the room, its gravity rendered truth by Evangeline's face.

"I know," Gail responded quietly.

"Can you try to like him?"

"Yes. I will. I'll try," Gail said.

"Good, because I need your help!" Relief washed over her face. "I would like to have a conversation with the man I'm to marry, without stuttering or blushing!"

"And you ask me to help you?" Gail repeated incredulously. "Dearest Evie, I do nothing but blush and stutter in public!"

"Oh, why is this so difficult? 'The tragedy in Norfolk is tragic?' How insipid I must have sounded! Normally, I'm, well, quite good at talking to gentlemen." Gail nodded in agreement as Evangeline continued, "But I have no idea what to say to Lord Fontaine. I have no idea how to make him smile, what his interests are, anything!" Evangeline flopped herself back down on the bed.

"Well then, you should ask him," Gail replied. She rubbed her chin thoughtfully for a moment, and clicked her fingernail against her front teeth. "You know," she mused, "Romilla is right about one thing."

Evangeline had the grace to look only slightly dubious.

"She has a *plan*. She is prepared with what we are doing, where we are going, who we will see, and has several topics of conversation at the ready—at all times!"

"Yes, she does have a plan," Evangeline considered, "but I can't let her take the lead in this. You saw today, both Lord Fontaine and I were rendered mute by her attendance. Apparently, having a parent present is not conducive to open courting."

"Then we must find some way for her to leave you two be. I know, I'll have some small wardrobe crisis and drag her off to the modiste's—"

"No!" Evangeline interrupted. "No, I can't have you leave, too. I want Romilla's presence removed, but I cannot be left alone with Lord Fontaine. If we were found alone together again it would cause a scandal in full force—not this little trickle of rumors that's happening now."

"I shouldn't imagine it will be a problem if you don't kiss him," Gail needled, but at the petulant frown on her sister's face, she acquiesced.

"Evie, don't fret. I'll stay with you," Gail said, reaching out to cover her sister's hand with her own. "Let me worry about Romilla, I'll find some way to make her vanish."

"And I'll make a list!" Evie cried triumphantly.

"A list?"

"A list of the questions I wish to ask Lord Fontaine. Just for reference. It's what Father would do. 'Go into situations with as much information as possible,' isn't that what he always says? It also has the added benefit of being conversation."

Although Gail was supremely skeptical about the idea of a list, she did think such a task would help put Evie at ease, and so walked to her writing desk and pulled a fresh piece of paper, quill, and ink. "Good idea," she said, handing the items to Evangeline. "Start with 'what makes you smile?'"

They stayed up until dawn broke against the windows, plotting ways to rid them of Romilla and writing questions to ask Max. "Give an account of the first time you fell off your horse," was particularly amusing to Gail. Evangeline's favorite was "Have you ever engaged in acts of piracy?" Evangeline had a strange fascination with pirates. However, the night's strategizing took its toll—hence the two very tired ladies descending the staircase the next morning at ten.

By the social world's clock, they were up and about remarkably early. By Romilla's standards, however, they were layabouts. Their stepmother met them in the drawing room, already deeply immersed in her morning correspondence, household accounts, and social schedule for the next several days.

"Girls, about time you were up. I've been revising our itinerary. Now, due to some unfortunate circumstances"— Romilla's eyes hardened—"we have not received the expected invitations to the Hurstwood party at Vauxhall." She faltered, then tried for brightness. "But we have half a dozen others." The set of Romilla's mouth told them that this was the first major slight they had received, and probably wouldn't be the last. "However, today, I need you both at your absolute most sparkling and pristine. Evangeline, later this afternoon we are going to call on the Garretts and Lady Jersey. Wear your blue walking dress with the light blue pelisse and be ready for some inopportune questions—she is a shrewd woman. Just laugh them off or act as if you have no idea what she's alluding to. Abigail . . . try to smile at least. And let me do the talking."

Gail wryly thought that Romilla never did anything but talk, but luckily caught herself before saying it aloud, embarrassed at her unkindness. Romilla moved about the room, speaking with her hands so expressively, Gail almost mistook her for Portuguese. Well, Lisbon was where father had met Romilla, after all; it wasn't surprising that she had picked up a few non-English habits.

Gail's musings were interrupted when Romilla said, "And I expect Lord Fontaine to arrive at any moment for his morning visit."

" 'Lord Fontaine?" Gail queried. "Already?" She had not thought to expect him until the next day. After all, they wouldn't want him to seem too attentive, would they? Surely, Evangeline needed more time to prepare.

"Well, of course. He said he would call today. Hopefully we will have some other gentlemen callers to divide our attention a bit. It was rather overwhelming, just the three of us and him yesterday wasn't it, but I fear . . ." Romilla paused for breath, and for the first time, Gail could see the cracks in her stepmother, the doubts seeping in.

"Well! We'll just have to see," she said brightly, smiling at the girls. Evangeline must have noted Romilla's distress as well, for she gave herself a little shake and offered Romilla a smile.

"Of course," she said. "I danced with a number of gentlemen last evening, and all were so agreeable. I wouldn't be surprised if half a dozen men turned up on our doorstep with flowers for Gail, for she has been catching some eyes, too."

Gail nearly snorted. Last night at the Carmichaels', she had barely moved from her position by the punch table.

"Tell me, Mother," Evangeline continued. "Do you think this dress will do? I do so hope to look nice for the Viscount." Evangeline pirouetted in her fitted gown, the color of green apples. It had mid-length sleeves, and the full skirt, covered in a gauzy white chambray, fell in beautiful folds to the floor. Romilla complimented the dress and asked to see how the shoes they had ordered to match fit. The conversation continued, Evangeline successful in switching topics to one their stepmother could engage in without fear or hesitation. Say what you will about Romilla, Gail thought as she excused herself for a moment to find Mrs. Bibb, but no one could fault her taste in, or enthusiasm for, clothes.

* * *

LATER, while waiting in the drawing room, Gail's stomach grumbled. The breakfast room had been cleared already, keeping with Romilla's odd schedule. Over the past six months, Gail and Evangeline had learned that if they wanted breakfast, they would have to be up and about early. Sometimes however, sleep was just too precious. Luckily, Romilla's habit of mid-morning tea, and a few of Mrs. Bibb's fantastic scones would stave off Gail's growing hunger.

She had just buttered one of those deliciously steaming confections when Lord Fontaine was announced, along with an unexpected guest.

"Lord Fontaine and Mr. William Holt," Morrison's voice boomed out, as he admitted the two gentlemen to the drawing room. Romilla quickly shot a reproachful look at Gail, who reluctantly put down the hot, buttery raspberry scone and rose to greet their guests.

The new gentleman Max had brought looked to be very amiable. His countenance was pleasing, blond shining hair and smiling blue eyes, and he held himself as a man who took joy in every aspect of his life. The contrast to Max was startling. His shoulders were as strong as his friend's, but Max looked as if he carried the weight of the world and didn't quite know what to do with it. His dark hair was windswept, and his cool green eyes took in the whole room, a raven's gaze that momentarily locked with hers. Gail looked away quickly, not wanting to be caught staring. She was surprised by the little spiral of awareness that went down her spine. Very surprised.

"Lord Fontaine!" Romilla exclaimed. "How lovely to see you. You're just in time for tea."

Max and Will took in the full tea service and the tiers of pastry and sandwiches. In their minds, it was still breakfast time. "Tea, madam?"

"Yes, we serve tea at half past ten in this house," Romilla answered. "I see you brought a friend. Mr. Holt, it's good to see you again."

"My pleasure, ma'am. I enjoyed your party last week. Quite the loveliest affair."

Romilla fluttered prettily at the compliment, her manner warming to accept the new addition.

The gentlemen sat, more than eager to take part in some mid-morning victuals. They were male after all, Gail thought, so food was always a welcome sight. Gail reached for her own abandoned scone, but a quick glance from Romilla stopped her from indulging in such a messy treat in front of the gentlemen.

"Tell me, Mr. Holt, how is it you came to be friends with Lord Fontaine?" Romilla began, taking the lead, as she had yesterday. Gail feared that she would talk over them again, but Mr. Holt seemed able to hold his own in any conversation. He smiled easily and launched into stories of two mischievous youths, growing up on the Bristol coastline. He told of boyish adventures, tree climbing, playing in the woods—tame stories that satisfied the party's need for conversation, but were obviously only shadows of the actual exploits.

Twenty minutes passed, without anyone but Romilla and Mr. Holt speaking. Occasional questions were directed toward Evangeline, so she had to pay attention, smiling and nodding when appropriate, but Gail had nearly nodded off while sitting upright. Only a discreet pinch from Evangeline kept her from slumping to sleep.

One of the maids entered to clear the remains of the tea tray, and Gail looked wistfully as she took away her now cool, uneaten scone. Romilla's voice was becoming raspy from carrying the weight of conversation, and a shared look between Gail and Evangeline cemented the need to put their plan into action.

The maid who had been clearing up the tea service was given a quick wink—the signal had been sent. She, in return, gave an almost imperceptible nod, and just as silently gathered the rest of the cups and saucers and left the room.

Two minutes later, a beautifully anguished shriek rent the air. Romilla stood up so quickly, she overturned the small stool near her left foot.

"What on earth . . . ?" she said as she trotted to the door. Mrs. Bibb opened the drawing room door before Romilla could, nearly braining her mistress in the process. Luckily, they both had reflexes enough to stop before any further pratfall could occur.

"Oh, Milady!" Mrs. Bibb said, breathless. "Might I have your presence in the kitchens? There's been an emergency."

Before Romilla could protest, Mrs. Bibb had taken off down the hall again. Romilla, torn between her duties to her house and the need to chaperone the girls, hesitated for two seconds, indecision showing on her face.

"Girls, I won't be but a moment. Please keep our guests entertained," she said, and ran down the hall after Mrs. Bibb, making certain to leave the drawing room doors open, lending at least some propriety to the situation.

The party had risen from their seats when Romilla had excused herself. Now they all held their breaths.

It was Max who broke the silence.

"She'll be back shortly, I presume."

A quick mischievous glance between Gail and Evangeline did not go unnoticed by their guests.

"Or perhaps not . . ." Max said, an eyebrow rising.

"I doubt she'll be back for at least an hour." Evangeline sat, waving for the others to follow her example.

"A problem in the kitchen will take an hour to rectify?" Will frowned as he took his seat. "I do hope it's nothing serious."

"Oh no! It isn't dire!" Evangeline exclaimed. She turned to her sister. "I think Gail could best explain."

Gail froze. She hadn't expected . . . she didn't think . . . She looked at the three faces focusing attention all on her: encouraging Evangeline, curious Mr. Holt, and a highly skeptical Lord Max Fontaine. He looked as if he couldn't believe that

Gail could or would plan anything properly. Her eyes narrowed.

"Well, the difficulty in the kitchen is that tonight's supper has gone completely awry, as I suspect a dog from the street has snuck in and stolen the joint of beef. It takes time to restructure an entire meal, arranging sauces and side dishes to go with whatever Mrs. Bibb can get at the market at such an hour. Up to, oh, twenty minutes to rearrange. Then I'm afraid my stepmother will discover a problem in the hedgerow in front of the house—the very same rogue dog dug up the beautiful crocuses she had specifically ordered and placed in a widening flow by the daffodils. Seeing to the reordering of flowers and new planting design will have to be done immediately—she would never let such a thing sit. It will take another twenty minutes at least. Then of course there is a very important letter of correspondence that has gone missing from her desk."

"Rogue dog, again?" Will asked.

"Not to worry. It should turn up in another twenty minutes. All added, Romilla will be unfortunately entangled in domestic problems for at least an hour," Gail concluded, her cheeks tinged with red at admitting all their deeds.

Max and Will looked at each other, clearly impressed.

"When did you have time to, er, come across this stray dog?" Will asked, the corners of his lips twitching.

"This morning. Gail asked Mrs. Bibb to, ah, keep an eye out for such a beast," Evangeline answered.

Max grinned in spite of himself. Soon enough, a small chuckle escaped.

"Well," he said gruffly, "uh, that's very interesting."

"Yes, interesting!" Will exclaimed. "So much so, that I think someone deserves a gift for such an *interesting* occurrence."

Will reached into his breast pocket and pulled out a bulbous handkerchief. He unwrapped it, and held out a raspberry scone.

Gail gasped with unexpected pleasure, smiling brilliantly at Will. So focused was she on her treat, she didn't see Max's brow crease into a scowl.

* * *

AS it turned out, Gail and Evangeline's elaborate schemes
were to be unnecessary.

Romilla was exasperated. First, Mrs. Bibb and Cook insisted a dog had run into the kitchen and stolen the joint of
beef that had been planned for dinner. If it hadn't been Mrs.
Bibb making the claim, Romilla would have suspected foul
play. Next, that same dog (which no one had been able to
catch) had torn up the beautiful purple crocuses she'd had
planted just yesterday. She sent the gardener off immediately
for replacements, and when she finished, she noticed a letter
she had started that morning to her bank was missing from
her escritoire. She inquired of the footman if he had accidentally sent it off with her other correspondence (which would
have been disastrous, as she was not yet finished), which he
had not. She was about to knock on the library door and see if
she had left the letter there, when the door suddenly opened
from the inside.

"Ah, my darling! Exactly the person I needed!" Sir Geoffrey took his wife by the arm and pulled her into the library,
shutting the door behind them.

"Geoffrey, what on earth . . ."

But Romilla was silenced by a long, fervent kiss from her
husband. As always, she was a bit shocked by the thrill this
man made her feel, as if she were a girl of seventeen again.
All too soon, he pulled away, leaving her breathless.

"We should start every conversation that way," Sir Geoffrey said, a bit breathless himself.

"I agree," Romilla mused, licking her lips, held in her husband's trance. She shook herself, remembering her responsi-
bilities in the house—time and efficiency must be maintained.
"Dearest, I'm looking for a letter I was writing this morning.
Did I happen to leave it in here?" She pulled away from him
reluctantly, straightening her frock as she began to search the
room.

"Forget that for a moment," Sir Geoffrey said, following
his wife to his desk, where she rifled through the papers. "Ro-

milla, I've just received the most interesting communication. From the Duke of Wellington."

Romilla stopped rifling immediately. "The prime minister?" she repeated.

"Yes! He has just sent a missive; apparently he has received a letter from Barivia, which he enclosed." He handed both letters to his wife, her own quite forgotten.

"It says I am to be placed in charge of trade relations with the German principality of Barivia. And that an emissary from that country is coming next week."

"Darling, I have spent the last twenty years of my life in Europe, and I have never heard of Barivia."

"Neither had most of England, until recently," Sir Geoffrey replied, smiling, and launched into his lesson on Barivian anthropology.

Barivia, it seemed, was an extremely small country in the German states, on the northwest coast. So small in fact, that even though it is on the North Sea, it was mostly ignored by shipping routes for larger ports of call such as Hamburg, Amsterdam, and Copenhagen.

Barivia was fairly unchanged during the Napoleonic wars, mainly because people on both sides plum forgot it was there. Everyone in Barivia grows their own food, uses the same plows and tools and homes that their parents and their parents and their parents used—Germanic construction being, of course, quite sturdy. The only two products they ever exported were chocolates, which were decidedly second-rate next to Bavaria's—and suffering from the similarity in the two countries' names, Barivia's chocolate profits were sadly undercut. The second export was Gunter Roffstaam, a painter of no importance historically or to this story, so it's not surprising that no one has ever heard of him, unless they visit his parents' farm, where his mother shows everyone the lovely portrait he did for her birthday and his father grunts about having only three daughters and one worthless son. But, as it's been stated, he's irrelevant.

What was relevant however, was that after eons of being the quiet, simple, forgotten country, Barivia suddenly found itself being spoken of in the highest echelons of the British government.

While tending to his herd of goats, farmer Bjorn Roffstaam—a distant cousin of the irrelevant artist Gunter (due to a lack of marital choices, Barivia is horribly populated by Roffstaams)—noticed one of his charges going into a craggy hole in a rock face near the coastline. While attempting to retrieve the errant goat, Bjorn discovered possibly the richest vein of high quality iron ore in Europe. It was malleable. It was pure. And England wanted it.

Romilla interrupted Sir Geoffrey there. "But why on earth would England want to import iron ore? We have loads and loads of it here—we don't need more . . . do we?"

"While it's true that we mine a great deal of iron ore"—Sir Geoffrey never missed a chance to pontificate—"the fact is, we use it to build parts for the textile mills and the new railways—and those don't require very high-grade iron. This is the purest stuff anyone has seen! Iron like this can undergo the reduction process necessary to produce sheet metal. And sheet metal is going to be a fantastic industry in the future."

Romilla was about to open her mouth with a question (for she always had questions), but Sir Geoffrey continued. "If Barivia started a manufacturing plant, it would take years and years—we already have the plants in place."

"Besides," Romilla added wisely, "we don't want Barivia to start into the iron industry—it would lower our prices abroad."

"Exactly."

"It so often comes down to money, doesn't it?"

"More often than not, my dear. Now, according to Wellington, both Hanover and France have made their interest in the ore known. We don't want them in the iron business either, and luckily Barivia has decided to contact us, by sending this emissary"—he consulted the letter in his wife's hand—"a Count Roffstaam."

"Another one?" Romilla asked in disbelief.

"My dear, I should not be surprised if everyone in such a small country is named Roffstaam. But he is coming next week, and Wellington has appointed me to the task!"

"Darling, I'm so impressed for you." Romilla beamed. "But why does not the Duke involve himself in something of such great import?"

"I suspect he would, but he's busy with the Catholics, and his whole cabinet is in an uproar. But if we get rights to the iron ore, it would be quite a feather in my cap. That awful business in Lisbon can be put aside . . . I could possibly receive an appointment to a ministry."

"Oh!" Romilla exclaimed, and threw herself into her husband's arms, kissing him fervently. When she finally stopped, she couldn't stop speaking. "That would be wonderful! You of all people deserve such an appointment! And it will happen, dearest, it will! We'll be the toast of London and . . ." Sir Geoffrey finally silenced her with another kiss.

After a time just beyond respectable, Romilla broke away and said, "What do we know about him? Of course he'll have to be entertained. Shall I organize a dinner party immediately? Where do I send his direction? Oh heavens, the things to do!"

Sir Geoffrey chuckled. "He will be staying at lodgings in Mayfair the Duke has had arranged. He's arriving next week, so you have plenty of time to organize a party. But darling, there is one thing I need to talk to you about . . ." He hesitated.

"Yes, dearest? What is it?"

"It's . . . Barivians are rather . . . sheltered . . . in their views of ladies and propriety. It is a country untouched by the outside world, we should not wish to shock them with our liberal, cosmopolitan ways. Wives, and er, daughters, need to be above reproach."

Romilla took this in. They needed Roffstaam. England needed Barivia. She could hold her tongue when necessary, but . . .

"Abigail," she said grimly.

Sir Geoffrey fought a frown. "And I am concerned about the situation with Evangeline and Lord Fontaine. It is most inconvenient, especially now."

"What should we do? Do you think we should speed up the wedding? Or perhaps send the girls to the country for the duration of the Count's visit?" Romilla worried her lower lip.

"No, I don't think we should do either," Sir Geoffrey replied. "If we rush the wedding, its reason will reach Roffstaam's ears all too quickly by my enemies in Parliament."

"And if we send the girls away, it will turn the rumors that are now sparks into full flames," Romilla finished.

"We must maintain present course. But make certain nothing else untoward occurs."

Romilla suddenly started. "The girls! Oh, I must get back!" She ran out of the room without a second glance, not even pausing to close the library doors.

She hurried to the drawing room, a scant look at the clock in the hall telling her she had been away from her charges for nearly forty minutes. Forty minutes! She dreaded to think what havoc could have been wreaked—or worse, what if there was no conversation? Evangeline seemed uncharacteristically dull of late, and they only had Lord Fontaine's word to bind him.

Romilla slowed to a brisk trot. As she rounded the corner to the drawing room, she was confronted with a sight she had never considered.

The four of them—Evangeline, Lord Fontaine, his friend Mr. Holt, and Gail were sitting quite amiably, laughing, talking of nothing in particular. Having a respectable, enjoyable morning.

What on earth was she supposed to do with that?

Thirteen

"YOU are the luckiest bastard on the face of the earth." Will lit a pipe once the door to the carriage closed. They had stayed at Number Seven for a few hours; it was well past noon once they took their leave. Other gentlemen who had spent last night dancing with Evangeline were arriving, ready to further their acquaintance with her and her sister. Both Will and Max had been reluctant to leave once they saw the mass of men vying for Evangeline's attention, but they were shooed out the door by Romilla, who claimed they had a hundred things to do that afternoon but insisted on their returning the next day and staying for dinner. Romilla had seemed newly distracted since the phantom stray dog had been unleashed, but she was nothing if not kind and escorted the gentlemen to the door.

Max could not help but scoff at Will's pronouncement. "Luckiest? That was the first time I've been able to say more than three words to her since . . ."

"Since being caught in a compromising position? But that's exactly what I mean. You are looking for a bride—any bride, just so you can save your fortune. And what falls in your lap? Only the most beautiful and pleasant creature Britain has ever produced! Lucky. Bastard."

"You don't think she's a little . . ." He searched for the right word. "*Boring*?"

Will looked at Max as if he had just swallowed a cricket bat. "Boring? Are you mad? She is incredible! She may be reserved, but over time, I suspect that will fade away. Her manners are impeccable, the sweetest nature—and a face like that could never be boring."

"Yes, I adore being spoken to about the latest fashions and hairstyles," Max replied sarcastically.

"That's what young ladies are told is polite conversation." Will shrugged.

"There is still the stepmother to contend with. And the sister," Max argued.

Will shook his head. "You're not marrying the stepmother. And as for the sister, I think you sold her a good deal short. Not bothersome at all. In fact, I found her to be quite pleasing."

"You liked her?" Max frowned.

"Of course! She may be shy, and the lesser in beauty—"

"She's not without beauty," Max protested, perhaps a bit too vehemently.

"True," Will agreed, an eyebrow in the air. "I never claimed otherwise. Also, she's quick. Miss Gail was the one who planned for our chaperone to be occupied, after all."

"Yes," Max drawled. "She is rather effective at creating small disasters." And doing a far better job of ridding them of the stepmother than he could have managed, he grudgingly admitted to himself.

Will simply smiled and continued on. "Pleasing smile, pleasing brown eyes. What's not to like?"

"Gold," Max said before he could stop himself.

"Beg pardon?"

"Her eyes—never mind. Good, I'm glad the two of you got along. You will be spending a great deal of time with the Br . . . er, Miss Gail."

Will sent his friend a devilish smile. "You say that as if it would be a hardship."

Max's jaw began working with fervor. Never in his life would he have expected Miss Gail Alton to be described as both shy and pleasing. He had half a mind to inform Will that Gail was the chit who threw him in the lake, but knowing his best friend, that would only make him like her more. "You really liked the sister?"

Will grinned. "Who knows? Maybe someday we'll be brothers-in-law."

An image flashed in front of Max's eyes: that smile Gail had given Will when he presented her with the scone. It was dazzling. And it had been directed at his friend.

For some reason, that thought set Max's teeth on edge more than anything else.

* * *

"THAT was absolutely brilliant!" Evangeline exclaimed in hushed tones, as she and Gail walked across Berkeley Square, Romilla six steps ahead as always. "You are the cleverest sister anyone could ask for!"

Gail blushed, but kept her eyes on Romilla's back, making certain she wasn't eavesdropping. It had been a surprisingly nice morning. Pleasant, companionable. And more confusing than Gail wished.

Max had been a gentleman: kind, inquiring, accommodating. It was difficult to alter her original impression of a boorish, overbearing lout to include this new dynamic. And his friend Mr. Holt had been such enjoyable company as well! Surely someone that nice could not be friend to someone who was not equally honorable?

"Gail? What are you thinking?" Evangeline inquired.

"Simply that . . . that Mr. Holt was quite nice," Gail managed to stutter out.

Evangeline blushed. "He was, wasn't he? Not to mention handsome and intelligent. I adored the way he described his home in Bristol. Right next to Lord Fontaine's! It must be beautiful there," she sighed wistfully. "Mr. Holt is possibly the most charming man I've ever met!"

"He, uh, seemed to bring out the best qualities in Lord

Fontaine, as well," Gail ventured, but only received a soft "hmm" as a reply.

"How are we to get rid of Romilla when they come to call tomorrow?" Evangeline said after a few moments.

"No idea—phantom stray cat?"

"Hurry up, girls!" Romilla said, not even turning her head around or pausing in her step. "We mustn't be late for Lady Jersey. Remember, leave all conversation to me, unless she asks you a direct question."

Evangeline suddenly grabbed Gail's arm. "The questions!" she whispered. "The list I prepared for Lord Fontaine! I was so nervous, I forgot to ask them!"

Gail desperately shushed her sister, but luckily, Romilla seemed blissfully unaware of what they were saying in hushed tones.

"You wrote them just in case there was nothing to talk about." Gail reflected. "Obviously the morning was going too well to need to employ them."

"But I should like to know the answers."

"I shouldn't worry. You will learn the answers eventually, in the course of normal conversation."

"One hopes I'll know them before my wedding," Evangeline worried.

"Evangeline! Pinch your cheeks. Gail, straighten your gloves."

They had stopped before Number Thirty-Eight, the residence of Lady Jersey, directly across the square from their home—a huge, marbled house with iron gates and bright daffodils growing in flanking pots.

"We're here."

* * *

AS it happened, neither Gail and Evangeline, nor Max and Will, had to invent some sort of elaborate scheme for the occupation of Romilla. She was much too busy preparing for the dinner party with Count Roffstaam to worry about the girls—as long as they were in Number Seven and together.

A boon had been granted—Lady Jersey had happily arranged for Evangeline and Gail to receive their Almack's vouchers. In thankful reciprocation, Lady Jersey, a vocal enthusiast of Barivian chocolates, had been one of the honored guests invited to the dinner party for the ambassador. Whether or not this proffered invitation had been any inducement to the giving of the vouchers was undetermined. To mention the possibility that a trade had occurred was highly indelicate. Even Gail knew that much.

Romilla spent the week readying her troops for the invasion. This would be a much smaller affair than the girls' coming out ball—but in many ways, it was far more important. Flowers had to be ordered, the courses arranged—a French cook was engaged for the sole purpose of making the pastries—another for sauces. Invitations had to be printed, and the seating arrangements between the Whigs and the Tories were a nightmare. The silver was still in good shape, since the ball was not a week past, but Romilla insisted on a repolishing of all the utensils, mirrors, candlesticks, and bric-a-brac that could possibly be viewed by their foreign guests. Entertainment had to be arranged. Romilla, naturally, had Evangeline practicing her pianoforte whenever possible, but was debating whether to engage a top soprano to sing an aria or two after the meal. Rooms that would never be seen, never even have their doors opened, were aired out, new linens were purchased, and, of course, gowns were arranged for herself and the girls. Not to mention the social rounds she had to make! Romilla was terribly busy, indeed.

Therefore, when they were unnecessary, Evangeline and Gail were left to themselves to entertain their callers.

Max and Will were the most frequent, having claimed tea at half past ten as their own. It was amazing how quickly everyone adjusted themselves to Romilla's busy schedule—she woke at dawn, no matter what time she went to bed, and therefore she considered anyone who lounged all morning sleeping as a hopeless layabout.

Max and Will would arrive at exactly teatime, with some flowers or a trinket in hand—always presented to Romilla, not the daughters. Occasionally they passed Sir Geoffrey on his way out the door, off to some important meeting of State. He would plant a perfunctory kiss on top of each of his daughter's heads, and squeeze his wife's shoulder before disappearing for the length of the day. Romilla stayed with the young people for approximately twenty minutes before she downed the last of her tea and ran off to her next imperative domestic task. She always left the drawing room doors open, and always made certain a maid or two was nearby in case of, well, in case of anything. When the girls left the house they were always chaperoned to the point of frustration, but at home in the mornings, after those twenty minutes, Evangeline, her secret betrothed, her sister, and his friend were left to their own devices.

Surprisingly, those devices were unaccountably tame. No one made a mad dash to the conservatory; no one spoke in low voices words only lovers said. They were far more likely to begin playing a game of whist than they were to embark upon a forbidden kiss.

And it was driving Max crazy.

It was Wednesday, and that evening the girls were to attend their first dance at the great hall at Almack's. Evangeline's enthusiasm was so catching that the gentlemen were reluctant to dampen it with their knowledge of Almack's weak punch and pallid music. Even Gail seemed to be interested in their expedition to the famous public gallery, following the conversation with interest, smiles, and even venturing the occasional question.

And therein lay the problem.

For the past week, Max had danced attendance every morning on Evangeline. He was prompt, courteous, and every inch the gentleman. And every morning, Gail was there.

How was he supposed to court his intended if her sister listened in on every word? She sat there, her golden eyes following the players like a tennis match, rarely speaking, never betraying her thoughts by showing an expression. She would smile sometimes, though, Max reflected. On the rare occasion when her attention would drift (generally when the gentlemen started talking at length about the latest neck cloth style), Gail would turn to look out the window. After a few moments, she would tuck a strand of rich brown hair behind her ear and smile privately to herself, lost and happy in her own thoughts, causing Max to pause in his own. Where did she go? What made her smile like that?

Yes, Max found it very difficult to focus on Evangeline with Gail at hand.

Worse though, was that Max felt like he hadn't actually spoken to Evangeline since that intoxicating night in the conservatory. Oh, they had been members of the same conversation, and even exchanged a few sentences, but they were of the "how is your father" and "did you enjoy the musicale last evening" variety. What he wanted was that feeling of closeness that had enveloped them that night—to catch her sighs and know their meaning.

Oh, he was well acquainted with her preferences in hair ribbons, but he knew nothing of her private thoughts, of her disposition toward marriage, home life, the Whig party—he barely knew anything of her personal history!

As they discussed Almack's, regaling the girls with carefully chosen, carefully edited stories of the various bits of scandal that had occurred there (lighter fare—that Lady Jersey had indeed denied the Duke of Wellington admission for arriving after the doors were closed, as opposed to the various cuckoldings and bastards conceived in its shadowed corners), Max decided that he had had enough. Romilla had run off nearly a half hour before, mentioning something about napkin rings. No one was going to interrupt him if he stepped beyond what they wanted him to do.

It was now or never.

Max moved from his wing-backed chair to the comfortable sofa where Evangeline sat next to Gail. It took Evangeline a moment to realize he was there, so intent was she on her conversation with Will, but when she turned to look at him, it was with some surprise.

He hadn't been this close to her since that night. He'd seen her every day since, but now he was sitting next to her, and impulsively took her hand in his. If possible, Evangeline's eyes grew wider, caught like a rabbit. He watched as she took a deep steadying breath, reined in her composure, and smiled at him.

"Miss Evangeline, would you do me the honor of a turn

about the room? I feel I could use the exercise," Max said directly into her enormous blue eyes. And for a moment, he didn't see an open-mouthed Gail looking over her sister's shoulder.

"Um, ah . . ." Evangeline hemmed, her gaze scanned the room and finally came to rest on his fingers surrounding hers. For a split second, Max feared she would pull away, when Will cleared his throat.

"Fontaine, you'll have to wait your turn," Will spoke up. "I fear a leg cramp myself. Miss Gail, would you care to join me?" Will stood and held out his hand. Gail had no choice but to take it.

Max exhaled. Holt had thankfully anticipated his needs and considered Miss Evangeline's comfort. He could speak far more intimately with Evangeline seated together on the couch without fearing Romilla's censure if she happened in, and Will in turn had removed Gail. Now all Max had to do was actually speak.

* * *

"WHAT'S going on?" Gail said very softly, so only Will could hear. They were at the far side of the drawing room now, near the large marble fireplace. At the pace Will was walking, they would reach the other end of the chamber around nightfall. Gail had to pull him to match her natural gait.

"Don't fret, Miss Gail." Will patted her hand, refusing to move any faster. "I believe Lord Fontaine merely wanted to speak to his fiancée on his own. You're surprised I called Miss Alton his fiancée? Don't worry—Fontaine tells me everything, I tell him everything, and neither of us tell anyone else. It's a system that's worked flawlessly for two decades."

"Flawlessly?" Gail questioned. "So I cannot count on you to relate any stories of Lord Fontaine's youthful indiscretions I can feed to my sister?"

Will smothered a chuckle, keeping his voice low. "Only if he deserves it."

Gail smiled and condescended to rest a little weight on Will's arm. She liked Mr. Holt—he was always pleasant, always smiling, but never in a leering or awkward way. He was a naturally happy person, and he was generous with his joy. Gail had difficulty understanding the bonds of friendship that held him to such a cynical individual as Max Fontaine. Gail listened down the length of the drawing room. She could barely hear the murmuring coming from the couch and certainly couldn't make out what was being said—but she saw it at the same time that Will did.

"Why does your sister have a piece of card in her hand?" He couldn't help but ask. "Is she reading something? A poem perhaps?"

"Very likely," Gail lied. "Evangeline is fond of poetry."

* * *

"SO, I uh, wanted to ask you, sir . . ." Evangeline started, glancing down at the crumpled piece of card she had pulled out of her pocket. "What is your favorite color?"

Max could only gape for a moment.

"My, ah, favorite color?" Max repeated, going a bit red in the face.

"I'm sorry." Her blush matched his. "That's a silly question, isn't it?"

"No, it's not a silly question—green. My favorite color is green."

Their first opportunity for unfettered conversation, and this is her chosen topic? His favorite color? This was not the beginning he hoped for.

"Oh," Evangeline replied. "Well. Um. My favorite color is violet. But I like all colors. In case you were wondering."

Evangeline looked down at the card again, affording Max a chance to peek at its contents. On it, he saw neat, even hand covering the card in the tiniest writing imaginable.

She had all these questions to ask him? What happened to the sweet, charming girl from the garden? Max nearly rolled his eyes, but something stopped their rotation.

Her hand was shaking.

"Tell me"—she cleared her throat—"what was the last book—"

"Miss Evangeline, I know you don't know much about

me," Max interrupted gently, as he reached out and plucked the card from her grasp, "and I know equally little about you. But I do know that I have been longing for the opportunity to speak alone with you for a week now, and I simply hope that we can sit, enjoy each other's company, and talk."

Evangeline flushed profusely, too much a female not to be softened by Max's pretty words.

"Talk? What, ah . . . what do you wish to talk about?" Evangeline stammered.

"You. Me. Each other. Us," Max said, his nerves unknotting as Evangeline's frame slowly relaxed.

"Your choice of topics is vast and far-reaching, to say the least." She smiled.

"Well, I have a feeling you are far more interesting than I—"

"That cannot be true," Evangeline said, laughing.

"We'll compare," Max declared. "What was it like growing up constantly abroad?"

And with that, Max and Evangeline embarked upon their first unrestricted and authentic conversation.

* * *

WILL had long since conceded to move at Gail's pace—it was a battle he wasn't going to win. They were on their fourth lap of the drawing room; nearly twenty minutes of uninterrupted time had elapsed since Gail had first seen Evie pull out her card of questions. It had since disappeared from view, which was all to the good, in her opinion. But that didn't mean things were going well.

"Why is she so uneasy?" Gail murmured. "She is the clever one with gentlemen. I've never seen her so awkward."

Will snuck a peek at the progress his friend and his friend's fiancée were making.

"Maybe because it's never mattered so much before," he whispered back.

For indeed, the flow of conversation, instead of being natural and easy, more closely resembled a gasping sputter. It started as a rush of words, either from Max or Evangeline, and often both at the same time, followed by a solid minute of silence. Both would look away during this time, searching the room for the next topic of conversation. Occasionally, Max's eyes would choose Gail to fall upon, and she caught him more than once watching her and Will circling the room. But then, he'd just as quickly shift his gaze elsewhere, and eventually one or the other's eyes would alight on some random object, which would spark a question, and another furious burst of talk would occur. And so it went.

Whenever Will and Gail circled close enough to eavesdrop with a degree of accuracy, they slowed down. But unfortunately, the seated couple always seemed to be in one of their silent stretches, and thus nothing was learned. Until . . .

"So you next traveled to Portugal then?" Gail overheard Max say. No doubt his eye had fallen on a Portuguese silk shawl draped over the chair.

"Yes, Lisbon," Evangeline replied.

"And did you enjoy it?"

"Oh yes," Evangeline said in a rush. Then she added, "However, I don't think I'm well suited to long travel."

"How do you mean?" Max questioned, the smallest hint of strain in his voice.

"Well, every time I go to a new place, I miss the old one desperately. And however much I enjoy the beauty of the new city or the friends we've made, I never feel . . ." Evangeline searched for the right word. "Settled." She looked to the side a moment, tracing the small flower pattern of the couch. "We were in the south of France once, traveling through a village with a beautiful cathedral. There was a man there, an artist, painting a canvas. He had dozens of them, all of the cathedral, all in different lights, different angles, different seasons. And I thought, how nice would it be to be able to sit in one place long enough to see it change. To paint the seasons. That's one of the reasons I'm so pleased to be back in England. We're finally here to stay."

"Oh," Max replied, sounding a little deflated. Gail and Will had stopped moving altogether now and had removed to a sideboard where they could listen in, unobtrusively. Will had the oddest, softest look on his face, but said nothing to Gail's questioning tug.

"But, at least you've had the experiences!" Max said, with perhaps more cheer than necessary. "I envy all the places you've been, all the wonderful things you've had the chance to learn."

Evangeline gave a smile, a bit strained to Gail's eye, but chuckled nonetheless. "Yes, of course! I should not begrudge the opportunities I've had for a moment. I loved the cities, the countryside landscapes, the music, oh, the art—the people especially, the new dances we were introduced to, the fashions."

"And the languages," Max finished, but Evangeline shook her head merrily.

"I'm afraid I'm hopeless when it comes to languages. English is my only fluency. My French is atrocious—broken at best, and we spent nearly two years there."

"Really?" Max suddenly got a mischievous look in his eye and cocked a lopsided grin. Gail knew that grin—it was dangerous. "So, if I said, *Vous etes la creature la plus belle dans le monde*, you would have no idea what I'm saying?"

Evangeline shook her head again, soft blonde curls dancing about her face. "What does it mean?"

"You truly don't speak any other languages?" he inquired playfully. "What if I said, *Quiero besar cada pulgada de su carne rosa*?"

Evangeline smiled, giving a small shrug.

Gail nearly choked.

Max had just said he wanted to kiss every inch of her sister's pink flesh, in what was, she grudgingly admitted, perfect Spanish. Before he had spoken in equally perfect French. Gail looked to Will to see if had understood either phrase. She could see he hadn't, but he was intent on Gail's obvious reaction.

"What about," he mused wickedly, *"Eu penso que nós devemos gastar menos tempo que falamos e mais tempo no jardim."*

Max had switched to Portuguese. While Evangeline blushed very prettily at a presumed compliment, Gail was red for an entirely different reason.

"Tu fondres pour moi quard je . . ."

"Stop!" Evangeline giggled.

"Yes. Please stop," Gail said, much more strongly.

Max looked up abruptly.

Gail fumed. She could only feel triumphant at the look of dawning horror on Max's face. How dare he? How *dare*—

"Gail, come tell me what he said." Evangeline turned to her sister, holding out a hand for Gail to come and join them. She was smiling. Max was not.

She should tell her, Gail thought. She should tell Evie exactly what Max had said, and then they both could kick this low, irksome creature out of their lives for good. Her words had worked this magic—and havoc—before. Why not now?

But she stopped herself. Evangeline, kind, nervous Evangeline, was flush with the relief of being able to laugh and smile with her fiancé.

Fiancé. No matter what, they were stuck with him.

And Evangeline had asked her to be kind. To try.

Gail glanced at Max. His eyes were not asking her to be kind. They begged. Pleaded. Laid himself at the mercy of his enemy.

"He said," Gail replied finally, "that you are the most beautiful creature he has ever seen."

"Oh!" Evangeline gasped, and turned to Max, clasping his hands to her bosom. "Lord Fontaine, that's lovely. Thank you."

Max responded with a relieved smile, but under that he turned his attention to Gail, and when their eyes caught, and held, Gail was certain she could read his thoughts.

Sure, he thought. *Just bloody lovely.*

Fourteen

"I'M desperate to know—what *did* you say to Miss Alton?" Will drawled as he sipped a weak punch. Almack's was all aglitter tonight, the Season in full swing. The long main gallery was bedecked in its customary finery: Crystal chandeliers dripped from the ceiling, marble columns flanked the walls in such a stately and military way, one felt certain that to break a rule here would merit a court-martial from all good society. The Patronesses, whose favor was necessary to gain admittance, were seated in a group at one end, holding court. Gentlemen dressed in formal knee breeches, hung about the edges of the throng in masses of black, pointing out the available girls on the marriage mart. Those young ladies were from the best families and had turned out in their finest white, ivory, ecru, eggshell, and if they were very daring, palest blue, evening dresses. Their mamas were distinguished by their darker colors and more calculating looks, as compared to the wide-eyed, wondrous faces of the daughters.

Max and Will stood at the very edge of the floor, watching the group of young, privileged couples finish dancing a country reel. Will was smiling into his punch. Max was not.

"What makes you think I said anything other than what Miss Gail reported?" Max replied, trying for bored tones, but failing abominably, much to Will's snickering pleasure.

"Oh, she hid your true meaning, make no mistake."

Max just grunted.

"Fontaine, you're very stupid, you realize."

"I beg your pardon?" Max intoned.

"They've lived their lives abroad! Chances are one of them picked up a phrase of French here and there!" Will replied.

"And Spanish? And Portuguese?" Max asked fervently. Then, sullen, he grumbled, "How many languages does she speak, anyway?"

Will shrugged. "I don't know. I didn't ask her. I doubt more than those."

"Well, let's hope you're right. Any more languages, and I'll run out of covert ways to whisper naughty things in Miss Evangeline's ear."

"I knew you were saying more than you ought this morning," Will muttered, his eyes on the glass of punch in his hand.

Max simply shot him a look out of the corner of his eye, smiled wryly, and checked his pocket watch.

"They are late," he declared.

"They are not," Will countered. "Look."

Will nodded toward the grand staircase, which led down into the gallery. At the top was a line of people waiting to be announced. Max looked up just in time to hear the announcer's booming voice say:

"Sir Alton, Lady Alton, Miss Evangeline Alton, and Miss Abigail Alton."

* * *

HERE we are, come and get us, Gail thought as she walked carefully down the massive staircase. Evangeline, of course, managed to float down the stairs with her easy grace, but Gail had to work very hard to keep her knees from wobbling and her feet from tripping. She was surprised at her nerves, given the number of balls and outings in society they had attended in the past week, but still, this was Almack's. This was the crucible of the Ton's activity. If Gail proved to be an embarrassment here, she was done for.

As they reached the base of the stairs, the hush that had occurred when their names were announced was quickly covered by a few whispers, a few titters. But mostly, everyone had resumed normal conversation. A vast improvement over the course of the week, Gail noted, and was not above smiling a little at their social acceptance. More than once that day, she overheard Romilla thanking God aloud that Lady Jersey was a fan of Barivian chocolates. Their admittance into Almack's had established their good name.

Their stepmother turned to Gail and Evangeline, quickly extracting the latter from a group of admirers, who had gathered with astonishing speed, and addressed her charges in businesslike tones.

"Girls, if you would follow me—we must pay our compliments to the Patronesses." Romilla patted Sir Geoffrey on the arm, who no doubt took that as his signal to leave everything to his wife and headed off in search of some refreshments and possibly a member of Parliament or two that he could wrangle into conversation. Romilla settled herself in between Gail and Evangeline, and together the three of them cut a swath through the masses of people—smiling and nodding politely as they did so, but intent on their destination.

"Now remember, leave the talking to me, and for the love of heaven, Gail, don't fidget!" Romilla whispered fervently as they approached the sofas where the queens of Society held court. "You'll worry the fingers off your gloves! Remember, you are lovely and proper and . . ."

"Lady Alton, what are you whispering to those girls?" came an imperious voice from a low red velvet couch. "Orders, no doubt, on how to simper properly and not give away a hint of intelligence!"

From the middle of the sofas, next to Lady Jersey, sat Lady Charlbury—resplendent in a gown of black jet, and wearing a mask of stern disapproval. She had a twinkle in her eye as she looked to Gail. Thankfully, she was without her cats for the evening.

"Lady Charlbury!" Gail could not help but exclaim. An elbow from Romilla had her remember her manners, and she curtsied. "It is such a pleasure to see you again."

"Yes," Romilla said, as she and Evangeline dipped into matching curtsies, "I had no idea you attended Almack's. What a pleasant surprise!"

"Oh, my good friend Lady Jersey drags me out of the house on occasion," Lady Jersey and the Altons acknowledged each other, as Lady Charlbury continued. "I daresay I worry about Old Tom dreadfully while I'm out, but someone has to keep an eye on these young things here. The notion of decency has fallen so low these days I hardly know what's what!"

"How is Old Tom?" Gail asked Lady Charlbury, who responded in warm tones. "He's up to his old tricks. Got into my face powder the other day, sneezed for hours. You must come and visit us again."

Gail smiled and moved to join her. However, before Lady Charlbury could wrangle Gail into another long, feline-centric conversation, Lady Jersey interceded.

"I'm sure Lady Charlbury will look forward to your visit, Miss Gail, but for now, you cannot make me believe young ladies prefer the society of two old matrons to the gentlemen here—who are eager to dance a waltz or two, I daresay." Evangeline blushed prettily, and Gail gave up hope of getting out of dancing by allowing Lady Charlbury to monopolize her. "Go and join them, and have a marvelous evening."

And with that the Altons were dismissed. Romilla escorted the girls back to the throng of gentlemen awaiting their return and was herself quickly distracted by some friend or other calling for her attention. Once she left, Evangeline whispered quick words to Gail.

"Why, that was easy!"

Gail blushed. "In truth I thought our interview would have been much worse. The way Romilla went on, I expected the Spanish Inquisition."

"Gail, you were marvelous. As soon as I saw Lady Charlbury, I knew heaven was smiling on us. But the best part of all—we were granted permission to waltz!"

"That is the best news I've heard all night," Max spoke as he came up behind Evangeline and Gail. He and Will made their bows, Max immediately offering his arm to the elder sister.

He looked like black fire tonight, Gail thought, veiling her eyes to hide how much she approved of his appearance. Indeed, Gail had to take a moment and remind herself he was a pompous ass. His dress was sober in comparison to many of the jades and fops there that evening, but his green eyes sparked and crackled in the candlelight. His black coat and breeches matched his dark hair, while the stiff white of his cravat contrasted sharply, like a ghost in shadow. His shoulders filled the cloth without the use of padding, as did his strong thighs. Must be from so much riding, Gail's brain mused on its own tangent.

"Miss Gail . . . Miss Gail?" Will was saying in her ear, and she blushed guiltily at having been caught on such an unseemly train of thought. Max and Evangeline had long since moved off to join the dancers on the floor. A quadrille was playing, and Gail saw that Evangeline and Max moved smoothly together. They were turning more than one pair of heads with their handsomeness.

Will offered Gail his arm. Ashamed to realize her mind was still dwelling where it ought not to be, she forced her attention back to her escort, and smiled.

"Would you care to join the dancers, Miss Gail?" Will asked, leading her to the floor.

"Happily, but Mr. Holt, I should warn you, I rely on you to keep me from total disgrace. When I trod your toes, please do your best not to yelp too loudly," Gail replied with good humor, causing a bark of laughter from Will, as they too joined in the dance.

* * *

"QUITE the pair, the young Viscount Fontaine and Miss Evangeline Alton," Lady Jersey remarked to Lady Charlbury, while keeping a hawk-like gaze on the dancing.

Having closed the doors to any late arrivals, and having been greeted most prettily by everyone in attendance, Lady

Jersey took pleasure in pointing out all the connections forming on the dance floor to her dear friend. The evening was
progressing splendidly, and Lady Jersey had much to gossip
about, mostly regarding people Lady Charlbury didn't know
or didn't care for. Her mind was drifting happily to her Old
Tom, when her ears suddenly perked up at the mention of the
Altons.

"Beg pardon, my dear? Lord Fontaine and Miss Alton?"

"Yes, Eleanor! Didn't you see them dancing earlier?" Lady
Jersey saw that indeed Lady Charlbury had not seen, and so
elaborated. "I'll have you know I *always* thought those rumors were rubbish. He stood up with her two turns in a
row—then of course he had to surrender her to the other
young bucks in waiting, but from where I sit, they move very
well together. Proper, respectful, and with grace."

"Proper, respectful dancing doesn't exactly speak of deep
feeling," Lady Charlbury grunted.

"And indeed it shouldn't. At least not at Almack's," Lady
Jersey answered, secure in her own rightness.

Lady Charlbury, on the other hand, remained skeptical.
She knew Lady Jersey's mind quite well. As devout as she
was to the rules of society, she still liked to see people
matched together, and she had in her mind that Lord Fontaine
and Miss Alton made a likely couple. And indeed, Lady
Charlbury grudgingly thought, they probably did, given their
constant company. It was by all accounts a good match. But
for her part, Lady Charlbury did not see the attraction. Something was missing. Evangeline Alton was fast becoming the
beauty of the Season—to that there was no question. But she
just didn't see a spark evident between them.

As Lady Charlbury scanned the crowd, she noticed Lord
Ommersley, whom she had never much cared for, barreling
his way across the room toward Miss Gail Alton.

"Tell me, Sarah dear," Lady Charlbury ventured to her
friend, who had spun off on a tangent about Barivian royalty,
or some such boring thing, "what do you think of the younger
Miss Alton?"

Lady Jersey took a moment to remember the face. When
it struck her, she said, "Tall, quiet. Pretty, though nothing

compared to her sister, which is unfortunate for her, I suppose. But she seems nice enough in spite of it. Sometimes younger sisters can be so hateful to the elder."

"You don't think she has a sense of wit? Or perhaps superior intelligence to recommend her?" Lady Charlbury ventured.

"La! Eleanor, you have taken to that girl simply because she asked after your cat!" Lady Jersey laughed. "No, my dear, I have seen no demonstrations of wit, although, in fairness, I have only had them call once, and the Misses Alton were barely given a chance to speak. She struck me then as she does now—a little awkward and overshadowed by her lovely sister."

"I will inform you now, my dear," Lady Charlbury said, "that my opinion differs from yours greatly."

"Well, it's lucky our opinions always differ," Lady Jersey said, smiling coyly. "Else I should be wounded by your dissension."

* * *

NO one would suspect Gail of being championed as a great wit of engaging personality by Lady Charlbury. She was, at that moment, where she often found herself: alone against the wall. Not that she minded! Of course not—Mr. Holt had been so obliging, dancing with her, fetching her tea, and simply being a completely amiable gentleman that she was surprised to find so many hours had passed. Of course, she couldn't dance solely with Mr. Holt, so after the first, she braved the dance floor with a surprising number of gentlemen. Her steps had been very careful and deliberate, and so she managed to dance without causing a major catastrophe.

Never had she so many partners, and nearly all the gentlemen enjoyed her company, as she did theirs. Although Mr. Leight would not be blamed if he never asked her to dance again. His toes might not survive it. Oh, she was actually having a good time! But the heat of the room and her extremely careful dancing were so wearying, that she begged Evangeline to take her next dance with Mr. Holt so she could sit and breathe for a moment. They obliged her, and Gail was left to her thoughts, as she had long desired to be.

She wanted to remember this moment. To remember the size of the hall, the beautiful gowns and dashing gentlemen, the men who had asked for her next, and the terrible, terrible refreshments. She wanted to be able to recall it all when she wrote in her little diary, and she needed to sit a moment and sketch it out. What a joy to be able to write of marginal social triumphs instead of complete disasters.

As she mused there, her eyes glazed over with thought, a dark shadow crawled its way up her face. The shadow's owner loomed above her, and addressed his quarry in a squeaky, breaking voice.

"Good evening, Miss Gail," young Lord Ommersley said, making a mockery of a bow toward her.

Gail jumped in her seat and looked up at her one-time accoster. She hadn't seen Ommersley since that dreadful night, for, once he'd come to, he skulked away from the party and back to his own house across the square. He hadn't come to call since, much to Gail's relief, and she had entertained the hope he would avoid her altogether in the future.

But now his skinny height loomed above her.

He looked appalling. She hadn't noticed his tendency for foppish dress before. Oh, his coat and breeches were appropriately black, but he wore more lace at his cuffs and throat than she did on her entire person. The particular shade of green he chose for his waistcoat matched his eye—the left one that is. The powder he had used liberally was ill applied, and the faded bruise that covered half his face was clearly visible. However, perhaps he thought his battle scars were to be worn with pride, or perhaps he thought himself the better of everyone else in the room, for his thin chest was puffed out to its fullest and his nose was high in the air.

The result was not unlike a sickly blade of grass trying to emulate a powerful, menacing oak.

Gail was so shocked by his appearance that she forgot her painstakingly applied tact.

"What the devil are you doing here?" she blurted, and then covered her mouth. It was one thing to be rude, it was quite another to swear in polite society. Fortunately, no one seemed to have taken notice of her.

Lord Ommersley grimaced at her unflattering greeting, then sneered. And then grimaced again. Making facial expressions must have still been a bit painful.

"Miss Gail, so *pleasant* to see you again," he smarmed. "Indeed, I've been looking forward to renewing our acquaintance."

"Well, I wasn't," Gail said. Normally, she would have made an effort to hold her tongue, especially fearing the consequences. But knowing how ungentlemanly Ommersley was, Gail could not be ladylike. "I can't say I thought of you much at all, and when I did, it was to wish you consigned to Australia."

"Tut-tut, Miss Gail—is that any way to speak to your dance partner?" He held out his hand for her to take.

She looked from his revoltingly offered hand to his face and saw the cold meanness that lived there. It scared her.

She pressed herself as far back against the wall as her chair would allow, but he stepped forward. He pursued, he leered, he positively hovered in her space. What could she do? She fought to keep her mind working as panic began to creep in.

"I'll not dance with you," Gail said, her fear showing in her voice. Ommersely gave a cold, hungry smile.

"But I have your stepmother's express permission. She's watching us even now."

Gail looked over his shoulder and found Romilla across the way. Gail pleaded with her eyes, but Romilla only smiled, gave a little wave, and turned her attention back to a friend.

"I'm not dancing with you," Gail bit out. "Leave me be."

"No! We have things to discuss, you and I." And with that, he reached forward and grabbed her arm, painfully tight.

Gail was about to disgrace herself and scream, when Ommersley's arm was removed.

"I'd listen to the lady, if I were you," Max drawled, his hand discreetly crushing Ommersley's fingers. He whimpered quietly while Max held his grip and voice steady. "Besides, she's to dance with me next."

Ommersley and Max straightened—nobody nearby seemed to notice any fuss. The best threats were always given in whispers, Gail noted. Max let go of Ommersley's hand, causing that young man to stumble back. A few heads turned at his ungraceful steps, so Ommersley quickly covered and made a bow to Max.

"Well, Fontaine. I see you have moved quicker than I," he said, as eyes turned back to their own conversations. "I shall have to content myself with the next dance," he said darkly.

"I'm afraid that one is spoken for, too," Max said. "And the one after, and the one after." He stepped forward, whispering menacingly into the gawkish fool's ear. "Anytime you get it in your head to ask her to dance, she is spoken for."

With that Ommersley darkened, his eyes growing hard and bright. But he again made a bow and turned on his heel and walked away.

Gail stood on shaky legs, her heart beating furiously. Max stared after Ommersley's retreating form, as if to make certain he had truly abandoned his pursuit. When Ommersley had faded from sight, Max's chest caved in a great exhale of pent-up breath. As if he hadn't breathed since he crossed the room. To save her. Again.

She reached out gently and touched his arm.

His head jerked around.

They stared.

She didn't know what to say to him. How could she thank him for another rescue? Her knees were still wobbly, and she couldn't remember ever being that frightened before—but she couldn't very well let Max Fontaine know that. She should say something smart and caustic. Unfortunately, all her brain could think was *thank God for you*.

He opened his mouth to speak, but stalled, his eyes searching her face. Would he reprimand her? Gail worried. Did he blame her . . . worse yet, what if he made fun of her? She would surely die.

Finally, after a time-frozen moment in each other's eyes, Max cleared his throat and asked, "Shall we dance?"

* * *

TAKING her hand in his, they took to the floor, joining the other couples as they waltzed. Max spied Evangeline in Will's arms, talking animatedly, Will smiling and laughing in return. Holt had always been the one with the gift of conversation,

Max noted, and promptly forgot about his betrothed. All his
energy was focused on the uncommonly pale, mute woman in
his arms. He fought the uninvited impulse to smooth her hair,
her cheek, and instead positioned them properly on the floor.
Max's left hand went to Gail's surprisingly small waist, her
hand perched tentatively in his right—but she put no weight
on that hand, almost as if she were afraid to touch him. Stiffly
they began to move.

She tripped once; he held her up. She trod on his toes; he
didn't say a word. After a minute of stony silence, Max's
worry was turning to annoyance. Her color had evened out,
and she was no longer the shaken, fragile creature afraid of
her own shadow. In fact, that side of Gail had been so fleeting,
Max began to wonder if he had imagined it. But she still
wouldn't meet his eyes. She was concentrating too intensely
on her feet, on dancing. When she misstepped onto his toes
for the fourth time, Max couldn't hold his tongue any longer.

"Are you trying to break my feet?"

That brought her eyes up from the floor to his face, flashing with challenge. The sight made Max smile with relief.

"I beg your pardon, good sir," she said with an edge of
sarcasm, "but one of us has to take the lead—and you seem to
be mincing more than moving."

"You want me to lead?" Max rose to the challenge. "Fine.
Try following. A few instructions: First, keep your eyes up, on
my face—don't look down at my feet. My feet are not going
to tell you where we move next."

She saw his dare and, smiling to herself a little, did as he
instructed, unnerving him with her direct and powerful gaze.
But he didn't falter. Instead, he continued.

"Now, put a little more strength into our clasped hands. I
need you to be able to feel me. You won't push me over, no
matter how much you want to." Once she had obeyed, he
pulled her a bit closer and lowered his voice into her ear.
"Now, do you feel my hand on your waist? My other hand
holding yours? I am going to tell you how to follow me, simply by touch."

"I think—" Gail started, only to be cut off.

"That's the problem. You can't dance while thinking about

dancing." His mouth was a scant inch from her delicate ear. "The act is about feeling, not thought."

And with that, he put the veriest bit of pressure on her side and spun her into a turn, which she executed with astonishingly perfect grace. Gail was so wide-eyed with surprise, she burst into a gleeful grin before she could suppress it. Her joy hit Max with such an explosion of warmth, it was like a dozen nails driven into his chest. He couldn't stop himself from smiling right back.

And then Gail tripped again.

She turned bright red and glowered at him. "You shouldn't smile at a lady like that," she remarked, after regaining the rhythm.

"Like what?"

"Like you want to eat her."

Now was Max's turn to trip, and Gail's turn to catch him.

After those initial stumbles, they spun around the floor, perfectly in tune with each other and the music. Max guided her expertly, surprised and pleased they moved together so well.

She challenged him to show her how to dance, and the fact that she thrived under his instruction was thrilling. And she was loving every moment. No matter how stern she tried to remain, she couldn't hide the light of joy on her face. And Max couldn't help but comment on it.

"If I didn't know better, I would say you were enjoying yourself."

That earned him a wry look, but she maintained dignity and would not be baited.

"Apparently you can be taught," he murmured in her ear.

She blithely stepped hard upon his toes and smiled serenely when he grimaced.

"I'm sorry, did you say something? I was too busy feeling and not thinking to pay attention to your chatter," she remarked, mischievousness alight in her face.

"You have the most amazingly selective hearing. Whatever I wish you to hear, you do not."

"And whatever you don't want me to hear, I manage to be listening," Gail finished for him, as he took them into another turn, Gail following easily.

Max frowned, and to his abject embarrassment, was unable to meet Gail's intensely direct gaze.

"You, ah, are referring to this morning, I gather," he said after settling his eyes on an innocuous potted tree.

"Your French accent was passable, but the Portuguese was atrocious."

"That is possibly because I have at least been to France, whereas I have not had the opportunity to visit Portugal."

"On your Grand Tour, I expect, after university?" Her eyes challenged him yet again. "I had wondered where you learned such language."

That brought his head back around quick enough. He lowered his voice and leaned in, his breath brushing her cheek. "The content of what I said was not intended for your ears." His hand had begun to move along the small of her back—his thumb caressing the silk ever so slightly, movement to match his low, seductive tones. "Come now, you must believe that had I known you could understand me, I should never have said those things. It was a stressful morning, and I was merely . . . amusing myself."

"Yes, gentlemen rarely think beyond their own amusement," Gail replied stonily. But then, with false brightness, "Do you know, I had intended to blast you for your appalling sense of decorum for even thinking, never mind saying, such things. Then it occurred to me just how utterly mundane your silly phrases were, it seemed almost pitiful to berate you for them."

Max heard some outraged gasping sounds—he was fairly certain they were coming from him.

"*Mundane?*" he repeated, shocked to his core.

"Uninspired, to say the least. Unimaginative. Uninteresting," Gail decided.

"For something so uninteresting, it certainly caught your attention," he shot back, but Gail waved it aside.

"Honestly, you are so British. 'I want to take off all your clothes' is the best you could come up with? The French are far more poetic—and more depraved, if that was your intention. And do you know how many words the Greeks have for the curve of a woman's flesh? I heard far more creativity dockside in half a dozen cities. You are not unintelligent, Max. I expected better."

His thumb stopped moving languidly on her back, as his hand fisted in the silk of her dress. A hundred thoughts flashed through his brain—not the least of which was images of a woman's flesh in Greece, depraved poetry in France, and the removal of clothing in Britain. So this is what the mind feels like when it's reeling, Max wondered dazedly. What disturbed him more was that the flesh he kept inter-continentally flashing to belonged to someone very close at hand.

"Where did you . . . how did you . . . ?"

Gail released a husky little laugh that shot straight down to Max's lower anatomy. "I listened. I've walked the lanes and avenues of every city I've ever been to. That's how I learn the languages. People say a number of interesting things when they think you can't understand them."

A lesson Max could take to heart after this morning.

"A young lady should not be exposed to the vulgar language of the general populace," Max said stiffly, trying to turn the conversation to something more comfortable, namely, Gail's faults.

"Actually, the most interesting phrases came from the 'gentlemen,'" she replied archly.

Max regarded this eighteen-year-old woman, who by all rules of decent society should never have been let out of the country—let alone admitted into that plane of thought where baser notions existed—yet she espoused her opinions with such a wide-eyed innocence, he had half a mind to tell her she knew not of what she spoke, and then, cravenly, inform her.

Instead, he said impulsively, "You must have loved it."

Her face warmed. "I did. I do. I miss it. I miss seeing new things, new places. Not everywhere thinks like England, you know."

"What do you mean?"

She shrugged. "I can't help but think we are far too impressed with ourselves and therefore think too lowly of everyone else."

Max smiled. "But then again," he debated, "most societies think their own is superior to all others."

"True," Gail conceded. "But England takes an almost childlike glee in having a world under its thumb. Why do we consider ourselves to own India? Or Australia? Other people were there first, some of them living in societies much further advanced than ours, but we won't let ourselves see beyond the differences. Take the Greeks for example, we have raped them of their very history, when young men like you go on grand tours and come back with antiquities, and . . ." She stopped when she saw Max's bemusement.

Her cheeks had taken on the most delightful hue of pink, her eyes the color of fire, and Max couldn't tear his attention away from the way her whole person warmed and moved when she was impassioned. His imagination highlighted other ways she could become impassioned before he could stop it.

"I'm sorry," she said, letting go the stream of fire she was building up in a sigh. "I tend to become heated about this subject."

Max was wholly entranced. "Young ladies aren't supposed to talk like you."

"You have just stumbled onto my greatest failure. I have too often spoken exactly as I thought, not as I should. So, it seems easier to not say anything."

"You have been truthful to the point of bluntness tonight, Brat," Max countered in a whispered growl, but Gail shook her head.

"I have long since given up any care what you think of me. It frees me to be honest." She tried to smile ironically, but the sadness in her voice struck at his heart. On the one hand, he was strangely pleased to have no cause for pretense with Gail. It was certainly freeing, and it made him feel almost special. But, he also realized the very intelligence that defined her was a trial to her. She wasn't allowed to speak her thoughts—because it wasn't what proper young ladies did. Or rather, she didn't have the thoughts of a proper young lady.

He pulled her an inch closer. If the matrons saw, they would have his head. But when he looked into her eyes, he saw a naked vulnerability he would have never guessed was there—not in this hard-shelled, wisecracking, insult-lobbing hellion. She looked like a woman who needed holding, and he wanted to be the one to hold her, just for a moment.

But as soon as he saw it, that transient vulnerability was gone, replaced by an up-quirked eyebrow.

"The music stopped," she said, breaking into his mind.

Indeed it had. The pairs of dancers around him had stopped moving and broken apart. Polite applause for the musicians sounded through the hall, as the young ladies and gentlemen moved about, changing partners, organizing themselves for the next dance.

Max slowly released his hand from Gail's waist and escorted her off the floor. They walked silently toward the edge of the room, where Will was already standing and chatting with Evangeline.

"You didn't tell your sister what I said," Max whispered.

"Hmm?"

"Thank you . . . for not revealing how mundane I am."

Her lips twitched up, and she blushed. "It's simply that I didn't—"

"One last question, Miss Gail," Max interrupted, before she could say anything further. "You have a knack for languages," he began, and she smiled impishly.

"Yes, I have, as you say, 'a knack.'"

"I have a talent myself. I took a First at Oxford in French, Spanish, and German," he said, not without some pride.

"How lovely. Is there a question coming, or shall I just fawn over your brilliance?"

"Feel free to fawn anytime," he replied, winning an approving smile, "but I meant to ask you how many languages you speak."

"A goodly number. How many do you speak?"

"Fluently? Or enough to get by?"

"Enough to get by."

He counted on his hands. "Six, including Latin. How many is a goodly number?"

She sighed the sigh of the long suffering. "Fluently, or enough to get by?"

"Enough to get by."

"Counting Latin?"

"Counting Latin."

"Because you realize it is a dead language; there is no present culture that speaks it as its main form of communication."

"I said, counting Latin!" But he kept his voice low, so only Gail could hear his ire.

"Fourteen," she replied immediately.

Max gaped. They had reached their friends' sides, but all his attention was focused on Gail. Will and Evangeline watched the exchange with wide-eyed interest.

"Name them," he challenged.

She sighed. "English, French, Spanish, German, Dutch, Swedish, Russian, Latin, Pig Latin, Portuguese, Arabic, Turkish, Hebrew, and Greek," she quickly supplied.

"Miss Gail, you speak all those languages?" Will interjected. She and Evangeline nodded in response.

Max was dumbstruck. Fourteen? But . . .

"Pig Latin? That's not a language," Max said curtly.

"Yes, it is."

"No, it's not—not a real one."

"But I require it in my list," Gail stubbornly defended.

"You have thirteen others!" Max burst out.

"But, Lord Fontaine," Evangeline stepped in, placing her hand on his arm soothingly, "thirteen is an unlucky number."

"Yes," agreed her sister, "and since you included Latin, I had to include Latin, and—"

"I understand!" Will said triumphantly. "You needed to count Pig Latin to make the number something other than thirteen."

"Precisely."

"May I ask, what did you do when you were thirteen years old?" Max said sarcastically. "Pretend to be fourteen?"

Gail looked to her toes. "Of course not," she mumbled. "But I did trip a great deal."

Max had to smile—but only a little. She was exasperating. But always surprising. He shook his head in mock defeat.

"You win, Miss Gail. I am utterly undone by your obviously superior mind." But Gail's face went cold, as pained as if he had struck her.

"I never viewed it as a competition, sir."

"Yes, hardly a competition at all, eh, Fontaine?" Will said jovially, slapping his friend on the back, trying to alleviate the sudden black mood. Max cracked a strained smile.

"You did not list Italian, Miss Gail," Max said finally.

"No, we never went to Italy," Gail replied, blinking.

"Well, thank God for that." He bowed and began to lead Evangeline to the punch bowl.

"Oh, Lord Fontaine!" Gail called after him, and as he turned, his eyes captured hers. And held them for an eternity.

"Thank you for the dance."

Fifteen

ALTHOUGH the world of Britain's social elite revolved around the Season, which ran from just after Easter to the end of Parliament's session on the twelfth of August, what greased society's wheels was gossip. So, as it would happen, as it should happen, and as it was always known to happen, the events of the previous evening were discussed over the breakfast table in every household of note. (And even some households of no note—but since they are insignificant in the scheme of this story, their reactions do not signify.)

So naturally, in the course of eggs, coffee, steak, kidney, and jam, the Pickerings mentioned the lovely decor of the great hall of Almack's, Lady Hurstwood's daughter gushed over her two dances with Captain Sterling, and Lord Draye said he was most impressed with this year's crop of marriageables. Young Lord Ommersley didn't say much that morning; he was nursing his head and his pride. However, polite conversation quickly turned more sloe-eyed and juicy, and everyone took care to mention Lord Fontaine. He danced a great deal with Miss Evangeline Alton, don't you agree? Why yes, Mother, I did see that, he stood up with her twice! And fetched her punch at every turn. What does it mean? Well, my dearest husband, I have no notion, only that Lord Fontaine has been continually in the Altons' drawing room since the Alton girls came out. But what about the rumors? Rumors? Bah, Miss Sally, I'll be tellin' ya whot—that comes to nuthin'—no proof—and the chit's parent's let 'im in tha house meantimes? Them rumors 're pure rubbish. Just some maid tellin' stories, dozy cow.

While this course of gossip was by far and away the standard for the day, a select few had noted something else in Lord Fontaine's behavior the previous evening.

Lady Charlbury had been one of the first to notice, because she had eyes on her person of interest all evening. It was odd, as someone who tried to avoid liking young people whenever possible, she found herself liking Miss Gail Alton. She watched as that odious Lord Ommersely backed Miss Gail into a corner (really, she must speak with Lady Jersey about his Almack's admission) and the subsequent rescue by Lord Fontaine. She watched as they danced—stumbling at first and then with a flair and intensity that sent a ripple of warm feeling through Lady Charlbury.

And Lady Charlbury was not a woman given to warm ripples.

They spoke animatedly, with arch looks and challenging postures. She couldn't hear what they were saying, of course, but she doubted the topics were restricted to the spring weather and the number of couples. They didn't move delicately, instead they made the dance a fluid battle, well worth watching. Lady Charlbury leaned to whisper something to this effect in Lady Jersey's ear, but thought better of it. This observation she would keep to herself and see how it developed.

The next person to note Lord Fontaine's remarkable waltzing technique had just recently walked in from the refreshments room, not being one for dancing.

Baron Rentworth, faithful informant to the Earl of Longsbowe, had stepped away from the tables of mutton and cheese for the opportunity to stretch his legs, and wandered into the crowded ballroom. He was surprised when he spotted the Earl's only son on the dance floor, for he had not known the young man would be there. The viscount was dancing quite remarkably well, Rentworth reflected, with a tall brunette young lady. Always aware of his duty to the Earl, Rentworth leaned over to the nearest person, a young man engaged in raucous conversation with his companions, and not at all inclined to assist a portly old man in stays and pink waistcoat. So when Rentworth asked who was partnered with Lord Fontaine, the young buck glanced at the floor, said the name "Alton," and returned to his jokes and laughter.

So this must be the upstart young lady the Earl was so disapproving of! The one Lord Fontaine was intent upon marrying. She seemed pretty enough, he supposed, but nothing uncommon. However, Lord Fontaine seemed utterly engaged by her conversation. Perhaps it wasn't so bad a match as all that, if he was keen on the girl. Rentworth hoped to get a better look at the future countess when the dance ended, but when it did, Fontaine led Miss Alton in the opposite direction, toward his friend Mr. Holt and another young lady. He tried to cross the room, but by then it was impossible, as another dance was starting in the too crowded space. He shrugged, committed the girl's features to memory, and retired again to the dining room.

The third person to take a wide-eyed notice of Gail and Lord Fontaine's fiery, mesmerizing waltz was someone who had the unfortunate tendency to think of Gail second, and therefore immediately taking notice of her seemed odd.

Romilla had been flirting harmlessly with an old acquaintance, keeping her sharp eyes on Evangeline and her sharp ears open to catch even the barest hint of malicious gossip about her girls. Although her intention had been to be the ever-vigilant chaperone, she could not help but feel the excitement of it all. Almack's! She hadn't had the opportunity to dance in these halls during her own season, oh so many years ago. Her marriage had been so quick, and her mother so disapproving . . . Then, her first husband had whisked her away to Europe mere hours after their wedding.

He had been an undersecretary to the ambassador of Spain—respectable, but certainly not particularly highborn (then again, neither was she). But together, they were working to become influential, to shape the world—he, having the ear of the ambassador, and she being his perfect hostess. Who cared if her letters home were always returned unopened? She was making great friends abroad, and one day, her husband would have his own appointment, then they would triumphantly return to England, he'd run for Parliament, and . . .

But then came the fever—and suddenly she was alone.

Now here she was, finally in the grand hall, over a decade past. She had buried a husband in Spain, lived through years on her own, and survived. But that part of her life was past, and here were the faces she'd missed and the ones she'd not had the chance to know. The English fashions and dances, the music—all of it called to her blood, saying, "Welcome home." It affected her so, there were a few times when she had to blink back tears.

So naturally, she missed it when Lord Fontaine took Gail to the dance floor.

Only the beginning, at least. While Romilla was laughing with a group of new friends, Mrs. Pickering tapped her on the arm with her fan and drew her attention to the dance floor, where her own twin daughters were dancing with Lord Whatshisname and Mr. Something or Other. Romilla had stopped listening the moment she saw Gail dancing with Lord Fontaine. In theory, there was nothing improper about it. Lord Fontaine and Gail were well acquainted, having been in each other's daily presence for a week now. Gail had received permission to waltz. Lord Fontaine was, in fact, to be her brother-in-law.

But the way Fontaine looked at Gail, the way he leaned in to whisper in her ear—the flash in his eyes when she said something—Romilla couldn't put her finger on it, but it made her very nervous.

Was he holding her a bit too close for propriety? Was his grip at her waist just a hair too tight? Was she . . . good Lord, was she *smiling* at him? Romilla glanced to her companions, but they didn't seem to notice anything amiss. Their eyes fell rarely on Gail, as they were looking out for their own interests. When the dance ended, Romilla began to breathe easier, but as Lord Fontaine escorted Gail to the side, there was still a palatable tension between them—was it only she who could see it?

Romilla prayed she was the only one to see it.

As Gail was deposited with Mr. Holt, and Evangeline was once again on Lord Fontaine's arm, Romilla returned her attention to her companions and slipped easily into their conversation. Luckily such inane chatter didn't require much of her mind. That was consumed by a much more volatile topic.

* * *

THE next morning, Romilla had the girls up at their usual hour, regardless of the fact that they hadn't gotten home until well past two. She was waiting for them as they came down the steps, holding hands and chatting with the speed and incoherence of youth. It was not yet eight o'clock, and Gail was dressed for her morning ride in the dark green habit, holding that wretched swatch of leather she called a hat. Both curtsied as they greeted Romilla.

"Abigail, what is that in your hand?" Romilla asked, ice freezing her voice.

Gail blinked. "'Tis my hat, ma'am," she replied.

"And you actually intend to wear it?" Romilla mixed incredulity and sarcasm, and watched as Gail shrunk into herself.

"I . . . I only wear it riding, ma'am, in the mornings." Gail had brought it to her chest, clutching it like a mother protecting her child.

"You have a hat that matches that habit, do you not? I know so, I purchased it for you. If you will not wear the appropriate hat, you will not go riding, whether it be in the early morning or at high riding time."

Evangeline's jaw dropped, and she held all the tighter to her sister's hand. Romilla feared she had gone too far, and that Gail might cry. But only for a moment. The child then straightened her spine and looked down her nose at Romilla (easily done, considering their height difference, but haughtiness was not a posture Gail often tried with her stepmother).

"Fine," was the reply, as she let go of her sister's hand. "I'll go find the *appropriate* hat."

Gail turned from her stepmother with the bone-deep strength of a queen and did not slump or look behind her as she climbed the stairs. When she was out of sight, Evangeline turned to Romilla, her eyes fiery, her lips so tight they were white.

"That was uncalled for," she said quietly.

Romilla turned innocent eyes on her eldest stepdaughter. "I know your sister has some silly sentimentality for that hat, and it does you credit to defend her feelings, but it *is* inappropriate. Evangeline, dearest, you know it is. She needs to learn how to dress and act correctly."

Evangeline shook her head. "That was not a lesson in propriety." She pointed to the empty spot where Gail had stood. "That was a lesson in control. And it was little, and mean." Evangeline turned up the steps. "I have some letters to write," she said over her shoulder. "I'll take my breakfast upstairs."

Romilla stood at the base of the stairs alone for a full minute. She was shaking, but her fury was directed at herself. Why had she said that? Why had she lashed out in such a horrible way? She had intended to take the girls into the breakfast room, find some way of speaking to Gail alone, and ask her calmly about the dance last night with Lord Fontaine. But the minute she had seen that hat . . . her mind went black, all her good intentions had gone out the window. She could only think that this girl continued to defy what was right, what was proper. So she said something mean and made Gail, and herself, feel small and wrong. Romilla laid her head in her hands. This was not the way she had intended to start the morning.

* * *

EVANGELINE knocked quietly on Gail's door. When no one answered, she silently turned the handle and stepped inside. It was empty. On the bed sat the brown hat that Gail had worn riding ever since the first time she had sat on a horse. Evangeline smiled a little at its ugliness. Next to it sat a newly empty hatbox, wrinkled tissue paper lying around it.

She would go riding after all, meanness be damned.

"Well done, Gail," Evangeline whispered, daring the walls to hear it.

* * *

TENSION can build in a household on incidents such as these, or it can dissipate. In Number Seven, it was simply put on hold. There was too much to do, Romilla surmised, than to worry over hurt feelings. The dinner for the Barivian ambassador was to be the next day, and the entire house was busy in intense preparation. It was a whirlwind of activity when Gail returned from her ride, muddy and flushed. She and Evangeline were immediately taken to the modiste's for a final fitting of their latest slate of gowns, as well as to acquire gloves, hats, underthings, and all the necessities to match. When Lord Fontaine and Mr. Holt called, for the first time in their acquaintance with the Altons, they were not admitted, for the ladies were not at home. In fact, they were told most seriously that the Alton ladies were scheduled for every minute of this day and, right up until the dinner party.

Max left his card and the flowers he had brought with Morrison and headed down the steps, almost at a loss as to how to spend this newfound time—so used was he to spending his mornings with the ladies.

Holt, with a surprise morning free, tried his best to shrug off disappointment, decided to head to the docks to check on some newly acquired ships.

"I still haven't any idea why Father would purchase such a light flier, no less three of them," Will said, frowning, "and now I'm to find some use for 'em. They've got good-sized strongholds, maybe they'd do well on moderate journeys to the Spanish coast."

He invited Max along to investigate the new purchases, knowing how his friend was enamored of the ships, but Max decided against it. He was behind in his own work. There were several documents he had been contracted to translate from German and Italian into English, and a novel waiting to be turned from English into French. Max spent the morning, night, and following day lost in his work, for he considered nothing more graceful than the study of words.

When he at last emerged from his hollow, he posted his finished work to the appropriate officials and publishers, was shaved and cravated, and turned from a scruffy intellect into a gentleman of breeding, arriving at the Alton's doorstep right on time.

Romilla was in place to greet him immediately.

"Lord Fontaine, welcome." She was striking in a deep plum gown with black jet beadwork. The feathers pluming out of her coiffure matched the gown exactly, the diamonds at her throat glittered discreetly. She was the epitome of a politician's wife, the first line of defense. Poised and confident, no one would guess if her heart was beating twice as fast as normal.

She welcomed him into the drawing room, where he had spent many a morning recently, but now it was cast in candlelight and peopled by a dozen formally dressed ladies and gentlemen. He was introduced to Mr. Fortings, who sat in the House of Commons, a "friend of the family," Lady Alton had said. As representative of a very powerful borough, he held several proxies and could sway just about any vote. Lady Jersey took Max's arm, as Romilla turned to greet newly arrived guests, and introduced him to the Duke of Wellington, who was somehow shorter than Max had always imagined him to be. Not nearly as short as Napoleon, mind, but the legend, it seemed, had a way of dwarfing the reality.

Lord Bambridge was an acquaintance of his father, the Earl; Lord Draye and Lord Pomfrey seemed to be the best of friends, as did their wives. A formidable alliance in the House of Lords—and they seemed to gaze with rapture upon Sir Geoffrey, who was leading them in conversation.

"Ah! Lord Fontaine!" Sir Geoffrey called out, beckoning Max over. They made bows and introductions. "I'm pleased you could attend."

"Indeed, sir," Max replied. "I doubt I could ever resist an invitation to your home."

"Of course. You are always game for a social call, aren't you?" Sir Geoffrey said, a silver glint in his eye.

Max sucked in his cheeks, determined not to rise to the bait. Sir Geoffrey's comment had the tone of disapproval, as if Max did nothing in life but attend parties. The others in their small circle were regarding him closely, eager to see what would occur next. But before he could say anything, gracious or otherwise, two arrivals happened in quick succession. First Evangeline and Gail Alton walked into the drawing room, capturing Max's attention. Evangeline looked her usual resplendent self in ivory silk. Gail, however, looked entrancing in a burnt gold, he thought, somewhat against his will. The glow of candlelight made her seem touched by Midas, his eyes followed her form automatically. And when she caught his gaze, the flush that spread up her cheeks made her glow all the more.

But then, on the heels of the girls, Romilla ushered in Count Roffstaam, ambassador from Barivia, the honored guest of the party, and his wife. Sir Geoffrey made his excuses to the group around him and headed over with warm greetings for the Count. Max left to seek the side of Evangeline Alton, but kept his eyes on the newest arrival. So this was the man who could open trade relations with England for his country. Again, Max had thought he would be taller.

The Count was a short man, but with a back so rigid, so very Prussian, he made full use of his whole five feet one inches. His dress was sober and impeccable, his nose high in the air, his sparse hair swept back in a surprising pink ribbon that matched his waistcoat. Indeed, it also matched his wife's dress. Pink, it seemed, was the official color of Barivia. The Countess of Roffstaam stood beside him with her nose just as high in the air. She was rather extravagantly dressed and making the same good use of her bony frame and full six feet. If they weren't so very authoritarian, Max thought, they would be funny.

No sooner had the honored guests murmured greetings than the bell rang for dinner. Sir Geoffrey took Romilla's arm, followed by the Count and Countess, the Duke of Wellington, and all the other assembled guests. Max gave his arm to Evangeline, but Gail was left unescorted. Max looked about the room for a second before realizing his friend Holt was not there, as he had not been invited. Was there no one to match the second sister? What kind of hostess would allow for a dinner party with an uneven number of males and females?

Max opened his mouth to offer his other arm to Gail, just out of politeness, of course, when suddenly, Mr. Fortings came from behind and took her arm. She curtsied and smiled at this old man, while Max watched. She looked wry. She looked in good humor. She blushed and nodded, as Fortings spoke something in her ear.

"Lord Fontaine?" A gentle voice at his side broke into Max's thoughts. He brought his head around and blinked his way back to Evangeline's enquiring face.

"Should we not follow the other guests?"

"Yes," he answered. "Yes, of course." He did not turn around to look at Gail one last time. Instead, he looked down into Evangeline's face, saw its gentle concern, and with a breath, smiled.

* * *

DINNER parties were, in Gail's experience, mundane affairs. The most anyone had to say was a politeness about the food or the decor, or the pleasurable activities in which they spent their days. Conversation was held with those to the left or right of you, never above a murmur. Mostly, Gail would converse minimally but politely with the matron on her left and comment on the forecasted weather for the shooting season to the gentleman on the right. If that gentleman were red-faced and portly, and the matron wore a jeweled turban and showed far too much cleavage, Gail would consider her night complete.

But tonight, the conversation was loud, intelligent, stubborn, and important.

"Why should we repeal the Corn Laws?" Lord Draye said boisterously. (He sported that red face and belly that lent itself to the boisterous.) "We must keep the price of corn stabilized in England. The introduction of the sliding scale last year is going to be an immense help."

"Ah, yes, Corn is King," said Mr. Fortings from Gail's left, quoting a satirical article in the *Times*. "Too bad it leaves the man who works the factory starving and the man who owns the land wealthy."

"Mr. Fortings, you own land. Indeed, I've been to your estate." This from Lord Pomfrey. "Are you saying you have more money to give the government?"

"Landowners are taxed, too, and quite well," piped in Lord Draye.

"I am well aware," defended Mr. Fortings, "but by keeping the price of corn artificially high, we are only doing damage to the economy and the families of factory workers."

"Bah! This is still an agricultural country! Parliament is not done over with industry folk quite yet!" Lord Draye said, banging his fist on the table.

"That Parliament does not represent them, doesn't mean they don't exist . . ." and such the argument would chance to go for hours.

At the other end of the table, Prime Minister Lord Wellington was amusing the countess with a wartime tale. "Oh yes, but when the troops had reformed the line at the field, we found the enemy had fallen back . . ." It was a tale oft told, but not by the general himself. Sir Geoffrey chuckled along with the countess, no doubt remembering his own part in the Napoleonic trials.

Gail didn't know which way to turn her head. Max was directly across from her, listening to Mr. Fortings debate with the House of Lords. Evangeline sat on his right and was making some comment about the beef course and how unfortunate it was Mr. Holt could not attend. (The girls had been quite disappointed when Romilla informed them Mr. Holt was not invited. He was in *trade*, after all.) Gail's attention eventually drifted to the Count, who was speaking in broken English to Romilla.

"Yes, my country is ze most beautiful. Farm and such pretty mountain, and ze field and ze coast. I cannot imagine my country ever being anything but . . . ah . . . ze word . . . nice. *Friedlich*."

The gentlemen involved in political debate had (quite

loudly) moved on from the Corn Laws to the relatively young government in America, and were not listening to the count's description of Barivia's pastoral beauty. The other end of the table had not broken their conversation either. Gail looked up and met Max's eyes. A small inclination of his head in the direction of the Count told her that Max had been listening, too. Indeed, besides Romilla, they seemed to be the only people attending to the Barivian emissary's words. Gail lifted an eyebrow as the count described his family farm, the beautiful castle nestled next to the hills, and the disappointment of only having second-rate chocolates. Gail noted Max's mouth quirked up at the sides, and Gail had to admit, hers did, too.

And then Mr. Fortings leaned over and asked a question about the empirical rights of Britain abroad, drawing her attention away from Max and the Count.

* * *

WHEN the ten courses were served, exclaimed over, and consumed, and every war story that the duke could reasonably tell was told, Romilla rose and lead the ladies away. What ladies did after dinner was one of the great mysteries to men—though not great enough to abandon their port and cigars and find out. Besides, this was the time for Sir Geoffrey and the Count to open the floor to negotiations. They needed to come to an agreement, and tonight was the first step.

The Count and Sir Geoffrey settled next to each other and began to talk. Pleasantries exchanged (I'm so pleased you came to London, and so on.), they started to discuss the iron ore.

"Yes. Ve are pleased vith the find. But ve are vary, as vell."

Really, the man should avoid Ws at all costs.

"Yes, of course, and I assure you, if you were to sell it to us, we would be extremely generous to Barivia financially."

The Count nodded, but in a manner that said he expected Sir Geoffrey to keep going.

"Ah," gruffed Sir Geoffrey, "we would, of course, help you set up the mining practices and the railway to run it to Hamburg for shipping—"

But the Count cut him off with a wave of his hand, much to the surprise of all the gentlemen. He then stuck a cigar into his mouth, puffed quietly, and refused to speak, no matter how anyone tried to engage him in conversation. After about ten minutes, Sir Geoffrey was getting quite worried, not that he would let it show. He moved away from the group of men's chatter, and went to the window, and stared out. In his diplomatic endeavors, Sir Geoffrey was used to difficult relations, although generally people did not simply stop talking altogether. This was just the first step. In times such as these, all he had to do was step away and think for a few minutes, and the answer would come to him.

"Ahem." A throat cleared to attract his attention.

Generally, of course, he did not have to contend with his daughter's suitors when doing his thinking.

"Lord Fontaine," Sir Geoffrey said, trying to maintain amiability, but failing miserably. "Are you enjoying your evening?"

Lord Fontaine decided to skip over the niceties. "I think I have a solution for you."

Sir Geoffrey took a puff of his cigar. He was thankful Romilla could not stop him from smoking here. It would be too stressful to go without tonight.

"Do you?" he inquired, and Lord Fontaine nodded. "You, who have so much experience in diplomacy, in foreign trade, in Barivian customs and concerns, have a solution that would allow England access to the purest source of iron ore on the continent?" When Max simply nodded again, Sir Geoffrey took another puff of his cigar. "Go to it."

"The Count, at dinner, was describing how pretty his country was," Max began.

"Yes, I know, and probably boring my wife to pieces with it."

"He was saying," the young man continued, "that he could not imagine it looking any other way. That it was *friedlich*—peaceful. I'm not the only one who noticed, Miss Gail heard it as well."

"So?" Sir Geoffrey questioned.

"You offered to build a railway to take the iron to Hamburg to be shipped here. If they wanted to build a railway to Hamburg, they would have sold the rights to the ore to Hanover already. But they don't. They absolutely do not want a railway cutting through their farms and ruining the countryside. They desperately want to hold on to, to protect, their traditional ways of life."

"What do you suggest?" Sir Geoffrey asked, now suitably intrigued.

"The ore was discovered in a rock face not half a mile from the shore, correct? Set up a small shipping port there—bypassing the rest of the country, leaving it be in all its pastoral beauty. It will be a shipping stop solely for use by the mine to run back to England."

"Interesting," Sir Geoffrey said, after a minute. "Very interesting idea. I was afraid for a moment you were going to tell me to offer him more money."

"Oh, he doesn't want your money," Max said, receiving a wry look from Sir Geoffrey. "Actually he does want your money, but he wants his country as well."

Sir Geoffrey grinned, taking another puff. "But where would we get a ship to run this route? A Royal Navy ship cannot be sent, it would raise the ire of the Hanoverians, and they would attempt to conquer Barivia if they think we are invading."

"A private line can be established."

"And at what cost? It would have to be small ships willing to take heavy cargo in smaller amounts. And only one product? Unheard of. Most of the companies I know have all their interests in the south seas and none in a piddly little country no one's ever heard of."

Max smiled. "I know of one that might be willing to take the job."

* * *

THREE days later, it was all arranged. After the dinner party, Max had run directly to Will's bachelor lodgings and pounded on the door until his friend was roused from bed.

"I have found a purpose for your new ships," Max had said.

"What the devil . . . ?" Will yawned. "Fontaine, what on earth . . . ?"

Max had quickly explained to Will the plan. Will may have been half asleep, but Max knew he was a shrewd enough businessman to be able to consider the opportunity presented to him.

"I don't know. Iron ore is not the easiest cargo; it's very heavy. That's why it's usually processed first, then shipped. Plus, my father was considering refitting the ships and using them to start a route to China. And while I'm not overjoyed about the prospect, Chinese goods are all the rage."

Max paced around Will's foyer, while Will sat slumped on the stairs in his dressing gown, nearly asleep.

"Forget China—it takes two years to return, over treacherous seas and indulging in some fairly shady trading practices. This is a product with an established market. Your new ships have strong holds, you said so yourself. There and back to the Barivian coast takes three weeks! And, while on one way you take iron ore to England, on the way back you take English goods to a new, untapped market," Max schemed. "How can you possibly say no?"

Will yawned. "Is this about helping the shipping line or impressing your soon-to-be father-in-law?"

Max's eyes hardened. "You'd be a fool of a businessman to pass up such a ripe prospect." His voice was clipped. "And you know it. And if Sir Geoffrey is impressed by the deal, 'tis nothing more than an added advantage."

Will was quiet for a few minutes more. Then, standing, he said, "Let's go talk to Father."

Talking to the senior Mr. Holt took two days, seeing as he was in Bristol, but the old man was easily won over, not only by the idea of a new exclusive line of trade but by his son finding a good use for the new ships.

"Maybe I can retire early!" his father had said, much to his son's shocked and pleased ears. In fact, Mr. Holt was so eager for the deal, he and Mrs. Holt accompanied Max and Will back to town to meet with Sir Geoffrey and Count Roffstaam.

* * *

"I am pleased vith this solution, Sir Geoffrey," The Count said as the papers were presented to him several days later in the library of Number Seven, "but I am afraid I cannot sign the papers yet."

The whole room looked up. Mr. Holt, Sir Geoffrey, the Duke of Wellington, and Lord Fontaine stared.

"I told my government I should not make my decision until I have spent a few veeks in zis country. Now, be assured, my mind is decided, but I must fulfill my promise to my government. If zey hear I did not, zey would look most unfavorably upon zis contract."

"Count Roffstaam," Mr. Gunnings, the undersecretary to Wellington who had drawn up the papers, began to sputter, "I assure you, ze . . . er, *the* contract is perfectly suitable, and no one in your country will think less of you for accepting such an excellent deal so quickly."

"It's not that," Sir Geoffrey spoke. "The Count knows the contract is sound and that it's a beneficial arrangement."

The Count nodded.

"What he's asking for, from the country that is going to be doing an immense amount of business with his, is some trust."

The Count inclined his head.

"We shall give it," Sir Geoffrey said, offering his hand. The count shook it readily. Mr. Gunnings sputtered, but the Duke raised his hand to his undersecretary, smiling, and stood.

The Count shook the Duke's hand, the undersecretary's, Max's, and Mr. Holt's in turn. The two countries were, as of now, if not married in trade, at least betrothed.

The Count was pleased. The Holts were pleased. The Duke of Wellington was so pleased, he promised the Minister of Foreign Trade position to Sir Geoffrey as soon as the papers were signed.

Max was chatting in German with the Count, when Sir Geoffrey sidled up to them.

"Count Roffstaam, may I borrow your companion for a few minutes?"

Max excused himself and followed Sir Geoffrey out of the library through the empty ballroom and to the terrace.

Sir Geoffrey leaned his hands against the stone railing and breathed deeply.

"Too stuffy in there, needed some fresh air," he said. "Too many men congratulating each other on a job well done."

Max leaned against the railing backward, facing the house. He crossed his arms over his chest, and waited.

"It occurs to me," Sir Geoffrey finally said, "that you are the one deserving most of the congratulations."

"I don't think so," Max replied, quietly pleased. "It was obvious, you would have thought of it, too."

"Yes—but it would have taken longer," Sir Geoffrey said. "Stomach your praise like a man and simply say thank you."

"Thank you," Max replied, letting quiet descend again. Sir Geoffrey reached into his breast pocket and brought out a cigar.

"What about fresh air?" Max asked, as Sir Geoffrey cut off the end and lit it.

"Overrated," he mumbled and took a deep puff. Once the smoke cleared, he eyed Max. "I misjudged you." Max looked up at Sir Geoffrey, who kept his gaze on the small garden. "I thought you were someone with no ambition beyond what you were born to. I apologize."

"Thank you, sir," Max said.

"What you managed to bring about in there," Sir Geoffrey motioned to the library, "well, it shows considerable intelligence. Diplomacy, even."

Max took this in. It was an immense compliment, coming from a man such as Sir Geoffrey. Another "thank you," was all he could strangle out, though.

"See, you're better at accepting praise already," Sir Geoffrey said, smiling.

"You sound like your daughter," Max said before he could stop himself.

"Gail?" Sir Geoffrey offered. "Yes, I do. But I'm surprised she spoke freely with you, she doesn't do that too often anymore. Gail gets all of her, let's call it *verbal ability*, from me. Evangeline takes after her mother: all sweetness." Sir Geoffrey looked away for a moment, a distinct shine in his eyes. He cleared his throat. "That's something I wanted to talk with you about." He paused, took another puff of the cigar, and plowed through. "You know Barivia is a conservative country. They don't even have the waltz there."

Max was silent, knowing Sir Geoffrey would eventually get to where he was going.

"I've decided," Sir Geoffrey said on a sigh, "that men in politics should never have daughters. When they are young, they bring the heart joy, but when they're older, they bring only heartburn."

Sir Geoffrey gave Max a knowing look.

"Sir." Max cleared his throat. "I need you to know that I have no intention of causing any, er, taint to your daughter's name. I never have."

"We will all be spending a great amount of time with the Count and Countess, and we need to be presented as honorable. As keeping our promises."

Max's eyes narrowed. "I do not appreciate your continual questioning of my honor. Now, I've said I'm going to marry your daughter as agreed. That's the end of it."

Max stared stonily at Sir Geoffrey, who met his gaze, and for several considering seconds, they sized each other up.

"Good!" Sir Geoffrey said jovially, breaking the silence as he slapped Max's back. "Let's go back inside and join the melee."

As they walked through the empty ballroom, Sir Geoffrey put a hand on Max's shoulder. "One last thing—I realize you are friends with young Mr. Holt, but how do you know so much of their business practices? How did you know they would have ships available so quickly?"

Max smiled wryly. "I'm an investor."

Sir Geoffrey viewed his soon-to-be son-in-law. "So, you'll not be hurt by the deal that was brokered today." He waggled his cigar in the direction of the library.

"That's not why I did it," Max replied, eye to eye with Sir Geoffrey.

"No, you didn't," Sir Geoffrey stated as fact. "I did underestimate you, didn't I?"

Sixteen

"I have a surprise for you," Max said upon entering the drawing room a few days later. Gail's head emerged from her book, and her eyes followed Max as he seated himself with athletic grace. Evangeline smiled politely and offered the gentlemen tea. Gail reluctantly marked her page and joined her sister on the settee.

"Surprise?" Evangeline replied. "What is it?"

He took a delicate sandwich from the tea tray and popped it into his mouth. He gave the curious stares he received a mischievous smirk as he chewed.

"I thought we might enjoy an outing today," Max eventually drawled. "After all," he continued, "it's been so long since I've had you to myself—I feel as if I haven't seen you in a week." This comment he directed at Evangeline, giving her an indulgent smile. Gail managed to refrain from rolling her eyes.

"Where are we going?" Evangeline inquired.

"I don't know . . ." he mused, twiddling his thumbs. "Maybe I shouldn't tell."

Evangeline looked to Mr. Holt, but he replied to her silent

question in the negative. "Don't look to me for help—he hasn't informed me of any of this."

Impatiently, Gail bounced to the edge of her seat. And Gail was not the bouncy sort. "Dispense with this nonsense and tell us where we're going!" she exclaimed.

"What makes you think you're invited?" Max shot back, but all he received in reply was an impressively arched brow.

Max cleared his throat. "Well, yes, you are invited." He then added beneath his breath, "But I don't know why you automatically think so, Brat."

"I heard that."

"No you didn't," Max insisted coolly, and moved on. "No, I don't think I'll tell you where we are going. I should like to make it a true surprise."

As Gail's brows drew together in a scowl, Evangeline tactfully intervened.

"A true surprise! This is a wonderful idea, Lord Fontaine. Gail and I have been cooped up in this house far too long. We could do with something resembling fun." She looked pointedly at her sister.

And though she was loath to admit it (out loud, at least), Gail knew this to be the truth. The house had been overrun for days. The Duke, the Count, and half of Parliament had been to call on Number Seven since the agreement had been reached. One couldn't sling a cat in Berkeley Square without hitting a politico, or one of the dozens of ambitious undersecretaries looking to impress Sir Geoffrey with sugarcoated congratulations. Word of his promised promotion had traveled fast. Romilla reveled in the attention of course, but Gail and Evangeline found it a bit trying. The Count liked to visit as well, and had a tendency to pop in at the most unusual times, such as half past seven, in the morning and evening. He always enjoyed engaging Gail in conversation, and although she liked him very much, she had the inkling that she was so often in his company because she was the only member of the household who was fluent in German.

Indeed, Gail could use a bit of air.

She looked up and met her sister's hopeful gaze.

"When shall we leave?" she sighed.

* * *

THE carriage pulled up in front of the sixteenth-century mansion in Bloomsbury, and the girls stuck their heads out immediately, eager to see where they had been carried. At first glance, it seemed your average building of wealth, the house was divided into wings, and the courtyard bloomed with early spring flowers. However, no one could miss the massive Palladian structure that was being built not a hundred feet away, crowding out the light—if there was indeed any light on this overcast English day.

"The British Museum?" Gail gaped. "You brought us to the British Museum?"

For indeed, it was the British Museum—of sorts. The ancient artifacts, natural history items, and royal libraries that made up the museum had long been housed in the sixteenth-century mansion, called Montague House. However, as more artifacts were discovered, and more of those artifacts donated, the need for more space became apparent. When George IV donated his father's extensive library collection, the need became immediate. So, whereas the natural history items were moved to a house in Kensington, the ancient artifacts and library remained in Bloomsbury, and Parliament had commissioned this humongous columned building to eventually house the treasures. An ambitious project that when completed would be larger than Buckingham Palace. Although only a few wings were finished, the most precious and interesting exhibits had already been moved into the new building. Oh, what worldly treasures were housed there!

"You haven't been yet, have you?" Max asked, after giving that lengthy lecture.

"No," replied Evangeline tentatively, "not yet, but—"

"Excellent! I thought it might be particularly interesting," Max said, walking ahead.

Will moved next to Evangeline. "Not to mention gets us

out of the house," he stage-whispered into her ear, eliciting an appreciative giggle.

Because the main exhibits were in the new building, Max led them there first. Gail's face shone with intellectual anticipation, and Evangeline's seemed more subdued, but not displeased. Indeed, Max thought, he should not be surprised if Evangeline could weather a plague epidemic with cool serenity. It was a comfort to know she was so steady of character, not given to ungoverned passions. Mild, he decided. Evangeline was mild.

He frowned. Why did that seem like a negative?

Max's grimace was quick lived, for as soon as they entered the mammoth building, his senses, as always, were assaulted by the past. It was as if he stepped from modern London into ancient Greece. The whole hall was filled with relics—the walls lined with bas-reliefs collected by travelers over the past hundred years. The niches that lined the main foyer were filled with statuary from the Townley collection of classical sculpture. He knew this, because he had memorized the guidebook. He pulled the tattered, dog-eared volume out of his coat pocket and made to consult it, but not before sneaking a peak at the faces of his companions. Evangeline was looking about with placid interest, Will's eyebrows raised, no doubt by the impressiveness of the structure, and Gail—her jaw had literally dropped. Her eyes moved left and right and circled with amazing speed, trying to take everything in.

"Well done, Fontaine," Will spoke. "Truly an excellent idea."

Evangeline murmured in agreement, but Gail still couldn't speak—something that Max found incredibly amusing. But before he could comment on it, a porter in livery and powdered wig greeted the party.

"Good morning," Max said, the large halls causing his hushed voice to carry with impressive imperiousness. He fished in his pocket for a card. "I made an appointment last week, for a guided tour."

"Guided tour?" A deep voice boomed out from a shadowed hallway. "Miss Gail Alton could give any guide on staff a lesson on what you see here!"

The party turned toward the voice.

"Mr. Ellis!" exclaimed Evangeline, as both she and Gail rushed forward to greet the older, somberly dressed gentleman, who held out his arms to the girls.

"I was wondering when you would come and give me a visit! Miss Gail, I'm especially surprised at you! You've been in London for how long—over a month now? And not once have you been here to lecture me. Is there no time in your busy lives for one sad and lonely old man?" He took a hand of each girl and kissed them, greeting them as if they were favorite nieces, then turned to address the porter. "The Alton family has a standing invitation. There is no need to confirm the appointment." The porter bowed, handing Max's card to Mr. Ellis before stepping away.

"And whom do you have with you?" Mr. Ellis asked, looking at the card. "Lord Fontaine, I presume?" Max nodded and gave a quick bow. "Henry Ellis, principal librarian of the British Museum, at your service."

As Mr. Ellis turned away to introduce himself to Will, Max could not conceal his amazement. Of course the Altons would be on familiar terms with the curator of the British Museum. Not just any curator, but Mr. Henry Ellis! This man who had traveled the world twice over, made copious notes on everywhere he went, authored books, and considered running the British Museum a form of retirement, was intimate friends with the family of his intended. Of course.

"You, sir, are a legend in your own time," Will was saying.

Mr. Ellis laughed, and Gail said, "Just don't get him started on his 'stranded on a desert isle' story. There isn't enough time in the day." She said it so adoringly, Mr. Ellis turned very nearly pink.

"Lord Fontaine, have you visited the museum before?" Mr. Ellis said, and Max snapped back to attention.

"Yes, it is most impressive."

"Good, then you know where everything is. Ah, I see you have the guidebook as well. Excellent. I'm afraid I cannot take you about myself today."

Gail's face fell.

"But do stop by the library wing before you take your leave. I'm afraid we still have a dozen volumes of Dr. Johnson's dictionary to sort through, and it's been a nightmare!"

And with that, Mr. Ellis disappeared up a massive staircase, mumbling about proper indexing procedures.

"Blimey, Fontaine, I'd wager you didn't expect to meet Mr. Henry Ellis today," Will said, slapping his friend on the shoulder.

"No, I didn't," Max ruefully admitted. "But then again, I've learned never to wager when it involves Gail Alton." He smiled toward Evangeline and Gail, who were already ten steps ahead, looking at an ancient sculpture of a woman draped in robes, holding an urn.

They joined the ladies by the stone woman and asked, "Shall we see some history?"

So they did. The rest of the morning and the whole of the afternoon were spent traveling through the wings of the museum (those that were finished), traveling through time, and imagining life in a different world. The party quickly split into pairs, and although Max had tried to stay with Evangeline, her short steps were no match for his intellectual appetite, and he found himself gravitating toward Gail, who, it turned out, really could teach the museum guides a thing or two. She whispered about the meaning scarab beetles had in Egypt, and lectured about mummification techniques. Max managed to keep up with her, surprising her with his knowledge of the matriarchal society that made women pharaohs before men. They warred with words, wit, and intellect. It's a wonder they didn't kill each other.

On the topic of the Rosetta stone, Max queried of his companion: "Don't tell me you could read it."

She sighed. "Sadly I cannot do everything."

"Surely not!" Max exclaimed, clutching a hand to his chest.

"I shall simply have to content myself with merely being able to do more than you," she responded dryly, and moved onto the next room, Max snickering close at her heels.

Sometimes they would stand and simply stare at a clay pot or a reliquary, and when they looked up, they would find that they had lost Evangeline and Will, who had already lost interest in one room and moved to the next.

"Where are Lord Elgin's Marbles?" Will asked, when they finally caught up with each other. "I should like to see them next."

"They are located in another building," Max said, "but it's attached to this one. This way." And he led them out a side door, under a covered walkway (for indeed, English weather had prevailed in its daily battle with the sun, and it was raining) and into a smaller Palladian building, made to match the large one, but housing only one exhibit.

"Why are they in here?" Evangeline asked.

"Because the room meant to display them hasn't been finished yet, but they didn't want to leave them in the Montague House, away from the rest of the Greek antiquities," Max answered as he led them in.

Inside, they were hardly the only guests. Indeed, the Elgin Marbles, the series of reliefs removed from the Parthenon in Athens, were a very popular exhibit. There were a few members of the Ton present, and Max and Will made bows while the ladies nodded and smiled in acknowledgment. There were also a few middle-class patrons, and some students of art, set up with easels and brushes, trying to capture the beauty of the story that was told on slabs of stone circling the room. Evangeline and Will moved immediately to the wall, to inspect one of the reliefs, but Gail and Max just stood for a moment, taking in the majesty and craftsmanship as a whole.

"They won't be able to do them justice," Gail whispered to Max. She nodded toward the artists. One young man's sketch had captured Evangeline's attention, and she was eyeing it critically.

Gail continued, "To have the warriors come alive, to really be able to see, they need to see the marbles in their proper place."

Max rolled his eyes. He knew he couldn't avoid this. "And have you ever seen them in their proper place?"

"No, of course not," she replied. "They were removed from the Acropolis before I was even born."

"Then how do you know they would look better there?"

Max took Gail's arm and led her to a frieze depicting two men on horseback.

"Because they are wrong here!" Gail nearly exploded, causing several to shush her. Mollified, she continued in a whisper.

"We English run over this world as if it were our private property. 'Oh here's something interesting and historically important to a different culture, allow me to take it away, for I am British and always right.' But by flaunting our superiority, we simply reveal our unwillingness to understand everyone else. By refusing to think anyone else could possibly be better, we show our inferiority."

It was a practiced speech, but Max knew she meant every word.

"I see," he said, watching her eyes flare gold. A sight just beyond Gail's shoulder caught his attention. "Yes, I do see. However, there is an inherent flaw in your logic."

Max took Gail by the shoulders and gently turned her around.

A family had entered the room. They looked to be of the middle class—respectable, proper, clean, but clearly not of the Ton. The mother had her hands full with a toddler in her arms pulling at the strings of her bonnet and a young boy clinging to her skirts. However, the father had a girl by the hand, she looked to be about eleven. Both father and daughter were enraptured by the sight and display of the marbles. The girl pointed and tugged her father's hand, he leaned down to answer her whispered questions. Sometimes they made him laugh—sometimes they made his brow pucker. But they were always answered.

"That girl there," Max said lowly into Gail's ear, "will, I doubt, ever have an opportunity to see Greece. It's just as improbable, that when she's grown, the world will ever afford her much opportunity to leisurely read a book on the subject. You yourself have just said that paintings will never do the Marbles justice. But today, here she is, viewing a masterpiece from a world beyond her own. She's asking questions, she wants to know about that world such treasures come from. Maybe, just maybe, the marbles were brought here because Britain is acknowledging that we still have a great deal to learn."

Gail watched the father and daughter move about the room, asking and answering questions in their turn. When the girl turned and saw Gail and Max watching, she smiled shyly at them—and Gail could not help smiling in return.

"I can see your point."

Max hummed in agreement.

"I still believe they belong in Greece."

"I never thought to change your mind," Max conceded.

Gail looked at the friezes in front of her. "I had never seen them before. They are beautiful, aren't they?"

Max smiled down at Gail, her face as enraptured as the young girl's. "Yes," he said. "They are."

They stood together for some time, the marbles holding their attention. The fall of cloth, the posture of a reclining body, the movement of battle—a whole story cut from impassive stone. In that silence one could not help but feel the wonder of it all.

Then Gail broke the silence.

"But, if they had been on the Parthenon when I was in Greece . . ."

He sighed. "Let it go."

Seventeen

ALTHOUGH the afternoon moved too fast for those of scholarly inclination, it was moving at a snail's pace for those whose interest waned early. Evangeline, while always one to enjoy a good portrait gallery or stroll in the park, had not her sister's love of all things historical. She tried to keep up with her fiancé, but by the fifth hour she was starting to wilt. Also, the new boots she had decided to wear pinched horribly. Really, when a man plans a surprise excursion, he should at the very least inform the lady of appropriate footwear.

She found Will was much of the same mind. Not regarding the shoes, of course (although if he had been wearing pinching boots, he, too, might have been a bit sour), but he didn't have his friend's interest in far off lands, different cultures, and random trivia.

"Really?" she replied curiously to this new information. "But you run a shipping line, I would think you'd enjoy life abroad."

"Not really." He shrugged. "I paid my dues on a ship, mind you, but what I do now is much more business related. I hate to disillusion you, but I'm not a swarthy pirate who rides the seven seas. I sit at a desk and take inventory and deal with merchants."

Evangeline couldn't help but giggle. "Oh, but I could picture you as a pirate. A patch over one eye, a peg leg, a propensity to say 'arr' at the end of every sentence."

"Sadly not." But he smiled and added, "Arr."

"Arr," she agreed.

As they moved to the next room, following in the wake of a very loud argument from Max and Gail about the historical ramifications of musical composers—they could argue about anything—Evangeline leaned heavily on Will's arm.

"Are you well?" Will asked concernedly.

"I'm perfectly fine. It's my shoes, I'm afraid. They're new, and . . ."

The rest of her protest was cut off by Will steering her to a nearby bench. "Let's sit down."

Evangeline seated herself, and before she could stop him, before she could even say a word in protest, Will had knelt down and loosened the laces of her boots.

Sweet relief. Evangeline breathed out a long sigh, letting blood flow back into her tortured feet.

"Better?" Will asked as he seated himself beside her on the bench.

"Mr. Holt," she said, her eyes closed and head leaned back in bliss, "that was most improper."

"Miss Alton, do your feet feel better?"

She nodded, feeling her face go pink at the admission.

"Then what's the harm?" He smiled rakishly.

There they sat, she and Will, in the middle of a room full of broken pottery from a time too long ago. The bench was quite small, and Evangeline could feel the length of Will's leg next to hers. And maybe, for just a moment, she gave in to the sensation of pressing hers a little closer—although if questioned, she would staunchly deny it.

The only sounds were the echo of steps of the other museum patrons (who thankfully didn't seem to have noticed any improper shoe-loosening) and the rushed whispers of disagreement from her betrothed and her sister.

"Do you think they'll ever be agreeable?" Evangeline wondered aloud.

Will turned to look at Evangeline, then back to Gail and Max, the former of whom was gesticulating so wildly, she nearly knocked over the only unbroken urn in the room. Luckily, Max caught her arm in time, but it didn't slow her argument's pace.

"I imagine they will. Given time."

"I hope so," she prayed aloud.

Will regarded her curiously for a moment, searching her face.

"It would be a hell for you," he said quietly, "if they didn't. The two most important people in your life, your sister and your husband, not getting along."

Startled, she brought her eyes up to meet his. No one outside of the family was supposed to be aware of the betrothal. William Holt had never given any indication that he knew the whole truth. But his simple statement and quiet countenance told her that this man understood the circumstances in which she found herself. She tried to find words, but her voice was lost.

He squeezed her hand—she hadn't even noticed when he took it. "Come," he said encouragingly. "Let us see if we can tear the Terrible Twosome away and head home. You can soak your feet, and Fontaine looks as if he needs to soak his head."

They stood, Evangeline taking Will's proffered arm, and crossed to the squabbling pair.

"You're insane if you think the fourth symphony is anything other than tragically beautiful, you naive, little—"

Will had to clear his throat rather conspicuously to gain Lord Fontaine's attention. "I believe it's time to end this excursion. I have dozens of things to do, as do the ladies, to prepare for whatever activities are scheduled this evening."

Max blinked owlishly for a moment, not quite yet seeing who had addressed him. Then he fumbled for his pocket watch, exclaiming, "Goodness—I had not realized we had been here so long."

I had, Evangeline thought ruefully.

Gail took the pocket watch from Max's hand (causing him to jerk forward, being attached to the watch) and remarked, "It's not all that late—indeed, we could stay a few—ow!"

As quickly as possible, Evangeline had crossed to her sister, attached herself to her arm, and pinched with all the strength her delicate fingers could muster. And her fingers could muster a surprising amount.

"Ahem." Gail cleared her throat. "I mean, I suppose we should search out Mr. Ellis and say our farewells."

Sadly for Evangeline's feet, they had to walk upstairs to do so.

When they found Mr. Ellis, he was deeply immersed with several other staff members in the organization of the *K*s, *L*s, and *M*s of the late King George III's expansive personal library. He tore himself away from his work, and expressed genuine surprise to see Evangeline and Gail depart—in his estimation—so early.

"This is unfortunate!" he said, polishing his spectacles (there was an uncommon amount of dust in the *K–M* section). "I was so hoping to give you the tour of the library wing. I should be more than happy to let you prowl through the parts we have yet to open to the public. Also, I should hate for you to miss the new private reading rooms. They are impressively appointed."

Evangeline felt momentarily remorseful—Gail would adore rummaging through the library's unopened sections. And from the enthralled look on Lord Fontaine's face, she wasn't the only one. Wistfulness hung about his frame like heavy clothes. Oh! She so hated to disappoint them. Her resolve to depart steadily weakened, until Will, who had been watching his companions' varied reactions with interest, cleared his throat.

"It's a shame to miss such an opportunity, eh, Miss Gail? Fontaine?" he said, his voice full of sober regret.

"Yes," Max replied.

"Absolutely," Gail said distractedly.

"So you should stay."

"Hmm?"

"The two of you," Will stated neutrally.

It was impossible to tell who spoke first.

"Beg pardon?"

"Excuse me?"

Evangeline looked at Will inquiringly, but he merely gave her an adorable conspiratorial wink and continued speaking in a steady stream.

"Fontaine, you have no pressing engagements, correct? Miss Gail, you have a few hours to spare? Good. I'll escort Miss Evangeline home—er, you mentioned something about a milliner's appointment, am I right? Excellent. And the two of you can explore the library to your intellects' delight. Mr. Ellis, it was truly a pleasure to meet you and see your museum. Fontaine, Miss Gail, I look forward to seeing you at the opera this evening."

And with that he took Evangeline's arm (for indeed she was too stunned to move of her own volition) and led the way down the stairs and out the door.

When they were safely out of earshot, Evangeline tugged Will to a halt.

"What on earth was that all about? You ran right over any protest."

Will grinned. "I knew that if I allowed one word to be spoken, it would be in protest, and then we should never have managed to leave your sister and Fontaine in the library."

"But why?" Evangeline exclaimed.

"Two reasons: First, they both desperately wanted to stay and explore. A blind man could see that."

"Well, yes, of course—Gail lives in books," Evangeline ventured, biting her lower lip.

"The second reason is more oblique. You wish for them to be on good terms, yes?"

Evangeline nodded, so Will continued.

"My father once taught me, the best way to get a cat and dog to tolerate each other is to lock them in a room together. Nine times out of ten, they will be friends when you let them out."

"Oh," Evangeline said, comprehension dawning. As Will handed Evangeline into the carriage, she suddenly squeezed his hand desperately.

"Mr. Holt, er, William . . . what happens the tenth time?" she asked, anxious.

"One will end up killing the other," Will answered gravely, but then his face split into a grin. "So your problem is solved either way. Now"—he stepped closer to Evangeline, making her breath catch—"what shall *we* do the rest of the afternoon?"

* * *

A stunned Max and shocked Gail were left standing in the main library, with Mr. Ellis looking on. Luckily, he was as absentminded as most librarians when in a library, and his attention quickly shifted back to the stack of papers being sorted by his assistants. With a strangled cry of "No! Those go under 'Land Management!' " he had run the twenty feet to his precious work, leaving Max and Gail on their own.

Max looked at Gail.

Gail looked at Max.

"Well," he said.

"Well," she agreed.

Silence.

"Ah . . . would it be improper . . . I mean to say, we can depart if you don't wish to stay."

"Oh, but I do!" Gail cried, then caught herself. A little more gently, she asked, "Er, don't you? Wish to stay, that is?"

"Yes, of course. I should like to see what treasures lie in this place. It's just . . ."

"Indeed," she agreed.

"Exactly," Max murmured.

"Well," Gail said, squaring her shoulders and putting on her familiar cloak of impertinent bravado, "if you can bear with my officious presence, I shall be your ticket inside. I'll even refrain from correcting your Greek when necessary."

An equally familiar scowl darkened his brow. "Your restraint shan't be necessary."

"Excellent. I find you far more pleasing when you are open to my correcting all your mistakes."

Mr. Ellis led Max and Gail into the back rooms of the library—those not yet open to the public. The shelves were in deplorable shape, piled high with texts not yet sorted by author, date, subject, or any system of classification one could easily identify. However, it was obvious that the books themselves were being kept in decent condition, the leather oiled and all bookworms eradicated by thorough maids. The room was free of dust and well lit by wall sconces and windows that had not yet received the spring cleaning the contents of the room had been subject to.

Mr. Ellis was quickly called back to his sorting duties, but left instructions for the pair to leaf through tomes as they pleased, confident in their ability and interest to respect the books and information they contained. But it must be noted that Mr. Ellis was not so remiss as to close the door. That was left open so anyone who cared to look in could see what the young Miss Alton and Lord Fontaine were up to.

Not that anyone looked.

For a time, Max and Gail lost themselves in the shelves. She began to sort through a pile of volumes detailing the family history of a baronet in Dorset in the late seventeenth century, while Max found himself flipping through the diary of a chaplain aboard a Royal Navy ship during the triumph of Queen Elizabeth versus the Spanish Armada. Deciphering the man's handwriting was difficult, but well worth the effort, for the chaplain had some choice words in his private ramblings for the "virgin" Queen. Max chuckled as he read.

"What are you laughing at?" Gail's voice came from the other side of the shelves.

"Oh, just enjoying the folly of a man who has an opinion on everything. Something you should know a little about, I imagine."

She appeared around the corner of the stacks, leafing through a small volume. Her eyes never left the page as she drawled, "And you consider this folly?"

"That he feels the need to voice it, yes. Who is this chaplain"—he held up the text—"to say anything against Queen Elizabeth?"

"Absolutely no one. Just one of her subjects, forced by law to bow to her whims."

The sarcasm was dripping from her tongue, provoking

Max, daring him to contradict her. Which he was more than willing to do.

"A pompous windbag."

"You call him that because he speaks his mind?" Gail asked, her voice controlled, deceptively neutral. She refused to look up from her book.

"I have a question for you," Max drawled. "This man, it seems, thought himself always right, and took care to make sure everyone knew. Don't you think his shipmates found him a bit, shall we say, annoying?"

Her head snapped up.

"If he was right, why should he care if others found him annoying?" Fire flashed in her eyes. "Personally, I can't imagine a life more revolting than compromising every opinion, desire, and truth I have to simply get along with others!"

Max opened his mouth to respond to that explosion of feeling, when a sudden change went through Gail. It was as if all the wind left her body, leaving her once blustery self hollowed, and tired. She smiled weakly. "Now, Lord Fontaine, I have a question for you: How long are we going to keep doing this?"

Whatever question Max was expecting, that wasn't it.

"Doing what?" he asked, befuddled.

"Fighting. Bickering. Get each other's back up. I don't know about you, but whenever we engage in our little battle of wills, I end the day exhausted."

For a moment, Max stood stunned. Then a great burst of air left him.

"God, yes, it's tiring."

Gail smiled in relief and then leaned forward, whispering as if taking Max into confidence.

"But fun, too." Her eyes twinkled.

Max grinned. "Fun, too. Sometimes."

She cleared her throat and straightened her back. "I think we need to find some middle ground, Max."

"I apologize if my earlier words were too harsh. I . . . don't know what the boundaries are with you," he said sincerely, meeting her eyes.

She nodded slowly, her mouth a grim line. "I don't know the rules with you, either."

"Half the time, we're sniping at each other, other times I, well I—"

"Want to kick my throat in?" Gail suggested wryly.

"Nothing so violent. I might wish you a prolonged bout of laryngitis, though."

Gail chuckled. It was a nice sound, deep and warm. Max smiled lopsidedly at hearing it.

"I propose," he said leaning on the shelves, relaxing a little, "that we let it go, just for this afternoon."

"Do you mean we pretend to like each other?" Gail lifted an eyebrow.

"Yes, just for today, you never pushed me off my horse into a lake, and I—"

"Never compromised my sister and are therefore not forcing her to marry?"

"Exactly." He nodded resolutely.

"But we start bickering again tomorrow?"

"Oh, absolutely."

Lit by the sconce on the wall, Max's eyes sparkled in good humor.

"Yes. I accept." Her smile broke forth like sunshine on that gray English afternoon. She extended her hand.

"Excellent." He took her offered hand and shook it once, in binding resolution. Never mind that it took him a second before giving it back.

They stood for a moment staring at each other, before each returned to the books they had been perusing earlier. Standing side by side in that row of shelves, each looking at their books, neither reading. Eventually, Gail, as was her way, broke the silence.

"Well, if we can't snipe at each other, what are we to talk about?"

Eighteen

AS it turned out, the temporary negotiated truce allowed for the most carefree afternoon that Max had enjoyed since the start of this torturous Season. He found that when she wasn't restricted by fear, or politeness, or a desire to provoke her companion, Gail Alton was quite pleasant company. Playing at being friends opened a wealth of curiosity each had about the other.

It started slowly. As Max was walking from one set of shelves to the next, he passed the open door and saw Mr. Ellis intently sorting papers.

"How did your family become acquainted with Mr. Ellis?" Max asked casually.

Gail looked up from her own volume. "He met my father in . . . India, I believe. They struck up conversation right away. After that, he would meet us in Greece, Egypt, anywhere our paths crossed. He quickly became a favorite uncle with us, popping up with toys and stories from his travels, always eager to listen to two little girls who moved around too much to have many steady friends."

"Both he and your father are well traveled. I imagine they have much in common."

"Not as much as you would think. They are friendly, yes, but they are forever in the middle of a row. Mr. Ellis is very liberal minded. He believes we should not attempt to enforce our British ideals on other cultures—that we really shouldn't engage them at all. He would say that the best way to learn about another place is to become part of it, blend in, meeting locals, learning the language, et cetera. Basically renouncing everything English."

"Sounds close to your own philosophy. And your father, the diplomat, is very much opposed to Mr. Ellis's extreme view," Max concluded.

"Such differing points of view can cause some friction," Gail conceded.

"Friction?"

"I believe furniture was thrown at one time," she admitted.

Max guffawed in disbelief.

"But in the end," Gail continued, "they respect each other and enjoy the fights. Healthy debate was the foundation of a solid friendship—as opposed to mutual loathing."

A skeptical eyebrow rose. "Thrown furniture is the foundation of a solid friendship?"

Gail shrugged. "It was merely a foot stool. Hardly worth signifying."

As Gail's attention returned to her book, Max allowed his gaze to drift over her. Her eyes moved rapidly over the text, her small pink tongue pressing into her upper lip, her face a picture of studious concentration. Max remembered how Sir Geoffrey had commented that Gail was much more like himself than Evangeline was. She didn't have her father's penchant for blustering or his ability to negotiate the intricacies of a peace treaty with a hostile but defeated nation, but she certainly seemed to have inherited his love of impassioned debate.

Smiling just a little, he turned his attention back to the shelves. After a while, all Max heard was the rustling of skirts in the next aisle over, the turn of a page. Since they had agreed not to bait each other, they were able to go about in companionable silence. Which was a nice change, he decided.

He certainly had never had any companionable silences with Evangeline, although silence itself was abundant. Whenever he was alone with Evangeline, the air was so fraught with awkwardness he could barely breathe. Luckily, they weren't alone too often.

"Do you know," Max began, and heard the distinct clunk of a book being dropped. "Did I startle you?" he asked, grinning.

"No . . . er, well, yes," came the voice from the side of the shelves. "But pray continue."

"I was simply going to comment on how I think I have been in your exclusive company far more than I have been in your sister's."

After a silence, she replied, "Well, yes I suppose you have. But there's alone, and then there's alone-kissing-in-a-moonlit-garden."

"We called a truce, remember?"

"Apologies," she said quickly. "What I mean to say is your current situation is predicated not on the amount of time you spent alone with a lady. It's based on your being caught in a compromising position. Really, you're quite lucky. Imagine if you had been caught alone with me at the ball when we were behind the curtain. In my state, it would have looked to anyone as if something untoward was going on, and then it would be *we* who were engaged quicker than you could say 'jackrabbit.' What a horror that would be, eh, Max?"

"Definitely," was the immediate reply, standard and ingrained. He was lucky that it was Evangeline he found himself attached to. But a niggling little voice in the back of his mind started to whisper. *What if?* What if it had been Gail?

Would it have been so bad?

"Besides, they don't worry about me," she said quietly. "Not like they do Evangeline."

"They should," Max answered automatically and honestly. More honestly than he cared to admit.

He could hear the eye-roll in her voice. "Max . . ."

"You shouldn't do that, you know."

"Do what?" She poked her head around the corner, her brow creased with confusion.

"Call me Max," he said clearly. "'Tis wholly improper. Your sister doesn't call me Max, and one would think she has more right to it than you."

Gail smiled reflectively. "Sometimes I call you Max to provoke you," she admitted, stepping into full view, leaning her long frame against the shelves, arms crossed over a book held to her chest. "But the rest of the time, I forget not to."

"Huh," Max said, nonplussed at her bold-faced honesty. "You do realize, such an intimacy would give me automatic leave to address you as Gail."

"But you won't," Gail stated.

"No," he admitted. "I probably won't. It wouldn't provoke you the same way 'Brat' does."

"And provoke it does," Gail said, her voice full of dry humor.

Max regarded her quizzically. "Does it truly bother you so much?"

"I hate it," she replied vehemently. "Almost as much as I despise being called 'Abigail.'"

"I'll stop, then."

She blinked at him a few moments. The corners of his mouth turned up. That certainly threw her off balance.

"But if you don't call me 'Brat,' I shall have to leave off calling you Max," she replied pertly, once she had regained her voice.

He lifted a shoulder. "Now that I know you do it to be provoking, it shan't provoke any longer."

"Your logic astounds me, Max."

"I should imagine it does, Gail."

"I thought you weren't going to call me Gail, either." She eyed him suspiciously.

Another shrug. "With 'Brat' and 'Abigail' off limits, I changed my mind about 'Gail.' Have to keep the field even, don't I?"

As she was reduced to laughter, Mr. Ellis stuck his head in and shushed them with all the gravity of the principal librarian. When he had again retreated to his classification system, and Gail and Max snickered their way to the next isle of books, Max realized that he was truly enjoying himself. How very peculiar.

Soon enough, each had a stack of books under their arms, and they made their way to the private reading rooms. The one they were directed to was about the size of a small drawing room, fully paneled in wood, with oil lamps and magnifying glasses available to assist detailed inspection. A small fire grate was lit and situated next to a pair of winged velvet chairs. A large table was in the center of the room, with sturdy chairs on each side. Max and Gail reverently placed their stacks of books on the table and began to sort through them.

Max was quickly engrossed in a collection of maps, drawn by the first explorers to the New World.

"Have you ever been here?" he asked Gail, drawing her away from a tome on the Greek system of congress.

"No." She stood closely behind him, looking over his shoulder. "We never traveled to the colonies."

"I don't suppose they take kindly to being called 'colonies' anymore." He flipped a page. "What about here?"

"The West Indies?" She shook her head. "No, never been there, either." An errant curl that had escaped her coiffure bobbed along with the movement of her head, momentarily capturing his attention.

"So, there is still much in the world left for you to explore," he said after clearing his throat.

"And I intend to see it all."

Silently Max agreed. He longed to see the tropical islands of the Caribbean, the shores of Boston, the pyramids on the Nile. But being an Earl, or next in line, with a huge property to maintain was not conducive to year-round travel. But then again, neither was being a single young lady.

"You're lucky to have seen all that you have," he ventured. "But what if your husband doesn't wish to travel?"

Gail scoffed. "If my nonexistent husband doesn't wish to travel with me, I shall go alone. There are some things that do not yield to the wishes of others."

Max shook his head. "You only say that because your

desires have never been tested. You will marry, have a brood of children—very impertinent ones—and find yourself ten years from now leg-shackled to the life you have, and the dreams of exotic places just that. Only dreams."

"That won't happen," she replied staunchly.

He simply looked at her, sad that for once, he knew more of the world than she. She seemed to understand his thoughts, for she replied adamantly, "In that case I shan't marry."

"Yes, you will." And though the thought gave him a moment's pause, he plunged on. "You will be married and subject to the rule of your husband. If he doesn't wish you to go, then . . ." He shrugged, allowing the sentence to trail off.

She quirked her head. "Is that what happened to you?"

His eyebrows shot up.

"Not the husband, exactly. But every book you picked is about some far-off place. And yet, beyond your grand tour, you never traveled. Why?"

Max sighed. "It's quite complicated. My father . . ." he trailed off. "Well, suffice to say, it's a long story."

"Oh, I have time," Gail said, seating herself in one of the large wingback chairs by the fire grate. "Indeed, the world seems to have forgotten us."

It was true. The private reading room lived up to its name. No one had come to check on them. Mr. Ellis and his assistants were engrossed in their work, and Evangeline and Will had promised to make their excuses to Romilla. They were completely alone, and no one seemed to care.

"The door is closed," Max said, dazedly.

Gail waved off his unspoken question in her very Gail-like way. "They saw us before in the other room. They don't worry about you and me."

Unbidden, *they should*, again flashed through his brain. Instead, he said, "I doubt your mother would be much pleased by that closed door."

"Stepmother, and you are purposely avoiding the subject. I have settled into a somewhat comfortable chair for the promised long story. I suggest you do the same."

Max weighed his options before her steady golden stare and realized he might as well admit defeat. Gail's intense curiosity would not allow her to give up until she knew what she wanted to know.

And strangely enough, Max wanted to tell her.

"To understand my situation, I think you have to understand how I grew up," Max started as he settled into the chair opposite Gail. The firelight flickered against her hair, making the ordinary brown glow with red flame.

"I was raised in Sussex, near a small coastal town called Hollings. For such a small place, it has a fairly good-sized shipping trade in place. Holt Shipping established its first port there, you know." When she nodded, he continued. "Of course you know, you know everything. Well at any rate, I spent my formative years at Longsbowe Park. I spent a good amount of time by myself. My parents had separate lives. I had nurses and governesses. My father was still active in the House of Lords, so he wasn't in the country some of the time. But when he was . . . he taught me to fish in a stream on the estate. And to shoot. And about the lands that would one day be mine. My father . . . Longsbowe hasn't changed in generations, you see. Hundreds of years and the land, estates, it's all been exactly the same. I was taught the history of every tree, who planted it and why, the crops and how long we've been growing the same thing in the same place. Now, I enjoy history. Learning about new places and things and ideas that never landed on our shores is interesting—after all, without knowing what came before how can we advance? But Longsbowe *is* history. It can be . . ." Max's voice became a little too rough for his liking. He cleared his throat, and began again.

"Anyway, my father wasn't around often when I was young, and I was relatively alone, which isn't abnormal. I would run three miles into town as a boy and watch the ships go out to sea, and I adored it. I would ask sailors where they had been and what they had brought back, and they would laugh and tell me I'd be a devil of a sailor one day. And I wanted to be—Lord, did I want to be—but I was to be an Earl. That's the way it was, the way it is, and the way it always will be. And Earls are not common sailors. But I was very young. When the Holt family purchased an estate that was not too far from ours, I finally had a friend nearby. Their blood may not have been as blue as my father would have liked, but their money was certainly the right color—and amount. So now, instead of just me running into town, it was Holt and I harassing the sailors and fishermen."

"It made it easier, to have a friend along," Gail said quietly.

"Yes . . . and harder, too." He frowned. "I knew he was going to have the chance to be on a ship like that one day—and I wasn't. So when I was about twelve or so, I decided to run away. I packed a bag—mostly full of cheese and books I believe"—he smiled as Gail chuckled at his boyish folly—"and went to sign up as a cabin boy on one of the ships headed out to sea. The captain knew who I was, of course, and escorted me back to Longsbowe, where my father locked me in my room for a week. Never in my life had I seen him so angry. He yelled, railed, told me I was ungrateful for not wanting to stay and be who I was to be. That leaving the country was foolhardy. When he finally let me out, I was sent immediately to Eton."

Max's voice cracked, and he had to cough into his hand to cover the effect this distant childhood memory had on him.

"Eton wasn't too bad," he continued. "My father approved of it only because it's where generations of Fontaine men had attended, and it was nearly as stuffed with history and tradition as Longsbowe. I know some gentlemen emerge with only horror stories of ruthless pranks and strict headmasters, but I didn't mind so much. I was a viscount, with an ancient name, so the bullies were careful not to dunk my head in any chamber pots. Holt came up the same year as me, so we remained mates. And I liked to study," he said wryly, indicating the pile of books he had left on the center table. "When I went home for holidays, my father and I, we no longer saw eye to eye. I started to notice that he had changed. A little at first, then rather dramatically. He began spending all his time at Longsbowe Park, stopped attending the House. My mother died while I was at school, and . . . I know that they had little affection for one another, but having her gone I think gave him permission to stop being in London. In the world, really."

Max sighed, leaning forward on his knees, moving his shoulders as if to protect himself from imaginary blows. "I thought that if I waited until I was grown, I could do as I liked, and my father couldn't stop me. He was a recluse by now, what would he care if his son spent a few years abroad? But I was wrong.

"When I came down from Oxford, I was ready to see the world. Holt and I set out on our grand tour. However much my father objected, he couldn't very well forbid me—it was part of the consummate British experience, I had argued. I intended to go about Europe and maybe even Russia for at least a year. But two months into my travels, I received a missive that my father was on his deathbed."

Gail sucked in her breath. Max nodded in agreement. "As you see. I rushed home, at record speed, and when I arrived, it was to see my father sitting up in bed eating a luncheon of hearty stew. I spoke with the doctors—they had been gravely worried about my father's health, but it seemed he had beaten back the severe cold that had threatened to take him. I was relieved. I couldn't believe how much I was relieved," Max said almost to himself. "I stayed at Longsbowe with him for a month, every day he got stronger. When the doctors felt his health had been fully restored, I packed my bags, intending to rejoin my friends abroad. But on the eve of my departure, it rained. And my father showed his true colors. He stood outside in the damp the whole night. By morning, all the repairs to his health that had been made in that last month were undone, and he was on his deathbed again."

"That's horrible," Gail whispered. "Why?"

"Because he wanted me to stay! He didn't want me out of England, out of Longsbowe, and out of his control. It only took him three weeks to recover this time, but once he had, I called him out on his behavior. And we had the biggest row in our history—and believe me, my school days were peppered with some thunderous arguments. He accused me of not living up to my duties to Longsbowe. He thought I should remain in England, learn about the estate, become his drone, his copy, his Earl. As he was a copy of the one before him . . . I told him to go to hell." At Gail's taken-aback expression, Max smiled ruefully. "But I said it less politely."

Gail was on the edge of her chair. "What was his reply?"

A cynical smile twisted his lips.

Max remembered very well what his father had said in reply.

* * *

"YOU can't live without me boy! So you shall live where I tell you."

His father's gruff voice echoed in his head. They were in the study of Longsbowe Park, a grand room that had not changed in seven generations of Fontaine men. The high shelves of unread books were the same. The wood and leather were the same. Even behind the large mahogany desk was the same chair, in which the Earl sat, lord of all he surveyed. Including his son.

"You're cutting me off? Fine—I don't want your money," Max said with more bravado than he felt. He was still young enough to have the idealism bred in university, but it was quickly lost when he pictured having to face the prospects of a world that turned on gears greased with cash and prestige. His father simply cackled.

"You won't last three weeks in the world without what Longsbowe provides! You will stay here and learn to appreciate it, learn to run it, and learn to love it."

"You've drilled into me the lessons of running an estate since I could walk," Max fired back. In every one of his letters to his son, the Earl would include a detailed lesson on crop rotation, tenant farming, or the estate's maintenance. It had gotten to be a bit of a joke between Max and his mates, for every time a letter had arrived, they would ask, "What's the Earl's lesson this week?"

"Time to put them to use then. I'm not as young as I used to be. You will now run the estates. I will oversee, advise when I think you are going astray, but I will have the stewards take orders from you. You will become Longsbowe, lad."

And Max saw it. His future stretched out in front of him. All the new ideas he had drying up like dust. A long life of checking his work with his father, getting approval before proceeding. Always the Earl's son, never his own man. Never leaving Longsbowe. Never discovering a damn thing about anything. Max's throat closed in on itself, choking, suffocating.

"No," he whispered hoarsely.

"What?" His father, who had clearly thought the issue was settled, looked up from his desk.

"I said no," Max repeated, more resolutely this time.

"No?" the Earl asked, incredulous.

"I will not stay here and be your lackey."

"Do you know what you are saying?" Desperation crept into the Earl's voice. He sounded old. "You want to leave? Fine! You do it without my money! You won't last a week without an allowance. You have *nothing* that is your own."

It was the ultimate dilemma. His father refused to let go—but Max would die by inches if he stayed.

"I'm a sick old man," his father had pleaded in a weak voice. "What will happen to me if you leave England?"

Max shook his head. "England is a big place. It will have to be big enough," he said resignedly. "But I won't live here under your rule."

And with that, Max stalked out of the room. He calmly packed a bag and left the house, only venting his frustrations on an antique vase near the door. But that could have been considered an accident.

When he got to London, Max had only the money in his pocket and what was left of his last quarterly deposit in the bank. The Earl had been true to his word and quickly severed financial ties with his son. His father probably thought if Max couldn't live high, he would come crawling home. Well, he would have to show the old man he was made of sterner stuff. Max set up house in an unfashionable but respectable part of town and began going about the business of becoming his own man.

Independence was his goal. Now, while the gentleman in him abhorred the idea of working for a living, the twenty-one-year-old in him was much more frightened of the prospect of marrying for money. So he learned to economize and looked for work.

* * *

"INITIALLY, some of my professors from Oxford assisted me," he told Gail, who listened with rapt attention. "They had been impressed with my head for languages and liked me well enough, so they recommended me for some translating work. Then the government started commissioning similar work from me, as did publishing houses. I was soon earning enough money to pay my rent and expenses each month. But I wasn't exactly living very well. Holt convinced me to invest a bit of each of my payments into Holt Shipping. And the rest, as they say, is history. I live economically, but I can't say I want for anything. Very few people know I'm cut off. Most people just think I'm aloof," Max finished with a sigh, settling back into his chair.

Gail looked at him for some minutes, twisting a lock of hair that had fallen out of her coiffure between two fingers. Late at night, Max would think about that lock of hair.

"But that can't be the end of the story," she said quietly. He looked at her expectantly.

"You have your own money now. The only reason you stayed in England was your father's threat to cut you off. That's no longer a threat. So why do you remain?"

Max exhaled a long breath. He looked at an innocuous spot on the floor—Gail's gaze was too questioning, too direct.

"Fear," he whispered, barely audible.

"Fear of what?" she whispered back.

"What he'll do. I'm afraid he'll make himself ill again. When he was out all night in the rain . . ." His voice broke. "I was so frightened. I was so very frightened of what would happen to him. You haven't seen him. He's not . . . strong anymore. He used to be the strongest man I knew. I have to keep my end of the bargain. I will stay in England. The world outside of it is a foolish place anyway." He stared into the fire, forlorn.

His offhand comment made Gail frown. "That is your father talking," she spoke, her voice resolute but her eyes soft and forgiving. She walked over to Max, kneeled before him.

Placing a gentle hand on his arm, she drew his attention away from the grate.

"Max," she said in soft kindness. "Couldn't he see he was making you unhappy?"

Max was caught in her eyes, eyes that pleaded for that little boy, for that man who was still held back by the strong arm of his father. His voice came out lower, more hoarse than expected. "He can't see beyond Longsbowe, beyond keeping things the same, within his control. He . . . manipulated me then. He still does, just in new ways. But I can't risk it."

"But how long? You have shut yourself off as effectively as he did. How long can you hold your true self in? How long before you are allowed to live?" Her hand was grasping his, a lifeline he didn't know he needed. His other hand reached out, lightly fingering the softness of that errant lock of hair before seeking the warmth of the side of her neck and face. His thumb rubbed absentmindedly along her jaw, drawing her closer to him. Mere inches away.

"I shouldn't have told you all this," he whispered.

"I'm glad you did," she whispered back. "I think I understand you a bit better now."

"Then you have the advantage over me," he replied, lowering his forehead to rest against hers. It was a gesture of deep need and closeness. Both closed their eyes, taking comfort in the simple existence of the other. "Promise me that someday, you will tell me all about your deepest anxieties and frustrations. Then we may be on even footing."

Gail sniffled, followed by a short chuckle. "Do you have a year?" she asked with a smile.

Max brought his head up, regretting the space between them, even if it was only inches. He looked into her eyes (which had become decidedly shiny) and murmured, "The world seems to have forgotten us."

She kept her eyes locked with his, something shifting in her golden gaze. It became darker, molten. She didn't breathe. Didn't move. Indeed, it seemed as though she couldn't.

But Max could. The space between them slowly began to close. As his nose lightly caressed hers, Max could feel the light stutter of her breath warming his cheek. Her eyes became hooded and flickered closed, as their lips met for the first time.

It was warm. Gail was so surprised by the warmth that flooded her face, her chest, down to her toes at the simple brush of his mouth against hers. His hand slowly stole from her jaw to the back of her neck, pulling her even closer, deepening the kiss.

As for Max, he felt the fire of her, and it inflamed him. His mind raced, filled with questions: How could he do this? How could he not? How long had he wanted her just this way? But he refused to answer any question as long as he could simply *feel* Gail—on his lips, beneath his fingers, all around him. Her hand wound its way into his hair—slowly, softly gripping him to her. A shot of lust went straight to his groin, and he grabbed her arm, pulling her onto his lap.

This shift from gentle and sweet to hot with need thrilled Gail as much as it frightened her. She could not have stopped him, and found that she didn't want to—especially when he opened his mouth, his tongue inviting hers to come out and play.

So *this* was kissing, Gail thought, as she tentatively met his movements in equal measure. Before, she hadn't understood its appeal—why the maids blushed and giggled, why the matrons were so rigid in their belief that it was a sin—and that wasn't the only thing rigid right then. Gail could honestly not blame anyone for what was deemed base desires, because the only desire she had as she felt his hands running over her back, holding her to him, was *don't stop*.

A sharp knock on the door broke the spell, freezing Max and Gail in their heated explorations.

"Hello? Miss Alton?" Mr. Ellis's voice broke through the door and their warm, insulated little world. Max watched as Gail's eyes went from heavy lidded and dark with lust, to wide with shock and, regrettably, horror. Her mouth a small, silent *O*, she lifted herself from Max's lap, cool air rushing into the growing void between them. Max could see that she wanted to absorb their actions, process them, try to make some sense of it, but there was no time for that.

Quickly she moved away, straightening her shoulders and ruthlessly combing her hair with her fingers. She was acting with speed and caution, both correct for this situation, but Max couldn't help but be saddened by it. Could she really let go of him so quickly? Only a few seconds had passed since the knock interrupted them, could she already regret?

Gail, satisfied with her hair, picked up a book from the table, and Max arranged himself more suitably just before Mr. Ellis opened the door.

"Ah! Miss Alton, Lord Fontaine. You are in here, excellent. I despaired of ever finding you. It's six o'clock. The museum is about to close."

If Gail's face was more flushed than normal, her eyes shinier, her lips redder, and Max's seated pose more carefully arranged, Mr. Ellis did not comment. Max dug for his pocket watch.

"Six o'clock! Already! Ga—er, Miss Alton, we seem to have lost the entire afternoon. Your parents will be curious as to your whereabouts."

"Lord, yes!" Mr. Ellis exclaimed. "Although I, too, have lost many an afternoon in these rooms. I daresay, if one of my assistants hadn't reminded me, I would have accidentally locked you in here all night. What a kerfuffle that would have been, eh?"

Mr. Ellis smiled at his own humor, while Gail and Max exchanged a glance.

A kerfuffle, indeed.

Nineteen

WHEN Max escorted Gail back to Number Seven Berkeley Square, Evangeline could tell right away that something had shifted between the two, and she for one, was ecstatic. William (as Mr. Holt had insisted she call him) had been correct! His plan had succeeded, and now Lord Fontaine and Gail would be friendlier. Didn't he smile at her as if they were on good terms? Didn't they not once snap at each other with caustic comments?

Truthfully, Evangeline had been more than a little anxious. When she and Will had arrived back at the house (at five o'clock, nearly two hours later than they left the museum, although there was no reason to inform anyone of that fact), Romilla questioned them as to Gail's whereabouts. Evangeline explained that Gail was perfectly safe, being escorted by Lord Fontaine and under the watchful chaperonage of their friend Mr. Ellis. Evangeline had thought Romilla would suffer a fit of apoplexy, so unhealthy was her color. Obviously, Evangeline surmised, her stepmother had noticed the acrimonious relationship between the two, and thought the same as she—that they would tear each other to pieces. But now,

Romilla would see that this was the absolute best thing they could have hoped for from the situation.

* * *

HOWEVER, Romilla had seen, and she did not consider it the absolute best thing. Far from it. When her errant stepdaughter and escort entered Number Seven, did Lord Fontaine's hand linger just a moment too long on Gail's arm before releasing her? True enough, they did not exchange any hard words as had become their custom, but animosity had been the only thing keeping one at arm's length from the other, and now . . . This new "friendship" worried her deeply.

Then, Romilla laughed. This was silly. It would turn out to be nothing. And what was Mr. Ellis always saying? Oh yes, that she was making a mountain out of a molehill. It wasn't as if Lord Fontaine was about to throw over one sister for the other. Especially if that first sister was as divine as Evangeline.

Still, 'twas best to remain shrewd and alert.

* * *

THAT night at the opera, Romilla was convinced her feelings on the matter were an overreaction. Any expression of sentiment she thought she had seen that afternoon had disappeared like smoke. Lord Fontaine was a guest in their box, as was Count Roffstaam and his wife. Lord Fontaine sat in the front, next to Evangeline, being everything that is kind and attentive. He paid no attention to Gail beyond what was polite. And as Gail was enjoying speaking in German with the Count, she and Lord Fontaine seemed content to ignore each other. Maybe they had reached an understanding of sorts, like Evangeline had hoped, wherein they never spoke to each other again. And Romilla, more than pleased with that, settled herself comfortably next to her husband to enjoy the performance of *Don Giovanni*.

* * *

WHEN the curtain came down on the first act to thunderous applause, the real entertainment of the evening began. Gail watched as the Ton flitted between the boxes, visiting with the occupants to comment on the ladies' wardrobes, who was sitting with whom, and which gentlemen were vying for attention from what lady. Naturally, the Altons' box became crowded quickly.

Romilla was receiving a visit from Lady Hurstwood, who had so viciously snubbed her a few weeks ago by not inviting the Altons to her Vauxhall party. Now, here she was, dancing attendance on their stepmother! Gail shook her head—would she ever understand the politics of society? Half a dozen young admirers stopped by to visit with Evangeline, crowding their way past the MPs who wanted a word with Sir Geoffrey. Every occupant of the box was beginning to feel the crush—especially those smashed against the wall, as Gail soon found herself.

"Miss Alton," Count Roffstaam addressed Gail in his thick Barivian accent. "It iz very crowded, iz it not?"

"Yes, I confess it is," Gail replied, lightly fanning herself with the libretto—not easy, as her elbow was pinned to her waist, unknowingly by the portly Lord Draye.

"Come," the Count said, offering his arm. "Let us go and seek some refreshment."

Out in the elegantly appointed hall, it was still quite populous, but at least there was room to move. The swish of silks against the plush carpet, the murmur of voices on top of voices echoed through the chambers as Gail and the Count made their way to the refreshments.

"I think my vife vill like—cham . . . champagne?" asked the Count.

Gail nodded, although she herself was repulsed by the prospect of any spirits, and instead requested a simple punch. "Really, Count Roffstaam," she said listening to his stumbling English, "we can speak German if you like. I don't mind, truly."

But the Count would not hear of it. "You have indulged me enough tonight in German. I am in England, I should practize mine English, yes?"

"Yes," Gail laughed and accepted the punch that the Count handed her.

"Besides," said a familiar voice from behind, "an evening such as this calls for Italian."

They turned, and the only man in the house, in the world, who could have spoken that comment bowed before Gail and the Count.

"Don't you agree, Count Roffstaam?" Max asked, looking beyond compare in his stark black and white evening kit. Gail had seen him dressed this way before, but never had the sight sent a frisson of feeling straight through her chest. He looked . . . beautiful. Gail's face flushed hot. She shouldn't be thinking this.

"Ja, I do," the Count spoke. "German is mine tongue, and ze tongue of ze composer, but Italia, it iz like a stream. Deutsch, it iz a bevy of rocks."

"Yes, exactly," Gail smiled.

"You seem to be enjoying the opera, Miss Alton."

"I am, Lord Fontaine."

They had begun to walk down the gallery, Gail still on the Count's arm, Max holding himself three feet away. He did not move any closer. She wished he would.

"Even though you do not speak Italian?" Max inquired, interrupting her thoughts.

"Ah . . . one of the best things about opera is that no matter the language it's written in, the meaning is universally understood."

"True. And you have the translated libretto."

"And I have the translated libretto," she agreed matter-of-factly.

"*Wie bitte?* Ah, pardon me? You speak ze English so fast," the Count broke in.

"Oh!" cried Gail. "Forgive us. We didn't mean to exclude you, Count."

"Yes, beg pardon, sir," Max added, but the Count simply held up his hands.

"No, no, you forgive me. I am old man, vith slow ear. Speak as you vill. I take the champagne back to my vife."

The Count headed back to the box and his wife, leaving Gail and Max alone in the middle of a crowded hallway. With no other recourse left available to them, Max offered Gail his arm, which she took. They began to follow after the Count. Slowly.

"I assume you trust implicitly whomever fetched you that punch?" Max asked as she took a small sip.

"That depends," Gail answered, once she had swallowed. "How much do you trust a short man with spotty English and a large moustache?"

A tight smile broke through his serious expression, mirroring her nerves.

"Strange how the Count's English is especially spotty sometimes, and less spotty at others," Max ventured. She looked at him questioningly, and he explained, "In his negotiations with your father, his English was easily understood. Also, that comment about German being like a bevy of rocks? Very poetic for someone with only a passing knowledge of our language."

Gail considered this. "I suppose you're right," she murmured. Then, unable to think of anything else to say, Gail said nothing, letting silence descend upon them.

Max cleared his throat. "Uh, are you enjoying the opera?"

"Yes," Gail answered, flushing hot. "As I told you before."

"Right." Silence. "So you did."

The porter came out and rang the bells, letting the guests know it was time to bustle back to their seats for the second act. As people began shuffling around them, Max pulled Gail to a stop.

"Just a moment, Gai—, er, Miss Alton," Max stuttered, Gail watching him, wide-eyed, "I didn't come out here to discuss the opera repeatedly. I wish—nay, I need to apologize for this afternoon. Once I reflected on the events, I realized I took some liberties I shouldn't have, and I'm sorry for it."

Gail turned as red as the velvet stage curtain.

"Don't." She held up a hand.

"Don't?" Max asked, his eyes lifting from his toes to her face.

"Don't you dare apologize. I realize I may not be fantastically beautiful or captivating, but when a girl finally receives a really good kiss, the last thing she wants is to have the man say he's sorry for it. It's insulting."

"I didn't mean to be insulting!" Max replied, almost grabbing her arms to keep her from walking away, but managing to keep them at his sides. "Gail—Miss Alton. I just meant it's my fault, my doing that it occurred in the first place. It was very warm in the room, and . . ." He coughed and started again. "I'm certainly not importuning the *quality* of the kiss, but more bearing the responsibility for it in the first place."

"Oh," Gail replied, unaccountably relieved. "I don't believe you to be responsible. We were both there."

"Luckily we were the only ones," Max grumbled. And then, with an imploring look, "it can't happen again, Miss Alton."

Her eyes shot up, wide. "Well, of course not. I know that." Her cheeks stained with remembrance of his hand on the back of her neck, the zip of warmth at his lips on hers. "No. Absolutely not," she stated firmly.

"So, we're friends?" Max asked, holding out his hand.

Gail smiled. "At the rate we're going, we'll need to repair our relationship every fifteen minutes. But, yes, we're friends." When she shook his outstretched hand, he took hers and wrapped it around his arm, and they began walking back to the box.

Gail smiled, glad to be at ease with him again, in silent harmony. They were nearly at the door of their box when Max again pulled her to a stop.

"What do you mean, you finally received a 'really good kiss'?"

Gail rolled her eyes. "I was so hoping you missed that."

"Not a chance," he said with satisfaction and that lopsided smile that made her heart flutter. It was highly annoying.

She sighed at his preening. "Well, simply put, every other time I've been seriously kissed, I found it rather fishy."

The preening stopped. Max's mouth hung open wordlessly before he sputtered a reply. "You're eighteen! And you've been kissed by other men before me?"

"Only two. I lived in Europe, Max," Gail said, as if that answered everything. Although clearly it did not, because Max's jaw was still agape.

"Max," Gail sighed. "Have you been kissed before?"

"Yes."

"How many times?"

"I doubt I could count," he answered, bewildered. The lights were getting very low now.

"How old were you when you were first kissed?" she continued, even as other couples made their way past them to be seated for the next act.

"I guess I was thirteen or so. Sally Smithson. Milkmaid." After a wistful pause, Max asked, "What is your point?"

"I'm simply trying to do the math," Gail explained. "This is a societal double standard I have never been able to understand. Men have been kissing since they were quite young, and have kissed many times, and this is considered normal. Yet, women are expected to keep their lips to themselves until they are ready to be married. But if this is always so, who are all these men kissing? Either the world is blindingly unrealistic in its expectations of women, or young boys are practicing on each other."

For a short moment, Max couldn't speak, and then the laughter came, bubbling from his chest until it threatened to echo across the whole opera house.

"Sssh!" Gail whispered furiously, covering his mouth with her hand. "What on earth did I say that was worthy of this?"

Max gently removed the hand across his mouth, placing a gentle kiss on the palm before lowering it. "Oh, Miss Alton—to hell with it. Gail. I'm so very glad I am not grouped with your fishy European kissers. And I am delighted that we are friends." Max smiled, his chuckles continuing as he escorted a bemused Gail back into the box just as the curtain was about to rise.

* * *

THEY each took their seats, no one in the box the wiser to their conversation, no one commenting that Gail had left with one gentleman and was escorted back by another. That's not to say it went unnoticed. In the back of the box, Romilla's eyes shone and sharpened as she focused not on the opera playing out on stage, but rather on the drama of the young couples seated in front of her.

Twenty

AND thus the unusual friendship of Gail Alton and Max Fontaine came to be. They didn't stop bickering with each other, as some had hoped, nor did they fall dramatically into each other's arms, as some had feared. Rather, when they bickered over intellectual pursuits, it was all in good fun (even though Max was known to get rather red-faced every time Gail corrected his pronunciation of some arcane past participle translation), and they found they could speak more freely with each other than any other person in their lives. When they were in public, they were uncommonly well mannered and were known to seek out the other's company, but nothing beyond what was considered appropriate.

However, the whispers still began.

At a card party hosted by the Fortings, Gail was sitting in on a rubber of whist, with Max at her table. As he divested himself of his three of diamonds, he chanced to look up at Gail, and saw on her face an expression that took his breath away.

She wasn't looking at anything in particular. She was lost in her own mind, remembering some other place and time, and it caused her to smile in a wistful, long-off sort of way. A little upturn of her lips, promising secrets. What was she thinking of? Max wondered. Exploring the ruins of Athens? Riding her horse wearing that silly hat? A joke that she holds on to just for herself? Him?

Gail suddenly snapped back to reality when Lady Charlbury prodded her with her walking stick. Gail played her card and turned to Max. Seeing that he stared, she blushed. After he played another card, he leaned in and said very casually, "I saw that."

Gail tried to school her features into impassivity, but failed, smiling even as she kept her gaze on her cards.

"So what?" she spoke just as casually, but with a hint of bold humor. Her turn had come around again, and she played. "Why shouldn't I smile and laugh? It's not illegal, after all."

"No, it isn't," Max agreed and played another card. "I'm simply glad I got to see it."

Lady Charlbury kept her smirk hidden behind her cards. She was intrigued to see such an easy exchange. She kept her countenance about the friendly manner between Lord Fontaine and Miss Gail, but most certainly felt justified in her earlier observations about the pair. However, Mrs. Fortings, who made up the table's fourth, did not have Lady Charlbury's foresight, nor did she have her desire for reticence. Later that evening, when all the guests had left, she took a moment to mention the exchange to her husband, adding, "But I thought he had compromised the elder sister."

Later the same week, at a musicale hosted by Mrs. Brenton, Max had taken refuge from a truly horrific young flutist making her stage debut by hiding in a far, darkened corner of the room near the refreshment table. He was edging his way toward the door and freedom, when a low whisper reached his ears and a gloved hand took hold of his.

"Don't you dare leave." Gail's fingers squeezed his palm, holding him still in his steps. The darkness veiled such a familiarity, and he felt the warmth surge through their connected hands.

"Where did you come from?" he whispered, taking a silent step toward her.

"Behind the potted palm," she replied. "I got up to use the

powder room before the last concerto, but Mrs. Brenton came in, and so I had to return. I thought if I hid back here I could at least put my fingers in my ears and no one would see."

Max looked at the potted plant. It could conceal one person easily, but not two. Just as he was entertaining notions of squeezing back there and standing very, very close to Gail, the young flutist hit an obscenely sharp note, causing all the guests to visibly cringe.

"I think my ears are bleeding," Max hissed, once the fatal note had passed.

"The worst of it is, my father specifically said we weren't going to attend this musicale," Gail whispered. "But I suppose Romilla got a hold of the social schedule, and . . . here we are."

The flutist paused, and the pained audience took the offered chance to applaud loudly, hoping to end the torment. Unfortunately, the girl was so very pleased with this reaction, she immediately launched into an encore, thus starting the torture all over again.

"I will pay you if you help me escape," Max pleaded lowly to Gail, who grinned evilly.

"And what would you be willing to forfeit?" she asked too charmingly for his peace of mind. Oh, the images in his head, the innocence of those golden eyes! Before he could explore that tantalizing line of thought, she shrugged and turned her gaze back to the performance.

"If I'm forced to stay, so are you. We'll bear the torture together."

"What good is that? You bear the torture, and tell me about it later," Max countered, but Gail rolled her eyes.

"Men. Honestly, you get squeamish at the veriest bit of pain and leave women to do all the hard labor."

At that moment, the flutist was the worst torture Max could imagine, so he readily agreed. "Yes, you are correct. Men are weak and cowardly in the face of bad music. Women are strong and resolute. Now may I sneak off?"

"Well, since you asked so nicely . . ." Gail said sweetly, "not a chance."

At his answering cry of outrage, heads turned, and the

music fumbled. However, Max gave credit to the performer—she rallied, playing louder than before in the hopes sheer volume would cover any mistakes of technique. A few sets of eyes, including Mrs. Brenton's, scanned the darkness near their hiding place. But soon enough, everyone's attention returned to the unblinking horror before them, and Max felt safe enough to exhale.

Gail smiled at Max in the darkness, her hand still grasping his. She leaned up, her mouth very near his ear, her breath warming his cheek.

"Learn to enjoy your torture, Max. It's the only way to get through it." Her voice was barely more than a series of breaths. Max's head turned, his eyes searching her impish ones in the darkness. It was really no more than a matter of inches, to lean down . . .

The "music" stopped. Mercifully, the applause began, and the extra candles were employed, quickly bringing up the light in the room and cutting off the performer with the finality of a long-hooked cane.

Mrs. Brenton was the first to whip her head around, looking for the source of the recent distraction, and spied Lord Fontaine and the younger Miss Alton, nonchalantly picking up glasses of refreshment. As she commented to Lady Hurstwood later that week, Lord Fontaine was spending a great amount of time with the younger Miss Alton. Wasn't he courting the elder?

It was unfortunate that when this comment was being made over hatboxes on Bond Street, Romilla was within audible distance, concealed behind a pile of striped cambric.

* * *

AND so it was, that when Gail hopped down the steps on a Tuesday morning shortly thereafter, her stepmother met her at the bottom.

"Good morning," she said, in a cheery tone. "Am I late for tea?"

"No, Abigail," Romilla began, meeting her happy countenance with a sober resolution.

"Excellent. I should hate to keep Lord Fontaine and Evan-

geline waiting. We are to go to the botanical gardens today."
As Gail smiled and began to move past Romilla toward the
drawing room, Romilla caught her arm.

"They aren't waiting," Romilla said quietly.

Gail turned inquiringly to her stepmother.

"I sent a note to Lord Fontaine last evening that he should
escort Evangeline out at ten o'clock, so she wouldn't miss her
afternoon appointments."

Gail's mouth worked for a few moments without any
sound. "They've already gone?" she finally croaked out. At
Romilla's nod, Gail sputtered, "But who will see them at ten
o'clock? And what about a chaperone?"

"They've a maid with them," Romilla replied.

"You . . . you said they needed to have a family member
with them, to ensure that it seemed the family was accepting
Max."

Gail realized her mistake, even before she saw the scowl
blacken Romilla's face. She shouldn't be surprised to see
steam pouring out of her stepmother's ears.

It was a few moments and one visibly deep breath before
Romilla spoke.

"Abigail," she began, her voice pitched low and soothing,
"I'm glad you are getting along with Lord Fontaine now. It
would not do to have bad blood stand between him and this
family. But being friends doesn't allow such extreme familiarity as calling him by his Christian name, does it?"

"No, ma'am," Gail mumbled, her eyes downcast.

"I think it's time," her stepmother continued, taking Gail
by the arm and leading her toward the drawing room, "that
we allow Lord Fontaine and Evangeline to go out in public
alone together. Now that everyone knows our family wel-
comes him, we shall show society that we trust him. Don't
you agree?"

"Yes, ma'am."

If this was all part of Romilla's grand plan, then Gail had
no choice but to go along with it, but, for some reason, it hurt.
She had been looking forward to this outing ever since Max
had suggested it.

"Now, shore up your disappointment, my dear," Romilla

said with forced enthusiasm. "If you still desire to see the botanical gardens, I will have your father escort us next week. Will that do?" Gail could only nod numbly, and Romilla forged ahead. "Besides, we have quite the morning planned ourselves." She flung open the drawing room doors. "Look who's come to visit us! Mrs. Pickering and her two daughters. We shall spend a delightful tea together, and after, Mrs. Pickering has promised to take us to the most adorable new millinery, where we'll find some excellent ribbon for your new green frock."

Gail could only smile weakly. Mrs. Pickering and her twin daughters, Lilly and Lavender, sat in the front parlor, yawning into their hands. These girls were easily the simplest, most empty-headed females in the northern hemisphere. Add their company for shopping for ribbons—Gail could not picture a more horrendously boring waste of time.

She forced her shoulders back, perfectly straightening her posture.

"What fun," Gail said, smiling tremulously at the ladies before her.

* * *

BY three o'clock that afternoon, it was Romilla, not Gail, who was ready to throttle the Pickering ladies.

Being this insipid must be a crime. Oh, they were nice enough, she supposed, but there was not a single original thought in their heads. They debated shades of gray, as if they were discussing matters of life and death, for heaven's sake! While in Markham's Millinery (which Romilla was quite unimpressed with, as she had been there at least thrice before and never found what she wanted) Lilly had been threatened with not being allowed to attend the next Almack's assembly if she did not make a decision between two gray-colored velvet ribbons. The weight of the decision had the girl near to tears, and even Romilla, who prided herself on her fashion sense and attention to detail, wanted to scream: *What does it matter? It's just a silly ribbon!*

Indeed, it was just a silly ribbon, singular. Gail pointed this out, when she noticed that Mrs. Pickering was unknowingly holding up two ends of the same length of gray velvet. Romilla wanted to cheer her daughter for putting an end to the circuitous hell of choosing between the same ribbon, but alas, Mrs. Pickering picked up two more, this time in revolting shades of pink and assaulted Lavender with them.

Luckily, time did not stop moving, as it often threatened to do on particularly horrendous afternoons, and the Pickerings and the Altons were soon forced to part company.

"We simply must do this again!" Mrs. Pickering said, clasping to her bosom the hand of her newest, best friend, Romilla, who was doing an admirable job of not yanking her appendage away.

"What a, pleasant afternoon, Mrs. Pickering. I'll look forward to our next meeting," Romilla replied, and, with a sharp kick to Gail, prompted a wry, "Can't wait."

"Such a pleasure!" and, "That green ribbon is perfect for you. Never had a better time shopping!" were the hurried good-byes from Lilly and Lavender, and the Pickerings departed the carriage and walked into their own home, Mrs. Pickering dictating to the footman about their parcels and to her daughters about their evening along the way. Once the door to Number Eight was closed, Romilla signaled to the driver to go forward the sixty feet to Number Seven. Silence reigned in the carriage, until Gail, as was her marked habit, simply had to say something.

"Please tell me we are never doing that again."

Romilla shot her stepdaughter a quelling glance, but then weariness pushed all the bluster out of her.

"Never in a million years would I subject us to that again," she intoned seriously.

Gail smiled. And then she chuckled. And then she laughed. And Romilla couldn't help it—she laughed, too.

"Why?" Gail asked through her laughter. "Just, *why*?"

"Oh, they are nice enough when we see them at parties"— Romilla was nearly crying, she was laughing so hard—"or when we've had them over for a morning with a dozen other people, for only a half hour at a time—but a whole day? Of undiluted Pickerings? I must have been mad!"

"Oh, that is too cruel, Romilla! They weren't all bad. Lilly took quite an interest in hearing about Lisbon." The carriage had rolled to a stop, and Romilla and Gail headed up the walk.

"Yes," Romilla agreed, "but you may want to correct the impression you left that all Portuguese women have extra toes."

"Oh!" Gail clapped a hand over her mouth. "I had nearly forgotten!"

Over tea that morning, in an effort to stay awake, Gail had engaged Lilly on the subject of foreign travel. As Lilly had never been out of the country, she didn't have much to contribute to the subject, instead inquired about the fashions in France, Vienna, and Portugal. Gail was caught, as she had no real interest in the subtleties of fashion, but knew enough to note that in Lisbon, the ladies' shoes were cut a bit wider.

"That's curious. Lavender, isn't that curious? How strange to have wider shoes. I wonder why?" Lilly pondered aloud. Gail couldn't help but murmur, "to accommodate their extra toes?"

Lilly did not note, or perhaps did not comprehend, the sarcasm. Instead, she leapt upon this information, peppering Gail with questions about other deformities of foreign people.

Really, the girl was quite macabre.

Before a stunned Gail could set any assumptions to right, Romilla intervened, declaring it time to go to Bond Street.

"I suppose I'll have to invite them over for another afternoon," Gail mused, delighting in Romilla's aghast expression. "I should hate to leave Lilly with a false impression."

Romilla chewed her lower lip as they walked through the front door. "Consider for a moment," she finally said, "how often is that girl going to meet a real live Portuguese anyway?"

Gail laughed again, and Romilla joined in, visibly pleased. Could it be that they were easy together? Maybe even *enjoying* each other's company? How surprising—and yet, how wonderful, too.

As they handed their coats and bonnets to Morrison, he informed them that Lord Fontaine was in the drawing room with Miss Evangeline. Romilla, seeing Gail's pleading look, figured that the young couple had enjoyed plenty of their own company for one day and waved the girl to the drawing room, saying, "Go ahead and join them. I'll be by in a moment, but first I want a minute with your father. Is he in the library, Morrison?"

Morrison nodded.

"Good," said Romilla.

Gail didn't even hear the last part. She gave a quick curtsy to Romilla and shot off down the hall to join her sister and friend (for that's what Max truly was now) to tell them all about her deliciously awful afternoon.

But when she opened the doors to the drawing room, she was thrown completely off balance.

Max and Evangeline sat on the couch entwined in a lover's embrace. They were so very close to one another, knees touching, Max's hands around Evangeline's neck. She was looking up into his face, his back to Gail. The embracing couple took no notice of the new arrival to the room, until Gail gave a small involuntary gasp.

"Gail!" Evangeline cried, extracting herself. "You're back! How was—" But the sentence was to never be finished. With a ruthlessly brisk gesture, Gail cut her off.

"Romilla's on her way. Probably best to cut the lovemaking short." And with that, she closed the drawing room door and took off down the hall.

Gail found herself in the warmth and light of the conservatory before she realized she was crying. She sat on the stone bench by the fountain and let the tears flow.

Twenty-one

MAX left Number Seven that afternoon, a confusion of feeling, growing for some time now, massed into a giant knot in his stomach.

He had, in accordance with Romilla's request, arrived a half hour earlier than usual that morning, ready to take Evangeline and Gail to the botanical gardens. When Romilla told him before he even had the chance to take off his hat that she and Gail had plans for the day, and that this was his opportunity to escort Evangeline without familial supervision, he should have been thrilled. Or at least, a little relieved. But all he felt was uncommonly let down, as if he was a lad whose favorite mate had to stay in and do chores instead of coming out to play.

However, he put those feelings aside the moment he saw Evangeline, a vision in a light blue pelisse and matching dress. Max began to rationalize his situation. This was good, he thought, this was progress. He would have the opportunity to spend more time with Evangeline, getting to know his bride-to-be. After all, they had been courting for three weeks now—soon, people would be expecting an announcement. It was best to know as much as possible about his partner in life before the wedding . . . or was it after? He always mixed up that proverb. So Max and Evangeline set forth in his hired (but beautifully appointed) phaeton, to enjoy the warm day at the botanical gardens and each other's solitary company.

Max should have been able to enjoy himself. Even a little bit. But the more he was in Evangeline's company, lovely and kind as she was, the more Max found himself at odds. They had very little in common. Max loved books. Evangeline loved art and sketching more. Max loved to go riding. Evangeline barely ever touched a horse. Evangeline delighted in the country—Max considered himself far more citified. One would think that a devoted couple would easily overcome these things, but in two people so undetermined in their feelings but locked into their fates, such differences acted as bricks, stacking one on top of the other, into a wall between them. There was no movement, no room for debate. With Gail, there was always debate, Max thought, but at least it was interesting. Evangeline was just . . . not interesting to him.

Even though spring had bloomed into its lush green glory, the botanical gardens were quite empty that day, and Max counted only a few other couples as they toured the grounds, too engrossed in the various plants or each other to give more than a passing glance to Lord Fontaine escorting Miss Alton. As they toured through hothouses of blooming exotic flowers, tall palms, and winding mahogany trees, Max's memory was drawn back to Number Seven's conservatory and a particular moonlit night.

"This place reminds me of when we first met," he said, attempting a smile, pulling a flower from a vine overhead and offering it in what he hoped was a besotted manner to Evangeline, but she simply bit her lip and looked at her toes.

"Lord Fontaine," she said, not looking up, "I do wish that you wouldn't bring that up."

"How we met?" Max asked, lowering the flower.

"Yes," Evangeline said, now worrying her gloves a bit, her eyes warily darting to the sides. "It's terribly embarrassing. I don't usually act that rashly, and the consequences thereof are already known to both of us. It was wholly out of character, and . . . it is not a moment I take pride in remembering."

Max felt the air leave him. In his head, he recalled the night he met Evangeline as magical, filled with moonlight and romance and hope. In fact, he had clung to their first meeting as the sole evidence of their mutual attraction, the proof they could possibly enjoy each other. But to hear that she did not feel the same, that she considered that moment not worth remembering, regrettable even . . . it destroyed the already crumbling illusion of that night as completely as sunlight would have.

They walked on through the hothouses quietly now, silent in their defeat. Max still twirled the small flower he had picked in his fingers. Offering it again to Evangeline, she smiled sweetly and accepted it, with thanks.

However, when tucking the flower into her buttonhole, she did add, "I don't think we're allowed to pick these, though."

They left the gardens sullenly, not finding anything further to distract them from having to converse with each other.

Later, making their way up Bond Street, they stopped for ices at the public rooms. Since the intent was to be seen in society together, Romilla had made certain their itinerary had included this stop, and Max, for one, was glad for it. It gave them something to focus on other than each other.

They were in the public rooms not five minutes before Will Holt came to greet them.

"Fontaine! Miss Alton! A pleasure." Will bent over Evangeline's hand as she smiled widely at the new addition to the party. Will stayed with them for nearly a quarter of an hour, regaling them with stories of how his father and Count Roffstaam were fairing since the ambassador had abandoned his rented apartments to become a guest at the Holts' London residence. However, it seemed the only person in the house who spoke passable German was the Holts's French cook, who, it was discovered, was of rather dubious origins.

"So the Count, who really is quite a jolly chap, if a little stiff (can you believe he took me to task for wearing trousers instead of breeches!), is every five minutes in the pantry, asking the cook to come up and translate something or other, and the cook is ready to beat him about the head with a chicken for interrupting her work. This, naturally, has my mother in fits and my father in giggles," Will recounted to a laughing Evangeline, who had somehow during the course of the conversation transferred herself from Max's arm to Will's, and was now the picture of ladylike flirtation. Max stood some two steps away, enjoying Will's story, but more pleased by the fact that for the first time that afternoon, Evangeline looked to be enjoying herself.

It was odd, really, Max thought, frowning. He should be jealous. He should be protective. But he wasn't. He liked Evangeline, he did, but it just didn't go further than that.

Would it ever?

Before Max could ruminate further on this latest and most disturbing of thoughts, Will was bowing over Evangeline's hand to take his leave.

"Are you certain you can't join us back at Number Seven?" Evangeline asked with a pretty pout.

"Alas, no," Will answered with real regret. "I am due at Jackson's, then the Holt offices. But I look forward to our next meeting."

Evangeline's light and joyful demeanor immediately fell when Will left. She and Max both attempted to buoy the conversation, but by the time they reached Number Seven's drawing room, they had once again dissolved into silence. The only thing that broke the tedium was when Evangeline leaned forward to grab a biscuit from the tea tray (besides affording Max a slight peak of cleavage—and how had the situation deteriorated when even that didn't inspire him beyond mild interest?), and her necklace, a precariously delicate looking thing, became unclasped and landed on his shoe.

"Oh dear," Evangeline cried, placing a hand to her now unadorned neck. "It was my mother's. Is it broken?"

"I don't believe so," Max said as he retrieved and examined the small gold chain and cross that adorned it. "It looks unharmed. Just came undone." He held it up for Evangeline to see, and her worried face broke out into a relieved smile.

As Evangeline tried and failed to clasp the necklace back in place herself, Max scooted closer on the couch and offered assistance. Taking her hands in his, he said, "Here, allow me."

As he fastened the chain back in place, Evangeline sat very calmly and still. Max was overcome with the realization that this was the first time he was touching Evangeline, really touching her, in any manner that might be deemed inappropriate since that fateful night in the conservatory.

And he felt nothing.

He had his arms wrapped around her neck, his face inches from hers, and any sane man would have taken the opportunity to pull such a delectable morsel close for a kiss. But he didn't. Nor did he care to.

He really must be going mad.

Of course, the fates being what they are, the doors opened at that moment.

And then Gail's stunned and crestfallen face appeared.

By the time he took his leave, Gail had not returned, and Max was deeply mired in his own conflicting thoughts. One thing remained clear, though—he wanted to speak with Gail, alone, at the next possible opportunity.

And there was only one time and place that Max knew he would have the chance.

* * *

"NOW, Jupiter, I know you are excited to see your beloved again, but I beg you: This time, try not to charge her down."

It was far too early in the morning for anyone of quality to be taking a ride, which, as Max had been informed by Jimmy, was exactly why Miss Gail took her rides now. He was also furnished with a general sketch of Gail's morning routes through the park's lesser-worn paths by the accommodating groom—along with a wink and a nod. Jimmy, it seemed, understood the situation better than Max did himself.

So, Max found himself on a winding path of the park, the dew still wet on the ground, waiting for Gail to appear.

She seemed to be taking her time, Max grumbled to himself, as he tucked his hands under his arms to keep them warm.

He checked his pocket watch, his breath still visible in the cool morning air.

It was obscenely early. *Duels* were fought this early. Maybe, Max considered, one was being fought today, right now, in this very park. If Gail was going to be a while it might be interesting to watch a duel, provided he could find it. Maybe near the Serpentine.

"Ruminating, my lord, when you should be watching your horse? No wonder you end up in lakes."

Her voice broke through his reverie, just in time for Max to take up the slack in Jupiter's reins, who was all too eager to greet QueenBee again.

"Whoa! Whoa there," Max said, calming his besotted mount. Once Jupiter was back in line, Max turned his attention to Gail.

All gold eyes and wry quirks of the mouth. A flush heightened the color of her cheeks, as if she had just come off a good run, breathing heavily. The deep green velvet habit was expertly cut emphasizing her surprisingly striking figure and the rise and fall of her breasts. A fetching froth of a hat in matching green topped the pile of her thick hair, completing the picture. Max was struck by how pretty she was. He always thought her nicely put together, but now, he couldn't stop staring. Did she even realize it?

Max caught sight of movement behind Gail and saw Jimmy sitting atop a gray mare. He was giving them a respectable distance, Max realized, while trying to stifle a grin. Again, Jimmy saw things Max himself was blind to.

Remembering his manners and purpose, Max tipped his hat in greeting. "Good morning, Miss Alton."

"Good morning." She nodded, that open humor never leaving her face. "Dare I ask what you're doing here at this hour?"

Max opened his mouth to reply, but could not find the words to his well-practiced speech. Instead, "Where's your hat?" fell from his lips.

"My hat?" Gail replied, reaching up to pat the smart green cap pinned to her coiffure.

"Not that one. The, uh, the squashed brown one."

"Oh." She looked embarrassed, smoothing a hand over her hair. "Don't you think this one's better?"

"Well, yes. And no. This one's very nice, but it doesn't seem very, er, you," Max answered truthfully.

Looking acutely uncomfortable, Gail forced her attentions back to QueenBee's nervous prancing.

"Why are you riding so early, Max?"

"In the hope of meeting you."

She blinked at him. "Well," her voice finally came, sounding a bit strangled, "your quick honesty is becoming unnerving, Max."

"I wanted you to know," Max began, then cleared his throat and nerves, and began again.

"You should know that, yesterday, when you arrived back at the house, you did not see an indiscretion."

"I know," Gail replied quickly.

"Your sister's necklace had fallen and I was helping her put it back on."

"I know," she repeated, stopping Max short. "Evangeline told me once you had left. After brief consideration, I came to the conclusion that you might have learned your lesson about attempting to ravage young ladies—at least in their own homes."

It was a cautious joke. It teased him and yet boldly invoked their encounter in the library. When he laughed, he watched a visibly relieved Gail join in.

Max walked Jupiter forward, so now he was face-to-face with Gail. Reaching over, he lifted her gloved hand from her reins and kissed it.

"Thank you," he said. He didn't release her hand.

"You're welcome," she returned. "For what?"

"For forgiving me. For being my friend." Max met her eyes, sincere.

"Max, there is nothing to forgive! You said it yourself, it was wholly innocent. Besides, you're to marry—" He cut her off with a wave of his hand.

"Gail, what you saw, no matter how innocent or indiscreet, gave you a shock. And above everything else, I never want to hurt you."

Gail didn't breathe for a moment. "I . . . I wasn't hurt," she lied.

Liar, he thought, but held his tongue, and with a final squeeze, released her hand.

So it followed, and nothing seemed more natural than that Gail and Max should spend the early morning ride together. Max allowed Gail to lead the way, who chose to pick various paths at random. The morning grew brighter, as the dew slowly began to lift from the grass in tufts of mist. When they reached fields with enough space, they raced. When they came to a path with only enough space for two riders walking closely, they used it to their advantage and talked.

"Why don't you ever speak?" Max asked.

Seeing as Gail had just given him a lengthy discourse on the perils of shopping with the Pickerings, she was understandably confused.

"In public," he clarified. "You have improved since I've known you, but you are still too often silent when out in society. You'll speak to me, to Holt, your family, and Lady Charlbury. And God knows you'll lecture to anybody who stands still long enough when in your cups, but in every other situation, you shrink back against the walls, into a shell."

"I have found that my tongue gets me into trouble," she replied, suddenly preoccupied with twisting a lock of hair.

"But you're brilliant," Max countered, pushing aside a branch. "You should be the darling of every dinner party."

"Don't call me brilliant," Gail said, blushing quite furiously now. "It'll go to my head."

"Maybe some things should go to your head," he argued.

Gail, her face scarlet, dropped her hand from her hair. "I'll go too far."

Max pulled Jupiter to a stop, and QueenBee followed suit. "Why do you think that?"

She sighed, admitted defeat. "You're asking to know the worst of me," she whispered.

"You already know the worst of me," Max replied softly.

Gail held his gaze for a full minute, as the sway of a light breeze through the low branches mixed with the caw of far off birds.

"I can trust you," she breathed softly. It was a statement, not a question.

Max nodded imperceptibly. That was the first truth of their young friendship. Even when they had hated each other, they had trusted. Turning her head forward, Gail gave Queen-Bee a light nudge, starting a slow canter along the path. Max silently kept pace.

"About a year ago, my family was in Lisbon," Gail began. "My father was assigned to the British Embassy there—in particular, he was asked to make friends with and earn the confidence of a man in trade relations, Don Basti. He was invited to our house often for dinners and parties as was his son Josef. We had only been in Portugal a few weeks when we first met them, so I didn't know the language yet. As time went by, I picked it up, but the Bastis remained unaware of my knowledge. I was so newly out of the schoolroom, I guess I didn't know my limits, but honestly, I shouldn't have tested them."

Gail paused to take a breath and shot Max a nervous smile. He didn't smile in return, but he nodded, let her know he wanted to hear more.

"About this time," she continued, "Romilla came into our lives. She met my father at some function, and they took to each other. She was always visiting, on the pretense of having taken a liking to Evangeline and me, but we knew—she always had eyes for Father.

"One afternoon, while Romilla was over for tea, the Bastis stopped by, this time accompanied by the second son, Paul. Don Basti went to speak with my father, but the younger 'gentlemen' joined us. When taking tea, Paul said in a low voice, and in Portuguese, that Josef had been right, Evangeline and I would be fun for what he termed a 'double-toss.' "

Max nearly fell off his horse. "He said what?"

"A double-toss. I took it to mean he wanted to seduce both of us at the same time," Gail explained baldly.

"And what"—Max nearly choked—"left you with that interpretation?"

"He went on to categorize our various differences. Light and dark, short and tall. Some other anatomical contrasts I'd like to avoid repeating." She shrugged. "Variety is the spice of life, apparently."

She told her story with a detached, uninvolved air, but Max knew that was for her own protection. It still made her angry. It still hurt. He was suddenly overcome with the desperate desire to hunt down the Basti brothers and dismember them. His shoulders shook with the effort of keeping control. But in his anger, Max remembered his own drawing room conversation in different tongues.

"God, you must think me an ass."

She looked up sharply. "Why?"

"Because of what I said that day—the, uh, mundane things. In other languages. I'm amazed now that you didn't slay me down to size. I certainly deserved it. Hell, I'd box my own ears if I could."

"Oh." She blushed. "Well, as I said—you *were* terribly mundane, Max. Hardly worth a comment."

Knowing that he had been forgiven for one of his earliest stupidities, Max reached over and squeezed her hand. "Please," he managed, "continue."

"Well, you have likely guessed by now that I was the only one in the room who understood what they said." At his nod, she went on. "My face was burning. I was so angry, but Evangeline and Romilla were laughing and being entertaining with Josef and Paul because they didn't know. That made me angrier than anything—it was like they were laughing at us."

What was it she had said? Gentlemen had proved to be far more vulgar than any commoner. This must be a key piece of evidence in her theory.

"When my father entered the room, with Don Basti, they looked inordinately pleased. Only later did I find out they had just come to terms on a deal. Don Basti made the suggestion that we all go out that evening together. And when Paul had the audacity to take my hand and ask me if I would enjoy such an excursion—"

"Oh no," Max moaned.

"Oh yes, I'm afraid," Gail replied. "I told him, in English, that I would sooner swallow my own tongue than willingly spend an afternoon in their company."

Max's jaw dropped. "Oh, God."

"That alone would have been bad enough, but I added, in Portuguese, a few less than complimentary names I picked up from my rambles around town. The, er, dockside, in particular."

That was, Max thought, without a doubt, the cruelest, sharpest, and most deserved slight he had ever heard. He could well imagine being so young, so angered to have lost one's temper, but Gail's brand of retort was an art. He had to laugh.

So he did. Long and loud and with his full body. But this time, Gail did not join in.

"Please don't laugh," she pleaded weakly. "It was a terrible, mean thing to say."

Max immediately sobered, and but for a hiccup or two, sounded appropriately subdued.

"You regret saying it, don't you?" he asked.

"Yes. No. They were abominable, awful men, and the way they looked at Evie made my skin crawl. But afterward, I learned that what I say can have serious repercussions. I had my ears blistered for days. Even after I had explained what the so-called 'gentlemen' had said. A week or so later, Don Basti changed his position on the exporting agreement. My father was so frustrated . . ." Her voice trailed off, lost in her own thoughts.

"Sometimes I think half the reason he married Romilla was to have a female around to teach me how to be a lady," she said. "The other half was so she wouldn't spread the tale of my uncouth behavior. She has tried to teach me, you know. How to demur, how to be gracious and flattering. It hasn't worked very well. It's just so much easier to sit in a corner and be quiet." She finished her discourse with a noncommittal shrug, as if to distance herself from her feelings by pretending nonchalance. But the air of sadness permeated her being, and Max, for one, would not stand by and let her pretend it didn't hurt.

"You should never temper yourself. No, listen to me." Max approached Gail, reached out and took her head in his hands, forced her eyes to meet his. "You felt as you did and spoke accordingly. And very bravely, too. God save me from simpering females who never speak their minds—I would go mad. You are a clever, witty, cynical, passionate gale force wind and you can't hide that under a bushel. So, please, for my sake—don't even try. Besides"—he smiled—"this is the worst of you? I've heard nuns speak with more bite."

Gail smiled in return. "Well, nuns are married to God. That offers them some protection, don't you think?"

His fingers were burning from the electricity of touching her skin again. But more he was burning from the liquid gold of her eyes. Jimmy was nowhere to be seen. They were wholly alone. Her scent as she passed him in the drawing room, her smile and sparkling eyes when she laughed at something only he understood, the torment of remembering her warm mouth opening to his had been torturing him for weeks. And now, here she was, so close, and he was touching her. His rough thumb caressed the soft skin at the nape of her neck. He looked into her eyes, and saw them go dark with passion. With hunger.

With fear.

Fear won out. Gail broke eye contact, instead searching the surrounding woods.

"Where are we?" she asked, her voice a pitch too high for his liking.

Max searched her face, and reluctantly let his hand fall. It was a loss, the cool air now separating them, the longing to touch again. But he pulled back.

Turning Jupiter about, he took stock of his surroundings and was amazed at what he found.

"I've been here before," Max whispered, awed. Somehow, in the course of the rambling paths and deep conversation, Gail had led them to the long forgotten grotto. The sun now rose in the sky instead of setting, but it was unmistakably his same grotto. The ruined Grecian gazebo stood, now with vines in full leaf twining up its columns. The silence here was overreaching. No breezes brushed through the trees, no clip-clops from horse hooves in the soft earth. The only sounds were their own breathing and the faint rustling of some birds hiding in high sycamore trees that edged the magical place. The colors of a deepened spring were in full life here, and Gail was open-mouthed in her appreciation.

"It's beautiful," she breathed.

Max dismounted, then helped Gail down. As Jupiter and QueenBee nuzzled each other and munched on the grass, Max explained how he had come across the grotto before. "I looked for it again every day, but I never found it," he finished.

"I can understand your quest," Gail replied. They walked to the gazebo, simply reveling in their surroundings. Max suddenly realized that he had never relinquished Gail's hand from when he assisted her dismount. He also noticed that she did not ask for its release.

"Do you know," Max said, regarding the gazebo, "I have no idea why it was so popular to build something that is crumbling."

"It is silly," she conceded. "But it's romantic, too, for an illusion. We're meant to pretend that this gazebo is just as old as the trees." Gail offered a grin, although the light did not reach her eyes.

"You're still thinking about it, aren't you?" Max asked. "Lisbon?"

"A little," Gail hemmed. "I just worry too much about making a mess of things."

Max squeezed her hand. "I am suddenly overwhelmed by this feeling that you will be just fine."

"Why is that?" she questioned.

He laced his fingers through hers. "Because when no one's watching," he whispered, "you're fearless."

A blushing smile of honest and brilliant light overtook her face. And suddenly every nerve in Max's body was tingling.

Just as suddenly, the crows in the trees sang their fierce cry and an amount of rustling predicted they would soon take flight.

"Oh!" Gail said, looking up into the air, "Crows! Max, quick, how many do you see?"

"Ah." Max spun around, his ears breaking as cries rent the perfect tranquility of the grotto, but he couldn't actually see any birds in flight. Suddenly, a small blur of black lifted from the top of the sycamore and crossed through the sky.

"One," he answered, looking back to Gail. She faced the other direction, her eyes scanning the treetops.

"I only saw one, as well," she said ominously. "That's not good."

"Why ever not?"

"Crows! You have to count them. 'One for sorrow, two for joy, three for a girl and four for a boy, five for silver, six for gold, seven for a secret, never to be told.' "

He pulled her closer. "A bit superstitious, aren't you?" he asked, a laugh in his voice.

"What makes you say that?" Gail countered, her eyes still desperately roving the treetops.

"The crows. The dire need to avoid the number thirteen."

"Oh. That's not superstition, Max. I simply prefer not to tempt fate." She worried her lower lip. Max was tempted to roll his eyes, but instead he took hold of her neck with his free hand, his thumb caressing the sensitive line of her jaw. Her eyes stopped scanning the skies, and after closing them blissfully, briefly, she turned her gaze to his.

"Don't worry, Gail. You saw one, and I saw one. That's two for joy." His voice was a low, warm rumble.

"That's not two," she argued. "That's one for you, and one for me. Two sorrows cannot make one joy."

"Yes, they can." His eyes grew dark, feral. Hungry.

"How?" she asked, barely a whisper.

The glint of a challenge flashed through him, and his mouth descended to hers.

Twenty-two

IT was too much. It had to be too much. How could there be so much feeling bound up in one kiss?

When Max's mouth met hers, it wasn't a tentative exploration like before—it was an explosion. His hands had roughly pulled her body to his, the warmth of his taut muscular frame pressing through the layers of clothing between them. Those same hands moved over her body, wound their way into her hair, shaking pins free and tossing the little green hat ruthlessly to the ground.

Gail's own hands clung to his coat, itching to crawl up his back to tickle the hair at the nape of his neck, to feel the stubble on the line of his jaw, but . . .

"Take off your gloves," he said roughly, breaking his mouth from hers just long enough to speak, his breathing ragged. "I want to feel your hands on me."

He recaptured her lips as she divested herself of the offending accessories. Once her hands were free, she let them do just as they pleased, running up the soft wool of his coat, finding that small bit of flesh at the base of his ear, teasing with feather-light touches.

Max, who had been burning with his own desire, immediately became hard as stone upon feeling Gail's light caresses and pulled her closer, forcing her soft curves to melt and meld into his hard planes.

He kissed her closed eyes, her temples, ravaged the soft flesh of her earlobe, worshipped the long lines of her neck. When his explorations met with the high green velvet collar of her habit, nimble thumbs made quick work of the top three buttons—exposing the sensitive skin of the notch at the base of her throat, already rising and falling with rapid, erratic breaths.

"Please," Gail breathed hoarsely, "I . . . I want . . ."

He knew. Max kissed her again, their tongues mating in a rhythm of pure, burning, unrestrained lust.

All wits were gone. All sense of propriety, of time, of what was correct fled in the face of what felt right. Gail felt her hands move from Max's neck, to the front of his jacket, to under that layer of wool. She ran them over the strong muscles of his shoulders, pushing the jacket off as she went—all the time feeling, feeling, *feeling* the incredible strength and sensation of this man.

God, how she wanted him. The thought flashed into Gail's brain with all the welcome of a bucket of cold water. She wanted him. In every way it was possible to want another person. How on earth did that happen?

Max felt her stiffen immediately. Nerves, he thought. He'd wager neither of those European fellows had kissed her like this. He smiled against her mouth. She was Gail. She was warm and alive and in his arms, and the only way this could be any more right was if she was on the ground and beneath him.

Which seemed a fine idea to Max.

Slowly, he began to bend at the knees, his mouth never leaving Gail's, soothing her into pliancy. She bent with him, into the soft moss of the spring ground, her mind still reeling with the implications of her own realization.

"Max . . ." she moaned. "Max, stop for a moment."

He pulled away, but only for the space of time that allowed

him to divest himself of his half-off jacket and lay it on the grass behind her.

Seeing this, Gail's eyes grew wide with surprise. Still kneeling, Max kissed her neck, his hand working a few more buttons of her habit's jacket.

"Max, we should . . . I think we should stop."

Gail felt his hand inside of her habit, caressing the rise of her breast. Immediately, her nipples tightened, peaked with want, and she instinctively arched into him.

"Oh God, don't stop," she gasped.

Wicked triumph flashed in his green eyes. His body had been craving this for weeks, and finally his mind was willing to acknowledge it. Succumb to it. Gently, Max lowered Gail back onto his hastily laid out jacket. His arousal strained against the prison of his breeches, his skin hot to the touch. Gail Alton had been driving him crazy since they met—now it was his turn to drive her mad.

Slowly, and with infinite patience, Max let his weight settle on top of Gail's long body. Her massive skirts billowed about them, making a nest of green velvet and white lace underthings.

His weight was thrilling. The warm rumblings at the pit of her belly became throbs as his right hand caressed and fondled her breast while the left undid the remaining buttons of her jacket. Pulling aside the lapels, Max grinned wolfishly as he revealed only a light lawn chemise.

"No corset," he said roughly.

"Well, honestly, have you ever tried riding in a corset? It's imp . . . ohhhhh . . ." He had pulled down the neckline of the chemise, and the rest of her argument was lost to the mind-bending sensation of his mouth on her breast.

Her rapid breathing, the small little noises at the back of her throat were so unbelievably erotic to him—they were the sounds of innocence giving way to knowledge. And he had so much he wanted to teach her.

Max let his mouth drift farther down her body, dropping kisses through the chemise onto her ribcage, her stomach, just below her navel.

Her body was shaking.

Running his lips back up her body, Max looked into Gail's eyes. While his had nearly gone black with need, hers shone with curiosity, desire, and fear.

"Don't be afraid," he whispered between kisses. "I won't hurt you."

And she knew he wouldn't. But still she clung to the back of his shirt like it was a lifeline, as he kissed her deeply. Slowly, he drew up the hem of her skirts. The cool air brushed against her stockinged calves, her knees. His hand ran over them lightly, relishing the feeling of her strong, well-made limbs. Max groaned against her mouth at the sudden image that flashed into his head: Gail's long naked legs wrapped around his equally naked torso. He had to lift his shaking hand from her knee just long enough to ensure that he wouldn't force her legs apart and plunge into her right then and there. When he thought himself calm enough, he allowed himself to continue the explorations of her underskirts.

She was so soft. When he had first kissed her, he had been surprised at such a sharp person having such soft lips. The memory of that softness had kept him awake at night. As he reached the edge of her stockings, tied just above the knee, Max found skin that was even softer. The inside of her thighs nearly made him lose control. His blood was racing through his veins, urging him to go further, to take more, to make her his. But she was an innocent, he thought savagely, struggling to keep his body in check.

That is, until Gail, the little vixen, pulled his shirt out of his breeches and ran her long fingers down the smooth flesh of his back, dipping them just under his waistband, feeling the top of his buttocks.

All sense of decency flew from Max's brain as he tore at the buttons of his breeches.

He kissed her with a ferocity that pushed her firmly into the wool of his coat, into the moss of the ground. God, no one's touch had ever undone him like this. Not Sally the milk-maid when he was thirteen, certainly not Evangeline . . .

Evangeline.

Oh, God.

He froze immediately. He lifted himself away from her.

Each inch that separated them was hell, his every nerve crying out in protest, simply wanting to sink deeper and deeper within Gail, until it was impossible to tell where she ended and he began. But he couldn't. It nearly killed him, but he couldn't.

Finally, he managed to remove himself completely and sat on the ground beside her. But he wouldn't look at her, for he knew what he would see. Her lips full and bruised from his kisses. Her hair a glorious mess. Her jacket open, that little chemise doing nothing to hide the round glory of her breasts, rising and falling rapidly with her uneven breathing. Her eyes—oh, God, her eyes would still shine with the force of her desire, but cloud with confusion and disappointment. They would mirror his. But she had no idea what had been *inches* from occurring.

What the *hell* had they been doing? Max's mind flashed angrily. He was engaged to Gail's sister, for God's sake. And here he was, Lord Fontaine, English gentleman, about to take her on the grass in the middle of Hyde Park! He wanted to laugh. He wanted to beat the living daylights out of something. Instead, he settled for raking his hands ruthlessly through his hair.

"Max?" Gail's tentative voice broke his self-control, and he answered with a barbaric yell, full of all his rage at himself. All of the crows in the trees took flight at his outcry, and he stood up quickly, pacing like a caged beast.

"Max?" she tried again, but he would not stop pacing, would not look at her.

"Max?" her voice broke.

"No!" he yelled, making her jump. "Cover yourself," he said sharply.

Shaky hands closed the buttons of her jacket, straightened her skirts, fruitlessly smoothed her unruly hair. When she was presentable again, Max turned to her, but still was too ashamed of himself to meet her gaze.

"Gail," he began, then coughed, and started again. "Miss Alton. That was . . . We can't . . . I . . ."

He couldn't finish, because he quite honestly didn't know

where to start. She seemed to understand though, and said quietly, "I know."

He turned to look at her then and saw the pain, the guilt, the sadness in her face, and it sliced at his heart.

"It's my fault," he said quickly.

"No, it's mine," Gail replied. "If I hadn't felt that way—"

"It's mine," he cut her off ruthlessly, brooking no argument.

Then, softly, Gail whispered to herself, "This is the worst thing I've ever done."

Every nerve in Max's body was screaming that it was in fact, the best thing he'd ever done. He was still hard for her, and he wanted to shake Gail for her stupidity, take her in his embrace and soothe her worries, kiss her until she agreed with him, but he couldn't. He couldn't put his arms around her and assuage her guilt. He couldn't tell her everything was going to be all right and normal and *fine*. It wasn't. He was marrying one Alton girl but wanted, needed, craved the other.

It was going to hurt.

"Miss Alton, I can't be near you anymore," Max said curtly.

She gave a small guffaw of disbelief. "How, Lord Fontaine," she said sadly, "do you propose we avoid each other? You're at my home nearly every day."

"I don't . . . I don't know," he said to his toes.

Silence threatened to swallow them, if their own rampaging thoughts didn't trample them first. Finally, after what seemed like achingly long minutes, Max's head snapped up.

"I have to go," he said, and he gathered Jupiter from a nearby patch of grass. He mounted, rather uncomfortably, but was kept from leaving by Gail's small cry of "Wait!"

She stood and crossed to him.

"Your coat," she said, holding the garment out to him. He took it—it smelled like her. Max could not avoid Gail's direct stare or the determined set of her jaw. The fire of her eyes was banked now, but her hair was still mussed from his ministrations. It made Max's mouth go dry.

With a quick nod, he sank his heels into Jupiter's flanks and sped away from Gail, and away from temptation.

* * *

ALONE now, Gail let the silence of the grotto envelop her. The crows had flown, there were no more to count. Gail picked up her hat and did not cry. She gathered her horse and absolutely did not cry. She located her gloves, found Jimmy some half a mile away, and refused to cry all the way home.

* * *

ON the other side of the park, Lord Hurstwood, having recently quitted a duel where sadly no one was shot, crossed a large meadow that gave way to a lake. There, as he told a friend later that morning, he was certain he saw Lord Fontaine diving fully clothed into what must have been freezing water.

Twenty-three

AND thus the unusual friendship of Gail Alton and Max Fontaine fell apart.

It wasn't with a war of words or a fading away as time and distance came between them. It was abrupt, forced by their own consciences.

They no longer spoke. When circumstances caused them to be in the same room, they barely did more than acknowledge the other's presence. And every moment of strained politeness was a turn of the knife.

The problem of avoiding each other proved to be nothing more than a trick of scheduling. Max called less frequently at Number Seven, and when he did, Gail somehow managed to be spending that day about town with some new friends.

"She's where?" Romilla blurted out one afternoon.

"Shopping," Evangeline answered, "with Lilly and Lavender Pickering."

"Willingly?" Romilla asked incredulously, but Evangeline just shrugged.

This news gave Romilla serious pause.

But alas, she did not have much time to focus on Gail's

odd behavior, for almost directly thereafter, things began occurring one on top of the other.

The first Event of Note was Count Roffstaam announcing his day of departure. Mrs. Holt, who had taken to her guest, but was yet so happy to have him leaving her beleaguered cook alone, announced a ball to be given in his honor.

"Another one?" Evangeline and Gail cried in tandem, only to be put off by a wave of Romilla's hand. She had promised Mrs. Holt to jointly host the affair and spent a great deal of time with that lady preparing the guest lists. The Holts's May-fair residence, while purchased with "trade money," as Lady Charlbury called it, was quite grand and perfect for hosting an intimate reception for more than five hundred people. Upon seeing the impressive residence and being greeted most warmly by Mrs. Holt, Romilla quickly decided that despite the acquisition of wealth through labor, the Holts could be worth knowing. She spent nearly every afternoon with that good lady finalizing preparations, often dragging the girls along with her. Gail was bored to tears by these outings, but Evangeline took to Mrs. Holt as easily as Romilla did, albeit without such mercenary motives.

The second Event of Note occurred soon after the announcement of the Count's imminent departure. Sir Geoffrey received his appointment to the ministry. It was done quietly, and without fuss, only a dinner party of fifty of their closest friends to celebrate the event and a front-page announcement, courtesy of an editor friend at the *Times*, discreetly below the fold. By now Romilla had become quite adept at throwing a dinner party at a moment's notice, and she did so with ease and flair. "Grasping" was no longer a phrase that befell them—at least not as often. For Romilla was fast becoming one of London's most sought after hostesses—a position that unabashedly thrilled her. The Duke of Wellington even stood up and toasted his newest foreign minister, saying that he was never so happy as to have such an intelligent, honest, and upstanding gentleman working for the good of England.

Lord Fontaine was of course invited, and this time, his

opinion was listened to with interest and consideration. He was seated, at Sir Geoffrey's behest, near enough to him to partake in any conversation, the elder gentleman making certain to show the audience his undoubted approval of the younger.

While Max enjoyed this attention, his mind was occupied with things other than his future father-in-law's approval. Indeed, he had difficulty concentrating on the conversation, with Gail seated across from him, not meeting his gaze, not sharing a laugh with him when someone misquoted Shakespeare. Not saying a word to him at all.

* * *

NO one should for a moment infer that the actions (or inactions) of Miss Gail Alton and Lord Fontaine went unnoticed by the other players in this piece. They weren't necessarily connected, however.

Romilla was, as always, the shrewdest of the lot. It had begun to prick at her curiosity that Lord Fontaine's visits had become less frequent. The month of courting was almost up, soon they would have to announce the betrothal. She began to worry that he had lost interest in Evangeline and would go against his word and jilt her. Oh, what a fiasco that would be! Sir Geoffrey's new appointment could be taken away, or his power considerably lessened if his family were embroiled in scandal. Indeed, now that he would have the position, they had to be more careful than ever. Thinking that Lord Fontaine was distracted from his ravishing bride, Romilla approached her husband.

"But what would you have me do about it? I have the boy's word," he said gruffly, pouring over papers in his library. Romilla sighed. She had interrupted him to discuss the invitation list for his celebratory dinner party, and he was barely paying attention! Really, ever since this Barivia business, Geoffrey had become more and more embroiled in his work, Romilla thought. It would be nice if he'd at least look at her when she spoke.

"You should make it known publicly that you approve of

him, make his ties seem very close with the family. That kind of public support will place him more firmly in—"

"Our clutches?" her husband finished.

"For lack of better phrasing," Romilla replied haughtily, "yes. At the dinner party. Make certain it is known you think very highly of Lord Fontaine."

"Fine," Sir Geoffrey sighed. "Seat him near me. He'd be a good one to ask about these translations, anyway," he said, rubbing his eyes and indicating the papers.

"You could ask Abigail," Romilla ventured. At her husband's look of confusion, she added, "Gail. Your daughter."

"She's off having fun. Besides, I thought you wanted me to talk with Fontaine."

"Yes, yes, of course," Romilla replied quickly. After a considering pause, she spoke again. "Speaking of, I'm a little worried about Abi—I mean, Gail."

"What about her?" Sir Geoffrey grumbled, his eyes on his work.

"Well, it seems she's spent the past few days with the Pickerings . . ."

Sir Geoffrey blinked at his wife. "What of it?"

"It's just . . . I know she's not particularly fond of the Pickerings," Romilla continued, realizing even as she spoke how weak her argument sounded.

"Nonsense," Sir Geoffrey scoffed. "If Gail didn't like someone, she wouldn't waste time with them. They're silly, but harmless—and it's good for Gail to make some friends. I really wish you wouldn't bother me with little worries like this, my dear. I've a mountain of work to do." And with that Sir Geoffrey returned his tired eyes to the papers in front of him.

Romilla nodded and left her husband to his work. After she shut the door, she realized sadly that he hadn't noticed she was wearing his favorite frock.

* * *

BUT Romilla was far too busy a woman to reflect sadly on anything overlong and so went about the business of assisting Mrs. Holt with the Count's ball, once the dinner party was out of the way. Therefore, she was not in the house when the next Event of Note occurred.

In fact, none of the family was at home except Gail.

Sir Geoffrey was at his new offices, as always, and Romilla had left just after tea to pay a call on Mrs. Holt, Evangeline in tow. After some discreet questioning, Gail found that Will Holt was expected to be there, which therefore raised the chances of Max being in attendance considerably. Accordingly, Gail had claimed she had fallen behind in correspondence (a bald-faced lie, but surprisingly no one questioned it) and stayed at home with a book.

Having just settled into blissful solitude with a copy of the latest gothic novel, she was greatly alarmed when someone began knocking furiously on her bedchamber door.

"Oh, Miss Gail, you must come downstairs at once!" Mrs. Bibb said when Gail answered the door. "There is a caller."

"Mrs. Bibb, I told Morrison to tell all callers no one was at home," Gail said, perplexed.

"We tried that, but he won't go away—and he's not the type o' gent one can easily dismiss," Mrs. Bibb replied, worrying her hands.

"Who is it? The duke?" Gail ventured as Mrs. Bibb, unable to wait any longer, grabbed her young mistress's hand, dragging her down the steps.

"Nay, miss," Mrs. Bibb answered. They came to a halt before the drawing room doors. "I sent a note to your lady stepmother, but someone needs to go attend him now." Mrs. Bibb pulled Gail to face her, ruthlessly smoothing her hair and brushing out the wrinkles in her skirts.

"Is it the king? Mrs. Bibb, stop that!" Gail said, swatting at the housekeeper's hands. "Really, I cannot imagine who would be worth all this fuss."

Satisfied with Gail's appearance, Mrs. Bibb opened the door to the drawing room, and shoved her through.

"Dratted girl! Shut that door. This house is drafty as a tomb."

The old man sat by an abnormally high fire, his sharp green gaze glinting as he looked her up and down.

Gail took his measure.

"You must be the Earl."

* * *

"SO you know me, do you girl? You've been forewarned, then?" The Earl kept his razor-sharp gaze on his quarry as she coolly moved to take the seat across from him.

"Not yet! Come closer. Let me get a good look at you," Gail obliged, standing under the Earl's scrutiny for a full minute in silence. She met his gaze and did her own assessment. He was old, she realized, so much older than she had imagined. He must have fathered Max quite late in life. The blue tones of the drawing room that brought out Evangeline's complexion made the Earl's already pale skin take on a deathly pallor. His posture was hunched in on itself, and his gnarled hands rested on a gold-headed cane. But in his face, in his eyes, was the active, shrewd mind of a man half as young.

"Good, good. Healthy child," the Earl murmured. "Although perhaps too tall for my liking." He waved his hand for Gail to take a seat, all the while regarding her with an aloof manner that could disarm royalty.

"To answer your earlier question, I was not, er, forewarned about you. You rather unmistakably have your son's eyes," she said, nervously settling back into the chair.

"It is he who has my eyes, and don't you forget it, missy."

And his officious manner, apparently.

The fire crackled and sparked in the hearth, while Gail searched for something . . . anything to say.

"I must apologize," she stammered, unused to playing hostess, "you have caught my parents and sister out of the house, but they will be back directly. Would you care for some tea, or . . . ?"

"No, no." He cut her off with a wave of his twisted hand. "Didn't come to speak with them. I came here to see you."

An eyebrow shot up. Why would the Earl wish to see her? Unless . . . but that was impossible. Gail knew Max had little to do with his father, how would he . . . Could he know about what occurred in the park? And at the museum . . . Gail suddenly flushed.

"You should blush," the Earl's eyes narrowed, "for what you've done to snare my son. But for some reason, the idiot seems to care for you, given his devotion, so I wanted to see what the next Countess of Longsbowe was made of."

Ah, that was it. Gail didn't know whether to be relieved or cry. The Earl thought she was Evangeline, that it was she who would marry Max. Gail opened her mouth to correct the Earl's assumption but was interrupted again.

"You had better have some good tricks up your sleeve, my girl, because you're not pretty enough to hold his interest six months together."

Anger suddenly flared to life, brighter than what burned in the hearth.

"And what do you know of your son's interests?" she asked, her voice deceptively low.

"I know my son," the Earl stated.

"No you don't. You don't know your son at all." Before she could stop it, Gail's tongue was off and running. "Did you know he nearly single-handedly brokered a trade deal with a foreign country? That he speaks six languages, including Latin? That he for some unknown reason thinks Beethoven is the best composer to have ever breathed? No, of course not. If you did know your son, you would have realized that cutting off his allowance wouldn't stop him from living. You wouldn't call someone who is so obviously brilliant an idiot, and you certainly wouldn't dare attempt to fit him into some untenable mold of your officious, overbearing self."

The Earl went white with rage. His hand tightened on his gold-headed cane.

"You dare insult me in such a manner?!"

"As you dared insult me *in my own home*," she said, leaning back in her chair and steepling her fingers in a dead-on imitation of her father at his most imperious. And although she looked to possess that steely calm, her mouth was dry, her palms sweaty, and inwardly Gail was quaking. What had she done? She had let her tongue run away with her, that's what. Almost immediately upon seeing the Earl, all of the progress she had made in the past few weeks, all of the happy manners she had learned to affect, gone with one insult.

The Earl's hand shook as he waggled a finger at her. "You should be more careful how you speak to the father of the man you will marry," he said menacingly.

"I'm certain I shall," she retorted, "but luckily, I have no call to impress you." At his surprised look, she explained, "I am Gail Alton. Max is to marry my sister, Evangeline."

The Earl grew silent with this new information, but she could see the gears turned rapidly in that still sharp brain. She had grievously insulted the Earl . . . she had spoken so far out of turn Max would have her head for what she revealed. All those things he had told her in confidence! But she would not be sorry for defending him to the man that was staring at her so intensely, the crackle of the fire the only sound in the room.

Gail, in turn, stared back.

She was about to go and ring for a servant—even if the Earl didn't want tea, she needed something, anything to do—when he cocked an eyebrow (so like his son!) and gave a smirk of dawning understanding.

"If you . . ." He stopped, cleared his throat, and began again. "You defend him," he said simply. She replied with a curious nod. "You defend him," the old man elaborated, "with a good deal of feeling."

Gail felt the blood drain away from her face. "I . . . I . . . well, Max, er, we've spent a great deal of time . . ."

A wolfish smile cracked the Earl's wrinkled lips, revealing a skeleton's grin. "And yet, you will be condemned to a life as merely a sister. Won't you?"

Abruptly she stood. "It is none of your concern. Now if you will excuse me, I'll check on the tea tray." She moved to the door, but a beleaguered cry of "Hold on there, girl!" stilled her hand upon the knob.

She turned her steely gaze to the source of the cry. The Earl had stood up too quickly on shaky legs, walking after her while leaning heavily on his cane, his breathing labored.

"I'll . . . chase you down, child . . . don't . . . doubt it," he said with shuttered breaths.

Gail, far from being coldhearted, could not help but be affected by the Earl's state. Her features softened as she hurried to the Earl's side. Taking his arm, she led him back to the fire and assisted him in taking his seat.

"Thank you, my girl," the Earl said, sounding so rusty that Gail wasn't sure the man had thanked anyone in the past fifty years. Gail smiled tightly in reply, leaning over the Earl to adjust the cushions. As she did, he caught her arm, stilling her movements and bringing her attention to his face. He regarded her again for a breath of time, not judging, but with consideration.

"You have more heart than I've seen in a woman for many years," he said quietly.

Gail quirked a brow. "You met me but ten minutes ago, sir, and I've spent a good part of that time insulting you." She gently removed her arm from his grasp and resumed her seat.

"Still, if I ever had anyone defend me the way you did my son . . ." He let his voice trail off wistfully. Then he shook his head, as if to clear himself of troubling thoughts.

"My son," he declared in a strong voice, "is a fool."

"Lord Longsbowe," Gail bit out in protest, but was interrupted before she could start her argument again.

"Miss Alton. My son and I may be estranged. We are different people, which is a fact that I was forced to contend with long ago. But I still have eyes, and I can still call him a fool if the occasion warrants it. And I assure you, my son is a fool." The hardness had returned to his green gaze, and Gail, for one of the few times in her life, thought better of voicing her opinion on the matter. Her temper was pricked, but so was her curiosity. It was on the tip of her tongue to ask why Max was so foolish, but just then a sharp knock on the door interrupted the tension of the room. Mrs. Bibb entered, bearing the tea tray. She placed it on the small table next to Gail, and with a pointed look at that young lady, left. However, when Gail made to pour, the Earl held up a hand.

"I cannot stay," he said, making to rise. "If you could . . ."

She was at his side in a trice. Helping him stand, she took a good deal of the Earl's weight as she assisted him to the doors.

"You are too strong for a female," the Earl grunted. Gail simply smiled and took more of the old man's weight.

"One of the many benefits of being unfashionably tall. Also, I can block people's views at the theater."

"And too much cheek," the Earl retorted.

Once at the door of Number Seven, the Earl transferred his weight with dignity to his valet, who had been waiting in the carriage. Gail said her farewells with a curtsy, while the Earl simply inclined his head.

"Good-bye, Miss Alton." He bent his creaky frame into a bow.

* * *

WHAT a curious exchange, Gail thought as she quietly banked the fires in the overheated drawing room with an iron. The man had been here but minutes, yet he left her with a great deal of conflicting thoughts. In her ill-advised defense of Max, Gail had listed any number of things that the Earl might have denied, yet he did not. His actions regarding his son, trying to hold him back, were *deplorable*—there was no other word. And yet, when the facade of steel and stone cracked, Gail felt more than a little sorry for the old man.

She sat in the chair she had previously occupied and stared into the fire, conscious of the swollen emptiness of the room without the Earl sitting opposite. He thought he was acting in the best interests of his fool of a son, Gail realized. He had probably always thought that, even when his actions were the most grievous. Perhaps he saw the pain he had caused in the past. He certainly saw a great deal when she had slipped and defended Max. Gail felt the heat rise in her cheeks, in no way related to the height of the fire. She worked so hard to make certain her feelings didn't show, and yet this stranger had seen through her as easily as water. She *was* condemned to a life as the sister of the perfect Evangeline. How could he call Max a fool, and not she?

Before Gail's thoughts could follow down this troubling path any farther, the drawing room doors burst open, admitting a breathless and somewhat harried Romilla. Evangeline followed just as impatiently at her heels.

"Abigail! The Earl! Is he here?" Romilla asked immediately.

Gail rose from her chair and reverie. "No, ma'am. Er, he sends his compliments, but could not stay long."

Romilla's face fell. "Oh dear," she said, on a great exhale. After a moment she shrugged, picked at the knot of her bonnet, and moved to the couch, Evangeline following suit.

"Now, you will simply have to tell me everything you and Lord Longsbowe spoke about. Heavens, it is warm in here, is it not? Oh thank goodness, you've ordered tea—Mrs. Holt, the dear woman, is unfortunately saddled with that German faux-French chef who tried to serve us sausages slathered in the most curious sauces for luncheon! Her son kept sneaking his to the dog. Mrs. Holt said it was unfortunate Lord Fontaine wasn't in attendance, for he is the only one that can convince the chef to cook a good English meal. Abi—, I mean, Gail, please pour and start at the beginning."

Gail's head swam from trying to follow her stepmother's lengthy speech, but one thing had stuck. As she prepared cups for her sister and stepmother from the tray that Mrs. Bibb had placed for the Earl only minutes before, she turned her innocent inquiry to her sister.

"Lord Fontaine was not in attendance?"

"No," replied Evangeline. "William—Mr. Holt—said that he was locked in his rooms on Weymouth Street, working on some new translation. William, that is, Mr. Holt declared that if he had been there, he would have run here to intercept his father faster than horses could carry us."

"As he should, Evangeline," Romilla lectured. "I don't understand your betrothed half the time. He should have introduced us to his father long ago. I had no notion the man was even in town! But now that the Earl has visited, hopefully it means he is accepting of the union."

Suitably cowed, Evangeline ducked her head and took a sip of tea. Satisfied in her daughter's deportment and a proper English cucumber sandwich in hand, Romilla again addressed the issue of Gail's conversation with the Earl.

But on that subject, Gail found herself deeply conflicted

and could not honestly relate what had been said. So she re-sorted to making up a number of vague compliments and in-quiries, which would not satisfy Romilla nearly as much as the cucumber sandwich.

* * *

"EVIE?" Gail knocked on her sister's door quietly before sticking her head in. She saw her sister by the window, staring as the carriages and people went by in the late afternoon traf-fic on the square. It took a moment before Evangeline became aware of her sister's presence, but once she turned, she smiled genuinely for the company.

"I . . . I was wondering if you wanted to hear more about the Earl's visit this afternoon," Gail began, as she seated her-self on her sister's bed. She was the tallest female in the house, and yet Evie's bed was so high, her feet dangled off the edge, making Gail feel extremely childlike. To be honest, she didn't think there could be anything more to be said about the Earl's visit—it had been extremely short, after all—but it was the best way she had come up with to introduce the topic she des-perately needed council on: Max.

For, in the intervening time since the Earl's departure, Gail's mind had been swimming with all the truths that man had presented her. And the largest, most looming one was the fact that if she let her emotions have their full rein, she would be condemned to a life as a sister. She didn't want to spend her life pining for what she couldn't have. Therefore, the only way she could see herself ever moving past her feelings, was to confess them.

To Evangeline.

She knew that in time, she would get over these silly no-tions. She also knew, that in time, her sister would forgive her for developing a friendship with and subsequently an inap-propriate affection for her husband. And she knew that all of this would only occur with a first step.

Still, it didn't mean that step would be at all easy.

"Yes, the Earl," Evangeline was saying, breaking into Gail's nervous reverie. "Romilla is right, it is appalling that we haven't seen him until now, but now that he's called, we can return the gesture. Do you think we should stop by during our rounds tomorrow and leave a card?"

"I don't think that's the best idea," Gail replied quizzically, her brow furrowed. "Ma—er, Lord Fontaine and his father are not on the best of terms."

Evangeline looked questioningly at her sister.

"But surely, you know that," Gail finished.

"Actually," Evangeline said, looking to her toes, "I didn't know that. Obviously."

Gail was about to open her mouth, about to start stumbling over her confession, when Evangeline's head came up, and with watery eyes, made one of her own.

"I guess I'm not a very good fiancée, am I?"

"Evangeline, darling—that cannot be true."

"Yes it can," her sister continued. "I assure you it can. As evidenced by the fact that I did not know of Lord Fontaine's relationship with his father, nor did I care to find it out."

"Evie," Gail began, wishing to reassure her sister, "all that stuff comes with time—"

"I know!" Evie cried. "Time is what we were given! Granted the boon of a full month, spent in each other's company, in an attempt to get to know one another, to become comfortable with each other—and the only thing discovered in that time is a gulf of differences and disinterest."

"I fear," Gail ventured, gulping, "that some of that gulf, a, er, good deal of it, actually, might be my fault."

"No, Gail"—Evangeline waved off her protest—"I asked you to be present, remember? I asked you to be my support, and support you have! I am dissatisfied through my own efforts, believe me. None of this is your fault."

Gail could only stare at her sister—this was certainly not how she intended this conversation to go. "Surely—surely, you're not so unhappy?"

Evangeline stood now, began pacing, wearing the carpet with her eyes as much as her feet. "No, but I . . . I just wish I'd never ventured into the conservatory."

"Oh, Evie!" Gail sighed, hating that she had on more than

one occasion wished the same thing, and hating her task now, "but that night, with the moonlight—you said then it was magical, entrancing . . ."

"Yes, darling, but the problem with moonlight is one has to live in the day. And that's the fundamental difference between romance and love. Romance is moonlight, it's the trappings of desire . . ."

"And love?" Gail could barely pitch her voice above a whisper.

It was many moments before Evangeline could answer. But when she did, it was with great, still feeling. "Love . . . love is understanding. Love is knowing that other person so well, you can anticipate them. Like if someone knows you're uncomfortable, and they loosen your boot strings. Or if he knows you're deeply worried about something, and does his best to remedy it and soothe your fears. Love . . . is need! Needing that person in your life, day after day, whatever ups and downs may come, wanting their presence, and they wanting yours, because it's the only way either of you will ever feel whole."

For a moment, Gail couldn't speak. Then, "And . . . and Max does not make you feel this way?"

Sadly, Evangeline shook her head. "No. He does not. And I doubt I inspire any such feelings in him."

She looked to the window for a moment, her figure framed in the falling light. "I am reconciled to the fact that I will not love my husband. I'm certain, that . . . that we'll have an amicable enough relationship. I know, he's not a bad person. But Gail," her voice became hitched as the deep pools of her eyes threatened to spill over, "is it so wrong, so foolish, to wish for something more?"

"Maybe." Gail shrugged. "Because the love you describe, giving yourself so completely to another, it sounds rather frightening."

"Yes, it does," Evangeline agreed, sitting beside her sister on the bed. "But maybe, just maybe, it's worth it. Now," she said, bearing herself up and shaking away any hint of tears, "I may not have the chance to find out, but I don't want you thinking that way."

"Whatever do you mean?" Gail frowned.

"I know you," Evangeline said, a small smile playing at the corners of her mouth. "I don't want you to feel like if I'm dissatisfied, you should be as well. I don't want you to be afraid of happiness just because I failed to achieve it!"

"I have the impression you've been practicing this speech," Gail drawled.

"For approximately eighteen years. Gail. Darling sister. Your life is your own. You don't have to wait in line behind me. Now, you have to promise me—that if a chance at happiness comes your way, and you think you might love somebody, really love them, not just some foolish inclination, you have to take it."

"This is terribly melodramatic, you know. It might help if you threw a joke or two in to break up the darker bits," Gail chided, aiming for some levity, but Evangeline simply shook her head.

"Do be serious for a moment! Gail, I'm not going to have the opportunity to experience love, real love. I wasted any chance I would have on a foolish moonlight kiss. But I would very much like to have my sister, one day, tell me what it's like."

Gail was speechless for a full minute, until with a sniffle, she found her voice and luckily, her sense of humor. "What if I fall madly in love with a goatherder? Or a red Indian in America? Or one of the awful Basti brothers in Portugal?"

Evangeline burst out laughing—the first full laugh Gail had heard from her sister in days.

"All right. First of all, you wouldn't dare fall for a Basti brother. The other two are far more easily imagined. And if it is a red Indian, you absolutely *must* tell me everything. I should require details."

Gail laughed at that. "Evangeline!"

"But beyond your jokes and my ridiculous bout of melancholy," Evie continued, still smiling, "if you loved someone, really loved him, why shouldn't you try for happiness?"

In that moment, Gail knew she would tell Evangeline everything. About the kisses, the dances, about the first time she saw Max in the lake, the magical grotto, and all her feelings, even if she could not be sure of his. But as she opened her mouth, as her voice sounded the first syllable of her long past due confession, a knock sounded at the door.

It was Mrs. Bibb, with Polly, ready to assist with all manner of buttons and hairpins.

"Time to dress for the evenin' m'ladies, your lady stepmother says the schedule is tight tonight, so we best hurry," Mrs. Bibb spoke as she bustled into the room, lighting the sconces to replace the daylight that had since left them.

And with that, the return of real life, Gail's hard-won courage left her, and the confession died on her tongue.

Evangeline was quickly at her dressing table, ready to be made into Miss Alton, jewel of the Ton.

It could be left for tomorrow.

Twenty-four

TOMORROW, and tomorrow, and tomorrow. All too quickly time fled, and with each passing moment, more of Gail's conviction left her. After all, who was she to disrupt everyone's plans? They say confession is good for the soul, but who is this "they"? And why on earth should Gail take their word? No, it seemed far more logical to bottle all that feeling and put it aside, concentrate on other things.

Romilla and Evangeline continued their attentions to the Holts' ball, which was shaping up to be the grandest event of the season. And if she couldn't take whole credit, Romilla seemed content being a cohostess. Gail continued to spend an inordinate amount of time with the Pickerings, who, while exasperating, did throw her into the company of more and more new people, some of whom she enjoyed. Indeed, it was an oddity, but Gail had quickly found herself with a busier social schedule than that of her oft-sought-after sister. It made time pass more pleasurably than she had thought possible. She began testing her caution and voicing her opinion more and more.

Max had been right: Her easy wit, so long as she kept the

lectures and insults to a minimum, made her extremely well liked. Her outburst with the Earl had been a rare display of emotion, and Gail continually wondered why it occurred. Maybe it was simply Fontaine men, she mused. They bring out something in her that other acquaintances were spared from.

The night of the Holts's farewell ball for Count Roffstaam, Gail was amazed to find herself surrounded by many new friends seeking her favor.

"Mr. Belling, you shan't be pleased with my company any longer once we dance. Your toes will forbid it."

But Mr. Belling had simply laughed and escorted Gail to the floor, followed by Captain Sterling, Sir Quayle, and Mr. Thornley (a trio that couldn't seem to have one do something without the other two following). Granted, none of them asked her to dance again after their first painful experience, but all were more than happy to sit and enjoy her company, laughing loudly enough to draw the approving attention of some of the matrons, including Romilla.

The great ballroom of the Holt mansion was a jewel in the landscape of London that night. Never had there been an equal. Indeed, the guests, comprised of the most jaded, unimpressed, upper upper crust of society, were open-mouthed with astonishment at the sight of the room.

It was bedecked in flowers. Boughs and strings of newly bloomed pink and yellow roses hung from the immense height of the ceiling, which had been painted with a fresco of the sky at sunset just for the occasion, little cherubs flitting between the pink-tinged clouds with delightful abandon. The whole room was built of polished honey-colored wood and pink marble. This, along with twinkling candles and the sunset fresco, lit the atmosphere with a golden glow. Its only rival in decoration was the dining room, where tables were set with white tablecloths, embroidered with gold filigree, and the plates and utensils all in gold. Small personal bouquets of pink roses sat at every place setting, as opposed to overbearing arrangements at the table's center. It was rumored there would be fireworks after dinner. But for everyone that came to dance, the real treat was the full orchestra, stolen for the evening from the most prestigious opera house in London, and the excellent acoustics of the hall that let the melodious sounds travel throughout the whole enchanting space.

It was a splendid affair, and everyone in attendance could not help but enjoy it.

That is, of course, unless they had some troubling thought on their minds, such as having to marry one sister while lusting after the other.

Max stood on the edge of the ballroom, watching Gail being stuntedly whirled across the floor, a broad smile on her face. She was magnificent, the bloom of popularity livening her countenance to something ethereal, something that glowed. It made his stomach turn.

He watched her every move, every slight tilt of the head, every time her eyes sparkled with mischief when she joked with her partner. She clapped her hands like a child when delighted, and the men surrounding her responded by grinning like besotted idiots and swelling out their chests.

How could she be having so much bloody fun when he felt like nothing more than a hollowed-out shell?

Although one would have to look closely, Max was not as composed as he seemed. In an effort to make him more wretched, his appetite had left him. His eyes were tired from forcing himself to work constantly—if he achieved a state of total exhaustion, he wouldn't dream. And although Harris had bullied him into shaving and his evening kit, he was paler than usual, and his posture uncompromisingly rigid. In the whirl of gaiety and color around him, Max was stark and immobile.

He managed to put on a good face, for it would never do to let people know one's true thoughts. He danced with Evangeline, the first two as required, and then handed her off to Will. He chatted at length with various acquaintances he didn't really know about things he cared very little for, smiling politely all the while. Cornered for ten arduous minutes by Romilla, Max listened as she rambled about how busy he must have been recently, and how much they had missed his frequent visits. Max had nearly started laughing. If she only knew the reason, she would bar him from the house and have him dragged through the streets!

He finally freed himself of his future mother-in-law's company and managed to make his way to an inconspicuous spot of wall, when a new voice assaulted his ears.

"Well, young man, you look ready for the gallows."

In the sea of black coats and sickeningly smiling faces, Lady Charlbury, cheerfully cantankerous, had managed to hunt him down.

"You're too thin by half—and those bags! Such are the marks of drunkards and wastrels. Have you become either a drunkard or a wastrel since I saw you last?" she inquired, all feigned concern.

Instead of releasing a pent-up sigh of frustration as he longed to do, Max simply bowed in greeting and replied in the negative.

"Ah," Lady Charlbury decided, "both then."

That pent-up sigh of frustration finally won its way out of Max's lungs, causing Lady Charlbury to chuckle with malevolent glee.

"My lady," Max bit out, "are you enjoying your evening?"

"More now than ever," she replied. "I suppose that Mrs. Holt did well enough in her decor, but is the orchestra really necessary? One cannot hear themselves think, let alone speak to others."

Judiciously ignoring the old woman's slight of his best friend's mother, Max took a sip of punch. "As luck would have it, most people don't think at all while conversing."

Lady Charlbury nodded wryly. "Right you are, my boy. Now, why don't you tell me why you're such a sourpuss?"

But before Max could gracefully dodge that line of questioning, another couple joined their party. And Max's face became sourer.

"Ah! Here you are, vith the Lady Charlbury! Mr. Villiam Holt said so, correct Miz Alton?"

Count Roffstaam stood before them, Gail Alton smiling with the radiance of pure pleasure on his arm.

She looked even more irresistible up close. It was all Max could do to hold himself from sweeping her into a dark corner of the room, kissing the smile off her face and replacing it with one just for him. How *dare* she be having a good time?

Unwilling to feast his eyes and torture himself further, Max turned pointedly away from Gail and gave the Count a deep bow, inquiring politely how he was enjoying the festivities in his honor.

"Oh! So lovely!" the Count replied. "Ze food, and ze flors, ve have nothing in Barivia like this."

"I was just telling Lord Fontaine that the flowers and gold are so excessively overdone," Lady Charlbury interrupted. "The whole effect is like being in a sneeze-inducing, over-warm, overcrowded peach."

"You're having a good time then?" Gail ventured with a half smile teasing her lips.

"Never had more fun in my life," Lady Charlbury answered, eyes twinkling. Suddenly, the orchestra struck up a waltz, and a titter went through the crowd as gentlemen sought out their partners for the dance.

"Ah, that awful orchestra!" Lady Charlbury cried, making to cover her ears, but no one paid attention to her actions. The Count was staring at the dance floor in wonder.

"A Valtz? I have heard, but never seen such dancing." He spoke more with curiosity than condemnation.

"Really?" Gail asked. "But I thought the dance was created in your part of the world."

The Count smiled under his moustache. "My country is very, ah, alone—ve do not see much of the lands beyond Barivia. And they do not see us." His eyes followed the dancers around the floor. "Clearly, ve have missed much."

"Well, perhaps you should give it a try, then," Max drawled.

"Oh yes, it's quite an easy dance—no intricate steps to learn, just a count of three, and, er, leading and following," Gail added, trying not to blush, and failing.

"I never have liked the waltz," Lady Charlbury piped up. "Men and women standing far too close for decency's sake."

"But, zey are on a dance floor. Iz proper, ya?"

Gail and Max judiciously avoided each other's eyes.

"Absolutely."

"Of course."

"Miz Alton, you vill show me."

"I should be delighted," she replied, moving to take the Count's arm.

He shook his head. "No, I know not ze steps. Ah, Lord Fontaine, vill you dance vith Miz Alton, so I may see?"

Max had a good notion to refuse, for there were any number of couples already on the floor that the Count could observe, but the way the Count was looking at him, straight-backed, with that immobile mustache, told Max that this was not a request.

So, with Lady Charlbury's sharp eyes watching with unabashed interest, Max bowed to Gail and led her to the floor. They were too intent on each other to see the Count throw a wink to a smirking Lady Charlbury.

* * *

THERE was none of the awkwardness, the learning involved in their first waltz at Almack's. Now, they knew all too well what it felt like to be in each other's arms. It was like touching fire. The lightest brush of her glove seared his shoulder. His fingers branded her skin through the silk of her gown.

They moved with more fluid grace than either had thought capable. She could feel him move before he even did so. They were perfect.

But any joy or pleasure that Gail had portrayed throughout the evening fell away. She kept her gaze steady over his shoulder; he kept his jaw set. There were no smiles. Only the warmth of his hands, the music propelling them around the floor in time.

Realizing some conversation must be had—even a very little would suffice—Gail gathered her courage and spoke first.

"I'm surprised I haven't stepped on your toes yet."

There. A simple comment on the dancing, wholly innocuous. Never mind her heart was racing.

"Perhaps you have improved through your ample practice this evening," Max retorted snidely.

Nothing would ever be simple with Max, it seemed.

"Perhaps," she conceded coolly.

"You've been having a grand time, haven't you? All laughter and jokes. You have Sterling, Quayle, and Thornley jumping through hoops. Be careful though—they are more out to impress each other than you." His eyes came to her face now, the bitterness of his words shining through them. He threw her violently into a turn, but she held on.

"Do you have a point, Max? Or are you simply enjoying a bit of spite?"

"My point is that for a fortnight, I've been wracked with guilt, while you've been out making friends and enjoying yourself. I've been in a hell of my own making, and you have been laughing and flirting! You have no feeling at all, do you?"

Tears stung her eyes, but pride stung more.

"You begrudge me any happiness I might find, then?" she said, her voice unsteady.

"That's not the point," Max replied curtly.

"You don't know my feelings! For your information, I made friends *because* I was avoiding you. Because I *had* to. With your calling on *Evangeline*, I could not be in the house. And did you know? Other people make it easier to not think about my own stupid actions. So do not begrudge me them, because they are the only reason I'm able to be here now." The tears choked her, making her voice thick with emotion.

"I cannot avoid your home," he said brokenly. "But I have made a very concerted effort to visit less, or meet with your sister elsewhere. You should have been able to enjoy your solitude."

"Yes." Gail let out a bitter laugh. "And still I cannot escape you. You are quite the topic of conversation. Romilla schools Evangeline daily on the importance of being a good wife. I could not call on the Holts for fear you'd be here. And the one afternoon I had to myself, your father arrived at my door."

For the first time all evening, Max stumbled in his steps.

"You met my father?" he asked, incredulous. At her affirmative nod, Max's face darkened.

"Lord Fontaine," she began carefully, "I know you and your father don't get on, but he's not . . . Max, please, that hurts."

The hand that had unconsciously tightened about hers slowly, deliberately loosened.

Gail let out a breath she hadn't even known she was holding. But before they could regain the pace of the other whirling couples, Max abruptly pulled her off the floor and to an innocuous corner shaded by a particularly low-hung bough of roses.

"What did he say to you?" Max loomed over her, so close, so intense, Gail's mouth went dry.

"He . . . he said he wanted to meet me."

"Why?"

"He confused me with Evangeline."

Swearing under his breath, Max demanded that a wide-eyed Gail recount the whole of her conversation with the Earl. She did so, judiciously editing out the Earl's insight to her own feelings. She told herself such information served no purpose, but secretly knew she was protecting her own heart.

As Max listened to her finish the careful speech, his jaw clenched tighter.

"And after he called you a fool—he left," she finished.

"Nothing new there," Max growled.

Tentatively, Gail reached out a hand, resting it lightly on his arm.

"Your father . . . he's not such a bad man."

Max shuddered a little, recoiling at her words as if struck.

Gail braved her way further. "It seemed to me he just wanted to know his son's choice of wife. He may be a bit dictatorial, but I think . . . I think he cares for you."

"No. No!" Max yelled, causing no small amount of turned heads. Only Gail's hand on his arm kept him from stalking off. Fury and panic read clear as day in his green eyes.

"Don't dare take his side. He cares about me only as an extension of a name he refuses to give up control of. You are one of the few people who know . . . He did this on purpose. He approached *you* on purpose. He'll try to manipulate you and through you, me. You cannot trust his motives. So don't you dare feel for my father, because God knows I don't."

Unaware he was ranting, unaware of the tears that swam in front of Gail's eyes, Max pulled his arm free of her grasp.

Music and laughter continued around them as long moments passed, Gail's heart cracking not because of Max, but rather for him.

"If you just talked with him . . ." she tried again valiantly, futilely. But Max backed away from her outreached hand as if it were diseased.

For a moment he looked as if she had hit him, hurt him. But then eyes hardened, and he allowed his spite to flow in low menacing tones.

"You talk and you talk and you talk, but you never listen, you foolish little girl. No wonder you were such a disaster all your life. You cannot mend fences that have been blown to splinters. I don't give a bloody damn about my father. He can rot in hell for all I care. And you can . . ." He paused for breath and faltered.

He had her backed against a wall—Gail was not too proud to admit that she was slightly frightened. His face was a deep red, his muscles tensed to a snapping point. His brow was drawn down into a menace, but slowly, slowly, Gail saw horror and pain dawning over him. He let out his steam in one long hiss.

"Blast," he finally breathed, before abruptly walking away.

Gail stood for some moments in shock, blinking back the tears that threatened to fall. She had no idea his father had burned him this badly. She was quite certain Max didn't either. As she brought her hand to her flushed cheek, she took a surreptitious peek from behind the bough of flowers. A few discreet nearby heads turned away quickly, but Gail couldn't bring herself to care. She was mostly surprised to find that the dancing, the laughter, the music, all continued.

Nothing, and everything, seemed to have occurred.

After a quick trip to the powder room, Gail found her way back to her circle of friends, ready to laugh and feign happiness until she could leave without giving offense, in approximately an hour. If she managed to tear her hem or stub her toe, she could escape in possibly half the time. She was just about to make an accomplice of a nearby chair, when Count Roffstaam approached.

Politely extracting her from Lilly Pickering and Mr. Belling, the Count pulled her to one side.

Gail was rather tired of being pulled from place to place.

"Zat vas a very short valtz," the Count said, watching closely as Gail worried a lock of hair.

"Count Roffstaam, I apologize if Lord Fontaine and I did not demonstrate the dance properly for you," she began tiredly. The waltz was the last thing on her mind right now.

"May I offer advising?" the Count asked. At her sullen nod, he continued. "My vife and I"—he nodded toward the Countess's tall pink form across the room—"fight like bears. But, never are we letting arguing go without the sun."

Momentarily befuddled, Gail asked, "Do you mean you never let the sun go down on an argument?"

"Ya, ya." He nodded excitedly.

"But Max . . . Lord Fontaine and I do not, er, have a relationship of that nature."

The Count stared baldly at Gail until her cheeks burned with the rightness of his assumption. As she looked to her toes, the Count took Gail's hand between his two.

"My country may not understand the waltz," he said, consolingly, but with surprisingly little accent, "but they understand each other. Two people must mend before sleeping. Go and offer the apology."

"But Count Roffstaam," Gail replied, tired but resolute, "it is he who owes me an apology. Of that I'm certain."

The Count leaned in conspiratorially and whispered.

"Then go and be there to receive it."

* * *

HE'D be damned if he apologized, Max thought as he downed a third glass of whiskey. He sat alone in Mr. Holt's private library, aware of the lull of music and laughter that went on just beyond the huge mahogany doors.

He'd poisoned her, was Max's only panicked thought. She spoke in defense of his father, and that was as damning a betrayal as Brutus to Caesar. Even as the pain of it sliced through him, he remembered, cringing, the look of wide-eyed fear on Gail's face.

She'd never forgive him, anyway. He poured a fourth. He'd been so bloody mean—as mean as his father on his worst day. So there was no point—he was unforgivable.

The only bright side of having Gail hate him was that she would never speak to him again. Max chuckled a raw, pained laugh. How low had he fallen when *that* was a bright side?

He was about to enjoy the fourth glass when the library doors opened, and on a flood of music and chatter, Will Holt entered the room, a small scrap of paper crumpled in his hand and a grave expression on his face.

"Fontaine, here you are." As Will started toward him, his eyes fell to the bottle at Max's side. "God—you've . . . you've heard, haven't you?"

"Heard what?" Max slurred, again raising the glass to his lips. Will stayed his friend's hand.

"Fontaine . . . Max. You may want to be sober for this." Will gently removed the glass, bringing a bewildered Max's attention to his face.

"Goddammit, Holt. I'm in here trying to drown my sorrows, and I bloody well can't do that without whiskey." Max reached for the glass, but Will held it out of reach.

"Fontaine! Damn it all, stop!" Will yelled, trying to hold the whiskey and hold him steady at the same time. "Max! Your father died!"

Everything stopped.

He went absolutely still. All the noise in his head, all other thoughts, stopped. Ceased to exist. The world had halted on its axis, leaving Max the only one turning, dizzy. Will held out the crumpled bit of paper to Max, who took it dully, automatically.

Max looked at the writing, not really seeing what it said, not able to make out the meaning. He held it for some minutes, as the words *Father* and *expired* finally registered in his brain. Max looked up to Will.

"I'm sorry," his friend ventured softly. But as Max met his eyes, the bubble of laughter that escaped Max's throat cracked through the air like a whip.

"Nothing to be sorry about, old chap," Max said, the cynicism dripping with each word. "I just inherited an Earldom and my freedom with one blow."

Will cringed. He didn't see the piece of paper clutched in a fist closed so tightly it shook.

In fact, only one person noticed that white-knuckled fist.

In his haste to reach Max with the news, Will had neglected to close the library doors. Gail, sent on her quest by the Count, had located her quarry. What she saw left her speechless.

However, it didn't leave Lady Hurstwood speechless, who was passing from the powder room. She may not have noticed the fisted, shaking hand, but she noticed everything else.

Twenty-five

LADY Hurstwood's gossiping tongue did its work at record speed. She told the tale of the earl's passing and his son's callousness with such relish, it was amazing to many that she managed to keep a sober look on her face. However, Gail was too busy at the moment to frown over Lady Hurstwood's facial expressions. She had to get to Max. And since Will had put him immediately into a carriage, the only way to do that was to get out of the ball. So, instead of returning to the ballroom, she turned into the dining room, where she intended to reach her father before the gossip or Romilla did.

Sir Geoffrey sat at one of the tables, indulging in a cigar and some conversation with Mr. Fortings. He was chuckling as his daughter limped to him.

"Father," she said, with what she hoped was a tired but happy expression, "I wanted to inform you I'm headed back to the house."

"What? Oh Gail! What's this? Going home already?" Sir Geoffrey asked, looking only a little peeved at her interrupting the masculine conversation.

"Yes. I've danced and danced, and now I've bruised my

foot in the process. Romilla has said it's quite all right, but I should ask you for either the carriage or hack money."

It would, of course, be terribly crude for Sir Geoffrey to send his daughter home in a hack, so Gail soon found herself in the possession of the carriage, with the strictest instructions to send it back for the rest of the family. Then, with a perfunctory kiss on the cheek and a dismissive wave, Sir Geoffrey turned back to his conversation with Mr. Fortings before he could see his daughter remove herself quite speedily and without so much as a trace of limp.

* * *

ELSEWHERE in the mansion, Romilla was idly sipping punch when the news of her prospective stepson-in-law's father's demise reached her ears. And by none other than Lady Hurstwood herself.

"And I don't suppose we'll ever see him married now," that lady conspiratorially whispered.

Romilla took a calm sip of punch. "Why do you say that?" she queried nonchalantly.

"Oh, everyone knows it was his father that was pressuring him into marriage. The Baron Rentworth is a, er, close friend of mine, and he said the old Earl (God rest his soul) had actually threatened to cut the boy out of his inheritance—the part that was not entailed, which is quite a large portion. But now that the father's gone"—here she interjected a heartfelt sigh to her narrative—"there's no reason for the son to hunt a bride."

Romilla, a credit to her social skills, managed to remain cool as iced tea as Lady Hurstwood delivered her parting line.

"It's a pity someone didn't snag him sooner—especially if that young lady strived to the point of compromise to secure him."

* * *

AND so it was, for the second time in a quarter hour, a female family member interrupted Sir Geoffrey during his conversation and cigar.

"Romilla!" he cried. Seeing his wife approach with a placid smile, he tried to shove his still-burning cigar into the hands of a very amused Mr. Fortings.

"Here you are, dearest," Romilla said easily. "Mr. Fortings, do you mind if I steal my husband away for a few moments?" At that gentleman's acquiescing nod, her husband stood and placed Romilla's arm through his, commencing a leisurely stroll to a private alcove out of sight and earshot of the other diners.

"Darling, it wasn't my cigar, I swear, Fortings just asked me to hold it a moment . . ."

"Don't talk to me now about such a silly thing as cigars, we are about to be undone!"

As Romilla told him of the Earl's demise and the gossip that had ensued, Sir Geoffrey's face went from white to red, to black with anger.

"All this time . . . it was just for his inheritance?" Sir Geoffrey asked disbelievingly.

"Dearest, whatever his motives, it is immaterial now. The point is he's going to cry off!"

"He gave me his word," Sir Geoffrey said darkly. "We must impress upon him the importance of keeping it."

"We must do more than that; we must force him." Romilla took a deep breath and imparted her plan. "We have to announce it."

Sir Geoffrey stroked his chin. "But even if we announce the engagement, it will appear after the news of the Earl's death—it will seem a desperate act on our part."

"Go and wake up your friend at the *Times*. Have him pull all the papers that were to be distributed in the morning and reprinted with the announcement. This is the material point: It must seem as if we placed the announcement before the Earl's death. And make it known they've been secretly engaged for a while."

"But . . . I've already given the carriage to take Gail home."

Romilla was so exasperated she nearly shook her husband.

"Then, hire a hack, for goodness' sake! In fact, t'will be better if you do—no one will spot our carriage where it should not be. I'll make your excuses. Just go, now!"

And with that last command, Romilla dispatched her husband to go and awaken his editor friend from his well-earned slumber. She returned to the ballroom some minutes later, wholly composed and graceful, keeping her eyes on Evangeline as she danced, speaking quietly with her in the interim. Although she seemed to be calm and blasé in the sea of gossip swirling around them, Romilla's mind was far too engaged on the predicament at hand to dwell very long on why her second daughter had left the party early, and unescorted.

* * *

TO carry off her hastily put together plan, Gail required the assistance of two particular servants. One was Jimmy, the groom, who as a longtime observer of the tenuous relationship between Miss Gail and "that Lord Fontaine bloke," and a bit of a romantic to boot, was more than willing to assist the young mistress. The second was Gail and Evangeline's ladies' maid, Polly, who, as luck would have it, was Jimmy's sweetheart.

After entering Number Seven and making a show to Morrison and Mrs. Bibb of her intention to retire for the evening, Gail went to her room. There, with the assistance of Polly, she quickly changed out of her ball gown and into the darkest clothing she owned, which she discovered was her dark green velvet riding habit. With a black hooded cloak draped about Gail's shoulders, Polly ushered her down the servant's fortuitously empty corridors and out to the stables. There, Jimmy was waiting with QueenBee.

Covered by the cloak and the darkness of night, Gail went to the front door of Max's rather modest dwelling and knocked softly.

She waited a full ten seconds before impatience had her trying the door handle. It was unlocked.

The lodgings were completely still. She moved quietly, keeping her eyes peeled for any servant, anyone who should acknowledge her presence, but none emerged. It seemed as if her very breath would disrupt the frozen house.

Had she guessed wrong? Maybe Max had not come back here, maybe he had gone to Longsbowe House in Mayfair.

Maybe he had already left for his estate. Maybe he had . . . Gail poked her head into the rooms on either side of the small corridor, finding a cozy, messy study, and a small, tidy drawing room, but no sign of life. She nervously played with a curl of hair, wondering if she should check the back of the house, when the slightest flicker of light caught her eye from under a door on the far side of the drawing room.

Gail froze, mesmerized by that faint glow of light. To slip into a man's house in the dead of night was foolish, impulsive, and tantamount to ruination. To seek him out in his bedchamber *was* ruination.

And yet, she'd come this far, with one purpose: Max. She didn't know how, didn't know why, but she knew he needed her to be his friend tonight.

Love is need.

It was the easiest decision of her life to cross the room and seek the light.

Her soft footsteps came to a stop before what she'd guessed was Max's bedchamber. When soft knocking elicited no response (and neither did loud knocking), Gail held her breath as she tested the handle, easing open the door.

He stood by the bed, his back to Gail. His stillness mirrored that of his rooms, as he stared at some random spot on the counterpane, lost in his thoughts.

She stepped into the room, but kept her hand on the knob, as if to hold her from fleeing.

"Your doors are unlocked," she ventured softly. He was so still, she couldn't know if he heard her. "Where is everyone?"

"The maid is only here once a week. I sent Harris to Longsbowe Park, to prepare for my father's arrival." He spoke in monotone, keeping his back to her. The light she had followed was a single candlestick, resting on a table by the bed. It flickered softly as his breath passed by, all too soon returning to stillness. As her eyes adjusted, Gail could see various articles of clothing lying neatly on the bed, a pair of boots on the floor. Max had not changed out of his impeccable evening kit, having only removed the dark black coat. Next to the clothes sat a small opened valise.

"You're going away," she said softly.

"I must. I have a parent to bury."

"Are you . . ."

"I'm fine," he said curtly. "You can go."

"No," Gail whispered, her heart in her throat. "I don't think I should."

He turned to her then, his eyes unreadable in the dark, but his jaw set and angry.

"Think?" he replied mockingly. "God forbid you ever try it. Get out of here, now!"

Gail's hand tightened on the doorknob, warring with the strong impulse to turn and run. But she held her ground.

"You told me your father tried to manipulate you in the past . . ." she began stiltedly.

"I don't wish to discuss my father with you," he warned, his tone low, his broad shoulders working fiercely under the taut expanse of his shirt.

"You should know," Gail continued bravely, "that whatever your parent's methods, I believe in the end his intentions were good." She let go of the handle, taking a step away from the door. It creaked softly shut.

"When you first told me of him, I thought him a monster, and you thought him a monster, too, I believe. But I met him. He was just a man, Max. A lonely, old man, broken by time and his mistakes. I think . . . I think he came to understand that you were your own person. And underneath all that, he was your father."

She stepped closer as she spoke, coming to rest in front of Max, who refused to raise his head and meet her imploring, sincere eyes. She was close enough to touch him, but dared not reach out.

"Max . . ." she whispered, the sympathy in her voice bridging the space between them.

"No!" he cried so sharply, Gail took a step back. "Why on earth am I plagued with such a nosy creature? Do I have to be cruel to be rid of you? Fine." When she took another step back, he stepped forward, pushing, pursuing. "At the museum, I told you about the meanness of my father to get under your skirts. You had been twitching about the stacks all day, driving me mad, and I preyed on your surprisingly eager sympathy. You should have seen yourself, too, when I told you how my father made himself ill to get me to stay in the country—you were so ready to comfort me in my grief I could have tossed you on the floor, and you would have made no argument. In fact," he crowded her as her back hit the wall, "you would have enjoyed it."

Gail sucked in her breath, finding she had no farther to go. He put both of his hands on either side of her head, effectively caging her in.

"Is that why you're here now?" he murmured. "To . . . assuage my grief?" One hand left the wall to graze over the velvet of her jacket. "I can't see you in this habit without thinking of how easily the buttons come free."

The want in his voice mingled enticingly with the menace. She felt his breath on her lips as he leaned in closer, and closer. Then in an instant, he pushed himself off the wall and stalked away from her, back to his packing.

"Get out of here now, Brat, before I take what your very presence here offers."

Gail stood frozen to the wall, but not with fear. A great calm had settled about her, an understanding. Her voice was clear as she spoke.

"He missed you."

She saw his shoulders tense, but he remained silent.

"All that you said tonight, on the dance floor, here in this room, I know it's not true."

"I don't give a damn about my father," he said as he ruthlessly stuffed shirts into the valise.

"Bullshit," she replied, clear as a bell.

He turned, openmouthed in surprise.

"Where did you learn that word?"

"I know lots of words." She moved toward him, her confidence growing with each measured step. "You've encouraged me to speak up, so I shall. It's bullshit."

"My father was an old manipulative man, and I *never* gave a damn about him," but his voice lacked the conviction it had before.

"What ho, methinks the gentleman doth protest too much,"

Gail said, her steady gaze penetrating him. "If you don't care about him, if you *never* cared, then what have you been doing in London all this time? You could have traveled the world twice over, and yet you remained here. If you didn't care about your father, then you must have been simply waiting around for him to die."

"Don't say that!"

"You stayed," she replied, her voice louder than his, stronger with its certainty, "because you did care. Because you were worried. You had to leave Longsbowe to survive, I understand that, but you stayed close enough so if he needed you, you'd be there. You loved him."

All of Max's arguments died on his tongue. All he could do was watch Gail as she approached him, listen as she gave voice to the tumult of his feelings.

"He loved you, too. Everything he did might have been warped and misguided and foolish . . ."

"Stop it," he croaked.

"He was still your father, Max. He was still the man who taught you how to fish, who shared his love of his lands with you. He cared about you. If nothing else, believe that. It's all right to be sad." She had reached his side by now and impulsively laid a gloved hand on his tense wrist. He simply stared at it. "If you're mad, if you want to scream. You're allowed to miss him."

"No," he whispered. "No! No! Stop, right now!" he yelled, shaking off her hand, turning away, pacing furiously.

His face was a portrait of pain and anger, of confusion and grief, as he stalked in long strides the length of the carpet. Suddenly he crossed to her, breathing heavily.

For a moment, Gail thought he might hit her, but she refused to flinch. Then, a decision made, he grabbed her arms and pulled her roughly to him, kissing her fiercely, bruising her lips with his.

She did not move. She refused to let her shaking knees fold into him, but also did she refuse to back away.

He kept kissing her, pushing himself against her soft but unyielding frame, trying desperately to feel something, anything, but this breaking in his chest.

Soon enough, Gail felt something wet fall against her cheek. A tear, but it did not belong to her.

Max was crying, no longer pressing his intentions against her mouth. His grip was still fierce on her arms, and he fell to his knees, unable to stand anymore, such was the violence of his sobs. She pressed his face to her stomach, holding him there, the dam finally broken.

They stayed like that for some while, Max holding firmly to Gail's waist, she soothing his head and shoulders, as he mourned for the father that had died tonight, and the one he lost so many years ago.

Twenty-six

IT was still pitch dark outside, and Gail was drooling on his chest.

Sometime during the emotional haze of the night, they had transferred to the bed. It was unclear to Max how they managed to end there, wrapped around each other, but it seemed right somehow. Peaceful repose would not have been achieved any other way.

They were both still clothed, of course. Gail's heavy, voluminous skirts belled out around her, her feet tucked under and lost in the sea of green velvet. It made her seem impossibly small. She seemed so peaceful, so delicate in sleep, Max thought. Considering how she had stood up to him so fiercely such a short time ago, it was another impossibility to add to the ever-growing list.

For instance, it was impossible that he was in love with Gail, and yet, he knew it to be true. While eventually exhaustion had caused Gail's eyes to flutter into sleep, Max had remained awake. She curled up against his chest, unwilling even in sleep to let go of him, and Max let his attention wander over the course of his life since he had come to know this annoying, nosy, curious, beautiful, intelligent, witty creature at his side. The minute he felt the cold wet patch of her drool hit his chest through his shirt, and he didn't mind, he knew he was in love.

She challenged him at every turn. He had been floating along, just making do until he met her. For the first time, he wanted more, wanted to be more. For her. He wanted to be the reason for those secret smiles that constantly lit her face.

He smiled just thinking of it, a great sigh leaving his chest. Unfortunately, such motion roused the weight of slumbering female half-situated on said chest. Her eyes fluttered open.

"Hello," he murmured.

"Hello," she replied, realizing as she moved her mouth that fluid had escaped. She blushed readily.

"Oh goodness. I'm so sorry." She wiped her mouth.

"Don't worry about it," he said, his hand pushing an errant lock of hair behind her ear.

"I don't usually drool, I swear." She took a bit of sleeve and dabbed at his shirt, causing him to chuckle.

"Good to know," he replied dryly. While indeed, Max didn't mind at all now, he shouldn't like to be drooled on for the rest of his days.

She stilled in her ministrations. Good lord, had he said that last bit out loud? She raised her lids and met his steady gaze. Or could she simply know his thoughts? A moment of heat passed between them, intense and very real. But then, with a flush of her cheeks, Gail looked away, coughing nervously, and blinked about the room, clearing herself of sleep.

"How long was I dozing?" she asked, attempting to pull herself up to a position resembling respectability, which, on a bed with a gentleman, was of no use.

"Not too long," he replied, ushering Gail's head back down to his shoulder, stroking her hair. "'Tis not yet day."

He could have her long, warm body lay in the crook of his arm forever. She seemed more than content to be there. After some minutes, Gail raised her head to look into his eyes.

"Are you all right?" she asked.

A mix of emotions flashed through him, but anger and hurt were no longer among them.

"I think I will be," he said after some deliberation. "And

that's to your credit." For indeed, a sense of peace had come over Max. In the course of his musings, his thoughts turned to his father, his mind clearer. Maybe he hadn't understood the old man at all. And maybe, even though the Earl had passed, it was time to try to do so.

But not this very moment. This moment was for Gail. That bewitching creature was looking up into his face with shining eyes, searching his face with concern and love. She leaned up and laid a soft kiss on his lips, one that asked nothing, but gave everything.

When she pulled away, it was to see that love reflected on his face.

"Would you like to know how I'm feeling right now?" he asked.

A moment passed before that wisecracking half-grin bloomed.

"A man *offering* to speak his feelings? This must be a first in the course of human history."

"Minx. You don't wish to know then?"

Her face softened. "Tell me."

"I feel like I've been thrown into cold water—" he said as she settled back down against his shoulder.

"If this is about the lake . . ." she warned.

"It's not about the lake. Although it was cold." She slapped his chest playfully, but he caught her hand, his fingers drifting over her wrist and opening her hand like a flower petal. Then he edged gently across her palm, lacing her fingers with his.

"I've been thrown into cold water, and all I've got to hold to is your hand."

His eyes burned into hers as he said this, the depth of his feeling expressed for the first time. So powerful were those words, that all she could say in that moment was, "Oh."

He leaned down, kissing her as lightly as she had him.

When he pulled back, it was to see the light of her humor back in her eyes.

"That was awfully poetic," she said.

"Yes," he agreed wryly.

"Are you sure you haven't been tucked away here, study-ing Byron for the past few weeks?"

His eyes crinkled at the corners as he regarded her with faux outrage.

"Are you mocking me? In my great moment of honesty you mock me?" She giggled in reply, the sound lightening his heart. "I am wounded, through the core."

"Oh, Lord Fontaine," she replied, stifling a giggle, "I am so very sorry to have bruised your obviously delicate feelings. Had I but known! Had I but seen!"

"And your apology insincere!" he cried, and turned his face away.

"Max!" she laughed, but he refused to look at her. So, mischeviously, she leaned up very close to his ear, whispering his name. At the same time, her free hand began to dance a seductive pattern on his chest.

"Max . . ."

Her breath blew across his ear, and immediately lust shot through him. He held still as long as he could . . . which was about two and a half seconds.

Flipping over with lightning speed, Max was suddenly laying on top of his laughing quarry. His face a hair's breadth from hers, she saw a flicker of roguish humor play over his features before his mouth met hers.

What began playfully soon turned passionate. Hands in her hair forced the long-maligned pins out, hands on his shirt found and undid quarrelsome buttons.

Freeing the full length of her tresses, Max lifted his head long enough to spread her hair out over the pillow. In the past he had seen it wet and tangled, he had mussed it, causing it to fall about her face in charming disarray, but never before, he realized, had he seen its full length. Surprisingly it came past her elbows. A smile of pure greed lifted his lips. Who would have thought that practical, sharp Gail would have something as feminine and beguiling as long, lush hair?

She was the most complex person he was ever likely to meet, he thought as he tenderly traced her eyebrows, her jaw. The quirks that made her strange made her whole.

"What is it?" she asked, confusion, nervousness in her voice.

He smiled, intent upon putting her at ease. "I was just thinking: Is there anything you aren't? You are witty, strange, superstitious, strong, brave—so many wonderful things to me. So is there anything you aren't?" he asked softly. "Anything you cannot do? Because quite honestly, you overwhelm me."

A tremulous blushing smile accompanied a barely audible sigh of relief. When he had pulled away, she was terrified she had done something wrong. Now, she knew there was no wrong here. Only what felt right.

Why shouldn't you try for happiness?

"Well," she breathed coyly, "I'm afraid I don't speak Italian."

His eyes blazed. His lips curled. "On that, I can instruct you."

He dove for her—she dove with him.

There was no restraint, nothing holding them back from each other. In this room, in this time, only they two existed. He kissed her eyes, her neck, her jaw, everywhere there was flesh. And when he found his pursuits obstructed, he went about exposing more. The buttons of her habit came free as easily as Max had remembered. The chemise underneath was silk, and when the erotic feel of it was replaced by his lips, Gail cried out in surprise and pleasure.

She could feel his grin against her breast at her outcry, but before she could protest his very male sense of victory, his lips came together again, and he began to suckle.

After that, it was really all she could do to not buck off the bed.

One hand threaded its way through his dark, thick hair, the other held firmly over her mouth.

"Darling, stop biting your hand," he said, lifting his head. "There's no one to hear you cry out."

She shot him a look through her daze of lust. "*You'll* hear me."

"I," he replied with a grin, "want to hear you."

Before she could come up with a clever retort, which Max liked to think might take a few seconds longer than normal, given her current state, he slipped one hand up under her skirts quickly, cupping her most private of places so intimately, she cried out again.

His eyes grew black with desire, with triumph.

"That's not fair!" she squeaked, as she felt his thumb do things that surely thumbs didn't normally do.

He grinned as he said, "Never said anything about 'fair,'" and lowered his mouth to hers again, feeding her fierce passion with his own, melding her to his body, only their clothes keeping them from each other now.

Then he stilled, withdrawing his hand. A small spasm of pain crossed his face as he watched her small frown.

"Darling. Gail, look at me." Her clouded eyes met his, ablaze with so much passion that he wanted to slit his wrists for what he was about to do.

"If you want me to stop, tell me now," he said, as he bit his lip, frustration, fear, and pain all crossing his features at once. "What comes next . . . I won't be able to stop."

For the space of a breath, for the space of an eternity, he thought she might come to her senses and make him end their play. That twisted a knife in his side. No, this was no longer playing. This was everything. And while his honor had warred with his body, honor had won, and left him in the balance as she decided his fate.

Then, a smile. That playful, wicked smile.

"And miss my Italian lesson?" she proclaimed innocently. "Not a chance."

Pure, unadulterated relief flowed from him in waves. Through a shaky smile, he replied, "I did say I'd instruct you, didn't I? Very well." He sat up quickly on his heels, immediately missing the feel of her next to him.

"This," he said, indicating his shirt that hung open, "is called a *camicia.*"

"*Camicia,*" she repeated.

Never letting his eyes stray from hers, he removed the *camicia* and tossed it on the floor.

An eyebrow shot up at seeing his bare chest, hard planes and muscles that played over his shoulders. A spattering of dark curly hair danced its way down his chest, over a hard, lean stomach and into a tiny trail that disappeared into his trousers.

So this was the body of a boring, bookish translator, eh?

He watched the flush rise to her cheeks, as her gaze traveled over his body, and if he thought he had been hard before, he was throbbing with need now.

"Now this," he said, fingering the open ends of her habit's jacket, "is a *giacca*."

She sat up, her eyes never leaving his face, the set of her jaw telling him, daring him to remove the *giacca*. And he was never one to back down from a challenge, especially not one so enticing.

Once that garment was tossed to the floor, Max's hand traveled to the waistband of her skirts. He found the row of buttons, and undid them each with a flick of his extremely adroit (as Gail was aware) thumb.

"This is a *gonna*." As he attempted to pull it down her body, Max realized she was also encased in about half a dozen petticoats. "Good Lord, woman, how many *gonna* are you wearing?"

Gail shrugged, a glint of mischief in her eye. "As many *gonna* as are required."

"Well, they are not required here. In fact, we are firmly against them," Max replied, as he worked her lushly rounded bottom out of the voluminous garments. "Oof," he said as he heaved them onto the floor. "That is the heaviest damn outfit I've ever seen."

"Yes, I believe I've mentioned that before." She smirked.

He remembered that first day at the lake, a waterlogged imp so weighted down by sopping wet velvet she couldn't even stand.

"So you did." He smiled, and lowered himself down on top of her once more.

Stockings and a chemise. *Calza et biacheria intima.* When they fell to the floor onto the pile, Gail felt wholly exposed, in body and mind. Although that could simply have been an effect of being completely naked. And it felt glorious.

His hands, his mouth, took in every plush curve, every

lean, long muscle, every sensitive bit of flesh, content to lazily feast. But inside, low in her belly, the desire, the need for more built a hunger she could not ignore.

Her hand reached for his trousers.

"What are these called?" she asked shyly as her fingers undid the top buttons.

His hand grabbed hers with such a fierce grip she thought fleetingly she hurt him—and by the look on his face, maybe she had.

"Not yet," he mumbled, and again kissed her, but she would not be deterred. Her deft fingers flicked the second button open before he could stop her.

Max groaned and he lifted himself on his elbows, staring down into her face.

There it was, she thought. His own little war. She had given him permission, and was about to give him everything, but still his honor demanded he question it.

Softly, and with infinite gentleness, she asked again, "What are 'trousers' in Italian?"

"Pantaloni," he said at long last, and in the space it took her to repeat the new word, they had joined the pile of clothes on the floor.

"Oh," she breathed, taking him in wholly with her eyes.

He was beautiful.

He was magnificent.

He was at full attention.

And he was far too large for this to be even remotely feasible.

He saw the fear, the uncertainty cross her face. Goddammit. He knew it was too soon—he didn't want to scare her. Now all he could do was allay her fears.

A predatory smirk lit his eyes. Good thing he knew exactly how.

She cleared her throat nervously, as she struggled to sit up, causing him to smile all the wider. "Um, ah . . . Max, I'm not . . . that is . . . how . . . ?"

"You at a loss for words is the best compliment I've ever received," he replied, grinning like the cat that ate the canary.

Her mouth formed an *O* of outrageous shock. He was

laughing even as his hand snaked up her thigh and began to caress her in a way that made her eyes go dark and dreamy.

"I promise you—and I always keep my promises—this will work. And quite well, too."

As he touched her intimately, that hunger that had been building began to burn. When a finger slid inside her, she burst into flames. When he slid down her body and replaced his thumb with his tongue, the fire consumed her.

It was rather fortuitous that Max had given her leave to cry out, Gail thought dazedly as a torrent of shudders wracked her body in waves. For surely, she was making noise enough to wake the neighboring county.

She was exquisite, he thought, watching her in the throes of passion. And he was the one to do that, he grinned with relish.

Before the little spasms of pleasure had ceased, Max angled her for his entrance. And found himself at the gates of paradise.

"What was that?" Gail asked between heavy breaths.

"That was the beginning." He grinned down at her.

"There's more?" Her eyes went wide as he nodded. He pushed himself forward, just a little, sliding so easily into her slick, welcoming entry.

"What is this?" She raised an eyebrow.

"Everything else," he replied, easing himself forward more.

The long eyelashes fluttered closed, as she gave herself up to the feel of him.

This was the tricky part, he knew. In theory, anyway. Having never deflowered anyone, he had to go on what he had been told about the process as a lad.

He really should have studied up more recently, he thought grimly.

Slowly, gently, he made his way. When he finally reached the barrier of her innocence, he lifted his head from their current distracting ministrations.

"Gail, love." Her eyes fluttered to meet his. "I, ah . . . I'm told this part hurts a bit."

"Told?" Gail said sharply. "You haven't done this before?"

"Of course I have!" he replied indignantly. "But, well, not

with anyone who hasn't also done this before. So if it does hurt, I apologize in advance."

Again, before she could voice one word of question, remark, or protest, Max plunged forward and broke through.

He stilled above her, desperate to see if she was all right, if she was in pain, if she was going to kill him for this. He watched as she took a series of slow, steady breaths, keeping her eyes closed. And then she opened those eyes.

And smiled.

Feather-light kisses rained down upon her face. And when he kissed her deeply, so deeply she felt it in her soul, she tilted her hips up, inviting him in farther.

That was all he needed. Her hands roamed over his strong back, his buttocks as he moved himself within her, holding her to him. Every time he pulled away, he came back, faster, deeper, until that pressure, that hunger, that fire built within her again. She matched his pace, his passion. He whispered words in her ear, *"Caro mio, amoré."* Words she didn't know but somehow understood. He took her thighs, her hips, lifting her to him, all the while caressing, feeling, feeling her to his goddamn toes. When she burst, she said his name.

And when her climax shook about him, he took one last plunge, and fell.

* * *

IT was a good time later that they finally decided to move. Not terribly far, however. Reluctant to quit that contact that had proved so powerful, Max simply rolled over, taking his lady with him. The sun had yet to peek above the horizon, so it could not account for the light in either Gail or Max's eyes.

"I confess," Gail said, breaking the lazy silence that cocooned them, "had I know Italian was so interesting, I'd have taken care to learn earlier."

"Perish the thought!" Max replied. "It is my estimable pleasure to teach you." He leaned up and kissed her damp brow.

"Is there any other subject you require instruction on? I should be happy to oblige," Max asked cheekily, as he wrapped Gail still tighter in his arms.

"We-ell . . ." she began, toying with a lock of hair near his ear, "I'm afraid I don't sing or play well."

"Hence your atrocious disregard for Beethoven as the musical genius time will prove him to be, but go on. Ow!" he exclaimed, as she tugged hard on the aforementioned lock.

She grinned and continued, "And I don't have a hand at painting. And I have never been able to make a single piece of embroidery that resembled what it was intended to. I cannot play chess to save my life. And I am absolutely abysmal at higher-level mathematics. Calculus completely escaped me."

"Lord, woman. That's quite beyond me. Who can do all that, honestly?" Max replied with a small laugh. Gail, however, was not laughing. She was regarding him with a furrowed brow and a quirk of her head.

"Evangeline."

Max stilled quite suddenly. "Really?" he asked, mildly perplexed.

"Yes." She nodded. "She's actually quite accomplished."

"But, er, what young lady is not accomplished?"

"She's not simply accomplished—she outstripped our tutor in mathematics by the age of fourteen. She's sold paintings to galleries in Paris." With a small, disbelieving laugh, Gail leaned up to look him quizzically in the eye. "Didn't she tell you she loved art?"

Max, more than a bit disgruntled to be discussing his intended bride with her sister with whom he had just made love, frowned in discomfort.

"Er—ah, she might have mentioned it, I suppose I wasn't paying much attention. Gail"—he began stroking the soft skin of her back in smooth, calming motions—"You shouldn't think that because your sister can do these things she's better than you. It's impossible."

Gail smiled nervously. "You asked me if there's anything I'm not. I'm not many things, Max, things that every lady should be. I know it. Evangeline outstrips me in many ways."

She paused for a moment, clearly awkward in her confession of her various lacks.

"Darling," he began, but Gail regrouped, clearing her throat.

"However, that's not the reason I was frowning. Max, it has just occurred to me that you didn't get to know Evangeline at all, did you?"

A moment of disbelieving realization passed in front of Max.

"No, I don't suppose I did. I was too busy falling in love with you."

Max's confession fell from his mouth with surprising ease.

"I have long since come to the realization that one evening, nay, twenty minutes, in a moonlit garden bespeaks nothing more than infatuation," he said, "which doesn't last beyond a real conversation. I confess, I never thought of Evangeline as more than a beautiful girl in a garden. I fell in love where and with whom I least expected. And, my darling girl, it took longer than twenty minutes."

The object of his affection looked down into his face, openmouthed with shock and wonder. Fortunately, she did not drool.

"Then again, maybe falling had only taken an instant," he whispered, warmth flowing from him.

For many moments, Gail could not speak. Then, "You love me?" she squeaked.

"Yes," he replied with a grin and a squeeze round her waist. "And you love me."

"Well, of course I love you, but trust you to take the upper hand in the conversation!" And with that, Max laughed loudly, kissed her soundly, and forgot himself enough to mumble more words in Italian. For which Gail insisted on translations.

* * *

SOMETIME later, night still cocooning Weymouth Street and its occupants, Gail lifted her sleepy head from her beloved's chest.

"Max . . ." she whispered.

"Hmm?" was the lazy, sated reply, which elicited a small smile from Gail.

"How is this going to work?"

At that he opened his eyes, met hers. "We'll make it work."

"Really?"

"Yes, really." He ran a hand over her long dark hair, easing her to rest on his chest again.

"Don't worry so. Everything will be sorted out."

Right before Max's eyes closed, he saw Gail's lashes flutter down.

"You'll see, my love. You'll see."

Twenty-seven

IF logic were rule, Max and Gail would have lived happily ever after from this point on. However, it's sadly true that logic and love rarely have anything to do with each other.

Max had departed for Longsbowe Park a few hours later than planned, and Gail had kissed him good-bye with longing. They murmured promises for the future and speedy returns between their kisses. And then he left.

Gail crept up the servant's staircase of Number Seven as dawn began to lighten the sky. Polly led her to her chamber, where a blissfully dazed Gail fell into bed, too exhausted to contemplate the night before, too happy to avoid doing so. She drifted to sleep, certain that life was, if not perfect, then full of perfect moments.

Of course, that sense of contentment quickly dissolved into confusion upon Gail's arousal from slumber.

She awoke much later than usual. Bleary-eyed, Gail blinked at the clock on the mantel, certain she read it wrong. Eleven! Impossible—Romilla would never let her sleep so late! 'Twas past tea!

Hurriedly she dressed and thrust pins into her hair while running down the steps. Oh, Romilla would have her head, she knew it. There was, however, one silver lining—if anyone had guessed what she'd been doing or where she'd been doing it the previous night, they would have hauled her out of bed by her ears. The fact that she'd been allowed to sleep meant that most likely, she had been forgotten.

That impression was reinforced when Gail entered the drawing room and was assaulted by the voices of a dozen chattering women and the scent of every variety of flower the London hothouses provided.

None of the ladies looked up at her arrival, save her sister, who flanked Romilla in the middle of the hubbub.

"Gail!" Evangeline cried, parting the sea of feathered bonnets and flowered bouquets to take her sister's hand, giving it a hearty squeeze. "You're awake at last. Polly said that you had danced yourself to exhaustion last night. I hope it wasn't the noise that roused you." Evangeline's voice spoke all innocuous pleasantries, but her eyes pleaded for sisterly support. Gail was more than ready to give it, but . . .

"Evie, what's all the to-do? I didn't know we were expecting so many callers," Gail inquired as Evangeline pulled her back to the couches. The ladies burst into a gale of titters.

"La, child, didn't you know?" Romilla said as the girls took their seats. "The announcement was put in the papers yesterday, and ran just this morning."

"And we are all agog! 'Tis an excellent match," Mrs. Fortings said.

"Quite," said a tight-lipped Lady Hurstwood.

"Announcement?" asked a bewildered Gail, and found Romilla's hand close over hers, squeezing rather tightly.

"Of your sister's engagement, of course," Romilla said very clearly. She beamed a smile at Gail, who could only smile weakly in return. "Gail's known about it for ages of course, the only surprise to her is that it's a surprise to anyone else," she said with an eager grin to the group.

"Indeed," said Lady Hurstwood. "I find it terribly surprising given that Lord Fontaine—I'm sorry, Lord Longsbowe now—that the announcement occurred so close to his father's demise."

"But Fanny, we discussed that before we got here," Mrs.

Fortings piped up. "The paper's deadline for announcements and the like is five o'clock the day before it's to run. The announcement was placed before he knew of his father's death."

The whole crowd murmured in agreement as Lady Hurstwood's lips grew tighter.

"Yes, yes, quite the sad affair," Romilla broke in. "Had we known earlier in the day of the late Earl's demise, we would certainly have asked Lord Fontaine—I'm sorry, Lord Longsbowe—to wait until a more proper time to place the announcement. But what's done cannot be undone, and I know, had the old Earl met my darling Evangeline, he would have found no fault in the next Countess of Longsbowe."

Evangeline smiled and received the accolades that followed of her style and beauty with the grace befitting a future Countess. Gail, on the other hand, felt certain that the floor had given way beneath her.

"Ma—er, Lord Longsbowe placed the announcement?" she asked softly of Romilla.

"Well of course, dear, who else should?" Romilla replied quickly, then returned to Mrs. Fortings's description of St. Paul's as a likely place for a wedding as grand as surely this one would be.

What's done cannot be undone. The phrase echoed in Gail's head, the merry chatter that surrounded her reduced to an ebb and flow of squawking likely to drive her mad.

Oh God, what had she done—what had he done? Max wouldn't . . . wouldn't announce the engagement to Evangeline and then spend the night whispering words of love in her ear . . . teasing her body with his . . . making her belong to him in every way. Max wouldn't do that . . . would he?

And Evangeline looked so beautiful, so perfect in her grace and future position. She practically glowed with every renewed good wish and congratulation. It made Gail crave to be alone, so she could cry and scream all the cries and screams building within her.

Suddenly, Lady Hurstwood's clipped tones broke through her deep reverie.

"I do wonder where Lord Longsbowe is. One would

imagine he should call on his bride the day the engagement is announced."

"He can't," Gail murmured before she could think better of it.

Lady Hurstwood regarded Gail with a fixed eye. "Why ever not, child?"

"Because he's in Sussex," replied a masculine voice from the door. The group of ladies turned to see Mr. William Holt, looking particularly fine in a morning coat and buckskin breeches. Evangeline was the only one who did not greet him with a smile.

"My friend Lord Fontaine . . . good gad, it's dashed hard to call him Longsbowe, but we must get used to it, I suppose—bade me come and tell you that he had to repair to Longsbowe Park, for obvious reasons. He left directly after the ball last night."

Much shuffling occurred to make room for Mr. Holt on the couches, but he held up a hand.

"I'm afraid I cannot stay long, ladies. A tradesman's work is never done, it seems." A few mouths pinched at the mention of Mr. Holt's occupation, but the moment passed quickly.

"Miss Alton," he said, bowing, "I understand I am to wish you joy."

Evangeline, her smile faltering for the first time that morning, never let her eyes leave Will's as she asked, "Do you mean that?"

A moment fell between them before Will replied, "Of course. I hope you are happy, Miss Evangeline."

"Of course," she repeated, a small frown creasing her brow.

"As I hope for all ladies to be, on this most glorious of mornings," Will said cheerily, smiling at the group. The not-so-easily smitten matrons of the Ton smiled back in appreciation of Mr. Holt's good looks and charm. He tipped his hat to them and started for the door.

"Wait!" Gail cried out, extricating herself from the group. "I'll see you out."

As she left the room on William Holt's arm, Mrs. Fortings leaned across Evangeline to whisper to Romilla that the Altons might have cause to plan two weddings this season.

Evangeline, who for a moment seemed slightly green, smiled at Mrs. Fortings, and returned to the topic of lace veils.

* * *

OUT in the hall, Gail and Will discussed the peculiarities of the last evening for a few short moments, until Gail came to her decided topic.

"The announcement this morning was a bit of a surprise."

"Yes," Will replied on a cough. "I admit it was."

"Did Max . . . er, did he mention his intention of placing it in the papers to you?"

"No, he did not. But he rarely discusses his actions with me until after he's acted." Will regarded Gail quizzically for a moment. "We were expecting this, you know. It was simply a matter of time, and time was up."

Gail managed to smile at Will. "Yes, of course. But even the expected can seem sudden."

"Miss Gail, I could not agree more heartily."

"I . . . I think my sister will be a perfect countess," Gail stammered. "Don't you?"

Will's brows came together for a moment. "Your sister has no claim to perfection, Miss Gail. Sometimes it seems she's too easily led. Also, she's too short for fashion, and . . . and one eye is slightly bluer than the other . . . she has those two freckles on her left earlobe . . ."

Gail's eyes slowly grew wider, as his ramble trailed off.

"Oh, Will," she sighed. For what else could be said on the subject?

Will leaned into a bow, kissing Gail's hand. He was nearly out the door when Gail caught his arm.

"Mr. Holt, do you happen to have Lord Longsbowe's direction? Evangeline, we, may wish to contact him while he's at his estate."

"Certainly," he replied, a small furrow on his brow, but provided Gail with the exact address of Longsbowe Park. He then said his farewells, leaving Gail in the foyer. She did not linger, nor did she return to the drawing room. While she felt for William Holt, she had her own difficulties to address. So instead she ran upstairs, and with a deep breath and a shaky hand, began to pen a letter.

* * *

LETTERS written in a shaky hand are notorious for their ability to be misdirected. Therefore, since he had not chanced to see a copy of the *Times* before he rode out, Max was fated to remain unaware of all of London's happenings, even those regarding himself.

He became so deeply entrenched in the estate, the home he had not visited in seven years, that an extra week went by before Max realized he had stayed longer than he predicted to Gail.

That's not to say he never thought of his lovely, fire-eyed Gail. Quite the contrary. He found his mind flitting to her randomly. He sensed her presence while sorting through papers in the library with his father's secretary, Mr. Merriot; while riding Jupiter hard over the land; and especially at night, when his mind freely wandered to the loneliness of his large bed and how well she should fill it.

When his father was put into the ground, only Mr. Merriot, the vicar, and a few local gentry were there. Baron Rentworth was among the attendees, of course, but he had been too distraught to do much more than blubber. As he watched the first clump of dirt hit the coffin, Max had the strangest notion that Gail was standing right by his side. It was the most peculiar sensation, a wisp of wind, of warmth. He turned, but saw no one.

He almost left for London that day. He needed to see her. To hear her voice tell him he was a complete nob and that she loved him for it. But he couldn't—not yet. It tore at him, but Max had the unconquerable feeling there was still something left undone at Longsbowe Park.

And so it was that he found himself in his father's study, his study now, going through old correspondence with Mr. Merriot.

"Your father never threw so much as a scrap of paper away," Mr. Merriot said, as he set down two more bundles of papers on the desk with accompanying thuds. Mr. Merriot was a portly, hearty gentleman, at least ten years Max's father's senior. It amazed him that the old gentleman was so robust, that his memory was wholly intact. A little too intact, actually. The man could tell stories for hours about great aunts Max had never met, and he never missed an opportunity to do so.

"I remember a time that Timmons—you remember Timmons, don't you, my Lord? He was underbutler when you were a lad—Timmons was about to use a bit of paper that had a list of old dinner menus written on it as tender for the fire. Suddenly, your father pounced on him—never thought the Earl could move that quick in my life! He grabbed that paper out of Timmons's hand and cried, 'Don't throw that away! How will I know what I ate last week?' " Mr. Merriot finished with a great guffaw, happy in his memories, but Max wasn't listening. He had happened on a letter that perplexed him greatly—a letter addressed to Maximillian Fontaine.

"Mr. Merriot, would you be so good as to tell me what this is? It is addressed to me but is dated whilst I was in the cradle." Max handed over the letter to Mr. Merriot, who looked over the tops of his spectacles at the missive.

"Not you, my Lord, your uncle. This was written to your Uncle Maxim from your father." Mr. Merriot flipped the envelope over. "Was returned undelivered."

"I have an Uncle Maxim?" Max asked, bewildered, taking the letter back from the secretary.

"Had. He died, oh, you couldn't have been more than three or four at the time."

Max's heart thudded in his ears. "How is it I've never heard of him?"

Mr. Merriot's face turned grim. "When he died, your father . . . he told us not to speak of his brother. Even took his portrait down in the gallery."

Max's mind flitted to the long gallery above stairs, which held portraits of the Fontaines at Longsbowe for generations. There was a space, he recalled, near his father's portrait. It was large enough for a medium-sized picture, and in Max's memory, nothing had ever filled the vacancy.

"What happened to my uncle?" Max asked quietly.

Mr. Merriot frowned, obviously debating his words. He let

out a great sigh and removed his spectacles, rubbing his eyes. "It's not a particularly happy story—nor is it particularly sad. Time has passed enough to make it only what it is. The same thing happened to your uncle that happened to too many Englishmen. He was a good ten years younger than your father, but they were the best of friends. You were named for him, my Lord.

"Being a second son, Mr. Fontaine had to make his way in the world. Your father would have preferred he put his education to use at the law or stay near home as a vicar or cleric. But your uncle had a taste for the world. He chose the Royal Navy. He died battling the French at Trafalgar."

Max took this in. "But why would his name and portrait be banished? He was a hero."

Mr. Merriot put down his glasses and folded his hands over his ample belly, regarding Max with a serious eye.

"Your father . . . was a good employer, and a man I respected. But he did have his faults." Max managed to keep his face blank as Mr. Merriot continued. "He was very . . . disappointed by your uncle's choice of careers. I think he felt as if he were being abandoned. He never cared much for life beyond England's borders, but after your uncle left, he outright despised it. When we received word Mr. Fontaine had died, the old Earl began to fold in on himself."

"He hated my uncle because he left him. Enough to wipe his memory away," Max stated dully.

"No," Mr. Merriot replied simply. "I think he removed the portrait . . . because he didn't want to be reminded. It hurt, you see."

Max chewed on this as Mr. Merriot continued.

"It worried us for a time. But you were there, and your father delighted in you when you were small. Your mother tried to be consoling, but she rarely left London . . ." Mr. Merriot trailed off.

Max sat there silent for a time. Mr. Merriot, his story told (in a rather expedient amount of time for that blustery gentleman), resumed shuffling papers and eyeing Max in turns.

"I was named for him," Max spoke in almost a whisper.

"And then I started to act like him . . ." Lost in his own thoughts, Max didn't notice when Mr. Merriot stood, replacing his spectacles on the end of his nose. Awkwardly he patted Max on the shoulder and left the room. The door closed with a soft click.

He could see it now. He could see the reasons, the whys and wherefores his father had leashed Max so tightly as a child. Why he had turned white—with fear, not rage—when he had attempted to sneak off and stowaway on a ship as a lad. That fear of losing someone, or being left alone, drove his father to some terrible actions. Max hated it—but at least now he understood it.

He turned the letter over in his hand. It was so very odd to see his name there, knowing it belonged to another man. How easy it was to slip his finger under the wax seal, cracked and weakened with time.

He had been the recipient of hundreds of missives from his father, but never before had he been so curious to see what he would say. *"My Dear Brother, I hope this letter finds you well and in a timely fashion. Remember, the post outside our borders is not to be trusted, but you should be courteous to whomever carries your letters . . . Young Max is nearly two now, and a right scamp at that . . .* the letter went on in that vein, and Max grinned ruefully. There was the same lecturing here that was in the letters he received over the course of his life, but this one he could see was tempered with affection and a little loneliness.

Did his own missives from his father carry those same feelings, and he just hadn't seen them?

Curious, Max sifted through the pile in which he had found his uncle's letter. There, mixed in amongst notes to his solicitor, lists of tenants, and old copies of the *Times*, Max found three more letters—all of which were returned undelivered. Looking at the dates, Max could easily ascertain why: They were written before his father was notified of the death at sea.

Suddenly unwilling to sit amongst all the paper and ledgers in the overstuffed study, Max abruptly stood and headed to his bedchamber, taking the letters with him. Once there, he locked the door. In the wardrobe, he located his valise, fished inside its depths, finally locating what he was looking for.

Over the course of his life, from Eton to Oxford to London, the packet of letters had grown to the size and weight of a brick. They had come weekly, always on time, never delayed. Even when he had hated the old man, Max had kept his letters, a habit he attributed it to his own inherited collective tendencies. He hadn't known why he had thrown the letters in the valise with his shirts and boots. Just a notion, a dim thought that maybe he would want them here.

He sat down in a large armchair by the window. The day was quickly turning to dusk, and in the early summer air, the hills of Sussex seemed to glow with warmth, with magic. Max held the letters to his uncle in one hand, the letters to himself in the other. He began to read.

* * *

A full day and night passed before he put down the last letter his father wrote him, the one prescribing marriage. That missive almost made him chuckle now.

Max stood, stretching his long body. There was a tray of food on a small table by the door, cold now, but Max didn't care. He was suddenly ravenous. He had read every letter, reviewed every emotion he had felt when he first received them—but now, he could view it with the aid of passed time. His loneliness when first at school, and how he used to pour over the letters, eager for news of anything familiar. The weariness that grew on him as adolescence fought the mold his father had tried to force him into. Every pull, every tear, every moment of rage was remembered. However, this time, he could not picture his father as a horned devil cackling as he wrote his missives. He pictured him much closer to how he had been. Growing old with loneliness, and growing lonely with age.

Such emotional journeys require sustenance, he rationalized, as he thoroughly decimated the cold chicken. After he was good and stuffed, Max rang for his valet.

"Have Jupiter saddled, Harris."

"Yes, sir," replied that good man. Then, tentatively, "Are you well, sir? The past day . . ."

"Has been illuminating," Max finished for him. As he pulled on his boots, he added, "And yes, Harris, to answer your query. I am well." He sighed and leaned back, feeling lighter than he had in quite a while. Harris bowed and turned to leave, but Max called him back.

"I have one other task for you."

* * *

IT only took Harris an hour to locate the portrait of Max's uncle in the attic. He was a Fontaine, Max said when he charged Harris with the task, and deserves to hang in the hall with the others. While Harris rummaged in the dusty garret, Max took Jupiter across the grounds, running as fast and meandering as aimlessly as the horse wished to.

The weight in his chest, the one that had settled in so deep for the past seven years, was gone. He felt the sunshine on his shoulders and finally felt peace.

When Jupiter's wanderings took them to the edge of the sea, Max pulled him to a stop. He looked out over the blue waters of the channel, the wind whipping through his hair with the briny smell of the sea whispering of adventure.

He had been a shuttered, angry young man for so long. Tethered, idle in his hiding. He had so often longed to flee across these waters. But now, standing by the edge of the sea, the title of Earl of Longsbowe resting firmly on his shoulders, he no longer wished to escape his life. He simply wished to start it.

* * *

BACK at the manor house, Max took a few moments to admire his uncle's portrait, sitting in its rightful place next to his father's. Then, he turned north to London.

Twenty-eight

IN Max's experience, even the most jaded of London Society did not offer up "congratulations" upon the death of one's parent.

So it was highly perplexing when upon alighting from his carriage in front of Longsbowe House (later than expected, as he had headed toward Weymouth Street before Harris reminded him he no longer lived there), no less than three sets of people passing by offered up their congratulations and best wishes for his future.

Unable to comprehend all the well wishing he received while wearing a black armband of mourning, Max simply shrugged it off as an oddity, as he had far more important things to do. Such as, after a change of clothes, repairing directly to the Altons at Number Seven.

He had told Gail he would sort everything out, and that entailed speaking with her father. Truthfully, he was not looking forward to the conversation. Remembering all too well his first interview with Sir Geoffrey when he applied for Evangeline's hand, he could easily imagine what the gentleman would think of his transference of affections. But it was best done as soon as possible, and Max was eager to see

Gail again. Just one smile, he thought. One smile, and he'd walk into Sir Geoffrey's library with no hesitation. Hell, he'd walk through fire.

These pleasant thoughts in his mind, Max almost knocked over Mrs. Pickering, who emerged from the door of Number Seven just as Max climbed the front steps, her twin daughters in tow.

Really, Max thought, those girls would never do well for themselves until they began to dress differently.

"Mrs. Pickering"—Max tipped his hat after he steadied himself—"good morning."

As the twins made identical curtsies, Mrs. Pickering cried, "Lord Longsbowe!" in a high-pitched voice that may very well have indicated delight. "Returned to town, how wonderful! The Alton ladies have been quite desolate without you. One Alton lady in particular," she finished with a roguish wink. Not many shrill women could pull off a roguish wink, but Mrs. Pickering managed superbly.

Max covered his perplexity with a polite smile. What did she mean by that? Unless, Mrs. Pickering was far more acute than she seemed, and Gail . . .

"Yes," the twin he thought was Lilly piped up, interrupting Max's thoughts. "We were all so thrilled when we learned of your engagement." After a pointed look from her sister, indicating his black armband, she added, "Er, and so sad when we heard of your loss."

Max frowned in confusion. What on earth were they talking of? He hadn't yet asked Gail to marry him, of that he was certain. He had it all planned, too. He would take Gail down to the lake where they first met, unceremoniously throw her in, and then, while she sputtered and raved, he would sink to one knee in the muck and beg for her hand. It would be . . .

A cold chill settled over Max's entire body, as the polite smile he kept pasted on his face began to crack. And then, he knew.

Engagement. The prescribed month of acquainting time had long since come and gone. It must have been announced. If the Pickerings knew, everyone did. He was officially engaged.

To Evangeline.

When at last, Max was admitted to the drawing room, Romilla greeted him with cries of rapture, Evangeline with a demure nod, and Gail with silence and a stony stare out the front window.

She most certainly was not smiling.

* * *

HE exited Number Seven an hour later, desperate to hit something. He had sat there, between Romilla and Evangeline, unable to do more than seethe, while Gail . . . Gail did nothing.

He placed the blame for this disaster exactly where he knew it should go: Romilla. Why was the announcement not discussed? Why had he not been at least informed? He managed to glean from some pointed conversation that the announcement had been placed in the *Times* a fortnight ago! How could he have been unaware that whole time?

You did this, his mind raged as he watched Romilla command the whole room like the conductor of an orchestra. *You brought this to pass.* Even though some bothersome little corner of his brain played devil's advocate, pointing out his own involvement in the affair, the rest of him was ready and willing to indict Romilla Alton on the unpardonable charge of unwanted interference. In fact, the only thing that kept him silent in his seat while Romilla and Evangeline chattered over him about lace or some such stupid thing, was the half dozen or so ladies that came to pay calls—all of whom were eager to offer their congratulations.

And all the while, Gail did nothing. She sat at the window seat, staring out onto the street, paying only enough attention to the conversation to give short, distracted answers when asked a question.

It was as if she had transformed back into that wallflower that had too little confidence in herself.

When Gail rose and left the drawing room, giving the excuse of a previous appointment, Max's hangdog gaze followed her out the door.

Romilla's gaze, on the other hand, followed Max's, with an expression decidedly more disapproving.

* * *

ONCE outside, Max tried to decide between running all over town looking for Gail or repairing to Jackson's Saloon to vent his spleen when someone familiar handed him Jupiter's reins.

"Jimmy!" Max cried, happy to find an ally. Although to be quite honest, Jimmy's expression did not read "ally" so much as it did "hostile."

"Sir," he said through tight lips, before turning away and heading back to the stables, causing Max to give chase.

"Jimmy! Wait. You must help me, I need to see Miss Gail alone. Er, again."

The young man turned, his eyes hard.

"Sorry, *sir*, I doubt the lady would want that."

"Jimmy, please," Max begged, adding impetuously, "I'll pay you. Fifty pounds if you bring her to me."

Jimmy, not even taking a moment to consider such a large sum of money, simply turned his head and spat on the ground.

Max took the gesture as it was intended.

"My apologies. That was insulting." He ran a frustrated hand through his dark hair. "Something became mixed up and turned around while I was away, I realize that. But please, help me see Gail. I only want to fix this."

"And how would you be fixin' it, *sir*? By makin' love to one girl and marryin' her sister?"

Max sighed deeply, but before he could explain the situation, Jimmy continued. "I shouldn'a helped ye before. I may only be a stable hand, but you, sir, are no—"

"I suggest you think carefully before finishing that sentence," Max said darkly, giving his best imperious glare. Apparently, the imperious glare of an Earl is far more effective that that of a Viscount, because Jimmy did indeed think twice about insulting him. The silence gave Max the time necessary to press his case.

"Please. I love her," was all he had to say.

Jimmy, ever the romantic, could not be unaffected, and considered Max thoughtfully for a moment. "You'll not hurt her? Not try nothin'?"

"Never," Max replied immediately. "You'll stay within sight at all times."

"Damn right I'll stay within sight at all times," Jimmy replied, "with a hunting rifle to boot." He rubbed his chin, considering. "All right, I'll help ye meet her. When an' where?"

Max felt such relief fill his chest, it was all he could do to keep from embracing the groom. "Thank you. More than words can say."

"Don't thank me," Jimmy snorted. "Half the reason I'm doin' this is so I can watch her order you to hell with me own eyes."

* * *

IT may not have looked like hell in the beautiful grotto, but Max certainly felt to be assigned to some form of perdition. Waiting was torture. He had ridden immediately to this place once deciding on it with Jimmy—a place that brought forth powerful memories for him, and he hoped for Gail as well.

He had found it instinctively this time, Jupiter's hooves following an invisible path to the hidden copse. The warming weather of summer had made the grotto lushly verdant, the sun dappled through the trees on this perfect afternoon, but none of this natural beauty could calm Max's racing thoughts.

What on earth was he to do? How did he fix this? What if Gail refused to see him? What if she came, but refused to see him ever after? Hours had passed in this way, Max pacing the ground, sitting in the gazebo, standing up again, pacing some more, his mind torturing him with "what-ifs." Jupiter munched on grass, obliviously content in the knowledge that he was a horse, and therefore not given to getting himself stuck in untenable situations. Or, at least that's how it seemed to Max.

Such was how Gail found him—pacing, sitting abruptly, standing, and shooting dark looks at his horse. She took a moment to watch him, too sad to smile at his antics. Then she emerged from the trees, Jimmy and his hunting rifle not ten feet behind.

Max immediately stilled, watching her alight from Queen-

Bee, who immediately joined Jupiter. She walked with measured paces, keeping herself from running either to or from him. He showed great restraint in meeting her halfway.

"Gail," he breathed, moving to embrace her, but she stiffly backed away. She did not meet his eye as she gave a formal curtsy, replying, "Lord Longsbowe."

So this is how it was to be, Max thought, breaking a little with the need to touch her, and yet not being permitted. She was too lovely to look at, in a new crimson riding habit.

"What happened to your other habit? The, er, green one?" he blurted out.

"I burned it," she replied, ice in her words.

Of the many small cues Max had received regarding Gail's state of mind, this spoke the loudest.

"You're angry."

"You're engaged. My congratulations. I can think of no better Countess than my sister."

"Oh yes, there is, there is her sister," Max retorted, only to see Gail's eyes narrow.

"Please, do not try to placate me with hollow promises. I have no sympathies left for you to prey on."

"Gail, darling." He reached for her again, this time she made a decided step back, maintaining the distance between them at all times. He slowed his step and his breathing. "I didn't know it was going to be announced, I swear. True, a month was prescribed, but no certain date attached. I would never have left London. I would have stopped it."

Gail looked at him like he was crazy. She felt the sudden urge to laugh. "You would have stopped it?" she sneered, disbelief dripping from her words. "Your Lordship, please don't plead ignorance, for I am not. You announced it."

"What?" he asked, startled. "How?"

"You sent notice to the papers. I realize that was a very eventful day for you, what with your father dying and deflowering me, but surely you can recall sending notice earlier of your impending nuptials."

"I did no such thing!" he stated vehemently.

"It was in the papers that morning!" she replied hotly. "That morning, after we . . ." A choke had crept into her voice, robbing her of the emotional detachment she employed like a shield. He watch as she swallowed her anger and summoned a wry tone of voice—but she could not stop her eyes from shining with tears. "I woke up, and there were all these people in our drawing room, congratulating Evangeline on snaring you. And I thought, this is a mistake, they've got the wrong girl. But then I saw Mr. Holt and the paper itself, and I . . . I knew myself for a fool. I've been silly and stupid and wrong before, but never have I been so damned ashamed of myself."

"Gail, I never thought . . ." But Max was lost in his pain for his Gail, for what she had been through. What he had abandoned her to.

"I was *so* convenient, wasn't I? Creeping into your room—silly me! Thinking I might be wanted. But who would want me?"

She raged blindly, anger spewing forth, cutting at him as surely as a rapier would.

"I want you. You know that," he tried gently, and in an added attempt at humor, "and I assure you, you are the least convenient creature in the world."

She simply stared off sadly. Coldly.

"When I never received an answer to my letter . . ." She shook her head at her own foolishness. "I half expected you to rush to London once you received it, but at the very least I thought you'd send a reply."

A lone tear trailed down her cheek, she kept her profile to him. He didn't reach for her.

"I never received a letter," he said quietly. Another tear rolled, but she simply shrugged.

"Does it really matter now?"

"Yes, it matters," Max replied, emphatic. "If I had, I should have seen your name and flown back here. The whole time I was away, you were not far from me. Every damn day I thought of you. Every damn hour."

For a moment it seemed she might believe him. Then she looked up at him, all the tears she had for herself gone from her eyes. When she spoke, her voice was bare.

"Where do I stand with you, Max? Where the hell do I

stand with you? One moment I'm the love of your life, and you mine, and everything will work itself blissfully out, but that's not what happened, is it? All that occurred was we stayed on the same course set out by circumstance months before, with you marrying Evangeline, no matter your feelings for me, or hers for you, or what you and I have known together."

He crowded her then, closing the space between them. "Do you think me so low that I should make love to you if I had the slightest intention of marrying her? It has been a long time since I knew that she and I would not suit." He refused to allow her to run away, framing her face in his hands, forcing her to meet his eyes. "And a long time since I knew that we would."

He kissed her then, fiercely, possessively, crushing her body to his. Only the knowledge that Jimmy was likely aiming his rifle at that moment kept Max from holding on to her forever.

Shakily, he let go, removed himself to arm's distance. A good thing, too, because if Jimmy had covered the last two yards, that younger, smaller man would have been at Max's throat. As it was, Gail, her face flushed and tear-streaked, dazedly waved Jimmy back. He returned to his post by the horses, but kept a sharp eye on Max.

Silence reigned for a time, thoughts reeling, eyes searching, breaths racing.

Finally, Gail spoke raggedly. "I . . . I do not think you so low as to . . . what you said." A faint smile played across Max's lips, knowing how difficult it was to disconcert Gail's speech, but she cleared her throat and continued. "Oh! But I don't know what to think! And even so, what is there that can be done now? You are as good as married to Evangeline. The rules—"

"Hang the rules!" he said so vehemently, even the birds in the trees were shocked into silence. "I have spent a fortnight remembering my life, and I realized something. I have spent the time following the rules of someone else. My father, Society . . . Gail." He came to her again, but only held her firmly by the arms, pleading. "Don't you find bowing to the dictates of the Ton abominably stupid? To hold our breaths for fear of what? We want to be together, but what keeps us apart? Not such conquerable barriers as language, distance, or time, no—it's gossip! I've been pushed around all my life. I shan't let it happen now." He cupped her chin, again bringing her eyes to his face. "You want to know where you stand with me? Gail, please, just stand *with* me! Come away. We'll fly to Gretna Green and be married, and no one will tell us how to act or who to be ever again."

It was so tempting. But . . . "You forget one thing, my Lord." She removed herself from his grasp and turned away, wrapping her arms around herself protectively. "'Twas you yourself that knotted the string to Evangeline. And now you would leave her flapping in the breeze? My sister, my family, would never recover from that. They live by the rules of society you are so eager to disdain."

Her stiff back to him, she looked to be made of solid rock—unmoving, and simply accepting of what happened around her.

"How can you be so accepting of this?" he asked, anger bunching his shoulders and pounding at his temples.

"I have had the last two weeks to become accustomed to the situation, my lord."

Max shook his head. "Two weeks, two years, two decades, I should still not accept it. I can't believe you'd give up so easily."

"I never had you to give up," she said dully.

He spoke softly now, so softly that Gail turned her head to catch his words, and in doing so, found his lips at her ear.

"You conceded your own happiness. You gave up on yourself. I will not."

Before she could speak, before she could open her eyes, he was gone.

Twenty-nine

Count Roffstaam,
I am delighted to accept your invitation to visit Barivia.
You have told me so much of its pastoral beauty that I
simply will not rest until I have seen the whole. I shall
arrange for passage as soon as . . .

A muted sound from the other side of her door interrupted
Gail's thoughts, and she lifted her quill. After returning from
the park, she had immediately fished the count's invitation
out of her cluttered escritoire, and began composing a reply.
She could not stay here. The entire situation was horribly
botched, and she knew her only recourse was to escape. She
refused to be the cause of her sister's downfall. Besides, every
time Gail laid eyes upon Max, a clamp closed down in her
chest, and she found she could not breathe. Surely, it was unhealthy to stay.

He said he did not put the notice in the papers. She wanted
to believe him. God, did she want to believe him. But to put
faith in his words would mean to give herself hope, and she
would not be able to bear it if it were ripped away again.

There it was again, that muffled noise. Curious, Gail rose from her desk. Yes, it must be coming from Evangeline's room across the hall. It sounded like . . . someone crying?

Softly, she knocked on her sister's door, but the only reply was a small gasp and the immediate ceasing of the sobs. Gail delicately turned the knob.

"Evie?" she said gently. "Are you well?"

Evangeline sat on her bed, the skirts of her afternoon dress pooled about her. She was clutching a piece of paper in one hand to her breast and a handkerchief with the other, trying to hid her sniffles, a picture of delicate, if splotchy, feminine distress.

"Oh, I . . . I'm fine, Gail." She dabbed at the corners of her eyes.

Gail marched over to her sister's side. "Liar. Evie, you are normally very beautiful, but it's a sad fact that such a pale complexion makes it rather simple for one to tell when you've been crying. And profusely."

Evangeline gave a watery sniffle. Gail sat beside her, comfortingly putting an arm around her shoulders. This had the adverse effect of what was intended, causing more tears to fall.

"He—he's leaving me! I thought I could do this, and . . . and he's leaving!" Such statements were made between wrenching sobs. Gail stiffened as her heart began thumping a mile a minute. Evangeline, disregarding her own handkerchief, wiped her nose on her sister's skirts.

"Wh—who's leaving you—what did you think to do?" Gail inquired.

"Oh Gail! My life is over! I've been such a fool!" Evangeline replied, dashing tears away from her eyes, as Gail pulled away, her own gaze locked on that piece of paper at Evie's breast.

Oh God, Gail's mind raced. He must have told her.

"Evie, I'm so sorry!" Gail hurriedly stood, unable to stop the confession she had held in so long from flowing. "I . . . I . . . we didn't intend for it to happen. I know I certainly didn't, but Max, he made me laugh, and then he kissed me, and I saw one crow, and he saw one crow, and that makes two, and it *was* joy, but then he went away, and I've been so afraid of hurting you, but he said he loves me, and I said he's engaged to you now and . . . I never wanted to hurt you at all." Gail stopped babbling lamely, petering out of words.

Evangeline blinked large, owlish eyes at her sister, shocked into silence.

"Please," Gail said meekly, "please say something. I'll . . . I'll go away if you want me to, I'll cut off my arm, well, maybe a finger, if you require it of me, just say something. Please."

Evangeline held up a hand.

"Let us be clear," Evangeline said in measured breaths. "You . . . love Lord Longsbowe?"

"Yes," Gail replied in a small voice.

"And he . . . loves you?"

"He says so," she whispered, barely audible.

Then, after the space of a heartbeat, Evangeline burst out laughing.

It was Gail's turn to blink owlishly, watching as her sister dissolved into giggles.

"Wha—what?" she sputtered.

"God above be praised!" Evangeline laughed, assuming a dramatic posture to thank her Lord and Master. "My sister loves Lord Longsbowe, so I don't have to!"

"Evangeline!" Gail sat down on the bed, her legs no longer willing to support her. "You—you didn't know?"

"No, I didn't! And you have no idea how happy you've made me!" her sister replied cheerfully.

"But . . . but, you've been so pleased since the announcement. I thought you were looking forward to becoming a bride."

"Well," Evangeline sobered for a moment, "I was, in a way. All the congratulations, all the parties and well wishing—'tis very exciting. But in my heart, my resolve toward entering a loveless marriage deteriorated by the day."

She giggled, relief flowing from her in invisible waves. It seemed that Gail had not been the only one burdened by secret feelings.

"But don't you see? We can fix this now!" Evie continued. "Lord Longsbowe can't mind my crying off if he'd rather marry you—and I would much rather . . . oh, Gail! Does he make you happy?"

"He makes me crazy. And happy. And it's just so easy being with him."

"Yes, that's exactly what it's like." Evie's voice shook with hope as Gail pulled her sister forward into a fierce hug.

"But I don't understand! What made you cry so?" Gail said, releasing Evangeline from the rib-crushing embrace. "Who wrote that note, if not Max?" Gail's eyes lit up. "Is it from—"

"Don't worry about that now," Evie interrupted, quickly folding the paper into her pocket before Gail could voice her suspicions. "You must tell me all about you and Lord Longsbowe. How did you come to love him? You two fought constantly!"

Too long had each been without the other's confidence, that now their stories came tumbling out—the fears, the feelings, the happenings—and when Gail arrived at one specific occurrence in her narrative, Evangeline's mouth dropped open in complete shock.

"You didn't!"

"We did," Gail replied, sheepishly blushing.

Gail courteously gave her sister a few moments to collect her jaw from the floor.

Once the shock receded, Evangeline smiled softly at Gail. "So, my cynical sister," she said, "you have fallen head over heels in love."

"Er . . . in a way," Gail replied. "It was slower than that, and yet there are times when my mind reels at how quickly all this took place. I've known him less than two months, and I've known him forever."

"Yes." Evangeline's smile became for herself alone. "I could not agree more."

Before Gail could inquire about that intriguing remark and enigmatic smile, Evangeline stood with sudden determination and marched to her dressing table.

"Now," she said as she began to brush errant locks of hair

back into place, "let's get ourselves unstuck from this quag-mire, shall we?"

"Society will skin you alive if the engagement is broken."

"Gail," Evangeline said as she turned from the mirror, "we are actively pursuing our own happiness for once. Yours, and mine, and . . . everyone's. We will talk to Father now. We are Alton women. Strong, intelligent—I for one refuse to consign myself to discontent without a fight."

Evangeline stood, regal grandeur emanating from every inch of her petite frame, her hand discreetly fingering the folded note in her pocket. "And Society—"

"Can go jump in a lake?" Gail supplied, archly.

Evie smiled at her sister, who for the first time in a fort-night, could return it freely.

"Precisely."

* * *

"ABSOLUTELY not," Sir Geoffrey said, and returned his eyes to the paper in his hand.

They had found him in the library, the only place he was to be found in the house these days. Parliament and the clubs owned so much of his time, and there were always so many women visiting and flapping about Number Seven, that Sir Geoffrey retired to his library for solitude.

He was invariably interrupted.

First, his wife had entered, *without knocking*, asking to share the paper with him. As long as she read quietly and did not attempt to engage a tired man in conversation, Sir Geoffrey didn't mind. But since she had joined him, perusing the society pages from her seat on the couch, Romilla had tried *three times* to ask his opinion on some silly matter. He was about to kick his beloved wife out of his masculine sanctuary when his daughters entered.

At least they had had the good sense to knock.

Evangeline, his eldest child, entered first, trailed by her sister. Both had looked serious and determined as Evangeline stated quite calmly that she no longer wished to marry the Earl of Longsbowe and would like to call off the engagement.

Once Sir Geoffrey had given his answer, he hoped it would be the end of the conversation. Unfortunately, the children did not share his hopes.

"Father, I do not believe you heard me correctly. I do not wish to marry Lord Longsbowe, nor shall I do so."

"And I don't believe you heard me, child." Sir Geoffrey sighed as he looked over the top of his paper. "I refused to allow you to cry off."

Evangeline fluttered wordlessly for a moment. She turned to Gail, who silently urged her sister on.

"N-no!" was the word Evangeline finally squeaked out.

Sir Geoffrey, seeing he was to remain in the company of his family for some time, calmly laid his paper aside. His wife owlishly watched the whole exchange from the settee.

"What is it, child? Is it nerves? That's understandable, but not cause to call the whole thing off. The engagement will be a long one, what with Longsbowe still in mourning. Plenty of time to become accustomed to the idea. Now, if you like, you can take your sister to the shops and purchase some new pigments and canvas. Won't that be nice?"

"Father, I will not become accustomed to the idea! I have come to the conclusion we will not suit—time will not change that!" Evangeline's petite frame squared, she looked up at him with such self-righteous defiance, it only served to deepen his scowl.

"You suited each other well enough all those weeks ago in the conservatory. If you wanted to remove yourself from the situation then, we would have weathered it, but now, the scandal of throwing over Longsbowe would be ten times worse than before! I will not countenance it, neither will your mother." He stood as he growled, his eyes never leaving his daughter's face.

"Geoffrey," Romilla spoke in a small voice from the couch, unheeded by her husband. The staring contest looked to be in Sir Geoffrey's favor, cowing his daughter, but at the last moment, Evangeline found a final ounce of resolution.

"I do not love him," she said with quiet strength.

Silence enveloped the library. They could have heard a feather fall, Sir Geoffrey was so shocked. He expected some silly sentimentality, but this! He had to laugh. His mirth began as a chuckle, soon becoming full-blown belly-clutching guffaws. Gail came and held her sister's hand, all the ladies cringing.

"You don't *love* him? Good Lord, child, did you expect to?" he said between laughs.

Evangeline's sweet nature could not face down Sir Geoffrey any longer. She turned helpless eyes to her sister. Gail, whose temperament was much closer to his, stepped with flashing eyes into the fray.

"You are too cruel to force her. What if . . . what if their affections are engaged elsewhere? Does Evangeline not deserve to be loved by her husband? Does he not deserve the same in return?" She stood eye to eye with him, her own height much the same as his. He saw such strength there—it was an admirable thing. But not when defying what was best for all.

"Affections and feelings no longer bear weight! Don't you see—it's not a matter of what they deserve. It is a matter of what is at hand! Happiness in marriage is entirely a matter of chance. And it's a chance they took when they agreed to become engaged to stave off a scandal nearly two months ago!" He turned nearly purple, his anger spewing forth.

It had been so much simpler when they were little girls. He'd adored having his daughters with him abroad. Evangeline and Gail had been angels, doing as he asked and not questioning. Now, they were home, and all there seemed to be were questions.

"Do you think any of us will be happy in this end?" Gail asked bitterly. Evangeline was silently sobbing behind her sister, who stared defiantly at her father. Sir Geoffrey sighed deeply, sagging against his desk. He hated yelling at his daughters. It cut him deeper than knives ever could.

"Of course I want Evangeline's happiness," he said calmly. "And, eventually, she will be happy, married to Longsbowe. This has moved too far forward to back out now." He eyed his younger, fiercer daughter. "That is how it must be. My entire career is based on public appearance. Don't you know how lucky we have been in London, Gail, especially after that botched affair in Lisbon? I am in the inner circle of the prime minister! If a taint besmirched our name now, in my new position, I would never be able to walk into Parliament again. Your mother should never be able to move about in society. Such an action is decidedly ungrateful."

"My dear," Romilla tried again from the couch, but one look from him kept her silent.

At the mention of Lisbon, a little of Gail's fire left her, and she shrunk back a bit. Her face fell slightly, but as her stubborn chin came up and her mouth opened, it was Evangeline who came back to face him, a zealous protectiveness filling her with strength.

"If I recall, *Father*," she said with the icy imperiousness only petite blondes can summon, "I will reach my majority in a matter of weeks. When I am twenty-one, I will no longer have to bow to your whims. You may be prepared for a long engagement, but I assure you, once I celebrate my birthday, it will be surprisingly short."

And with that last statement, Evangeline took her shocked sister's hand, and exited the library as quickly as her feet could carry her.

* * *

UPSTAIRS, Evangeline broke down in sobs in Gail's arms.

* * *

INSIDE the library, the battle was far from over.

Romilla, crossed to the desk, where her husband had resumed reading the paper.

"What on earth just happened?" she asked, her tone implying she knew exactly what had occurred.

"My dear," Sir Geoffrey sighed. "I'm tired. I'm irritated—more so now. So if possible, could we have this little discussion at another time?"

"I just witnessed a display unlike any I thought I'd ever see from you. You mocked Evangeline's feelings by trying to buy her off with paints. You made Gail ashamed by mentioning Lisbon—which you know good and well was provoked! I speak Portuguese, too, I know exactly what was said, even if you have conveniently forgotten how the girls were insulted!

What made you think that yelling bloody murder and intimidating your children was the best way to handle Evangeline's request?"

Romilla put her hands on her hips, her eyes boring through the paper until Sir Geoffrey had no choice but to put it down and deal with the third disgruntled female in his family.

"She's just nervous. She needed to know the engagement still stands."

"She's not nervous. I've never seen her more resolved in my life. Did you listen to her at all? She's unhappy. The situation, to her, is untenable. I, for one, would like to know why."

"Well, it's lucky then you haven't seen her all your life." Sir Geoffrey felt the ire rising again. "She'll follow along and do as she's told. Evie's always been a good girl."

"She's not a girl anymore, Geoffrey!" Romilla's volume matched her husband's. "She's a young woman, with a mind of her own, and feelings on top of it. Which you just told her don't matter! Evangeline is a young lady who knows her own self and, in my experience, is not in the practice of making idle threats."

Sir Geoffrey stilled for a moment, letting the meaning behind his wife's words sink in.

"My God . . . do you really think she would? Cry off when she turns twenty-one?" Sir Geoffrey rubbed his chin as Romilla shrugged in reply.

"She does not leave this house." Sir Geoffrey pointed a shaking finger to the doors.

"What?" Romilla's head snapped up.

"Evangeline. Keep her under lock and key. She does not leave this house, she does not leave her *room* until she can be brought to her senses!"

"My dear, no, I meant we should talk to her . . . get to the bottom of her thinking!" But her protests fell on deaf ears. Sir Geoffrey had already stormed into the hall, calling for Mrs. Bibb.

Romilla could only stare blankly at the utter stranger who had replaced the loving family man she had married.

Thirty

IT was decided that the Alton household would spend the evening in.

Notes were sent to the hostesses of all the parties they had planned on attending that evening, remarking that Romilla and the girls were so worn out from the social rounds of the past few weeks that they were taking a well-deserved respite. The hostesses were understanding and happily placated by the promise of invitations to the next Alton household event.

Evangeline and Gail had each retired to their rooms, Evangeline too deeply entrenched in her tears to think clearly, and Gail resolved to think long and hard about the situation. But she soon grew restless and found herself wandering the halls until, at last, she came to the conservatory.

Summer bloomed all year long in the indoor garden, and as the sun faded into darkness, the atmosphere must have been very much like the night Max stole the infamous kiss from Evangeline. The scene of the crime, Gail thought bemusedly, as she walked to the fountain, the sound of water flowing over the carved sprites soothing her mind. All of this madness because of one silly kiss. As she seated herself on the stone bench, her foot tapping idly on the head of a stone frog, Gail thought what would have happened if it had been she instead of Evangeline. Would she have let Max kiss her then? Would she have been engaged now? Would she have been happy?

It didn't matter what would or could have happened, Gail thought, shaking off those disturbing questions. What mattered now was what was to be done—and when the answer finally came to Gail, it was the clearest, simplest, truest thing in the world. In this whole mess it was the only thing that felt right.

Gail quietly slipped back upstairs, intent to visit with Evangeline and tell her what she planned—but was deterred when she saw Evangeline's door was still closed. Best to allow her some privacy, she supposed.

Dinner was served in each person's bedchamber, and all too soon, the sun dipped below the horizon. As Gail ate, she made her arrangements, finished her letter to Count Roffstaam, and afterward, crept downstairs to place it in the pile of correspondence by the door. When she saw the footman take the letters to be delivered, she again crept up the stairs, but this time, was confronted with the sight of Romilla by Evangeline's closed door.

Romilla paused, obviously wanting to say something, but unable to find the words. Gail took a breath and took the opportunity to ask something that had been plaguing her for far too long.

"Was it you?"

Romilla blinked at her. "Was what me?"

"Was it you who placed the announcement in the papers?"

"Gail, I told you, Lord Longsbowe—"

"Had nothing to do with it," Gail finished for her. "So I ask again, Romilla. Was it you?"

Romilla brought her head up and met Gail's cool assessing stare with one of her own.

"Yes," she affirmed, completely without shame or boastfulness. "Things were about to be ruined, so I had your father call in a favor."

The faint sound of muffled sobs emanated from Evangeline's room. Gail gave a small, cynical smile. "And you don't believe things to be ruined now?"

A frown crossed Romilla's brow, as she silently digested Gail's words.

Gail was about to turn into her own room, when Romilla found her voice. "Where were you?"

Gail turned back, looking at her stepmother quizzically.

"The night of the Holts's ball," Romilla clarified. "Your father said you took the carriage . . . why would you leave so early?"

Gail felt her cheeks go hot, and Romilla in turn went pale, and held up a hand. "Never mind. I don't think I want the answer to that question."

They stood awkwardly for some moments longer, staring at each other, until finally, Gail simply said, "Goodnight, Ma'am," and went into her own bedchamber. She didn't see Romilla poke her head into Evangeline's room, see the girl asleep on the bed, and remove the key from the inside of the door. Then she closed the door, locked it, and pocketed the key.

* * *

SO, it seemed to Gail there was nothing left to do but go to sleep. After all, emotional encounters tended to be physically draining, and today she had endured no less than three. While certain she would toss and turn all night long with the weight of her decisions, in truth Gail was asleep when her head hit the pillow.

* * *

SUCH was how Max found her—asleep in bed, dead to the world.

He was very thankful to see she was not drooling.

Sneaking into the back of Number Seven had been surprisingly easy. The wall was uneven brick, easily scaled, and the full moon had lent plenty of light to the operation. Climbing the one tree outside Gail's window, however, proved more difficult.

Reedy and covered with thorny vines, Max endured dozens of scratches and a few moments of real fear when the tree swayed so violently he was certain he would fall. But nothing would keep him from his beloved's side—not even Mr. Newton's principles of gravity.

Rescue the girl and save the day, my good man.

Finding the window unlocked, he tiptoed into Gail's room.

She was an angel drenched in moonlight, her long lashes casting shadows against her cheek, a small smile painting her soft mouth, and so deeply unconscious the only movement she elicited was the slow and steady rise and fall of her breast.

Max's mouth quirked mischievously. How best to awaken his angel?

He leaned down in the moonlight, softly kissing her mouth. Gail gave a small moan, but still remained asleep. Max deepened his kiss, drawing her through a haze of dreams into reality, assaulting her senses, waking her body before her mind had the chance to catch up. Max felt her slackened arms snake up around his body, through this hair, and . . .

POW!

And wallop him with a vase from her bedside table.

"Ow!" Max cried, barely remembering in time to keep his voice down. He fell back on the bed, hands clutching his skull, his vision reeling. Gail sat up immediately, readying herself to strike again, but Max quickly placed his hands before him in a gesture of surrender.

"Gail, stop! It's me!" he whispered hurriedly.

"Max?" She blinked the remnants of sleep and defensive attack away. Slowly, she lowered the vase. Luckily, it was only made of pressed tin, and bore the impression of Max's head, which was far preferable to the opposite situation.

"Oh, Max!" she cried, and flung herself into his arms. He caught her with an "oof," and another "ow" as her force knocked him over and into the bedpost. She gave him a hearty kiss to sooth his wounds, before pulling back and asking questions.

"What are you doing here? How did you get in? Did anyone see you?"

Max gently placed a hand over her mouth, gesturing for silence.

"No, I don't think anyone saw me, and I got in via one terribly unsteady tree. It's a hazard to lovesick swains everywhere."

"Max, don't be vexatious now, I beg you."

"I'm serious," Max continued, taking Gail by the hand and pulling her out of bed. "Look at me, I'm all scratched over, and nearly died twice. Kiss it and make it better?" He grinned.

Gail let a withering glare speak her reply.

God, she was lovely, he thought, his mouth going momentarily dry. The fantastically simple lines of her nightdress, the moonlight highlighting all the right curves through the sheer fabric. In fact, Max was so preoccupied by the vision before him, he didn't notice that the vision was speaking to him, and therefore had to resort to poking him in the arm.

"Max, what's going on? Why are you here?"

He shook off his current train of thoughts, fought his way back to the present. He grinned that lopsided, rakish grin that routinely made Gail's knees go weak. "I thought about everything I said earlier today, everything you said. I came to a conclusion."

"Yes?" she said, a catch in her voice.

"You're an idiot," he said softly, pulling her to him. "And it seems I simply cannot do without you." He held her still for a moment, locked in time, in the space of a breath. "So, you need to pack, quickly. We're leaving tonight."

"Leaving?" she squeaked, bemused, as Max opened her wardrobe. "You're *abducting* me?"

"Eloping. Eloping involves hurried packing. Abducting involves masked men and a burlap sack."

"Max . . ."

"Dress for travel, pack only what you'll need for a day or two. I'll buy you entire continents of wardrobes once we're wed, but for now, speed is of the . . ."

"Max," she said firmly. "Look down."

He complied, thinking maybe there was a particular pair of shoes from the heap that invariably collected at the bottom of wardrobes—but instead he saw a packed valise sitting neatly on the floor.

"As you see, I came to a similar conclusion. I can't seem to do without you either." Her face softened into a sheepish smile, and Max was awestruck.

"Besides, I was already aware of your idiocy," she shot back, grinning.

"You were going to abduct me?" he asked, that half smile playing across his lips.

"Elope," she replied coolly, but then she smirked. "But I was going to do so in the morning! After a full night's sleep."

He laughed aloud at her exasperation, unafraid of who would hear.

"Silly girl! Don't you know all proper eloping is done in the dead of night?" When she shrugged in reply, her nightrail slipped off her shoulder in the most innocent, beguiling way, that Max had to force his head to turn back to the wardrobe.

"Ahem." Max coughed, moving the valise to the outside and rummaging through the wardrobe's contents. "You need to put some clothes on, else we'll never get out of here. What's . . . ? I thought you said you burned this."

Max's rummaging hand had come to the very back of the wardrobe, and pulled out the deep green riding habit. It was balled and wrinkled, but most certainly not burned.

"Yes, well . . ." Gail cleared her throat, eyes askance. Max was suddenly overcome with the urge to grab Gail and kiss her thoroughly. So he did.

"I do love you," he said, after he finally pulled back, brushing an errant lock of hair out of her eyes.

"I didn't tell Evangeline," she admitted worriedly, looking up into his face. "About my plan to abduct . . . er, elope. I didn't know how, and she's the one who will be gossiped about, and snubbed everywhere she goes. Max, I don't want to cause her any pain."

He opened his mouth to answer, but a considerable amount of noise at the window caused his face to split into a grin.

"Good God, Longsbowe," Will Holt said as he stumbled into the room, "I nearly killed myself in that damn tree. I thought you said it'd be an easy climb."

"I wouldn't worry about Evangeline," Max said to an astounded Gail. "I brought her a gift, to sooth the pain of losing me."

For indeed, while Gail and Evangeline had spent the whole of the afternoon rehashing almost every single moment of the last two months, Max had engaged in a similar, albeit shorter, conversation with Will Holt.

He had found his best friend in his offices at Holt Shipping, imbibing a rare glass of brandy during working hours.

"I'm sailing on the morning tide," Will had said immediately upon seeing his friend.

Max, noting that Will's face was pale and drawn, sat down in a chair opposite and said, "You look horrid."

"You look fairly awful yourself," Will replied, sipping the brandy.

"I'm in love with my betrothed's sister. What's your excuse?"

Will paused, the glass halfway to his lips, and smiled in spite of himself. "Well, I'm in love with your betrothed. Brandy?"

That is all that was said on the subject.

Now, Will stumbled about Gail's bedchamber, banging into a delicate side table before his eyes managed to adjust to the relative darkness of the indoors.

"Miss Gail," he said, with a polite bow. Gail stood partially concealed behind Max—she was still in her nightgown, after all. "Do you happen to know where I might find your lovely sister?"

"Um . . . the door across the hall," Gail replied, blushing furiously. Once Will had made his exit, Gail turned triumphant eyes to Max. "So he *is* the one who wrote Evie's letter!"

"What letter?" Max asked confused.

"Never mind—I'm just going to bask in the glow of being right for a moment."

Max shrugged, grinning. "It wasn't a terribly difficult guess. Evangeline and Will are not as farfetched as say, Max and Gail. Don't worry about your sister. No one will laugh at the wife of the most successful shipping businessman in London and the sister of a Countess."

Gail looked to her beloved in wonder, before throwing herself into his arms and kissing him so thoroughly, he had to pinch the back of his hand to be able to pull away.

"Time enough for that later," he breathed. "For now, hurry and change."

She did, shaking out the green riding habit and donning it with the speed of a jackrabbit. She was just doing up the final buttons on the jacket when Will knocked softly and reentered the room.

"I beg your pardon, Miss Gail, but do you happen to have a key to Evangeline's room?"

"A key?" Gail repeated, confused. "No, Evangeline's door is never locked."

"It is now," Will replied.

Gail and Max crossed the hall with Will. Gail tried the knob.

"Well, it certainly is locked," she said grimly.

"Gail?" Evangeline's small voice came from the other side of the door.

"Evie!" Gail cried. "Can you open the door from the inside?"

"No, I can't find the key."

Gail knelt and looked through the keyhole, meeting Evangeline's similarly prying eye.

"Mr. Holt and Max are here to take us away," she said.

"I know," Evangeline replied, the corner of her eye crinkling with what must have been a smile. "William was telling me just now."

"Evie, tell me one thing—do you love him?"

"Yes," Evangeline's reply was clear as a bell. "I truly do."

"For heaven's sake, why did you let me ramble on and on about Max this afternoon, and you never said a word! No, you just sat there smiling enigmatically while I—"

"Uh . . . Gail," Max said from behind the crouching form of his soon-to-be-wife, "while I'm sure this discussion is of the utmost importance, do you think it could wait until we find a way to open the door? Do you happen to have a hair pin?"

"I have more hair pins than God." Gail stood. "Can either

of you pick a lock?" At the negative shakes of their heads, Gail rolled her eyes. "And I was so hoping one of us might have had a misspent youth. Can you get in her room like you got into mine? From the window?"

Again, Will shook his head. "The front of your home is a sheer face. There is no way to scale that."

"Then," Max replied, "we're back to the key. Evangeline, you didn't happen to put it somewhere and then forget about it? In a box or a reticule or some such thing?"

"No," was the muffled reply. "The key is normally in the keyhole. I never touched it, I don't have it."

"Then who does?" Gail asked.

"I do."

Romilla's voice floated from the end of the hall.

Thirty-one

WILL, Max, and Gail froze in the middle of the hallway, watching as Romilla, dressed in a wrapper and bearing a candle, approached with unearthly calm.

"Honestly, the three of you are the least stealthy people in the world. You could not have made more noise if you brought an orchestra."

For the space of a minute, no one breathed, no one made a sound. Gail was certain that Romilla was going to raise a hue and cry and then Max and Will would be taken to prison as trespassers and then they'd be sent to Australia—she and Evangeline would be locked in a tower at their country estate, until one day they managed to escape and sneak aboard a merchant ship and search the entire desolate Australian continent of thieves and murderers for their beloveds and . . .

Then Romilla did the strangest thing. Calmly, she parted the crowded hallway, walked to Evangeline's door, and to everyone's surprise, unlocked it.

Evangeline might have been the most surprised of all, but she did not hesitate in removing herself from her cage. She had already thrown on a day dress, cloak, and shoes. Warily, she edged past her stepmother to stand beside Will, who took her hand.

Romilla shut the door. Turning, she found she had the rapt attention of the hallway's occupants.

"Madam—" Evangeline began, but Romilla interrupted.

"You have special licenses?" she addressed the gentlemen of the party.

"Uh, yes, ma'am. Right here." Max brandished two pieces of paper from his breast pocket. Romilla gave them a cursory glance before nodding.

"Good. Elopement is one thing. Abduction is quite another," she said sternly.

"Yes, one involves burlap sacks." Gail couldn't help the little quip from slipping out.

Romilla turned her steady, unsmiling eyes to Gail. "Gentlemen," she said, her gaze immobile, "perhaps you should go and see to the carriage. I assume there is one? Good. I should like a word alone with my daughters."

Max and Will refused to budge, until Romilla rolled her eyes, and with an exasperated "Oh heaven's sake!" handed the key to Evangeline.

"There," she said. "I cannot lock her back in if she has the key. They will be down in a moment. I certainly cannot stop young fools in love from living their lives, so I refuse to try."

"It's all right." Evangeline squeezed Will's hand. "We will join you shortly."

A look passed between Gail and Max, the former giving the latter similar assurances. Once the gentlemen departed with last backward glances, Gail and Evangeline were left alone with their stepmother.

"Where's Father?" Gail asked before Romilla could begin the dreaded lecture.

"Locked in his bedchamber." Romilla gave a little smirk. "Evangeline's is not the only key in my possession."

"Ma'am," Gail began, "I know our actions are—" but Romilla held up a hand.

"I have put a good many things together in the past few hours. I should have seen this outcome long before, but I can only think that while I had my suspicions, I refused to see a depth of feeling that now is so plain." She turned to Evangeline. "Your father did not listen to what you were saying today, for that I'm sorry." Then she turned to Gail. "I fear I have not listened to you for quite a while, and for that I can only beg forgiveness."

Gail and Evangeline began to shake their heads, but again, Romilla refused to hear their murmurs of denial. She reached up around her neck and removed an intricate garnet necklace, handing it to Evangeline.

"For your wedding," she said, as she removed a matching garnet ring and handed it to Gail. "Each of you will require something old, something new, something borrowed, and something blue. These are quite old, and it would be an honor if you would borrow these from me for the occasion."

Gail, stunned, numbly took the beautiful ring from Romilla's outstretched hand. Evangeline had silent tears streaking her cheeks.

Romilla addressed both girls then, but peculiarly, kept her eyes on Gail.

"I know I've muddled some things—stepmotherhood is not easy, but I shouldn't imagine stepdaughterhood is either. But please know, that underneath everything"—the tears in her eyes broke the brim, and fell—"I wished the most for you to be happy."

Unable to hold themselves apart any longer, both Gail and Evangeline gathered Romilla into a fierce embrace. When finally they released their stepmother, all three were smiling through profuse tears.

"Mother, please know . . . the scandal . . . we wish it didn't have to occur," Evangeline stumbled over the earnest words.

Romilla simply waved this away with a watery laugh. "Bah! Gossip isn't worth the paper it's printed on."

"But," Evangeline replied with a frown creasing her brow, "gossip is said, not printed."

"Exactly." Romilla smiled.

Down the hall a great banging broke the simple honesty of the exchange.

"Romilla!" came their father's voice. "Why am I locked in? Drat it all! Morrison! Mrs. Bibb!"

Romilla wiped away an errant tear, as she turned back to her daughters. "Now, as to your father . . ." The banging continued loudly. "Come back in a fortnight, and I think you'll find that you've had his consent and blessing all along."

Gail squeezed Romilla's hand one last time. "Thank you, Mother." Romilla had to shoo the girls down the steps before she began crying again.

Once the girls were out of sight, Romilla returned to her husband's door and seated herself in a chair placed for that purpose outside the door.

"Darling, stop pounding, you're giving me a headache."

"Romilla!" came Sir Geoffrey's relieved voice. "Let me out of here."

"Not quite yet," she replied. "You and I need to have a chat about the girls."

"The girls? Are they all right? Where are they?"

"They are fine, dearest. And they are gone. When you next see them, they shall each be wed. And not to whom you'd expect."

"What!?" Sir Geoffrey cried.

"Dearest you simply must stop that infernal banging. I assure you it is fruitless. Now, listen. Yes, listen. I have noticed that since we came to London, your ability to pay proper attention to your family has gone into rapid decline. Listening to your daughters, in particular, seems to have been forgot. However, I have high hopes it is a skill you can regain without much injury."

Inside the master bedchamber, Sir Geoffrey banged against the door with all his strength.

Outside, Romilla sighed and rolled her eyes. It was going to be a long night.

* * *

GAIL and Evangeline emerged from Number Seven at a near run. The large black carriage sitting in front of Number Seven swung open its doors, and Max and Will each exited to take the hand of their chosen lady.

"Thank God," Max said to Gail, "any longer and we should have come back in with swords drawn to take you by force."

"Max, do you even have a sword?" Gail asked wryly.

"Well, a metaphorical sword." Once inside the carriage, Will rapped on the ceiling, signaling to the driver to drive at a breakneck pace out of the city.

"Where are we going?" Evangeline asked.

"A small church on the outskirts of London," Max replied to his future sister-in-law. "The vicar is an old friend of ours from school days."

Pleased with this, Evangeline settled back into her seat next to Will, content to be able to whisper sweet nothings at each other, a pleasure too long denied. Max looked to Gail, who had grown unusually quiet.

"You have grown unusually quiet," Max said softly, eliciting a small smile from his intended. "Are you thinking about your stepmother? What did she say to you? I promise, she will never be able to interfere in your life again."

Gail turned and smiled at the concern and protectiveness in Max's eyes. Then she saw that Max's question had drawn her sister's attention as well.

Gail and Evangeline shared a look, and a contented smile.

"She wished us to be happy," Gail said, fingering the garnet ring on her right hand. Evangeline placed a similar hand over the necklace around her throat.

Max and Will looked to each other and then to their future brides.

"And are you?" Max asked, taking her hand, lacing their fingers. "Are you happy?"

Tears shone in Gail's eyes.

"More than words can say."

Epilogue

IT would be a happy thing indeed to say that nothing resembling a scandal occurred. However, that would be a fib. It was the grandest scandal the Ton had ever seen—for about a month. When the announcement of the nuptials of Maximillian Fontaine, Earl of Longsbowe, to Miss Gail Alton hit the papers, Mayfair was in chaos. Lady Hurstwood repaired immediately to Lady Alton to inquire if the papers had misprinted the name.

She was told the papers were correct.

Lady Alton had no less than twenty callers that morning before ten thirty, all asking to stay for her famous early teas and to be told how such an outrageous elopement took place.

Indeed, only a few people were less than shocked.

Mr. Ellis at the British Museum glanced at the announcement, smiled to himself, and then returned to his filing.

Lord Ommersley was heard in White's sniggering that he'd known it all along, and if his mother allowed him to place wagers, he would have bet his inheritance that it was Miss Gail that Lord Longsbowe preferred, not Miss Evangeline. But since Lord Ommersley was not terribly well liked, no one paid him much heed.

Lady Charlbury went so far as to tie a leash to Old Tom and exit her house. She went directly to Lady Jersey's drawing room, where she proceeded to crow in triumph.

Count Roffstaam, who did not receive the *Times* in Barivia, was uninformed on the matter until he received two letters some three weeks later, the first describing a madcap plot to abduct a gentleman. The second told of its modification and success. He smiled and laughed (most unlike a Barivian) as he read, but nothing pleased him more than when he saw the signature of Gail, Countess of Longsbowe.

However, the vast majority of the Ton was agog at the affair. A few of the matrons began making disparaging remarks about Miss Evangeline now that she had been compromised and thrown over for her sister . . . until they chanced to read farther down the page and found Miss Evangeline was now Mrs. Holt.

And when the pair of couples returned to town in the prescribed fortnight, Sir Geoffrey was first in line to embrace them. Literally. As Gail and Evangeline knew, the man had the strength of a bear when engaged in an enthusiastic hug. Max and Will, however, were a bit surprised.

Romilla and Sir Geoffrey still find themselves constantly in demand in London. Scandal now seems to slip off them like water off a duck's back, a lesson learned when their daughters married and they had to deal with the fallout. The easiest way, it seemed, was to not care. Many matrons have been frustrated by this newfound breeziness, and yet many still court their favor.

Evangeline and Will settled at Will's family estate and are said to be disgustingly happy. She had seasons upon seasons to paint her beloved new home, and half a dozen children to pepper about the vistas.

The Earl and Countess of Longsbowe spent the first few of their many years together at Longsbowe Park, becoming acquainted with the estate, and much more acquainted with each other. After finding and training an eminently trustworthy steward (not surprisingly, Mr. Merriot's son was as adept as his father), Max took his wife and young sons to Italy, where that Lady was determined to add a practical fourteenth language to her list, and no longer rely on the dubious Pig Latin to round it out. It was whispered by those in society, accompanied by a wink and a nudge, that her desire to grasp the language was so desperate, the Earl and his Lady would retire during the hottest hours of the day, every day, for an Italian lesson.

But honestly, who listens to gossip?

EVERYONE agreed that Mrs. Phillippa Benning was a beau-tiful young woman. Stunning even, with her cornflower blue eyes and corn silk hair. One poetic gentleman had likened her teeth in shape to perfect corn kernels, but that perhaps was taking the metaphor too far.

Mrs. Benning simply sparkled. Her wit and humor and joie de vivre gave her entrée into the most exciting crowds in the Ton, a place that lady enjoyed and intended to stay. So, if she was occasionally seen as being too forward in her thoughts and too ambitious in her flirtations, it was easily forgiven as the capricious combination of youth and beauty, for when Phillippa Benning smiled, a sultry pout known to cause mar-ried men to forget their wives' names, no one could find fault in her.

Indeed, everyone thought well of Mrs. Phillippa Benning. And certainly would have done so even if she were not so rich, or so conveniently widowed.

All the world knew Phillippa Benning's short marriage had been the stuff of fairy tales, merely lacking the "ever after." And after mourning a full year for her husband of five days, Phillippa had discovered it was exceedingly pleasant to no longer require that smothering protection unmarried ladies lived under and took to her life as a young woman of independent means with verve.

She liked all the same things other women liked—but made them so artlessly hers. She read the latest gothic novels by M. R. Biggleys and Mrs. Rothschild, but whenever she commented that the hero of one was far too bland for her taste or the setting of another was spine-chilling, it was automatically taken as fact and quoted by ladies and gentlemen alike as such. She could affect sales of fabric as much as a drought or rainy season would affect a crop: If Phillippa Benning declared lilac watered silk to be déclassé, sales of such material would plummet—conversely, if she was seen strolling the park in mint green sprigged muslin and butter colored walking boots, two dozen such costumes would be on order at the best modistes the next day.

It was uncommon for someone so young to rule the Ton (she was just one and twenty)—but when it came to Mrs. Phillippa Benning, her position was unquestionable. Her favor could make or break a novel's success, a modiste's reputation, a hostess's event, a young debutante's popularity, or a young buck's heart.

And she knew it.

"I absolutely refuse to attend Mrs. Hurston's card party. She insists on wearing that feathered purple turban, and I have taken the trouble to twice tell her how it does not suit her," Phillippa said as she looked through her opera glasses, scanning the crowd lined up along the parade route.

Phillippa's best friend, Nora, clucked her tongue and shook her head, suppressing a delicate giggle beneath a tiny hand.

Nora was an adorable little creature Phillippa had picked up this year. She was eighteen, in her first Season, and could have turned out disastrously if not for Phillippa's intervention. Miss Nora De Regis was very rich, born and raised English, but suffered from a touch of dark coloring inherited from a Greek grandfather, and from a mother who refused to allow the child to dress in anything other than eyelet cotton and stiff corsets. Phillippa simply made certain the world saw Nora's dark eyes and olive skin as exotic, and steered her mother to more expansive modistes. Now mother and daughter alike would not be caught dead in anything but the latest fashions. Nora, at the beginning of the Season, also had a rather innocent and open nature, that Phillippa was teaching her to suppress.

Nora was proving a very apt pupil.

"No Phillippa Benning at Mrs. Hurston's party?" she replied archly. "She'll lose more face than if Prinny himself failed to appear. Maybe that will shock the good Mrs. Hurston into taking your advice more seriously."

"Really," Phillippa replied, lowering her opera glasses, "you would think they would know by now."

Normally, Phillippa was not one to partake in forced outdoor activities before noon. But then again, there were very few social events whose express purpose was the ogling of men, and a parade of militia was one of them. Patriotism was all the rage. Her companion, Mrs. Tottendale, could not be roused to attend, but Nora was always game for assessing young men's attributes. And besides, Phillippa's other best friend, Bitsy, her Pomeranian, could use the fresh air.

The red woolen coats slashed with gold epaulettes glinted brilliantly in the sun, but none of that distracted Phillippa from her view of a dashing gentleman in a dark green coat watching the processional from the other side of the thoroughfare.

"Did you spot him? The Marquis of Broughton?" Nora craned her neck, trying in vain to see over the throng gathered at the park.

"He's just across the street, to the right," Phillippa replied, never looking directly at him but always keeping him within her view. After all, she did have all of these dazzling redcoats to look at. Bitsy shook delicately in Phillippa's arms, his emerald collar jangling with the dog's nervous energy.

Nora went up on tiptoes and leaned over far enough into the thoroughfare to nearly be knocked over by an outside fife player. Finally, she spotted the object of Phillippa's intensely purposeful nonattention.

"Oh! He's simply delicious!"

"I know," Phillippa purred, letting a small smile play about her mouth, soothing Bitsy with long gentle strokes. "Where has he been keeping himself? The past few Seasons would have been so much more interesting if he had been around."

"The past few Seasons have not been dull for you, Phillippa, admit it," Nora replied, wide eyed and mocking.

It was true. Phillippa had thoroughly enjoyed her first Season as a widow. Oh, she had enjoyed her original Season, too, but it had ended rather abruptly with Alistair's death, and as such, Phillippa had been determined to regard her emergence from mourning as a fresh start. She knew she would marry again—the hazy vision of a quiet country life with rug rats loomed over her like a cloud threatening rain—but her first Season as a widow had been such an overwhelming success, she refused to settle down before giving herself another. She was accountable to no one. Her funds were her own, having inherited her trust upon her marriage. There was something unbelievably luxurious about being untethered. She could flirt with no dreadful repercussions. She could dance until dawn.

Oh, her parents were hopeful that she would make a match, of course, and provide them with a few grandchildren to dote upon and make heirs. But Phillippa informed them she required the perfect specimen of man for her to even consider marriage—rich, titled, a leader of the Ton. And until that man arrived, her parents could do nothing more than throw up their hands and go back to their own lives. Her father to the estates and playing the market; her mother to Bath or Brighton, where the waters were as invigorating as the men, she'd say.

But her parents would be very pleased when they learned of the Marquis of Broughton's arrival on the scene and of how very perfect Phillippa had found him thus far.

"Rumor has it Broughton's been locked up at his estate, poor thing," Phillippa pouted saucily.

"Which one?" Nora asked. "They say he has a dozen."

"Does it matter? It only matters that he wasn't here before, and now he is." A small, satisfied smile lifted the perfect bow of her mouth.

"Well," Nora conceded, "if he's as *delicious* up close as he seems to be from a distance . . . Have you been introduced?"

"Not yet," Phillippa said, as the last of the militia trooped past leading cheering revelers in their wake (luckily, the parade had been horseless, else the revelers suffer a misstep and a smelly fate). "But he'll introduce himself shortly."

Nora's brows shot up in surprise. "How can you know that?"

"Watch."

As the last of the revelers passed, Phillippa let go of her coyness, and turned, catching hold of the Marquis of Broughton's hawklike gaze and holding.

One . . . Two . . .

She arched a brow, slightly, allowed the faintest upturn to the corner of her mouth.

Three . . . Four . . .

Never did his eyes lift from hers. Never did she allow the heat of his gaze to cause more than the faintest of blushes to paint her cheek.

Five.

With one last fractional brow raise, Phillippa pointedly turned away and addressed Nora.

"He'll introduce himself shortly," she repeated. She didn't even attempt to hide the smugness she considered well deserved. "In the meantime, shall we get some ices? Its unbearably hot amongst all these"—she flitted her hand—"people."

Phillippa handed a squirming and eager Bitsy to his liveried attendant for walking, and taking Nora's arm, gently steered her toward the shops that lined the park. Out of the corner of her eye, she saw the Marquis of Broughton approach them. He was still a good twenty feet away, but moving like a hunter stalking his prey. Surreptitiously, Phillippa reached over and grabbed one of Nora's gloves out of her hand (well, she certainly wasn't going to let her own glove get muddy) and dropped it, all without Nora noticing. The marquis was behind her now, out of her line of sight.

She slowed, and then counted . . .

Five . . . Four . . .

He would be a few feet from the glove by now . . .

Three . . . Two . . .

Bending down, he'd have picked it up . . .

One.

"Excuse me, Madam?" an unfamiliar, deeply masculine voice addressed them, a warm drawl coloring his expression.

Phillippa turned, sly smile and coy looks at the ready to lay claim to . . .

. . . Someone who was not the Marquis.

"You seem to have dropped this," the incredibly tall man with the deep voice said, holding up Nora's small, now soiled glove.

"Thank you," Nora said, accepting the glove with a polite smile. "I hadn't realized I dropped it, Mr.—"

"Mr. Worth," he replied, before tipping his hat.

"Mr. Worth," Nora repeated, doing the conversation duties Phillippa had abdicated.

Abdicated, because her gaze had narrowed and locked on to the Marquis of Broughton, who, like them, had attracted his own barnacle of sorts, as she watched him hand a reticule back to a vaguely pretty female who lightly touched his arm at discreet intervals.

It seemed he had "accidentally" been bumped into by none other than the treacherous harlot herself, Lady Jane Cummings.

Enter the rich world of
historical romance
with Berkley Books.

Lynn Kurland

Patricia Potter

Betina Krahn

Jodi Thomas

Anne Gracie

Love is timeless.

penguin.com